Color OF Love

Color of Love

A Historical Romance

ANITA STANSFIELD

Covenant Communications, Inc.

Cover image: *Stately Home and Garden* © Cathryn Gallacher, courtesy istockphoto.com

Cover design copyright © 2017 by Covenant Communications, Inc.

Published by Covenant Communications, Inc.
American Fork, Utah

Printed in the United States of America
First Printing: January 2017

23 22 21 20 19 18 17   10 9 8 7 6 5 4 3 2 1

ISBN 978-1-52440-132-0

Chapter One
EQUALLY INDIAN

Wiltshire, England—1867

AMALA SAT ON A PARTICULARLY uncomfortable chair at the edge of the crowded and stuffy ballroom. While trying to keep her back straight—as a lady was expected to do—she fanned her face with the hand-painted lace fan that had been a Christmas gift from her father. He wasn't *really* her father, and everyone knew it. In fact, no one outside of the family ever referred to him as her father. But that was how she thought of him and felt about him, and the fan was something she treasured. In that moment she also appreciated the way it offered just enough movement of air in front of her face to keep her from feeling faint. The music was too loud, the room was too hot, and her corset was too tight. Her back ached nearly as much as her feet, and she longed to be at home in her own room, wearing a nightgown and getting lost in a good novel. But a glance at the clock told her it could be hours before that happened, and then she'd surely be too exhausted to read. She wished she hadn't been required to be here at all, but that was part of the price she paid for being given the gift of such a privileged life—especially when she knew that what her fate could have been otherwise was too unbearable to even think about.

Amala became distracted from her own misery when she noticed that one of the servants carrying a tray of champagne glasses was Indian. He was middle-aged and nice looking, and was wearing typical Indian dress rather than the conventional English suit that was worn by most manservants. She watched him discreetly, intrigued by what his background might be and what his reasons might be for being here. And why wouldn't she be curious? He was the first person she'd seen in years who had the same dark skin and hair as herself. He'd clearly come from the country of her birth. How could she not be fascinated? She wanted to talk to him but knew that having a real conversation with one of the servants would be considered entirely inappropriate.

A few minutes later Amala noticed another Indian servant in the massive ballroom, and then a third—except this one was a woman. They were all wearing traditional Indian dress. She felt intrigued with the woman's clothing especially, and thought that it looked far more comfortable than the chemise, corset, petticoats, and gown that were constricting her own body and making her sweat.

Katarina sat down next to Amala, sounding out of breath. "Oh, I could dance all night," her sister said with delight.

"I couldn't," Amala said. "My feet are screaming."

"We must get you some better slippers for such events," Kat declared.

"Little good it would do. You don't see any men lined up *wanting* to dance with me, do you?"

"They just don't know you," Kat said with her usual optimism.

"And they never will," Amala said, stating an obvious truth. Since Kat was English and not her blood sister, she could never fully understand either. But she tried, and Amala loved her for it. "It's just as it's always been, Kat. The color of my skin keeps people from even *trying* to get to know me. Therefore, you are my one and only true friend for life."

"Well, it's not fair," Kat said as if she'd never said it before. Amala couldn't *count* how many times she'd said it throughout the years they'd shared. "It shouldn't make any difference, whatsoever."

"It shouldn't but it does, and it's a fact of the world we live in. It's not fair but that's the way it is. There's no point making a fuss over something that can't be changed." Amala concluded the same speech she'd made countless times over the years, but Kat likely hadn't heard the last few words because a gentleman had asked her to dance and she was off again having a marvelous time. Kat certainly *did* love to dance. Perhaps it was a good thing that Amala wasn't terribly fond of dancing; perhaps that helped ease her disappointment somewhat. Perhaps it was better if she wore shoes that hurt her feet and kept her from wanting to be on the dance floor, caught up in the movement and color of the main purpose of this event. She told herself all of that was true, but in some tiny, secret place deep inside herself, this was one of those moments when she truly wished she wasn't different. At home with her family she wasn't treated as if she was different, but they only had to step outside of the house for her to become an oddity. The local people tolerated her at their social events because her father was a powerful and influential man, and no one would dare tell him that the orphan Indian girl he'd raised as a companion to his daughter was not welcome to attend their balls and picnics and bazaars. And so Amala went dutifully wherever her family went, but she most often remained on the outskirts of whatever was taking place.

"Are you thirsty?" she heard a male voice ask and felt a little startled.

"What was that?" she asked, pretending she hadn't heard him due to the noise in the room—which was perfectly believable. In truth, she just wanted to be certain he was talking to her.

"I asked if you're thirsty," he said, holding a cup of punch out toward her.

"I am, actually," she said, taking it after she'd set her fan in her lap. "Thank you. That's very kind of you." She took a sip, and he sat in the chair where Kat had been sitting.

"Forgive me if I'm intruding," he said. "But you looked rather . . . bored."

"I must try harder to be a better actress," Amala said and took another sip of the punch, realizing she was much thirstier than she'd realized.

"Not at all," the man said. "I don't believe in pretending. We should convey exactly who we are and how we feel."

"Perhaps," Amala said, feeling a little awkward in spite of his kindness. She noted that he was tall and as well built as he was well dressed. His hair was dark blond with a distinct wave to it that she suspected would be curlier if it hadn't been forced into submission for an event such as this.

"Forgive me," he said. "I haven't properly introduced myself. I am Henry Beckenridge. And you are?"

"Amala," she said and laughed softly to cover feelings of mild embarrassment, as she usually did when people asked her name. "I won't bother telling you the rest because you won't be able to pronounce it and you won't remember it. Unofficially I belong to the Hepworth family, but I was never actually adopted. I have always been considered a *companion* to their daughter Katarina. We are near the same age, and very close in every way. It works out nicely at home, but on occasions such as this, I . . ." Amala stopped herself. "I don't know why I'm telling you all of this. We're complete strangers, Mr. Beckenridge."

"We're becoming acquainted . . . Amala. And I know of the Hepworth family—of Willenbrock House—even though I confess I am barely acquainted. Dare I guess you were going to say that on such occasions you don't really feel like you fit in?"

"It's not a matter of what I feel, sir; it is a fact. I have lived in England since I was a child. Although it's impossible for me to speak—as much as I've tried—without betraying a hint in my accent that I am not English. I will never be able to look English, or sound English, and therefore I will never *be* English."

"And so you sit here and watch everyone else dancing and having a good time? Is this how you generally handle social events?"

"If you must know, yes."

He set his punch down on a little table and stood up. "Then you must dance with me."

Amala felt astonished. She could count on her fingers the number of times she'd actually been asked to dance, and never by a man so handsome. It was generally the homely men who felt out of place themselves who behaved as if they were doing her a great favor to dance with her. But this man genuinely seemed to want to dance with her.

Amala had to admit. "Truthfully, my feet are killing me, and . . ."

"Slip off your shoes," he whispered. "Push them under the chair and no one will ever notice. Come along. Dance with me."

"I must warn you," Amala said, liking this man more by the minute, "dancing with me could create a scandal. Consorting with a woman like me is not looked upon favorably."

"And I've never looked favorably upon the ridiculous notions of society that make absolutely no sense whatsoever." He held out his hand. "So, let's cause a stir, shall we?"

A waltz had just begun and Henry was quick to catch her up in the lively rhythm of the dance. His efficiency made it evident he'd had plenty of practice, but it helped make up for Amala's *lack* of practice. He swept her effortlessly around the dance floor while Amala was aware of her full taffeta skirt swirling around her and brushing against that of other ladies, who were all wearing skirts far too full to be practical for any purpose except this.

When the dance was finished everyone applauded, although the lace, fingerless gloves Amala wore prevented her hands from making any sound whatsoever. Unwilling to make any presumptions—or even the appearance of them—in regard to the attention Henry had so kindly offered, she hurried back to where she'd been seated and picked up her fan from the chair in order to sit down. But she was barely seated when she heard Henry say, "Did I frighten you? I must confess I was hoping for more than *one* dance."

"Perhaps later," Amala said, fanning her face. She truthfully stated, *"I* must confess that it's terribly hot in here." She didn't add that she thought it would be far better if he wasn't seen spending too much time with her. A vast collection of difficult memories supported her concern. "But . . . thank you, Mr. Beckenridge," she added in order to be polite. "You have been most kind."

"Please call me Henry," he said and again sat beside her. Amala felt concerned but couldn't force him to go away. In truth she was enjoying his company and couldn't help feeling pleased—however foolhardy his spending too much time in her presence might be. "And let me call you Amala . . . since you've not given me a proper surname I might use."

"Most people call me Miss Hepworth . . . even if it's only a formality."

"That all sounds very well and proper," he said, "but I prefer to call you Amala, and I would very much like to have a conversation with you."

"About what?" she asked as if he'd proposed something scandalous.

He chuckled with a sparkle in his eyes that made her stomach flutter, and she increased the speed of her fan.

Henry leaned slightly closer, as if he meant to tell her a secret, although he could have likely shouted and no one would have been able to hear what he said due to the din of music and laughter in the room. "I'm hoping you would do me a *very* big favor," he said, and for a moment she wondered if he *was* proposing something scandalous. "You see . . . I'm feeling a little . . . disoriented, and I do believe there is no one here I could talk to about it but you."

"Why?" she asked, hearing an abruptness in her voice that she knew wasn't customary for her.

Instead of answering the question, Henry relaxed in his chair and looked toward the crowded ballroom. "I saw you watching the Indian servants. Curiosity? Intrigue? You're probably wondering why they're here. I'm guessing you've been to a social in this home before, but these particular servants weren't here and you're wondering why. Well, I can tell you. The eldest son of the Roderick family just returned from India last week."

Amala looked sharply toward Henry but he didn't seem to notice as he continued. "The servants you see wearing their native dress are very dear to him, and given the choice, they wished to remain with him and come to England."

"And you know this because . . ." She purposely left the sentence unfinished.

"Howard Roderick has been my closest and dearest friend since we were children." He turned to look at Amala. "I went to India with him, and I too returned just six days ago."

Amala's vision blurred from the moisture that filled her eyes before she could even think to try to hold it back. The fragments of her heart that were forever tied to her homeland suddenly hung on every word that might come out of this man's mouth. The silence between them grew, but she couldn't speak without betraying how overcome she felt, and she didn't want to risk embarrassing herself.

Henry saved her when he said, "You told me you left India when you were a child. How much do you remember? I saw colors there like I've never seen in England—the flowers, the clothing, the decor. The streets of the cities were so noisy, but it wasn't at all the same kind of noise as the noise in the streets of London. The hills and valleys have a beauty there unlike anything that can be seen in this part of the world. And the—"

Amala was suddenly so overcome with emotion that she had only one thought. She had to get out of the room before she burst into childish sobbing. She didn't fully understand the source of the emotion roiling inside her, but its intensity was frightening, and she ran as if it might run after her like a wild animal in the woods. She ran through the huge open doors that led out onto an enormous veranda, and she kept running until she felt cool grass on her stockinged feet and realized she'd left her shoes beneath the chair. She slowed her pace and soon found a bench situated against some artistically trimmed shrubbery. She sat down and tried to catch her breath, all the while fighting to swallow back the emotion that had caught her off guard. This was neither the time nor the place to contend with such feelings.

"I seem to keep frightening you," Henry said, and she let out a breathy scream that verified the truth of his statement. Amala took a deep, sustaining breath, glad at least that it was dark. She was seated with the lanterns on the veranda behind her, which kept her face in the shadows, hopefully concealing any evidence of her emotion.

"Forgive me," she said, unable to think of a single word of explanation.

"I assume that something I said upset you," he said and sat down next to her. He held up her shoes, which were hanging from his fingers. "You forgot these."

"Oh, thank you," she said, taking them quickly to set them on the ground near her feet. "How silly you must have looked walking out of the ballroom carrying a pair of ladies' shoes."

He chuckled. "I doubt anyone noticed, but even if they did, what does it matter? Do you think I'll be the subject of gossip over tea tomorrow?" He raised his voice comically to mimic a woman. "'Oh, did you see the way he was carrying those shoes?'" He changed his tone only slightly to offer the other side of the imagined conversation. "'What on earth was he thinking to engage in such unseemly behavior? It's scandalous, I tell you. Utterly scandalous.'"

Amala couldn't help laughing, which eased her nerves and offered some perspective over her concerns. Following their laughter, a silence fell that threatened to become awkward until Henry asked, "How old were you when you came to England?"

"I was nine," she said. "And now I have spent more than half of my life in England."

"But still you don't *feel* English?" he guessed.

"In some ways I do," she admitted. "I've grown to love much about England, and I love my family. I am grateful every day that these good people made me a part of their family and brought me here. Otherwise . . ." She cleared her throat and sought for different words. "As I understand it, my situation would have been extremely dreadful following my parents' deaths."

Amala looked directly away from Henry and let out a little laugh that stemmed more from embarrassment than any kind of humor. "And again I am talking too much."

"I *want* to hear you talk," he said. "Otherwise, I wouldn't have asked. I find it ironic that I don't really . . . well, I'm very glad to be back in England, and I don't ever intend to leave again. But I feel as if I left a part of myself behind in India; I will never be the same. Would it make me sound inane to admit that—after the years I lived there—a part of me feels . . . Indian?"

Amala looked at him, hoping to be able to discern whether or not he really meant it. She was surprised that even in the shadows she could see—as much as she could feel—his sincerity.

"How long were you there?" she asked.

He chuckled and she wondered why he might find the question humorous. He leaned his forearms on his thighs and threaded his fingers together before he turned his face toward her and said, "Nine years." Amala let out a little gasp even before he put words to her own thoughts. "So, does that make us equally Indian? I may seem crazy, but somehow I feel like it does. If not for the color of our skin, would we not be? I hope that doesn't sound offensive; that's not how I intended it."

"Not at all," she said, wishing she could find words to explain how she felt so strangely drawn to him—as if they *were* equally Indian. Beyond her own family—who had also lived in India for many years—she had never spoken to anyone who understood that part of her. She had an awareness of many British people going back and forth to India, but she was not at all acquainted with any of them and had therefore felt that her memories of her homeland and the occasional strange longings she felt were something that she could only hold in her heart. Kat's memories of India were not favorable; she hadn't liked it there, which meant she didn't want to talk about it. Her parents had some fond memories of India, but they had also been aware of the depravity and injustice taking place on many fronts, and the topic couldn't be brought up without conversation inevitably veering toward such things.

Sometimes Amala would allow her mind to wander to her childhood memories, sifting through them to hold only to the good ones—the beauty and wonder and strangeness. It was all so unlike England, that the older she got the more her memories had come to feel like dreams—elusive and unreal. She realized now that her conversation with Henry Beckenridge felt very much the same— dreamlike and difficult to grasp. She thought of a hundred questions she wanted to ask him but couldn't settle on where to begin. Then the noise of other party guests talking and laughing grew very near and Amala's mind went to her biggest concern.

"You shouldn't be seen with me this way," she muttered and grabbed her shoes and hurried away, deeper into the garden that was splotched with a vast array of flowering shrubberies and rose bushes in full bloom.

"I *do* wish you'd stop running away from me," Henry said, showing up at her side while she walked briskly. "You forgot *this,*" he said, holding up her fan. "It's apparent you need me to follow you around and keep track of your belongings."

"Thank you," she said, taking the fan from him.

"Why should I not be seen with you?" he asked. Amala looked around, seeing that they were alone and that a high wall of shrubberies blocked their view of the veranda.

"My presence at such events is only tolerated because no one would dare offend my father by excluding me. But no gentleman would ever be caught in my presence longer than to participate in an obligatory dance here and there or to be moderately polite. At dinners I am always seated between my family members so that no one else will be required to be in close proximity to me." She heard him mutter a noise of disbelief, but she kept talking in order to say what she knew needed to be said. "If you have lived in India, then you should be well aware of the lines that are clearly maintained between your kind and mine. Those lines are the same here—if not even more vividly defined. My parents made a huge sacrifice to take me on when my mother and father were killed; they knew they would always be judged and criticized for it. Perhaps if they had me scrubbing floors and cleaning fireplaces, their caring for me would be considered acceptable. But they've told me that doing anything less than treating me as their own daughter would be dishonoring my parents. Yet, for all their kindness and efforts, they cannot change the society in which we live. I am different and I always will be, and *you* are a fool if you think that you can come back here and somehow magically change all of that. You've been very kind, but you must . . . seek conversation elsewhere."

"Why?" he demanded, sounding mildly angry. "There's no one else here tonight I have any desire to talk to. I want to talk to *you,* and I've already explained my reasons for that. Why can we not just . . . walk in the garden . . . and talk about our common passion for a faraway world that will always hold a portion of our hearts? Is that a crime?"

"Some might see it that way," she declared, even though she longed for such conversation.

"Well, no one is watching right now," he said in a tone that implied he wouldn't care if they were. He motioned toward a bench she hadn't realized they'd happened upon. Then he reminded her, "My lifelong friend lives here; I know this garden like the back of my hand. Sit with me, Amala . . . just for a little while. Talk to me. We won't be missed."

Amala thought about it for a long moment, then sat down. "For a few minutes," she said, and he sat beside her. She was glad when he began to talk about the things he'd loved about living in India, as opposed to asking her questions about her own memories. He also talked of the things he'd hated—most specifically the heat and the bugs. She enjoyed listening to every word that came out of his mouth, until the sense of how much time had passed shocked her to her feet.

"Oh, my goodness," she said. "I must get back." He stood beside her but didn't get a chance to speak before she blurted, "Thank you, sir. You've been so kind. I very much enjoyed our conversation, and . . . I wish you a good evening."

Amala ran back toward the house, making certain she had her shoes in one hand and her fan in the other so that Henry wouldn't have any excuse to come and find her again. Just before she came to the veranda, Amala stopped for a moment to catch her breath and put her shoes on, if only for the sake of propriety. She knew her stockings were surely ruined but she didn't care. Already the memory of the cool grass on her feet mingled in her mind with her secretive excursion into the garden with Henry Beckenridge, and the delightful conversation they'd shared.

Back in the ballroom everything appeared just the same as it had been when she'd left. It took only a moment of scanning the room to spot Kat having a wonderful time on the dance floor, and her parents were doing the same. Glad to know she'd not been missed, Amala was disappointed to find that the chair she'd been using earlier was now occupied by a rather large woman who was taking up a great deal of both chairs on either side of her. Amala walked discreetly in the other direction around the perimeter of the ballroom until she found a place to sit. She was glad to note how many people were caught up in the dancing; otherwise, there might not have been any vacant chairs.

The fresh air had felt good and had cooled her down somewhat, but it only took a minute before she flipped open her fan and began using it, rehearsing in her mind how Henry had told her he'd hated the heat and the bugs in India. She'd not remembered how much hotter it had been there in contrast to England, but it was one more reason to feel that—in spite of certain challenges—she was much more suited to England. If she could barely tolerate the heat of a crowded ballroom, surely the climate of India would undo her.

Recalling other bits and pieces of her conversation with Henry, she now wished she'd not rushed away so hastily. Now that she was here, sitting alone as she often did on such occasions, she missed his cordial company and the way they'd so quickly gained a comfortable rapport. She wondered then if she would ever see him again, and the thought saddened her. People came from all over for this sort of social gathering. She had no idea where he lived; for that matter she knew absolutely nothing about him—except that he'd spent nine years in India. And that Howard Roderick was his closest, lifelong friend. Henry couldn't live *too* far away from here, she concluded. Although the Roderick home was nearly an hour's drive by carriage from her own home.

Amala stopped herself from such silly speculations when the music ended and everyone applauded. A moment later her mother was seated next to her, patting her arm in her typical way.

"Oh, there you are, darling," Viola Hepworth said. "I was trying to find you earlier. Is everything all right?"

"Yes, fine," Amala said. "I only took a brief stroll in the garden to get away from the heat."

"How very brilliant of you!" Viola said and exchanged a wink with her husband, Oliver, who was chatting nearby with a couple of other men near his age.

Amala's unofficial parents were the most generous and loving people she had ever encountered, and she considered herself greatly blessed to have been taken into their home and their lives. Oliver was tall and thin with barely a hint of gray hair left on his balding head, but his lack of hair didn't detract from his fine features that had—according to Viola—only grown more handsome with age. Viola was also tall—at least compared to most women. But still she was more than a few inches shorter than her husband. Her hair had also gone gray, but it was long and thick and always looked striking no matter how it was styled. Right now a portion of it was pinned up artistically at the back of her head while the rest hung down her back in an array of curls. Viola had the hair of a woman half her age, which made her age show less in her face than did the ages in the faces of most women of her generation. Ironically her hair was styled very much the same as Amala's and Kat's—which was likely due to the fact that the same maid had done all of their hair earlier this evening. Since the style was certainly flattering on all of them, it worked well.

Viola had a well-rounded figure but by no means carried any superfluous weight. Together, Oliver and Viola Hepworth were a handsome couple, and any stranger only had to observe them together for a minute or two in order to conclude that they loved and respected each other. Amala felt sure that the love they felt for each other was so great that it had spilled over and made it possible for them to love her as much as they loved their own daughter. Whatever the reasons, she praised God every day for the way she felt such a place of belonging, love, and acceptance among them. For it was *only* among the Hepworth family that she felt that way. But if she ever took to feeling sorry for herself, she only had to imagine an orphaned Indian girl with no family, begging in the streets for her survival. While it hadn't been spoken of often, Amala knew from all she'd been told of her situation that it surely would have been that way. Some of her memories of India were vague and cloudy, but she had very clear memories of holding to her mother's skirts while they pushed their way through crowds of people on a narrow city street—memories of the beggars with their ragged clothes, their sunken faces, and their outstretched hands.

"I saw you dancing earlier," Viola said, bringing Amala out of her unsavory thoughts. "Given that it was a very lively waltz, I didn't get a good look at him, but from what I could see, he looked rather handsome."

"Yes," was all Amala could say, unable to deny the truth in Viola's statement. But Amala felt unnerved by the subtle fluttering in her stomach at the thought of Henry. She'd made up her mind a long time ago about the course her life would have to take. She'd accepted that the good life she'd been given came with sacrifices that simply had to be, given the society in which they lived. Feeling attracted to *any* man did not fit into her plans. She quickly convinced herself that Henry's appeal was based entirely in their common interest in her native country.

Fearing that Viola might speculate over the identity of the mysterious dance partner, Amala was relieved when one of Viola's friends sat down on the other side of her and they began to chat. Amala couldn't help noticing that the woman offered her neither greeting nor acknowledgment; she wasn't at all surprised, since it happened all the time. She only wished she could somehow become immune to the sting she felt every time she was left feeling invisible. She suddenly felt very tired and wondered how much longer they would be staying. Thankfully, her parents often left such events at a reasonable hour, in contrast to many who would stay on into the early hours of the morning. Still, since she couldn't see a clock from where she was seated, Amala had no idea what time it was, and she just wanted to go. She couldn't deny that her fear of encountering Henry Beckenridge again added incentive to her desire to leave.

Scarcely a few minutes later, Oliver approached and announced that he was ready to leave. He went to find Kat, who would surely be disappointed at having to give up on her continual opportunity to dance with one partner after another. By the time he returned with Kat, Viola had finished her conversation with her friend, and within minutes they were in the carriage on their way home.

As always, Oliver and Viola wanted to know if the girls had had a good time, and Amala was always glad to allow Kat to dominate the conversation with her talk about all the latest fashions the ladies had been wearing and all the men she'd danced with. She revealed which of those men she would prefer to never socialize with and which of them she would enjoy getting to know better.

"And what about you, my dear?" Oliver asked Amala. "Any young prospective beaus that sparked your interest?"

Amala felt like snapping at them; she wanted to say what should have been obvious—that the very idea of marrying, or even courting, an Englishman was absurd. They all knew it, and she wondered why they'd never talked about it. Did her family have some secret hope that all of the social disdain of such a prospect might magically go away? In her mind she committed to initiating that conversation with her family at a more appropriate time, if only so they would all stop expecting—and talking about—something that would never happen. For the moment she simply said, "No one."

"I saw you dancing more than once," Oliver said, as if that fact might help convince her of the magical transformation that had been implied a moment ago.

"Yes," Amala said. "It was delightful." Her stomach fluttered again at the memory of dancing with Henry. She hurried to add—as if it might soothe her family's concern over the fact that she hadn't danced nearly as much as Kat, "But my feet were hurting far too much to—"

"We must acquire more comfortable shoes for Amala," Kat said to their parents. "She shouldn't be kept from dancing simply because of poorly made shoes."

Amala thought about how she hadn't been wearing her shoes when she'd danced with Henry, and her skirts were plenty long so no one would have noticed. But she didn't comment.

"No, you're absolutely right," Viola said as if Amala's shoes were surely the entire source of the problem. "Before we attend another ball, we will get you some proper shoes."

Amala offered her mother an appreciative smile but said nothing. A bridge of silence lured Amala's thoughts to Henry's descriptions of the brilliant colors of fabric worn by the women in India and of the unique scent of spices in the air. His words made her childhood memories more vivid, and she held them close. She longed for more such conversation with Henry Beckenridge, but doubted it would ever happen.

"Oh, I forgot to tell you," Oliver said, interrupting her reverie. He was looking more at his wife, but his comment was obviously meant for all of them. "I invited someone over for tea tomorrow. Howard Roderick."

"Why, he's as old and crippled as any man could ever be," Viola said, astonished. "I thought he never left his house. It was his wife who hosted this evening's ball. I don't think Howard could have made it down the stairs or—"

"No, not *that* Howard Roderick," Oliver said. "His son; the younger Howard—although he has some strange nickname, something to do with his middle name. I don't recall it now. But I had a nice, long chat with the fellow. Very gentlemanly, he was."

"Oh, of course," Viola said with exuberance. "Tonight's gala was in his honor; he's just returned home after many years away, has he not?"

"That's right," Oliver said. "He's lived in India for years."

Amala's heart quickened as her mind made the connection. Howard Roderick, the lifelong friend of Henry Beckenridge. They had traveled to India together.

"We had a jolly good time talking of India," Oliver continued, "and so I invited him to tea, thinking we could go at it a great deal longer. I hope you don't mind, my dear."

"Oh, not at all!" Viola said. "It sounds delightful!"

"And I was thinking," Oliver said, and Amala realized he was looking at her, "that you might enjoy such a conversation, as well—to hear more about your homeland. I wonder sometimes if we shouldn't talk about it more. I'm not even certain what you remember."

Rather than try to discuss her memories or encourage any discussion on the topic itself, Amala simply said, "Tea with Mr. Roderick sounds lovely."

Amala felt a secret wish that it might be tea with Mr. Beckenridge instead—who had also just returned from India—but she immediately knew it was likely better if she never saw Henry again. She had no sooner thought it when Oliver said, "Oh, and he's bringing a friend; been friends forever, he tells me. They traveled there and back together. Did some kind of work for the viceroy, I believe."

"Oh, that would be Henry Beckenridge," Viola said, and Amala's heart quickened at the very mention of his name. "I've known his mother . . . well . . . since I first came here as a bride, I suppose. Although she's not one whose company I've ever enjoyed much. Cranky, I'd call her."

"And what of his father?" Kat asked.

"Oh, he died very young, when Henry was still a child, from what I recall."

"I believe that's right," Oliver interjected. "Which means that Henry owns the whole of the Beckenridge estate, which is no small birthright by any account."

"Then why do you suppose he went to India?" Viola asked.

"Perhaps to get away from his cranky mother," Kat said with a giggle.

"Indeed," Viola said and laughed with her.

"I suppose we can find out tomorrow," Oliver said. "It should be a delightful afternoon."

"Indeed," Viola said again, but Amala didn't know whether to feel thrilled or terrified.

* * * *

Henry sat alone in the garden long after Amala had rushed away, resisting the urge to track her down one more time. He tried and tried to find some plausible reason for his undeniable fascination with this woman. It couldn't simply be the fact that she was Indian; he'd been living in India for years and he'd had personal interaction with hundreds of Indian people. He couldn't deny that he'd always felt intrigued with the dark skin and black hair of the Indian women. Their exotic appearance in contrast to English women had fascinated him, but no more or less than the men and children of the Indian race. And his fascination with the people had always been much like his fascination with the culture and the landscape, the colors and smells, the very fact that so many things there had often seemed exactly opposite to so many things in England. He concluded that his intrigue with Amala was not simply the fact that she was Indian or that he was feeling somehow nostalgic for the country he'd just left behind where he'd grown to feel comfortable and at home. No, it was much more than that.

Henry wondered if it was the contrast of seeing an Indian woman in English dress, along with seeing her in the surroundings of a typical English social gathering. Still, that wasn't the reason either. While her dark skin and eyes and her silky black hair had certainly made her stand out among the crowd, it was Amala herself that made it impossible for Henry to stop thinking about her.

Henry finally returned to the ballroom, debating whether or not to try to find Amala and beg for one more dance before the evening ended. He imagined how she would protest and insist that he was a fool, but the thought only made him smile. She was far from the first person to call him a fool; he'd been a fool for far lesser things.

Henry felt a little skip in his heartbeat when he caught a glimpse of Amala across the room, but disappointment settled in when he realized she was with her family and they were leaving. He sighed and watched her from a distance until she was gone, then he looked around the room and couldn't think of a single reason why he wanted to stay any longer. On the other hand, he couldn't think of any reason why he wanted to go home. Certain he would find his friend Chit somewhere playing cards, he sought out the most obvious location, and, sure enough, he found a parlor containing a small gathering of men who obviously preferred a friendly game of poker over dancing or trying to impress the ladies.

Howard Chitworth Roderick—or *Chit*, as he'd always been called by close friends and family—was in the middle of a heated game, and Henry slumped into a comfortable chair nearby to wait for the outcome. It was only heated because of the way the men were playfully bantering in a way that mimicked a serious row. And since the bets being made were only small numbers of coins, there were certainly no stakes involved.

Chit was by far one of the finest men Henry had ever known, and he considered their friendship one of the greatest blessings of his life. Henry's own father had died when he was very young, his mother was barely tolerable company in only small doses, and his sister clung to every opinion that was exactly opposite to his own. Consequently, Henry had found comfort and security in Chit's home and with *his* family. Chit had always been of a portly build and had lost most of his hair in his early twenties; he wasn't known as being fair to look at, but his smile was infectious, and his charm was in his warm personality and his impeccable integrity. Everyone who knew him loved him. But Henry had the privilege of being Chit's oldest and dearest friend.

Henry laughed when Chit lost the game terribly. He slapped his friend on the shoulder and said, "This is why gambling with anything more than ha'pennies is not good for your health."

As he came to his feet, Chit laughed and declared he was bowing out of the next game. "I'm glad you're here," he said to Henry, easing him away from the crowd where they wouldn't be overheard. "I was afraid you might have run off before I had a chance to tell you."

"Tell me what?" Henry asked, already skeptical. Chit was known for making plans that included the both of them without first consulting Henry.

"We're invited to tea tomorrow," Chit said.

"Oh, you cannot be serious!" Henry declared. "What is this? You've got a fancy for some pretty young lass and you get us invited to tea? And of course you have to drag me along so you don't make yourself too obvious! And what if I'm busy? Or what if I don't want to go?"

"Oh, come on, old boy," Chit said. "It'll be grand! And it's nothing like that. There you go again, thinking you've got me all figured out. It was a kind old chap who invited us; used to live in

India. We had a fine visit and he thought it would be grand to have more time to compare notes, and all that. He came back here not long after we left; says he misses it sometimes—although he doesn't want to go back."

"I can agree with that," Henry said, not daring to hope that Chit could be talking about Amala's father. It was not at all uncommon for Britishers to go back and forth to India; there could have been a number of people present this evening who had traveled there and enjoyed talking about it.

"And just who are these people whom I have agreed to have tea with entirely against my will?" Henry asked, almost holding his breath.

"Oliver Hepworth," Chit said, and Henry almost laughed aloud. It was far too amazing to be a coincidence—at least as far as he saw it. "You know him?"

"Know of him," Henry said.

"Oh, and . . . he has daughters; perhaps they'll be lovely, eh? One of them is Indian, he tells me. Took her on when her parents were killed. I don't know about you, but it sounds like the perfect family for us to lounge about with for an afternoon. Oh, gotta go. Just saw someone I need to speak with. I'll be around to get you after lunch, old boy."

"I'll be ready," Henry said and briefly glanced heavenward, as if to acknowledge the sudden feeling he had that Providence had smiled upon him.

Chapter Two
THE UNWANTED SUITOR

AMALA HAD A STRANGE DREAM that night, in which her hazy memories of India mingled with the things Henry had told her of his own impressions of the country. She could hear the noise of vendors in the street and feel the soft fabric of her mother's sari that she clung to as they pushed through the crowds with a particular destination in mind, although she had no idea where they were going. Their clamoring through the crowds seemed to go on and on, as if they might never arrive. The throng of people became so thick—all moving in the opposite direction—that Amala began to feel frightened and clung more tightly to her mother.

Amala awoke with a quickened heart, as if the fear she'd felt in the dream had been real. It took minutes for her heartbeat to return to normal, but her thoughts remained with the dream—and almost against her own will, she couldn't keep herself from thinking about Henry. She reminded herself that he was charming and they had something in common, but she absolutely knew it could never be more than that, and she carefully put her frame of mind in place to keep her thoughts within proper parameters. They could be friends and nothing more; she could not lose sight of that. No other possibility could even be considered. She'd already considered carefully—over the course of many years—the possibilities of marriage and children for herself. And it simply would not, and could not, happen within this society. She had accepted it, and she was content to be grateful for the good life she had been given; she would not waste time mourning over what she could not have. The fact that Henry was coming to tea with his friend later today was of no relevance beyond their common interests and the possibility of conversation about shared interests.

Amala proceeded as normal with her day while she did well at remaining convinced that her inability to get Henry Beckenridge out of her head was simply a result of her anticipation of experiencing more of the stimulating conversation she'd enjoyed sharing with him the previous evening. If she had actually met Mr. Howard Roderick and had been given a chance to speak with him, it would have surely had the same effect on her. But for all the logic she was strictly imposing on herself, she couldn't find any justifiable reason for her nervousness in anticipating the visit of these two gentlemen. She considered the possibility that she might feel less nervous if she didn't feel as if her parents were attempting to match her with a possible suitor. In Kat's case, such efforts were completely appropriate, but Amala didn't understand why her parents couldn't see the obvious in regard to herself. No gentleman would align himself with a woman like Amala, and her parents seemed to think that the problems associated with such a possibility might magically go away. Amala made up her mind that she needed to speak with her parents and clear up the matter so there would be no further room for misunderstanding. But by the time Amala figured out she needed to have that conversation, lunch was over and there was no time for broaching such a delicate matter when company would soon be arriving.

At the time their guests were due to arrive, Amala was sitting in Kat's room, waiting for her sister to make certain her appearance was perfect. Kat speculated over what these two gentlemen callers might be like, as if every gentleman who entered their social circle might be considered a potential husband. Amala mostly listened, only commenting enough to be polite and let Kat know that she was paying attention. For a long moment Amala watched her sister primping and envied her fair skin and golden hair, only because they allowed her to hope for a normal life here in a country where Kat's appearance alone made it evident she belonged. At the moment, while Kat had good reason to anticipate any opportunity to get to know available English gentlemen, for Amala it was only a temporary distraction, and she knew it could never be anything more. She felt some anticipation in knowing that Henry would be here, but as much as she craved his company and conversation, her attraction to him caused far more unrest and confusion than any of the pleasant delight Kat was going on about.

Amala hurried Kat along, if only so she could stop dreading the official introduction to these gentlemen—which would inevitably bring up the fact that she'd become acquainted with Henry the previous evening. Amala followed Kat through the doorway of the drawing room and caught a glimpse of her parents visiting with their guests. It only took a second to see that Howard Roderick was not nearly as conventionally handsome as Henry, although Amala firmly held to what her parents had taught her—not to judge others by their appearance. She only wished that others might offer her the same courtesy.

At that very moment, Mr. Roderick was telling her parents something that was making them laugh a great deal, but Amala's focus was on Henry Beckenridge. She wished he *wasn't* so handsome, that the waves of his blond hair didn't seem to fall perfectly into place, that his features weren't so perfectly proportioned. But just seeing him brought back every feeling she'd been battling and more, rushing over her with such force that she almost felt a little unsteady on her feet for a moment.

"Oh, there they are!" her father said, noticing the girls near the door. He stood, which prompted the other two men to do the same. Oliver motioned the girls closer while he said, "Here are my lovely daughters. I told you, Howard, about my daughters."

"Indeed, you did," Howard said and stepped forward, holding out his hand. "This must be Katarina," he added, and Kat slipped her hand into his. He kissed it quickly and let go, smiling at her as he said, "You're every bit as lovely as your father described. It's such a pleasure to meet you."

"And you," Kat said graciously.

"And this must be the lovely Amala," Howard said, turning toward her to kiss her hand as well. "Your father has told me so much about you. It is indeed a pleasure."

"Indeed it is," Amala said.

Howard then introduced his friend, Henry, who also kissed Kat's hand and expressed his delight in meeting her. He then turned to Amala, and she wondered if they were meant to pretend they'd not met previously. But he offered a smile that brightened his countenance and took her hand, saying with enthusiasm, "Amala and I had the pleasure of meeting last night. She was kind enough to take pity on me and share a dance." He kissed her hand, then held on to it a few seconds longer than necessary.

While Henry gracefully guided Amala to a chair and when everyone was once again seated, he told the others how she had been kind enough to share some conversation with him at the ball and how much he'd enjoyed being able to talk about India, since he was still feeling rather disoriented after his recent return.

Everyone was apparently thrilled at the *delightful serendipity*—as Viola called it—of Amala and Henry having already gotten to know each other. Amala couldn't deny being glad to see Henry again, and when he smiled at her, it was impossible not to smile back. She thought of how comfortably they'd conversed the previous evening in the garden, and she couldn't deny that she already thought of him as a friend. The problem was that in seeing him now, what she felt went far beyond friendship—and she wasn't certain what to do about it. Concluding that this was only one afternoon and that for now she could do absolutely nothing, she relaxed and determined that she would simply enjoy the company of their visitors while it lasted.

Amala quickly liked Howard and could see why these two men were such good friends. They were both kind, thoughtful, and polite. And they were both rather amusing. They had a particular way of bantering between themselves that always made the others laugh, and she could understand why—when Howard had made the decision to go to India more than nine years ago—Henry had quickly been talked into going along. The two men seemed as inseparable as were Amala and Kat.

The subject of Howard's nickname came up quickly when Henry referred to him as Chit. When Viola asked about it, Henry explained that Howard's middle name was Chitworth and he'd been called Chit practically from his infancy. Since Howard and Henry had known each other nearly that long, Henry never called him anything but Chit except in the case of formal introductions. Oliver then clarified that he far preferred a lack of formality—especially at such informal gatherings. The visitors agreed, and Amala recognized her father's customary way of giving permission for given names to be used in his home. Amala had seen people respond to his declaration with varying degrees of shock and disgust; it seemed that for some people anything less than formality in *all* matters was practically criminal. Amala had realized years ago that such people were rarely invited back into their home. Her parents far preferred the company of people around whom they could all be more relaxed and comfortable. It was evident these two men fit easily into that category.

Amala and Kat mostly listened while the others talked of India, sharing their memories and discussing their reasons for going there and enthusing over the strangeness and beauty of the place. Amala felt deeply fascinated with the conversation, since she'd never heard her homeland discussed in such detail before. She even heard things from her parents she'd never before heard them say about their reasons for living there and the things they'd loved about it.

Amala sensed that Kat was mostly bored. Kat's memories of India were not favorable; she'd apparently never liked it there, and she had no interest in talking about it. Amala had often wondered if Kat's memories included difficult things she didn't wish to be reminded of. She'd once asked Kat if that was the case, wanting to understand why she felt the way she did. Kat insisted otherwise, declaring that she simply hadn't liked it there. But Amala wondered to this day if Kat had some hidden reason for disliking India. Either way, India was a topic that had become taboo in conversation between the two sisters. They could talk about anything and everything—except India. Amala respected Kat's wishes to avoid the subject, except that she doubted Kat had any idea of how Amala sometimes felt the need to talk about it, to explore her memories, to indulge in the reality that for all that she was devoted to fitting into English life each and every day, she only had to look in the mirror to be reminded that she was and forever would be Indian.

Amala wasn't at all surprised when Kat declared that she was feeling a little under the weather and made her apologies before gracefully bidding their guests farewell and leaving the room. Amala knew very well that Kat was simply bored and unable to bear the conversation any further. Amala couldn't fault her sister when she knew that she might likely do the same if such a gathering had the same effect on her. Truthfully, once Kat had left, Amala ceased to be distracted by the subtle signs of Kat's discomfort and she was able to relax even more and enjoy the stories these men were telling of their years spent on the other side of the world. Some of their adventures had been very exciting—even frightening. And some had been marred by sadness at the evidence of poverty and political difficulties. But Amala hung on every word and was surprised when it was actually time for tea to be served; she couldn't believe how the time had flown.

When tea was winding down, Amala dreaded the departure of Henry and Chit, certain they would soon express the need to leave. But Oliver mentioned a collection of Indian artifacts that he kept in his personal study. Chit enthusiastically said that he'd love to see them, but Henry said to Oliver, "Forgive me, but . . . I confess I noticed what a lovely rose garden you have, and I was rather hoping to get a closer look." He paused and stole a barely detectable glance toward Amala before he added, "Perhaps Amala would do me the honor of giving me a tour."

"What a grand idea!" Oliver said with a pleased expression, much like the one that appeared on her mother's face. She mentally noted the need to have that conversation with her parents, and soon, if only so they would stop implying that she might be courted by some proper English gentleman. But for now, nothing sounded more appealing than the idea of having some time alone with Henry to share conversation akin to what they'd shared the previous evening.

"If that's all right with you, of course," Henry said directly to Amala, and she appreciated the way he considered asking her opinion rather than assuming that the men could decide what a woman might want to do with her time.

"I'd be happy to show you the gardens," she said. "They *are* especially lovely right now with the roses all in bloom."

"Perfect," Oliver said and headed out of the room with Viola on his arm and Chit right behind them.

Henry turned to Amala and offered one of those broad smiles that consumed his face. "I feared it was too much to hope for," he said, "that I might actually have some time alone with you." Amala looked down, feeling unusually shy, and he added, "I'm glad your parents aren't the sort who think we would need a chaperone to walk through the gardens in broad daylight."

"No, they aren't that sort," Amala said, looking at him again. "They know I am capable of causing you great bodily harm should you attempt anything untoward."

He looked momentarily astonished, then laughed when he realized she was joking. She didn't bother telling him that she *was* capable; there was no need, given the fact that she already knew him well enough to know he was a true gentleman and that she felt completely safe with him.

"Shall we?" he asked and offered his arm.

Amala put her hand over his arm and guided him out of the drawing room and down a long hall to a door that exited onto the garden terrace. They walked across the terrace and onto the lawn toward a cluster of artistically arranged rose bushes in a variety of colors, all pruned to perfection and covered with blooms that filled the air with their fragrance. Amala stopped and closed her eyes while she inhaled the sweet aroma that to her was like the smell of summer. She opened her eyes and looked around, trying not to feel distracted by how much she enjoyed the opportunity to hold Henry's arm.

"It's very beautiful," she commented, focusing her gaze on a flourishing bush of yellow roses that was one of her favorites.

"It *is* very beautiful," he said.

Amala stole a glance at his face, surprised to find him staring at her. "You're not even looking at the roses," she said in a scolding tone.

"Oh, I looked at them," he said, completely unabashed over his attention to her. "They are very beautiful too."

Amala's heart quickened and she turned her back to him, letting go of his arm. "Henry, you mustn't," she insisted, feeling like a hypocrite.

"I mustn't what?" he asked. "Look at you? Tell you that you're beautiful?"

"No," she said without conviction, "you mustn't."

"How can I not when I have thought of nothing but you since you ran away from me last night?"

Amala resisted the urge to turn and face him, knowing it would be easier to say what needed to be said if she weren't looking at him. "You're very kind, sir, but you also have a very short memory."

Henry chuckled and moved around her so that she had no choice but to face him. "I think you just insulted me," he said.

"That was not my intention," she insisted. "Forgive me."

"There's nothing to forgive, Amala. I'm just trying to understand why you have such an aversion to my company . . . or you seem to . . . part of the time. It didn't seem to be a problem when we were sitting in the garden last night."

"No one could see us together there," she said. "But . . . I explained all of this to you. There is no good in our being seen together. It will only cause problems." Again she turned her back to him. "You should have gone with Chit and my father to look at the—"

"All due respect to your father, Amala, I don't want to see his mementoes of India. I doubt it's anything I haven't seen before. Chit likes that sort of thing. I, on the other hand, wanted to be with you. And I don't care what anyone thinks or says. It's just a walk in the garden. And this is *your* home, Amala. Surely here of all places you are not subjected to such ridiculous prejudice and—"

"Here in my home I am treated as an equal to my family members, but it's not my reputation that concerns me. The talk of servants travels quickly through the villages and from house to house."

"You speak as if our spending time together will taint me with leprosy or something."

"In regard to social matters," she said, "your analogy is quite accurate, Mr. Beckenridge."

"And now I'm *Mr. Beckenridge*?" He sounded vaguely angry. "We can't admire the rose garden together without regressing to such formality?"

"If you were only admiring the roses," she said firmly, "perhaps I would have no reason to be concerned."

Amala walked away, deeper into the garden and around the corner of a long hedge. She knew he would follow her, but she needed a moment to try to make sense of the turmoil rumbling inside of her. *This isn't supposed to happen*, she kept hearing inside her mind, but just the thought of what he'd said to her, and the way he'd looked at her made her knees feel weak and her stomach flutter. How could she keep having this argument with him when she wanted nothing more than to just soak in every morsel of his attention?

Amala was glad to make it to a bench before the weakness in her knees got any worse. She gripped the cold stone with both hands and lowered her head to try to draw a deep breath, but she found it practically impossible to pull air into her lungs. The same moment she realized she was crying, she looked up to see him standing nearby and knew there was no point in trying to hide her tears from him. Still, she turned her face away, and when he sat down beside her, she gripped the bench more tightly, as if doing so might save her from the effect he had on her.

"I've upset you," he said gently. "Forgive me. That was not my intention."

"It was not my intention to become upset," she said.

Henry held his breath until he had to remind himself to breathe. He felt as if he'd lost his mind—or maybe it was his heart. Or perhaps one malady was a result of the other. His mind had been consumed with thoughts of Amala ever since he'd laid eyes on her, and he'd hardly slept due to his attempts to reason away all of her logical and proper decorum over why they shouldn't pursue what he felt. But one element of the situation had completely eluded him. Until now. And now his heart felt as if it would explode out of his chest. He wondered what to do, what to say. He had no obvious answers either way, so he just took a deep breath and ventured to put a hand on her arm while he softly spoke her name. "Please look at me," he added. When she didn't, he said, "We haven't known each other long, but I believe we know each other well. You are a wise and practical woman, Amala. But I believe you are also as sensitive as you are sensible. We are two mature adults; I believe we've shared sufficient conversation to prove that we can talk about whatever it is that's upsetting you now. I hope you can believe me when I promise I would never be judgmental toward anything you share with me, and I would always hold everything you tell me in the strictest confidence."

"I *do* believe that," she said and sniffled.

"Please look at me," he repeated.

She turned slowly toward him, her eyes downward, tears streaking her face. Henry took out his handkerchief and couldn't resist the opportunity to wipe away her tears before he gave the hankie to her and she pressed it beneath her nose, muttering a quiet "Thank you." But she kept her eyes turned down, which made it impossible for him to even attempt gauging her thoughts.

"Until yesterday," he began with trepidation, hoping he wouldn't regret what he wanted to say, "I never would have believed it was possible—in a matter of hours—to grow to love someone."

At the mention of the word *love*, her eyes finally turned upward. He saw astonishment there. But he also saw something else— something she was trying to hide but couldn't—the very thing he'd been desperately hoping to see there. He couldn't hold back a smile as he stated the truth that was clearly visible. "You feel it, too."

He predicted that she might attempt to leave, and he took hold of her lower arm just before she tried to stand. "Don't run away from me, Amala," he said. "Just . . . talk to me."

Again she avoided looking at him. "This wasn't supposed to happen," she said and pressed the handkerchief beneath her nose again. "This *cannot* happen."

"This *has* happened," he said, "and you can't run away from it because I won't let you."

"To even *consider* acting upon . . . this *thing* that we feel— whatever it might be—is nothing short of madness. Nothing good could come of this. Nothing."

"Then we're not talking about the same thing," he insisted.

She sighed loudly and closed her eyes, and he could imagine her trying to think clearly and be rational. At the moment he felt anything but rational. He'd always struggled with being impulsive, and more than once in his life he'd made an utter fool of himself. But he'd never felt so strongly about anything—ever.

"Listen to me, Amala," he said, still keeping a firm hold on her arm— both because he wanted an excuse to touch her and because he feared she might try to leave. "I'm not suggesting anything irrational. I realize we only just met. I simply intend to ask for your father's blessing in courting you officially, then we can give the matter some time and—"

Amala shot to her feet so quickly it startled him, but he didn't let go of her. "You are completely and utterly out of your mind!" she snapped.

"I appreciate your faith in me," he said with sarcasm. "Please sit down and talk to me."

She *did* sit down, and it took no urging to get her to speak her mind. "Your interest toward me and your desires are an honor to me, Henry, but . . . there is no world in which what you are proposing is even remotely possible. For you to even *consider* courting an Indian woman tells me that you have not properly thought through the possible ramifications."

"I don't care about any of that," he insisted.

"You are speaking of things you simply don't understand!" she said, sounding angry. "Being an Englishman, you cannot have the slightest notion of what it's like for someone like me to exist in this society. The fact that you have not even lived in England for many years has perhaps distorted your perception of such things, although I'm well aware that such a relationship would be no more acceptable in India than it is here."

"Amala," he said with forced patience, wishing he could make her understand, "what can I say to make you believe that I don't care what *anyone* thinks . . . or says? It doesn't matter."

"It *does* matter," she insisted, still sounding angry. "I feel completely comfortable at home and I am treated as an equal, but I cannot step beyond the borders of this estate without being treated as grossly inferior, and you cannot comprehend the things people have said about me—and sometimes to my face. You can *say* that it doesn't matter, but this is the society in which we live. No human being can live a completely isolated life. You speak of courting me as if it were nothing out of the ordinary; I fear you would very quickly come to see it as an irreversible mistake. And then what? Courting implies the possibility of marriage. It's impossible, Henry. Impossible!"

"Change never happens if someone doesn't have the courage to do things differently. The fact that you are treated as less than equal to those who happen to be born British isn't right."

"It might not be fair or right," she said, "but you and I do not have the power to make such great changes."

"No, but we might make a little bit of difference for even a few people. However, this is not about making a change in the world, Amala; not to me. You're right. Courting implies the possibility of marriage. I don't know if it would come to that, but I hope it will."

"And what of the children who would come from such a marriage?" she asked as if he were on trial. "Such children are evilly persecuted and cast out in India. Do you really think it would be any different here? And don't tell me that the love of a good family could make up for whatever else they might face. Their entire lives would be *different* and filled with hardship because I would be their mother."

Henry felt his heart sinking further and further down toward the growing knot in his stomach. She had obviously given the matter a great deal of thought, but she was also shedding tears that mingled poignantly with her anger. He sat in silence beside her, taking in everything she'd said while she wiped the tears off her cheeks. She finally said, "You can let go of my arm. I'm not going to run away."

Henry *did* let go, but only so he could hold her hand. She seemed surprised but didn't resist. "What are you saying, Amala?" he asked as it all began to fully sink in. "That you intend to live your life as some kind of nun?"

Henry was surprised by the conviction of her answer, as well as how quickly it came out of her mouth. "Not officially, of course. But unless I leave my family and go back to India—which I will not— then I simply have to accept that marriage and children are not a possibility for me."

"I can't believe what I'm hearing," he said, sounding as astonished as he felt.

"Eventually you will *have* to believe it," she said, "because that's just the way it is. And in case it's crossed your mind that perhaps I could find a suitable match among people like the servants who came back from India with your friend, allow me to point out that this too would be considered inappropriate. If I were to marry a servant I would be considered a part of the serving class. I'm not against having to work, but it would sever me from my family. And they are everything to me. They are all I have." He heard her sniffle and realized she was crying again.

"You have me," he said, still holding her hand. "At the very least we are friends."

She turned to look at him—and he clearly saw his own thoughts mirrored in her eyes. She didn't want to be only a friend to him any more than he wanted to simply be *her* friend. Looking at her beautiful face while everything she'd just said rumbled through his mind, he felt as if he were locked in some ancient torture device. He didn't know how to talk her into changing her mind, and he couldn't deny his own naiveté and ignorance, which made it impossible for him to offer any reasonable argument. In that moment he could only hope that with time she would change her mind and allow him to court her.

As if she'd read his mind, she said while she squeezed his hand, "You must promise me that you will *not* speak to my father—or to anyone else, for that matter. You must promise me. If you care for me at all, you must promise me."

"I *do* care for you, Amala—more than I can say. But I heartily disagree, and my silence feels hypocritical."

"Do it for me," she said.

"I can't do it without the hope that something will change."

"You mustn't hope," she said with a conviction in her voice that was a complete contradiction to what he saw in her eyes. At least he didn't feel alone in his confusion.

Suddenly frozen as if they'd both turned to stone statues there in the garden, Henry could only stare into her black eyes and wish for some reasonable solution to the strength of all he was feeling. She didn't seem any more eager to look away than he did. It was as if they were trying to memorize each other, trying to hold on to this moment with the fear that it would be all they'd ever have.

Henry didn't think about kissing her; he just did it. The moment their lips met he could think of a hundred reasons why he shouldn't be doing this, but instead he chose to simply savor the experience, as meek and simple as it was. She offered no resistance, and her eyes were glistening with fresh moisture when she opened them to look at him. He couldn't keep himself from kissing her again.

Henry finally forced himself to some measure of rational thinking and drew away, turning to look straight ahead. He cleared his throat much louder than necessary and said, "Forgive me. That was completely inappropriate, and I'm sorry. I shouldn't have done that."

He felt the sting of tears in his eyes as he wondered if that would be the first and last time he would ever kiss her.

"Your apology is completely unconvincing," she said. "I don't believe a word of it."

Henry looked at her abruptly, even though he knew that meant she would be able to see the tears in his eyes. "How well you read me," he said. "I must confess . . . I'm not sorry at all. I can't dispute that it was inappropriate, but how can I regret it?"

She looked at him long and hard, as if she were desperately searching for something to say that might help assuage the wave of grief rushing over him. He was surprised by the way she put her free hand to the side of his face while she kissed his other cheek. She looked at him again and her voice cracked as she said, "Good-bye, Henry. If our paths cross again, it must be merely as friends . . . acquaintances. This must be the last time we speak of such things. I will never forget you."

She stood up and walked away, and he found himself completely incapable of going after her. There was nothing he could think of to say that might change her mind. The helplessness he felt had left him stunned and immobile. Knowing that he was completely alone and no one could possibly see him, he hung his head and pressed his face into his hands, weeping as if he'd just received news of the death of a loved one.

* * * *

Amala ran toward the house with the intention of hopefully getting to her room unnoticed so that she could follow Kat's example of claiming to not feel well, undress down to her chemise, and crawl into bed. Quickly assessing that she wasn't likely to get to her room without encountering *someone*, and also realizing that she couldn't get out of the dress, corset, and enormous petticoats without assistance, Amala impulsively took a different path and sneaked into the carriage house, where she knew there was only one person she might encounter there, and he would not fuss over her need to find a place to be alone and just think—or even cry if she needed to. The burning in her eyes and throat lured her to the likelihood that it would be the latter.

Amala was relieved to see Everett there, repairing one of the carriage wheels that he'd just removed. From his father, he had inherited the job of caring for the family's wheeled vehicles and thus had been born and raised on this estate. It was more home to him than to her. He was near her father's age, and rather nice looking with his graying dark hair. He wore a white shirt and dark breeches and boots—as he always did. In spite of having work to do to keep the carriages maintained, Everett knew he could be called upon to hitch up the carriages and sometimes drive them, which would require buttoning the cuffs of his rolled-up sleeves and donning a proper waistcoat and jacket. Right now he was at his most casual, and he only had to glance at Amala for her to know that he'd noticed her distress. He immediately let go of what he was working on and put his hands on his hips.

"What's wrong, child?" he asked in a way that she knew meant he hoped she would talk to him, but he wouldn't insist upon it. She'd been running to the carriage house to find respite and privacy for as long as she'd lived here, and Everett had become one of her truest friends. As close as she was to Kat, there were things they just couldn't talk about. But Everett had great wisdom and insight, and he never got upset or defensive about certain topics of conversation the way Kat did. Amala had come to see him as something akin to an uncle, and she knew that Everett saw their relationship much the same way. He'd been married in his younger days but had lost his wife and young son to disease, and he'd been alone ever since. He mingled comfortably among the other servants and was highly respected by them—as well as by the family. But he'd readily admitted that he'd grown to especially care for Amala and to feel some responsibility for her.

Everett's familiar expression of concern provoked Amala's tears to come forth. She'd learned long ago that the safety and trust she felt with him often had that effect. She could hold grief or sorrow inside for hours—or even days—until she spoke with Everett, and then it would just come bursting out of her.

Amala searched for words to try to explain, but they all felt too complicated. She settled for simply saying, "It's finally happened . . . just as you said it would." She knew he would understand exactly what she meant, so she left it at that and rushed to the deepest part of the carriage house and into an older vehicle that hadn't been used for years, where she settled into the cushioned seat in order to vent her tears privately. But a moment later Everett stepped into the carriage and sat beside her, putting a fatherly arm around her shoulders to offer silent support while she spent the tears of her sorrow.

* * * *

Henry entered the stable to see a man sitting with his back up against one of the stalls, whittling with a knife at what appeared to be the spoke of a wagon wheel. He glanced up at Henry for only a second before he said, "Stable hands are taking a break, but I can help ready your horse for you if you're needing it."

"No . . . thank you," Henry said. "I . . . should wait to leave until my friend has finished his visit with Mr. Hepworth."

"But?" the man asked with a boldness that most servants wouldn't dare assert with their employer's guests, although it actually made Henry feel more comfortable with him.

"But?" Henry echoed.

"But you're wandering around the stables?"

"I . . . wondered about leaving . . . but I really should wait . . . and I don't particularly want to go back into the house right now." Henry didn't add that he and Chit had a long-standing agreement that whenever a social engagement separated them—which it usually did— they would meet up at the stables if they'd come by horse, or in the carriage if they'd arrived in one, which only happened for more formal events. This prevented them from having to try to hunt each other down in large, unfamiliar homes or among crowds of people. "I'll just wait for my friend here," he said, "unless I would be intruding."

The man stopped his whittling and gave Henry a hard look, while Henry wondered if he should be ashamed by the likely evidence on his face that he'd been crying like a child.

"Might you be the man who reduced our sweet Amala to tears?" he asked, and Henry was so taken aback that it took him a good half minute to even blink.

His instincts told him he could be forthright with this man, so he tested the theory by confessing, "Might it be possible that it was the other way around?"

The man chuckled and turned his attention back to his work. "Yes," he muttered, "that certainly might be possible."

Henry didn't know if he felt validated or skeptical. Needing more information before he came to any conclusions, he asked, "Is it common around here for Amala to leave men in tears?"

"Never happened before to my knowledge," the man said, stealing a long glance at Henry before he again put his focus on the work at hand. He chuckled again, but Henry didn't find anything about this the least bit amusing. "Let's just say I suspected it would happen eventually. You can't blame a man for being just a wee bit pleased with himself for realizing he'd been right about something."

Henry didn't know what to say, but he didn't want to leave. If he couldn't talk *to* Amala, he figured the next best thing was to talk to someone who knew her well. And what little this man had said already made it evident that he had some insight, and perhaps some personal connection, to Amala. He'd admitted right off that Amala was in tears, but it had not been twenty minutes since she'd left Henry sitting alone in the garden.

While Henry just stood there, the man said, "The situation here is not easy for our little Amala. Those of us who have tried to look out for her have known it would likely only become more difficult when she came of age." He stole another quick glance at Henry. "Twas you and your friend just returned from India." He stated it as a fact, which meant this man knew very well who Henry was and why he'd come here today.

"Yes," Henry said.

"Which would have something to do with why you took a long walk with Amala in the garden."

"Something to do with it," Henry admitted.

"But apparently your conversation didn't end well."

"Apparently not," Henry said and ventured to clarify, "You said she was in tears?"

"Yes, indeed," the man stated. "At least she was when I left her to cry in peace. I came here to give her some privacy and sent the stable hands off. Don't much care for their company."

Henry surmised that this man had lived and worked here for a long time and held some authority among the servants. He clearly had some level of long-term relationship with Amala. But he felt confused on one point and asked, "If you help look out for Amala and you believe I'm the one who upset her, then why are you being so kind to me . . . and so forthright?"

The man looked up at Henry and stopped whittling. "Sit down, young man, before you fall over. You don't look like you feel too good." Henry sat down, unable to argue with him on that count. The man set his work on the ground beside him and folded his arms over his chest. "If Amala was crying because you'd been cruel to her, I doubt very much you'd look the way you look right now. I'm thinking it's more likely that *she* broke *your* heart."

Henry took a sharp breath, uncomfortable with the direction this conversation was taking. He tried not to sound defensive when he asked, "How is it possible for a woman to break my heart when I've not yet known her for twenty-four hours?"

"Who am I to judge matters of the heart?" the man countered.

"And who exactly are you?" Henry asked. "I'm sitting here talking to you of personal matters and I don't even know your name. Perhaps we should be properly introduced."

"Perhaps we should. You're Henry Beckenridge. You don't have to tell me that. And there's no need for you to act surprised that the servants of such a household freely discuss what's going on—as much as they're privy to. I can't get a cup of coffee around here without being told everything I don't necessarily want to know."

"So, you know who *I* am, and why I'm here, and that I've traveled to India. I know nothing about you, but you obviously know Amala very well."

"I'm known as Everett around here; been here all my life. Took over my father's job when he got too old; now he's long gone to our Maker. I take care of the carriages and everything else here that's got wheels on it. Sometimes I drive them, although they do employ a driver, but he has other tasks too, so we spread the work around different from day to day."

He sighed and took on a somewhat nostalgic expression.

"Of course, I was here when the good folks I work for finally came back from India to live in this place that had been vacant except for the serving folk for several years. Amala was quite a shock to the household and especially to folks about the county. The mister and missus, being the good folks they are, didn't pay any attention to what others thought or said, and they made it clear to those working here that any ill words toward Amala would see them dismissed immediately. They tried to keep Amala from knowing about any of that, but children are sharp, you know; and she was always sharper than most. She never wanted to hurt her parents by getting upset—her new parents, I mean; those that brought her into the world had gone to their Maker, of course. That's why she came here. But she never wanted to hurt anyone, so she'd hide when she was upset. And I guess she'd not been here very many weeks when she figured out there were lots of places to hide in the carriage house, and no one but me was ever here. Sometimes I tried to give her some words of comfort. Mostly I just let her cry. People need to cry, you know. Men and women, both. I think we'd all be better off for crying more, but who am I to say? I'm just a simple man. But a sensitive little thing like Amala, she especially needs to cry. If she held all those tender feelings inside, she'd likely die from all the hurt eventually. It's my thinking that all the crying when she's alone helps her stay strong when she's around others."

Henry lowered his head as Everett's candid opinions—and his insights into Amala's heart—tempted him to start crying again himself. Everett's belief that crying was good for people only made it more difficult to hold back the temptation to do so. But he was afraid if he got started he wouldn't be able to stop. There were a great many things in his life he'd never cried about, things that had nothing to do with Amala. And he feared that crying over the way he felt right now would eventually tap into a wellspring of unshed tears that had been accumulating for a lifetime.

"You know her well," Henry managed to say with a fairly steady voice.

"I'd like to think so," Everett said. "She's as kind and good-hearted a person as anyone I've ever known. She brings her laughter and joy to the carriage house as much as her tears. We've had many a good talk."

"And did she tell you why she felt the need to be alone and cry today?"

"She did," Everett said with a hint of challenge in his voice as if he were weighing whether or not he would divulge that information to Henry.

Henry felt the need to clarify, "I'm glad she has someone she can talk to freely. I would never want you to break any confidence you share with her."

"She didn't ask me *not* to tell anyone. I'm no gossip; quite the opposite, in truth. I've only told you what I have so far because I sense you're the kind of man who respects a person's privacy, and you're only concerned about Amala. I consider myself a good judge of character. I hope you won't prove me wrong."

"I'll not repeat anything you've told me, of course," Henry said. "I appreciate your candor more than I can say."

"Dare I ask if you have anyone you can talk to?"

Henry chuckled, but not with any humor. "Not really; not like this. Chit is a dear friend and the best of men. But I suppose I have a more sentimental nature, while he tends to take a more practical view. Our years together in India made that readily evident to me."

"How do you mean?" Everett asked, and Henry felt as if he'd known this man for years. Considering Everett's closeness to Amala and that he felt the same way about her, Henry couldn't help wondering if that was somehow a validation of what he was feeling.

"There is so much beauty in India. I could see it everywhere and couldn't help but comment on my observations. Chit always listened politely, but it was as if he couldn't see it, or it simply didn't affect him. By the same token, there was so much injustice and depravity—much of it caused by my own people. I would sometimes feel horrified or enraged, and Chit always allowed me to express my views to him without any judgment. But his response to such things was simply that life is what it is, and he considered it a waste of time and energy to be affected by such things. He could walk through a crowd of starving children on the streets, all begging for anything that might help them get through the day, and he didn't seem to even see them. I not only saw them, I wanted to take them all home with me. I took on the habit of never going out without pockets full of coins, believing I could help in some small way. And maybe I did. But the years proved that I'm just one man and I couldn't singlehandedly change the course of a mighty storm."

Henry sighed and repositioned himself on the horribly uncomfortable wooden chair.

"I believe Chit will go back to India, but I never will. Perhaps I'm just too softhearted and sentimental to live in a place with such extremes of beauty and horror. I'm not sure I could even handle going to certain parts of London. I prefer to hide out here in the country. Does that make me weak?"

"If you're asking my opinion—and it sounds like you are—I don't think that knowing what kind of man you are and choosing a life that suits you would amount to hiding *or* being weak."

"You're very kind, Everett. It's no wonder Amala has gravitated to the carriage house all these years."

Henry's compliment hovered in the air until it became mildly awkward, as if Everett didn't know what to say, and Henry was left wondering how to continue their conversation. He desperately wanted to know what Amala might have said to him before he'd left her alone in the carriage house, and perhaps Everett might even help him find Amala so that he could speak with her again.

Henry was just formulating the words to attempt crossing that bridge when Chit entered the stable and declared, "There you are, Henry, old boy."

Henry sprang to his feet, feeling as if he'd been caught doing something he shouldn't. He quickly checked himself with a reminder that only his sudden, overwhelming feelings for Amala might remotely fall into that category—or at least they did from Amala's perspective. But Chit knew nothing about that.

Henry casually introduced Chit to Everett, and they exchanged a respectful nod and a few words of appropriate greetings that Henry barely heard. Henry thanked Everett for the conversation, glad that Chit had no idea just how candid and tender their conversation had been. Within minutes Henry and Chit were riding away from Willenbrock House, away from what had been intended to be a casual visit. But Henry felt as if an invisible cord had wrapped itself tightly around his heart, tying him irrevocably to all that he was leaving behind, threatening to pull him back beyond his own will. He felt as if this place had become more home to him than his own home ever had been, and leaving caused him pain. Unconsciously he pressed a hand over the center of his chest as he rode and glanced back over his shoulder more than once, thinking of Amala sitting alone in the carriage house. And he knew he would never be the same.

Chapter Three
THE DECLARATION

ONCE AMALA HAD RELIEVED HER turbulent emotions enough to put on a brave face, she returned to the house, certain that by now Henry and Chit would have left and she didn't have to fear coming upon them. At dinner she listened to her parents discussing how delightful their company had been and how much they'd enjoyed the visit of these two fine men. Oliver had invited them back and declared his hope that both Henry and Chit would become regular visitors. The very idea tightened Amala's stomach. Viola was in complete agreement, certain that it was good for all of them to spend time with people who had so recently come from Amala's homeland. Amala remained polite but commented as little as possible. Kat, as always, had no interest in hearing about India, but she was *highly* interested in the prospect of more visits from these two fine gentlemen. She steered the conversation toward their admirable character traits, which led into a discussion regarding whether or not they qualified as potential suitors.

Amala had long ago become accustomed to the way marriage was treated as the most important factor in their culture and society. She assumed it was the same in any culture, even if the process through which it was achieved might vary greatly from one culture to another. But here in this society, all men and women of marriageable age were either preoccupied continually with putting themselves into the path of anyone of the opposite gender who was considered a suitable match, or they had to tolerate other people pushing them into that path. Once people were married, society seemed to constantly be interested in assessing whether or not it was a good marriage, which—as far as Amala could see—was based on evidence that seemed entirely superficial. A great deal of gossip could be nurtured out of any indication of infidelity in a marriage. But the measurement of a good wife seemed to be how well she added grace and support to her husband socially and whether or not she gave him children—especially a son who could carry on family titles and traditions. Amala rarely if ever heard any assessments of whether or not a married couple was happy or content with their choice. It was only here, within the walls of her own home, that such a thing seemed to matter. Oliver and Viola were obviously very happy in the relationship they shared. Amala and Kit had both seen evidence of many disagreements between their parents, and what they shared was certainly less than perfect. But their trust and commitment and mutual respect were evident. Still, among society in general, such priorities in making a suitable match in marriage were never discussed. She only heard about whether or not each party could bring wealth into the marriage, and exactly how much. Love was only mentioned now and then as something that wasn't necessarily important but that perhaps would grow after marriage, and if it didn't that was fine as long as the match was proper and suitable. And those were words Amala had come to hate, mostly because she knew that she was considered completely improper and unsuitable in every way.

Amala distracted herself from her own tumultuous thoughts by listening more attentively to her sister. She loved Kat dearly and knew her to be completely without guile, although she sometimes didn't come across to others that way. What Amala and her parents all knew—because they had discussed it privately—was that Kat had a very simplistic way of looking at life. She didn't think or feel as deeply as did Amala, and therefore she often didn't think through her ideas or feelings very well before speaking them—or even acting upon them. But Kat's intentions were never selfish or meant to be unkind. She had always been there for Amala; they had shared everything since that horrible day when they'd been together at the time of the tragic death of Amala's Indian parents. But Kat never wanted to talk about that; in fact, Amala wasn't sure she even remembered it. Oliver had once told Amala he'd heard that sometimes people's minds would block out something traumatic because it was too much to bear. And

Amala wondered if Kat had done exactly that, which had spilled over into her only seeing the good in everything and everyone, which in and of itself was an admirable trait—even if it made Kat somewhat naive in regard to the realities of the world.

Amala, on the other hand, could never forget what had happened that night. It still haunted her, just as other memories of her childhood did. But she chose to focus on all she had been blessed with in her life and to seek to find something joyful each and every day. She believed she could live a good and fulfilling life without ever marrying or having children of her own. It had to be that way. She knew it and she'd known it for a long time. But her time alone with Henry Beckenridge had made that knowledge more difficult to accept, which made it more difficult than usual to listen to Kat's assessment of the eligible bachelors who had visited their home earlier in the day.

Kat declared her conclusion that both Henry and Chit had admirable qualities, but she didn't know why their each having great wealth and prestige was the first notable point mentioned in that regard. Beyond that, Chit was friendly, charming, easy to be around, kind, and respectful. Amala agreed with all of that. Kat mentioned that he was not as pleasing to look at as Henry, but she didn't personally consider that a deficit when he was obviously a good man. At least Kat was much more sensible than most young ladies in regard to appreciating a person's character traits above and beyond his or her appearance. But then Kat went on to express that Henry seemed to have all of the same qualities of character as Chit, even if he wasn't nearly as talkative. And then Kat pointed out how very handsome Henry was. She went on and on about it with a zeal that actually made her sound a little silly while Amala found herself growing increasingly uncomfortable and fearing she might actually throw a tantrum if she didn't excuse herself and go somewhere to be alone.

While her parents discussed the fine traits of both Henry and Chit, inserting subtle hints of what *suitable* prospects they might be, Amala forced her inner turmoil to calm down, but she also knew that she couldn't wait any longer to declare to her family what she'd known for months needed to be said. She'd dreaded it and avoided it, but the appearance of Henry Beckenridge in her life made her fear that if she put it off any longer, a disaster could happen. What if Henry ignored her wishes and asked her father's permission to court her? Had her parents become so accustomed to seeing Amala as an equal in their home that they'd come to overlook the way other people saw her? Had Amala's efforts to keep from hurting her parents' feelings over the many hurtful incidents in her life done her and them a disservice over time? Whatever the reason, she had to stop it. And she had to do it now.

"There's something I need to say," Amala said, and all eyes turned to her. She didn't know if their astonishment was because she'd said nothing at all for several minutes, or if her tone of voice had been more agitated than she'd intended.

"Then you should say it," Oliver encouraged.

Amala took a deep breath and considered how many times she had weighed and measured the words she might use when this moment finally came. She prayed silently for God to help her find those words now. "You have all given me so much. Here in your home and as a part of your family I am more blessed than I can even comprehend, and I want you to know how very grateful I am for that. I am certainly not unaware of what my fate would have likely been if I'd been left on my own in India. We don't talk about it . . ." She sensed Kat fidgeting slightly but ignored that and pressed on. "We don't talk about it, but I will never forget."

Again Amala took a deep breath. "There are other things we don't talk about, either. But now that Kat and I have come of age, I believe certain issues can no longer be ignored. We must discuss the situation in order to avoid inevitable problems."

"What on earth do you mean, darling?" Viola asked, and Amala checked the expressions of Kat and their parents. Not one of them had any idea what she was trying to say, and their ignorance felt maddening to her in that moment. How could they possibly be so oblivious to her predicament? She reminded herself not to judge, knowing it was surely their love for her that had made them so blind to how different she was from them.

"I mean," Amala said, forcing a calm and even voice, "there is nothing good in pretending that a suitable marriage will ever be a possibility for me."

Amala heard all three of them gasp simultaneously. She looked at her hands in her lap to avoid having to see their expressions. "I'm well aware that no respectable gentleman would ever want to marry a woman like me, and . . ."—she thought of Henry and realized she needed to clarify the way she'd said that—". . . and even if he did, it would be foolish. It is simply not acceptable in our society, and such a marriage would bring nothing but grief to everyone involved. I could never, in good conscience, bring children into this world who would inevitably face such stigma and ridicule simply because being of mixed race is not acceptable and it never will be—at least not in the world we know."

A long moment of silence assured Amala that no one had anything to say, so she forged ahead. "I don't ever want to go back to India; I consider England my home, and you are my family. I want you to know that I've accepted what must be. I only ask that you respect what is clearly inevitable and that we all stop trying to pretend it could ever be otherwise. I am fine with attending socials if you wish me to go with you, and to be present when we receive guests in our home. But I need it to be clear that I am not seeking a suitable husband, because I would never consider bringing such obvious challenges and grief into the life of any decent man." She forced herself to draw air into her lungs and concluded, "There. That's what I needed to say. I should have said it a long time ago."

Again there was only silence, which implied to Amala that no one could think of any reasonable argument to her declaration. Of course they couldn't. Everything she'd said was true and they all knew it— now that they'd actually been forced to think about it reasonably. She finally found the courage to lift her head and look at each of them, only to find that their expressions only corroborated their lack of disagreement.

"I'm feeling very tired," she said with full honesty. She felt absolutely drained of strength. It had been an emotionally exhausting day. She came to her feet and set her napkin on the table. "I believe I'll go up to bed now. I will see you all at breakfast." She hoped her last statement would prevent any of them from coming to her room tonight to try to talk to her. Until she had some rest and some time alone, she just didn't have the strength to discuss this any further.

"Good night," Amala said and hurried from the room, relieved when she got to the stairs to note that no one was following after her. She wondered what they might say to each other following her departure. All she could imagine was more silence and perhaps some tears as the truth of what she'd declared settled into them. Any conversation that might be meant to try to convince themselves that she was wrong wouldn't go on for long, because she wasn't wrong, and none of them could deny it.

Amala had only been in her room for a minute when Pearl knocked lightly at the door, just as Amala had expected. Pearl was the lady's maid she shared with Kat. While both Kat and Amala had been taught to be independent of servants in most ways and to always be kind and appreciative toward them, there were certain things that were part of the culture in which they lived with which they simply needed assistance. Sometimes Kat and Amala would help each other into the ridiculously heavy dresses and huge petticoats they were required to wear much of the time. But Pearl was almost always somewhere nearby, willing and able to help whenever she was needed. And she was an expert at styling a lady's hair in ways that Kat and Amala could never do for each other.

Pearl had obviously been reading—as she loved to do—in her room across the hall, with the door open, waiting to hear any evidence that she was needed. She said little as she helped Amala out of the dress and petticoats and then unlaced the confining corset. Even though Amala had always refused to have her corset laced so tightly that it inhibited her ability to breathe deeply, it still always felt good to be without it. Once Pearl had given Amala all the help she needed, the young woman left, and Amala was free to finish getting ready for bed while she tried not to think about the scene she'd initiated in the dining room. By the time she crawled into her bed, placing her weary head on one pillow and holding tightly to another, a rush of tears refused to be restrained. But Amala managed to keep her tears silent with the hope that if anyone in her family peeked into her darkened room with the hope of talking to her, they would believe her to be asleep and leave her in peace. She only wanted to be alone and attempt to take in the reality that today Henry Beckenridge had shattered her hope that she would never actually fall in love. If she'd never felt such things, it surely would have been easier to live without them. She knew now that the way she would have to live out her life hadn't changed, but living with a broken heart was something to which she would have to become accustomed.

* * * *

Amala drifted in and out of sleep, assaulted with crazy, disjointed dreams that she couldn't quite recall except that they'd been riddled with anxiety. She woke up with a firm resolve to press forward in her life with courage and dignity and to find ways to be useful and positive and make her life worthy of all she'd been blessed with. But it quickly became evident that her family was not in agreement with her view on the matter she'd broached at the supper table. There were tears and strong discussion at breakfast, which continued when they all retired to the drawing room afterward to continue the drama. Kat and Viola were practically inconsolable, while Oliver just looked as if someone he cared for had died. Amala wondered how it had come to this. Had they truly been so oblivious to the way other people regarded Amala—or rather *disregarded* her? Did they believe that their own acceptance and unconditional love toward her all these years had somehow magically changed the way the community viewed her? Perhaps they did, but she couldn't fault them for that. She *did* feel accepted and loved. But she wondered now if she should have been more forthright about the things people had said to her when no one in her family was nearby, or the way she had been looked at and whispered about. She realized now that only Everett knew the whole truth—or at least more of it than anyone but herself.

Amala shared her realizations and admitted—both to herself and aloud—that this was not a new idea for her; she'd been considering the matter very seriously for many months, and perhaps longer. And she needed to give her loved ones a chance to catch up to her thinking, to realize the truth in what she was saying and accept it. They were grieving; the life they had expected her to be able to live would not come to pass. She had to allow them the time and opportunity to experience sorrow over that if they needed to. But when she heard them saying the same things over and over, expressing the same astonishment and sadness again and again, she finally had to say, "I know this is difficult, and it will take time for you to come to terms with it. I understand. I only ask that you not make any further implications to me or to those around us that my circumstances are different than they obviously are." She sighed loudly and stood. "I need to be alone. I'll see you at supper."

"Not lunch?" Viola asked and sniffled.

Amala glanced at the clock, seeing that lunchtime wasn't far off, given the amount of time this little family meeting had taken. Unable to bear this drama any further until things settled down a bit, she simply said, "I'm very tired. I think I'll take lunch in my room."

Amala hurried away before anyone could stop her or say anything else. She wondered if the sorrow of her parents would be so deep that they might wonder if they'd done the right thing in bringing her back to England with them. But she only wondered for a moment. She knew they loved her and they would not have left her to fend for herself under atrocious circumstances. She just had to remind herself that with time they would come to accept the present situation for what it was and find joy on her behalf in whatever path she chose for her life.

Instinctively Amala went to the carriage house. She found Everett there, standing on a small stepladder while he polished the shiny black exterior of one of the family's carriages. He took his job very seriously and expected perfection of himself. She admired that in him, along with so many other traits.

Without any preamble, she simply said, "I told them."

She knew he didn't require any further explanation, given the many previous conversations they'd shared regarding the matter. He'd encouraged her to talk to her family about the issue a long time ago. It was Amala who had put it off and dreaded it.

As if to declare how serious he knew this was for her, he stopped polishing immediately and stepped down from the ladder, tossing the rag aside. He faced her directly and put his hands on his hips. "And?" he asked.

"It went exactly how I expected . . . but worse."

"Worse?" he echoed. "And I thought you were being pessimistic."

"They're devastated," she said. "It's as if the prospect of marriage and children is the only possible path to happiness for me, and realizing it's not possible is like I've told them I'm going to die of some dreadful disease. Surely there are many valuable things I can do in my life and remain unwed."

"Of course," Everett said.

"Look at you," she declared, seeing him as a fine example of the point she wanted to make.

Everett chuckled and leaned against the carriage wheel. "I find meaning in my work, Amala, and I recognize that I'm much blessed, but don't be thinking there aren't things I have to force myself not to think about."

Amala wanted to ask *what* those things might be, but a moment's thought answered the question. He'd lost a wife and child. He lived a mostly solitary life. And yet he seemed content. Surely she could do the same.

"Would you like me to teach you my trade?" he asked with mild sarcasm. "Or perhaps you could take lessons in the kitchen."

"Perhaps I should," she said, certain in that moment that she'd far rather be able to do some kind of useful work than sit around and do useless stitching on cushions or crochet doilies.

"So, a change of wardrobe and lower yourself into servitude?" he asked, still in that voice tinged with sarcasm.

"Perhaps. Would I not be better suited to such a life . . . all things considered?"

"Not in my opinion," he insisted, very serious now. "And not unless you want to move away from here. Do you want to be separated from your family?"

"No!" she declared. "They are important to me above all else save my devotion to God."

"Then you'll have to find a way to live a meaningful life within the life you're already living and the limitations of your situation."

Amala took that in and smiled slightly at him before looking down. "You are very wise for being such an isolated old bear."

He chuckled at her teasing, and the comfortable relationship they shared eased the tension of the difficult topic of conversation.

Amala began to pace slowly, which always helped her think better. Everett leaned against the carriage and folded his arms. She appreciated the way he'd grown accustomed to giving her time to think and allowing her the silence to do so.

"Perhaps I could be a nanny or a governess. Working with children could surely fill that void in my life and give me purpose. I think I could be good at it."

"I think you could be *very* good at it, and you might be right about such a position offering meaning and purpose. But again . . . you'll not get hired by anyone in this county who already knows you as the orphan girl taken in by the Hepworth family. You would have to leave the area."

Amala also appreciated the way that Everett wasn't afraid to lay out the facts and tell her exactly what he thought—even if it stung. But he was right.

Before she had a chance to think any further, he added, "This is not a decision you need to make right now. Offering your family such possible solutions right now would only hurt them more . . . at least the way I see it. Just . . . give them some time. And give yourself some time. When they see how strong you are and that you can be happy with this, they'll feel better. And I think you'll feel a *lot* better not having to skirt around the issue with them."

"I'm sure you're right," Amala said and sighed. Then her mind went to Henry Beckenridge and she wanted to curse aloud to think of him ever showing up in her life. If they'd never met, she wouldn't continue to be overtaken by her mind's willful stubbornness in being determined to think of him; and her need to accept the circumstances of her life would have been difficult but certainly not so heartbreaking. Even now, the memory of their conversation in the garden lured hot, burning tears to her eyes, but she forced them back and swallowed hard, silently praying she would never see him again.

* * * *

Henry lay in his bed, staring into the darkness, counting the days and realizing it had been a whole week since he'd had that devastating conversation with Amala in the garden at her home. Since then, not an hour had passed when he hadn't tried to convince himself that she was right, that it was better this way, and that he needed to forget her. And not an hour had passed without him being utterly convinced that she was everything he'd ever wanted in the woman with whom he would choose to live his life. And forgetting her felt completely impossible. In the brief time they'd spent together, she'd had even more impact on him than all of his years spent in India—and the two felt so closely integrated. India had changed him, and so had Amala. Both had opened his eyes, his mind, and his heart to beauties and injustices he'd never considered before. Both had soothed his spirit and calmed his aching soul. And both had broken his heart.

During the intervening days, Henry had done everything in his power to keep himself occupied. The only other resident of his home—beyond the servants—was his mother. But she was even crankier and more disagreeable than she'd been when he'd left here nine years earlier, and now she was bedridden with poor health and he found it difficult to even step into her room, given that she would immediately complain and prattle on and on about the local gossip that came to her ears from her stuffy and arrogant friends who came to visit her regularly. When she wasn't complaining about the behavior of people who didn't meet her expectations, she was often engaged in demeaning dialogue about Henry's father. Henry's memories of his father were few and precious, and he had heard many people tell him what a good man he'd been. Everyone seemed to think so except for his mother and her friends.

Henry's mother also loved to complain about her own daughter— Henry's only sibling—who had married a man of great means while Henry had been in India. And she'd not returned home since. Henry had never been close to his sister in any way and therefore didn't regret her absence. In truth, he completely understood why she would have been glad for the opportunity to leave this place and want nothing to do with it. But Henry quickly learned that he couldn't say anything to convince his mother that both of her children were not ungrateful and selfish, and so he stopped trying. Every attempt Henry made at offering a more positive perspective on any topic was immediately discounted. His efforts to talk to her about his travels and all he'd experienced were always silenced with the statement, "I don't want to hear about that barbaric place! I told you not to go, but you went anyway. I don't want to hear about it!"

So, Henry checked in on his mother at least once a day, but he quickly determined that if he had any hope of not becoming utterly depressed, he had to keep a reasonable distance between himself and his mother. His going to India had partly been for that very reason. He decided that he was mature now, more seasoned and reasonable. And now he knew that his inability to tolerate his mother's company was not a character flaw in himself but rather due to the fact that she was the most miserable, negative person he'd ever known. But she was elderly and ill and he knew there was nothing he could do to change the way she saw the world. However, he *could* choose how he handled it, and the best way to do that was to try to be as good a son as possible, but avoid allowing her to poison his own moods with her venomous attitudes.

Henry was aided in not spending too much time at home by following Chit around on his escapades. His friend was surely the most popular bachelor in the area. His charm and good nature and stories of adventure easily made him the center of attention at teas and luncheons, soirees and balls. And Henry was always expected to come along, as if everyone took for granted that they were inseparable as friends. But of course that had always been true. They'd been friends since childhood, and they'd traveled to India together, where their work and their social life had been closely integrated. Although, Henry was finding that he felt less and less dependent upon Chit, and Chit seemed to do just fine even when Henry slipped away from nearly every social engagement early and left without him. He wondered if it was meeting Amala that had changed him, but he could look back and see that this had been slowly evolving for years now. It was just as he'd described to Everett: India had made Henry realize that he and Chit saw everything in the world around them much differently. And Henry felt more and more drawn toward being himself—however sentimental and sappy he might be—as opposed to clinging to a longtime friendship they both seemed to be outgrowing. He also knew that Chit likely planned to return to India, and Henry intended to live out his life in England. Their separation was inevitable; Henry could feel it settling in a little more every day.

However, he did appreciate the social distractions that were open to him by tagging along with Chit. It wasn't that Henry couldn't be adequately social all on his own; he'd never considered himself quiet or reserved in any regard. But Chit just had a way with people that seemed to evoke more invitations. Perhaps it was because Chit's parents had been more socially active. The reasons didn't really matter to Henry; he simply wanted any distraction he could find to keep him from thinking too much about Amala. But inevitably night would come, the parties would end, and Henry would find himself in the stillest part of the night wondering about her, longing to see her, to talk with her, *to marry her*. He knew there was truth and substance in all of her reasoning as to why they shouldn't pursue a relationship. But something inside of him just couldn't accept it. He wanted to believe they could love each other enough to overcome whatever challenges they might face. Perhaps his thinking was naive. Or perhaps he was right.

Nearly three weeks after meeting Amala, Henry awoke from yet another restless night, determined to see her again. He'd actually talked Chit out of accepting an invitation to dine with the Hepworth family, and another time Chit had gone there for tea and Henry had declined going along. He'd believed he couldn't bear to see Amala, knowing how her edict had been meant to banish him from her life. But now he felt differently. Perhaps enough time had passed that he felt renewed courage. Perhaps he'd lost his mind. Whatever the reason, he knew he had to see her, but rather than showing up as a formal visitor, he decided instead to go and speak with Everett. And on the chance that Everett wouldn't help him, or that Amala refused to see him, he wrote a lengthy and carefully worded letter to her that he would entrust Everett to pass along. At least then, one way or another, she would know exactly how he felt.

* * * *

Henry left his home after supper, knowing that with the time it took him to ride on horseback to Amala's home, he wouldn't arrive until after dark. He didn't particularly want to be seen coming or going; he only hoped Everett might be willing to help him. As kind as the man had been to Henry, he had no idea if this friend of Amala's would be willing to cross borders on Henry's behalf that Amala had so clearly put into place.

When Henry arrived he didn't even bother going into the stables, where he felt sure there would still be men working. Light coming from the windows and open doorway made that evident. But there was also light coming from the carriage house, which increased his hope of seeing Everett. Henry tethered his horse discreetly in the shadows and went to the door of the carriage house, taking a deep breath before he opened it as quietly as he could manage, wishing he didn't feel so nervous. Whatever grain of hope he'd been holding on to that this situation with Amala might change could well be determined by the outcome of this evening's visit.

Henry immediately saw Everett pausing in his task of sweeping the floor to look up and see who was there. He leaned on the broom and offered a subtle smile that increased Henry's hope slightly as he closed the door behind him. "I've been wondering if you'd show up here again." He resumed his sweeping.

"So . . . in your opinion . . . is my coming here a good idea . . . or foolish?" Everett didn't answer right away, as if he were thinking about it, and Henry's nervousness prompted him to add, "I assume you know *why* I haven't been back?"

"And why you're sneaking in under the cover of darkness," Everett said, still sweeping. "Yes, I know. You're not the first she's sent away, but seeing that you're the first who left her so upset, I couldn't help hoping that you might be the first to actually come back."

Henry breathed that in with increased hope. "And why is that?" he asked.

Everett stopped sweeping and leaned the broom against the wall. He gave Henry a hard stare and settled his hands firmly on his hips, a stance that seemed to imply he might kill anyone who hurt Amala in any way. But his voice was kind as he said, "A man not willing to fight for a woman like that could never be worthy of her, but in her case, the fight will be far more difficult than most men would ever consider taking on; no doubt about it."

"And you're wondering if I'm up for such a battle?" Henry guessed.

"I am."

Henry knew he'd get no better opportunity to declare exactly where he stood, and with any luck, his declaration would make this man his ally. He stated with all the fervor he felt, "I truly believe that with Amala at my side we could conquer anything the world might use as an assault against us. Once committed to her I would never back down on protecting her from the harshness of the world, and I would do everything in my power to make her happy. But how do I convince Amala of that? If my battle is *against* her, I'm not sure I can win."

Everett smiled, perhaps hinting that he liked what Henry had said. He glanced down and commented, "She's a stubborn one, but not without good reason."

"I know I can't fully understand those reasons, because I've never experienced what she's seen . . . and felt. But I observed much during my time in India that I believe gives me some degree of understanding. I'm only one man, and I can't change the way society's injustice impacts some people more than others, but I'd like to think I can make a difference for *her*."

Everett was thoughtfully silent long enough to make Henry's heart pound. He finally asked, "What would you like me to do? Although I can't promise there's anything I can do or say to her that might make her change her mind."

Henry reached inside his jacket and pulled out the letter he'd written. "Would you give her this? Discreetly? I'm certain she wouldn't want her family questioning her about it."

"I'm certain you're right," he said and took the letter. "I'll make sure that she gets it. And then what?"

"I'm not sure," Henry said. "I confess that for all my stewing over this . . . I'm just not sure. I've stayed away because I didn't want to upset her, but . . ."

"Come back tomorrow . . . same time. I'll do my best to convince her to see you, and perhaps you can talk."

"Thank you," Henry said, his heart beating quickly for an entirely different reason. "I'll be here." He nodded toward Everett, who nodded in return, and Henry forced himself to turn and walk back toward the door.

"Either way," Everett said and Henry stopped, turning back, "might I offer some advice?"

"I'd consider any advice you have to offer very welcome."

"You have other valid reasons to be social with this family, do you not?" Everett asked.

Henry thought of the invitations he'd turned down and the reasons he and Chit had been invited here in the first place.

Before he could answer, Everett added, "Word has it that the mister and missus very much enjoyed your company, and they are keen on socializing with people who share their love of India. They've wondered why you've not come back. So . . . pay a visit. You're a gentleman; you know what's socially appropriate and what isn't. I don't think you'd put on any falseness with the family in order to be around more, but . . ."

"No, I wouldn't. Of course not. I very much enjoyed the company of Amala's parents."

"So pay a visit," Everett repeated. "Visit often if it suits you and you're not wearing out your welcome. Perhaps if Amala sees that she's not going to drive you away, and she has the opportunity to get to know you better, she might soften up some. Can't hurt any, can it?"

"Thank you, Everett. Your kindness and wisdom mean more than I can say." He believed Everett wouldn't be so open with suggestions or a willingness to help if he didn't respect Henry or trust him to do the right thing. He wanted to say as much but wasn't sure how to do so without sounding either insensitive or arrogant.

"Glad to help," Everett said, which neatly summed up Henry's own thoughts. They shared another mutual nod, and Henry left the carriage house feeling encouraged and hopeful.

Riding toward home through an especially dark night, Henry was glad the horse could see better than he could and kept them firmly on the road. His mind was wandering to the possibilities before him that he'd been unable to foresee without Everett's sound advice. Perhaps he could yet win Amala over and convince her to at least consider allowing him to court her. And if she never changed her mind on where she stood, he could at least know he'd done everything in his power to make that happen. He could never move forward in his life without knowing he'd sincerely exhausted every possible effort to let Amala know how very much he'd come to love her, and that his greatest desire was to spend the rest of his life with her—no matter what that life might entail.

* * * *

Amala decided to get out of bed at the very first hint of daylight creeping into her room. She'd endured yet another night of fitful sleep, interspersed with chaotic dreams, and she felt even more exhausted than when she'd gone to bed the previous evening. After putting on a simple day dress and her most comfortable shoes, she barely pulled a brush through her hair and grabbed a shawl, certain a brisk early-morning walk would help clear her head. The sun had come over the horizon by the time she got outside, and she stood for several minutes with her face turned toward the blinding light, her eyes closed, allowing it to bathe her in its warmth.

Amala walked the entire perimeter of the house, which was no small undertaking, and by some kind of gravitational pull she went to the carriage house. There was nothing she could talk to Everett about that they hadn't already discussed over and over, but she always felt comfortable just being around him, even if they only shared meaningless small talk. He was the only person in the world who knew her completely, and therefore he knew the turmoil currently afflicting her while she attempted to accept that she'd fallen in love with a man with whom she could never share her life. She didn't know if Everett would even be here yet, but if he wasn't, she would enjoy finding respite in one of the empty carriages until it was time to go in for breakfast.

Amala entered the carriage house to find Everett there, but he was sitting on a stool, leaning back against a wagon used for transporting supplies from town, reading a book.

"No work to do this morning?" she asked, closing the door behind her.

"Worked late last night," he said and closed the book. "I was hoping you'd come out here before breakfast."

"You were?" she asked, surprised. He'd always been more than willing to be there for her and offer his friendship and wisdom, but she couldn't recall his ever making such a remark.

"I can't very well go hunting you down in the house in the wee hours of the morning," he added, and she felt all the more surprised. He then pulled an envelope from between the pages of the book he'd been reading and held it toward her. Hope and excitement battled with dread and fear inside of her, making her heart race and her breathing suddenly became shallow. She already knew what it was, even before he said, "Henry came by last night; asked me to give this to you."

"I don't know if I should even take it," Amala said, unconsciously pressing a hand over her heart. "Maybe it's better if I don't know what it says."

"And wonder for the rest of your life?" Everett asked, making a valid point. "I think the man at least deserves to have you read what he's taken the time to write, and he did come all the way out here to bring it himself."

Amala still hesitated to take the letter. "You like him," she stated.

"Can't think of a reason not to," Everett said and shook the letter, implying that he was growing tired of holding it with his hand outstretched.

Amala stepped forward and took it. She saw her name written elegantly on the envelope and just stared at it. "If I were an English woman, your recommendation of his character would mean everything to me. Given who I am, I think it only makes the situation more difficult. If you thought he was a blackguard or a scoundrel, my decision would perhaps be easier to accept."

"Have you ever considered the possibility that you might be wrong?" Everett asked.

Amala snapped her gaze toward him, astonished and mildly angry. "You, of all people, know that I did not come to this realization lightly. I'm only trying to protect the—"

"I know what you're trying to do, dear girl," he said, not even slightly ruffled by her agitation. "I'm just saying that . . . sometimes a situation changes; sometimes there's things you didn't count on . . . things you couldn't see coming. I'm not going to tell you what to do; I'd never tell you what to do. I'm just thinking that . . . it wouldn't hurt for you to consider that maybe there's something here you hadn't considered before."

"And what's that?" Amala asked.

"Maybe the *right* man, a truly *good* man . . . who loves you . . . could make possible what has always seemed *im*possible." Everett opened his book as if to end the conversation, or at least to declare that was all he intended to say on the matter. "I'm thinking you should read that letter now . . . before you leave . . . so I can tell him when I see him again that I know you did."

"You're going to see him again?"

"He's coming back here tonight," Everett said and turned a page. "About nine o'clock, give or take . . . on the chance you might want to talk to him."

Amala stood clutching the letter, unable to move or even think. The need to be alone finally set her free and she rushed to a long-unused carriage that was her favorite place to hide. She was glad to have sufficient sunlight shining from the carriage-house window into the carriage so that she could still manage to see her name written in Henry's hand. Minutes passed while she just held the letter and stared at it. Everything Everett had just said swirled around in her mind, mingling with her encounters with Henry and the feelings she'd been battling ever since she'd met him. She already knew the letter would be some attempt to try to get her to change her mind, and she already knew she had to remain firm in her resolve. It only took her a moment to reassess all of the careful thought and pondering and prayer that had gone into her decision. She would be a fool to change her mind now, no matter how her emotions might contradict what she knew to be right. Far better to hurt Henry a little bit now than to make his life miserable with all that would inevitably follow if they became romantically involved to any degree. Far better that she come to terms with her own sorrow over the matter in the present, as opposed to hurting others in the future.

Finally, Amala found the courage to break the wax seal and unfold the letter. She had to move closer to the light in order to more clearly see what was written. At a quick glance she was able to see that the letter began with *My Dearest Amala*, and that it ended some pages later with, *All the love my heart possesses, Henry.* The problem was that in between was such a beautifully detailed expression of his devotion that Amala kept having to dab at her eyes to keep her vision from blurring so that she could continue reading. When they had spoken in the garden, she had told him plainly and clearly where she had to stand on the matter of their attraction to one another, but she was now reading a genuine and sincere rebuttal to her every argument. It became evident through his words that he knew a great deal more about the issues of prejudice behind her motives than she'd given him credit for. He declared his firm belief that no matter what governments or society might try to dictate in this world, God surely saw all of His children equally, and that in God's eyes, surely they could find a way to be right with this.

Amala was completely taken off guard by how much her resolve had melted by the time she finished reading the letter, and after she'd read it through a second time, she was filled with doubt and confusion over matters that had previously seemed completely clear.

Chapter Four
THE SECRET

STARTLED BY THE SUDDEN REALIZATION of time passing, she wiped her tears, tucked the letter inside her bodice, and hurried into the house, hoping she wouldn't be terribly late for breakfast and draw attention to herself—or worse, have missed it altogether. She entered the dining room, relieved to see the family all seated there and just beginning to eat.

"Forgive me for being late," she said and sat down. "I woke early and decided to go for a walk and lost track of the time. Would you pass the marmalade, please?" she added quickly while reaching for a scone, hoping to distract them from any suspicion of the unrest she was experiencing.

"It's a lovely morning," her mother said, and typical small talk commenced, which allowed Amala the opportunity to put her emotional response to Henry's letter into perspective. At least for the moment she could set all of that aside, and being with her family reminded her of how much difficulty she could bring into their lives by making a foolish decision.

As the meal was winding down, Oliver said to Viola, "Oh, I almost forgot. I received a message this morning from Henry Beckenridge."

Amala coughed but managed to avoid choking, so no one seemed to notice.

Oliver continued. "You remember Henry? The lad who—"

"Of course I do!" Viola exclaimed with glee. "Such a fine young man!"

"Indeed he is," Oliver added. "Why, even in his youth I remember being very fond of him, and now that we've all got so much in common with the boy, I almost feel like he's one of the family."

Amala barely managed to keep from coughing again before Oliver went on. "He wrote to apologize for not accepting the previous invitations I'd sent to him; been rather busy settling in, apparently. As soon as we're done here I'm going to send a message back to him straightaway. I want him to know he's always welcome in our home and there's no need to stand on formality and all that. With any luck I can convince him to show up for tea—or even supper—as soon as he can manage."

"Oh, that would be splendid!" Viola declared and turned to look at Kat and Amala. "Isn't he a fine young man, girls?"

"He's very handsome," Kat said, "and kind . . . as much as I can recall."

Amala knew she needed to say something while she wondered futilely what Henry's intentions might be. She couldn't imagine him going against her wishes and saying anything to her parents about his feelings unless he had her permission first. Did he intend to make his presence in her home and in her life more frequent in order to further his cause? Forcing her mind to the present, she simply stated, "Mr. Beckenridge will be very amiable company, I'm certain."

After breakfast Amala excused herself and hurried up to her room, where she sat in the middle of her bed and read the letter again. The sincerity of his words became more evident, and she felt them wrap around her heart like a warm blanket on a cold night. She wanted to believe everything he was telling her. But it only took a glance toward a nearby mirror to be reminded that she and Henry were like oil and water; no matter how hard one might try to mix them, one always settled above the other. She wondered what she should do now. She wanted to see Henry so much it nearly caused her physical pain to think of it. But she feared what seeing him might do to her. If reading his letter had left her confused and losing all reason, how might she respond to being in his presence? She considered writing a letter in return and leaving it with Everett. A written response would give her the opportunity to consider her words carefully and therefore hold fast to her resolve over the matter. But then how might she respond to seeing Henry when he showed up for tea on any given day?

The dilemma was making her head ache, and she was considering the need for a nap when a knock at the door startled her. She stuffed the letter beneath her pillow and quickly laid down, trying to make it look as if she'd already been relaxed before she called, "Come in."

Kat entered and closed the door behind her. "Are you feeling all right?"

"Just a little tired," Amala said. "For some reason I woke up very early and couldn't go back to sleep. Nothing a nap won't set right."

"Are you certain?" Kat asked. "You just haven't seemed quite yourself lately, and it seemed a little worse this morning. I'm worried about you."

"I'm fine, truly," Amala insisted.

"Well, I don't believe you," Kat said and sat next to Amala on the bed, leaning back against the headboard. "You've seemed especially sad since you made your declaration that you have no intention of ever marrying. It makes me wonder if you've really thought it through as carefully as you should."

"I assure you that I've thought it through very carefully."

"But you don't want to talk about it at all," Kat said.

"There are things *you* don't ever want to talk about," Amala countered. "I didn't say my decision wasn't difficult, but I believe it's right." She thought that prior to reading Henry's letter she would have said that she *knew* it was right. Now, she mostly felt afraid—of her own feelings as much as of Henry's. But she fought to keep her expression noncommittal and her emotions concealed. Doing so was easier with her eyes closed. She *didn't* want to talk about it. The issue was simply something Kat could never fully understand. She was kind to a fault, but her way of thinking was often simple and limited, whereas Amala always felt the need to analyze everything to its core. She'd never tried to talk such things through with Kat for that very reason. She loved her sister dearly, but she accepted how very different they were.

When Kat changed the subject to talk of some gossip among the servants, Amala felt relieved, but Kat quickly tired of that topic and began speculating over the possibility of Chit and Henry coming to visit more frequently. Kat admitted she would like that very much; she was drawn to both men and would like to get to know them better, considering they each had fine qualities.

"I'm certain they are both fine men," Amala said, still keeping her eyes closed.

She was about to reiterate her need for some sleep if only to put an end to the conversation, when Kat apologized for chattering, seeing that Amala was obviously tired. Kat pressed her usual sisterly kiss to Amala's forehead and left the room. Amala was only alone for a minute before unexpected tears wet her closed lashes.

"Henry," she whispered as if he might be in the room and she could will him closer. She wanted to see him again so badly that the thought of doing so quickened her heart with a surge of something joyful that pushed away all of her reason and practicality. Tomorrow she might be filled with regret and feeling like a fool, but tonight she needed to see Henry, to talk to him face-to-face. While a part of her knew that any hope of them being together was entirely futile, for now she felt only impulsive and careless and undeniably in love. She had to see him! And she prayed that he would forgive her when he came to fully accept that there simply could never be any future for them together.

* * * *

As Henry set out again, right after supper, to ride to the Hepworth estate, he was initially overcome with a deep thrill that made his stomach quiver and his heart beat faster. But throughout the course of the ride, which took nearly half an hour, his excitement at the prospect of seeing Amala—and the hope that his letter might have convinced her to change her mind—settled into something akin to dread. If she refused him, he couldn't even comprehend how he would respond. He'd considered the possibility, of course. In fact, he considered it to be a more likely outcome. But he'd been unable to keep himself from hoping, until the hope had gradually drowned out any skepticism. And now he only felt afraid. He recounted all of his thinking on the matter these past few weeks, and by the time he arrived he had to acknowledge his fears, but they were combined with determination. Perhaps she wouldn't change her mind, but he wasn't going to give up without a fight.

Henry discreetly tethered his horse in the same place as he had done the previous evening. There was light shining through the carriage-house windows, but the windows were too high to see inside. He took a deep breath and willed himself to be calm before he went inside and closed the door quietly after him. He waited a long moment but saw no one, heard nothing.

"Everett?" he called. "Is anyone here?"

Henry held his breath when he heard a sound, and a moment later Amala stepped out from behind one of the carriages. Had she become more beautiful? Or had his memories not done her justice? Her black hair hung in long curls over her shoulders and down the front of a simple yellow dress, and she held a dark shawl around her arms.

"Amala." Her name came through his lips on the wave of his breath as his lungs forced him to let it go. "I was so afraid you wouldn't be here."

"I feel afraid of what the consequences might be of my being here," she admitted, and he saw her put a hand over her heart. "I'm not certain it's wise, but . . ."

"But?" he asked when she hesitated.

She looked away when she spoke. "Your letter was very convincing. You made some valid points, but . . . you need to know it doesn't necessarily change how I feel about the matter . . . or what I believe is best."

"Sometimes following your heart is not the easiest course," he said.

"As you mentioned in the letter." She looked at him again.

Overcome with a sudden desperation, as if she might run away again and never come back, he stepped toward her, relieved when she didn't back away. "I would do anything for you, Amala. With time I hope you will come to believe that's true."

She lifted her gaze to meet his, and he could see her shoulders rise and fall with her breathing. "I already believe it's true," she said. "But that doesn't necessarily mean that being together is the best decision . . . for us . . . for our families."

"You are wise and strong, Amala. But I hear you telling me the way things *should* be according to the dictates of our society. I hear you speak of the matter with perfect practicality." He lowered his voice to a whisper. "But what does your heart tell you, Amala?"

As soon as he asked the question, he noticed her teetering slightly, and he took hold of her upper arms to help steady her. She lowered her head as if she were dizzy and took hold of his arms in the same manner. When she lifted her head, he'd pressed his lips against her brow spontaneously, with no resistance on either of their parts. He pressed a lengthy kiss there and felt her hands tighten around his arms.

"I'm so afraid to speak what is in my heart, Henry. I've seen so much in my life that makes me believe only heartache and suffering could possibly come from our being together. How can knowing you so short a time make me question all of that? I don't know if I can ever balance out what I know and what I feel."

She looked up at him with raw vulnerability visible in her eyes, as if she hoped that he could give her all the answers; at the same time, they both knew he couldn't. But there was something he knew he *could* say, something he needed to say, one of the main things he'd come here tonight to say. "Amala, those are the things we need to talk about. I think we need to listen to our hearts enough to at least . . . give the matter some time . . . talk through the things we're feeling . . . and the things we're afraid of. I don't think I can go on with my life and have any peace if I don't know that I've done *everything* I could to be absolutely certain—one way or the other. That's all I'm asking, Amala. Please . . . don't turn me away without . . . giving yourself time . . . to at least consider the possibility. You've spent years convincing yourself you could never marry or have children. Surely we can take some weeks—or even months—to consider the alternative."

Henry could see in her eyes that her thoughts were racing; he could well imagine the internal argument taking place. But he kept his gaze firmly connected to hers, as if that in itself might keep her from saying no.

"I have one condition," she said, and a little burst of laughter came out of his mouth. His relief was so overwhelming he almost felt a little dizzy himself.

"Anything!" he said, fearing even as he said the word that he might regret doing so.

"I don't want anyone to know," she said.

"What?" he asked, not because he hadn't heard her, but because her condition was so contrary to his own vision of courting her and spending as much time with her as he possibly could. He'd only spent one afternoon in her family's home, and they already felt more like family to him than anyone ever had. How could they possibly keep anyone from knowing how they felt about each other?

"Until we both agree that moving forward in life together is the right thing, I need all of this to remain a secret."

"Why?" he asked, still holding tightly to her arms. "Explain to me how that's possible and give me a reason that I can live with."

"I have made it clear to my family that I would never marry," she said. "They're not happy about it at all, even though they understand my reasoning. To suddenly announce my feelings for you would cause confusion and upset. Also . . ." She looked down again, and he'd come to recognize that she avoided his eyes when she needed to say something especially difficult. "If it doesn't work out . . . I don't want people speculating or ridiculing you for having any romantic association with me at all." She looked up at him again, apparently having said the worst of it. She must have known he would protest because she put her fingers over his lips. "You haven't lived in England for nine years. Please trust me when I tell you that it's better if we keep it a secret . . . for now . . . until we know for certain."

Henry still wanted to protest, but she didn't move her fingers. A smile broke her solemn countenance and filled him with fresh hope even before she said, "You can make a nuisance of yourself by coming to tea and supper, and my parents will love every minute of your company. And you and I can take long walks in the garden and lounge about in the library while my family believes we're talking about India. And if one day we announce that our friendship has become something more, we will cross that bridge when we come to it."

Henry was feeling better about her *condition*, except for one thing. He moved her fingers from over his lips and kept hold of them. "And what if it *doesn't* work out between the two of us? Will any friendship gained with you and your family suddenly become awkward and I'll have to stay away without explanations, making myself a fool?"

"No," she said firmly and with compassion. "Whatever friendship you find among us will be forever. It is only the possibility of marriage that must be carefully considered. I believe we are both mature and sensible enough to move forward appropriately—either way."

Henry let that settle in for a long moment, amazed at how wise and strong she truly was. He didn't want to keep their feelings for each other a secret, but she was making a compromise in order to give him a fair chance, and he needed to respect her wishes. Knowing that she was the kind of woman who would honor her word and that they could all remain friends no matter what made him feel much better. He'd fallen in love with Amala, but he'd also loved the time he'd spent in her home with her family. He'd missed all of them since he'd last been here. In his heart he believed that he and Amala were meant to be together and somehow it would all work out. Either way, the prospect of spending time with her family warmed him—especially when his own home was so bitterly cold.

"Very well," he said. "I agree to your condition, but I have one question: Are we alone here?"

"Yes, of course," she said, barely getting the words out before he pressed his lips over hers, wondering how many times he'd imagined this moment since he'd last seen her. The response he felt in her kiss was more soothing to his soul than anything ever had been. "I love you, Amala," he whispered against her lips and kissed her again.

"I love you too, Henry," she said with a quiver in her voice. "Oh, how I pray we don't regret this. How I pray we're not just bringing more heartache into our lives by even considering this."

"Don't think about that now," he said and took her face into his hands. He'd longed to touch her beautiful, dark skin from the moment he'd laid eyes on her in a crowded ballroom. He threaded his fingers into her black hair while he closed his eyes to savor the way it felt, and pressed his forehead to hers. He wanted to kiss her again, but considering the intensity of his attraction to her, he resisted the temptation and focused on how good it felt to just be with her and to have the hope of sharing his future with her. Knowing, at the very least, that he would be able to spend a great deal more time with her and her family left him inexplicably happy. In contrast to how he'd been feeling the majority of the time since he'd returned from India, he basked in the sensation and didn't take it for granted.

"Come with me," she said, taking his hand. They went deeper into the carriage house, almost to the rear, where an older but well-preserved vehicle was located. Amala nodded toward the door as if he should know what to do. He opened it and took her hand to help her step inside before he followed her and closed the door behind him, accepting her invitation to sit next to her on an especially lush blue velvet seat that had also been well-preserved.

"Is this where you come to hide?" he asked. Although it was difficult to see her face in here, he still knew she was astonished by the question. "Everett told me you were keen on finding places to hide in the carriage house, which is how you and he became such good friends."

"Yes," she said, "this carriage is my favorite. It's comfortable, and it never gets used anymore—old as it is."

"I can think of much worse places to hide," Henry said, taking hold of her hand.

"My father considered selling it at one time, but Everett talked him out of it. I'm certain my father knew the reason for Everett's protest, even if he never said so. I believe my family knows there are times I just need to be alone, and they know I'm safe here. Which reminds me . . . as for Everett, he is the exception to our needing to keep all of this a secret. We can trust him. I discussed the possibility of this with him before you came. I told him he could speak freely with you; there isn't anything about myself I don't want you to know. But there are perhaps some things I would rather not tell you myself. He knows everything. He can be our liaison and our confidant—if you're all right with that."

"It's fine. I like Everett."

"And it's evident he likes *you*," she said. "I confess there were things he said that made me realize I should at least give this a chance."

"Then I am grateful to him," Henry said, letting go of her hand to put his arm around her shoulders. He loved the way she leaned against him, and he pressed a kiss into her hair.

"Oh, I've missed you," she murmured, and he felt as if he were dreaming. He refused to think about how it might feel if the dream ended when all was said and done.

"I've missed you too," he admitted. "More than I can say."

"How is it possible to feel this way, Henry, when—not so long ago—we didn't even know of each other's existence?"

"I've asked myself that question a thousand times," he said.

Long moments of silence ensued, as if they both needed time to simply accept this dramatic change in their relationship. Henry still wasn't keen on the idea of keeping all of this a secret, but he kept his thoughts steered toward his gratitude that she was at least willing to spend time with him and give what they shared a fair chance.

Trying not to think about the possible outcomes, he sought for a way to initiate conversation. That was what he'd wanted—the opportunity for them to get to know each other better, to become more comfortable with each other. Except for the secretive aspect of their arrangement, that was surely the purpose of courting. He just needed to look at it that way, even if their situation was far from conventional.

"I used to find places to hide in my home," he said. "When I was a young child, my parents could hardly be in the same room without arguing, and I hated it. I would try to get as far away from them as possible—grateful that it was a very big house—and I would hide until I knew the argument was over."

"What did they argue about?" Amala asked, sincerely interested.

"Everything," Henry admitted. "To be truthful, my mother is the most difficult and cynical person I have ever known. I don't say that to be unkind; it's just a fact. As I understand it, from talking to different people who knew them before the marriage, she was always that way, but she pretended to be very much otherwise in order to catch herself a wealthy husband. Once they were married her facade quickly disappeared, and they were never happy together. I remember never wanting to be around my mother; I much preferred my father's company. He was kind and genuinely interested in me. I don't remember very much of him, but I do recall how he told me I would one day inherit all that was his, and I could do whatever I wanted with it, but the only way to be truly happy was to use such great blessings to do good. Those are words I've tried to live by."

"What happened to him?" Amala asked, knowing his father had passed away many years ago.

"He died suddenly; an illness that came on very quickly. There was little warning. My heart was broken, and to make matters worse, my mother only became more cantankerous and difficult to live with. I spent a great deal of time in Chit's home and with his family. They were kind to me, but not necessarily warm. They're very caught up in appearances and gossip. So, I kept finding places to hide. I was barely a man when Chit talked me into going to India with him. Going to the other end of the world seemed like a very good way to hide. I made certain every possible provision was put in place for my family's care, and I left with hardly a second thought."

"You have family besides your mother?"

"One sister," he said. "But we were never close at all; she was almost like a ghost in my life. She made a good marriage while I was in India and moved far away. She has no contact at all with either me or our mother—in spite of our efforts to keep in touch. I believe she's severed her ties, and I don't blame her. In a way I did the same when I went to India. But I don't regret the decision at all; it made me a better man in too many ways to count, even if the path to becoming better has left me with memories that are haunting." He sighed loudly and concluded, "I returned to find my mother's health very poor and her mood even more foul. Of course, I knew all of that from the occasional letters we exchanged. She was well cared for—and continues to be. But I confess I've come to see that there is nothing I can do to be a good son in her eyes, and it's better for me if I just keep my distance. I check in on her every day and try to remain cheerful, but it's not easy. I don't know how my father did it. I believe the man was a saint."

"I believe you must be very much like him," Amala said.

Henry looked toward her in surprise, although he could barely see her face in the darkness of the carriage interior. "I think I've tried to be . . . although I was so young when he died that it's difficult to know exactly what that means."

"You're certainly not cynical and cantankerous like you describe your mother."

"Not that you know of, anyway," he said in a teasing tone that he hoped would lighten the mood and draw attention away from himself.

She laughed softly and relaxed her head on his shoulder. "Won't you be missed?" he asked, mindful of the time. He'd been hoping to speak with her for a few minutes. He felt blessed to be sharing this kind of time with her and hoped for many more such moments in the future.

"Not at all," she said. "They all think I've gone to bed. Sometimes Kat sneaks into my room late at night to talk, but she's not feeling well and went to sleep right after supper. Since Mother gave her a spoonful of what she calls the once-a-month concoction, I'm certain Kat is sleeping deeply."

"The once-a-month concoction?" he asked, and she let out a little laugh that sounded mildly embarrassed.

"Forgive me," she said. "My father is very comfortable—given that he has a wife and two daughters—having such things discussed freely in his presence. But I've been taught that it's not proper to talk about such things in front of those of the opposite gender."

"Men, you mean," he said, and she nodded. "Such things?"

She was slow to answer, as if measuring her words carefully. "The unique facets of womanhood that sometimes confine her to bed once a month."

"Ah," he said with understanding.

"Are you shocked that I would be so bold? My mother told me that any gentleman would be, but I don't think I believed her; obviously I didn't or I would have been more discreet."

"No, I'm not shocked, and I'm not naive. *You* might be shocked to realize how much men are aware of such things and really don't care. It's impossible to live under the same roof with a woman— whether it be a sister, a wife, a mother, or even a housekeeper—and not be somewhat aware of the days of their not feeling well."

"Or the days of being unusually petulant?" Amala asked lightly.

"That too," Henry said and chuckled. Her ability to be so candid and comfortable over the simple facts of life made him love her all the more. He felt certain that the more time he spent with her, the more he was doomed to just keep loving her more and more.

"Tell me about India," she said. "Tell me how you felt when you first arrived there."

"Oh," he drawled, "that's . . . very difficult to describe. I'd heard things, of course. Others who had been there offered a variety of descriptions—which varied mostly in relation to whether or not they'd liked it there. Some said it was a horrible, barbaric place.

Others said it was beautiful and exotic and remarkable. I found it to be both. But . . . when I first arrived, not really knowing what to expect, I think I was mostly just . . . shocked. Yes, I was shocked. It was so dramatically different from anything I had ever seen that it had simply been beyond my ability to imagine. I felt as if I was sleepwalking somehow for the first several days I was there, looking at everything through some kind of daze. And I remember a day—it was more than a year later—when I realized that I'd become so accustomed to everything about India that it was difficult to remember what it had been like to live in England."

"And how did you feel when you returned?" she asked. "Shock again?"

"In some ways, yes. But at least I'd been here before, I'd grown up here; I had memories of this place. It has been a very big adjustment, but it feels like home to me." Instinctively he tightened his arm around her and pressed another kiss into the softness of her hair. "Now more than ever."

Another stretch of silence made Henry realize he was getting tired, and the way that Amala was relaxed against his side let him know that she was as well.

"I think it's time we both got some sleep," he said, reluctantly removing his arm from around her. "I have a very important invitation to tea tomorrow." He felt delighted at the prospect of being able to return so soon to spend time with Amala and her family.

"How lovely," she said, letting him know she was pleased as well.

On their way out of the carriage house, Amala doused the lanterns as she'd promised Everett she would do. Henry walked her to a side door of the house, wanting to see that she got there safely. She turned to face him, and he felt the impending separation already saddening him, but he felt something else too and was quick to express it. "Thank you," he said, "for . . . being willing to see me . . . for giving me a chance."

"I pray you do not regret it," she said, putting a hand to his face.

"My greatest regret would be spending my life wondering if I could have tried harder."

He wondered if it would be improper to kiss her again, but she lifted her lips to his and he gratefully accepted her simple offering of affection.

"Good night, Henry," she whispered. "Travel safely."

"Not to worry," he said. "The horse knows the way home in the dark."

"Until tomorrow, then," she said and went inside.

Henry stood there a long moment, just trying to soak in the essence of her that she might have left behind. The evening had gone far better than he'd dared hope—except for his agreeing to keep their relationship a secret. But he had renewed reason to believe that his future would be bright and that Amala would be a very real part of it.

* * * *

Amala could hardly sleep when her mind was consumed with reviewing every moment of her time with Henry. Her temptation to ignore her own edicts and give Henry a chance had been clinched when she'd asked for Everett's advice and he'd told her that she'd never know whether or not she could trust her own heart if she didn't allow herself to open it up enough to really hear what it was telling her. Unable to argue with such a point, Amala had forced away her fears and realized that if she and Henry could get to know each other better without anyone around them being aware of it, she could feel comfortable exploring the possibilities of changing her mind. A very big part of her still felt doubtful that—in the end—she wouldn't still firmly believe that remaining unmarried was a better course. The practical part of her that feared bringing any difficulty into the lives of anyone she cared for believed that such a marriage could never take place and be worth the sacrifices. The same part of her believed that this experiment would eventually show Henry the harsh truth of how bad it could be for them. But for now, she chose to push all such thoughts away and do as Everett had challenged her to do: listen to what her heart was telling her and give it a fair chance to be heard.

Amala trembled with a delight she'd never felt before as she recalled her time with Henry. His kiss was as intriguing to her as the way they were able to share candid and respectful conversation. She was inexplicably grateful to know he would be visiting tomorrow, and she hoped they might be able to steal at least a few minutes alone together.

At breakfast Amala's father announced with glee that Henry and Chit would be coming for lunch, and it was Oliver's hope that the men would stay on through tea and perhaps even supper. Amala secretly shared his hope *and* his enthusiasm, but for entirely different reasons. She believed one of the biggest reasons her parents enjoyed entertaining company—at least when it was people they actually liked—was at least partly due to the restricted expectations of their place in society. Her father—like Henry and Chit—was a gentleman with ample wealth, and their family names and situations made it unseemly for them to engage in any kind of employment beyond matters of their estates, which were mostly taken care of by well-trusted overseers. The result was that the majority of this class of people—both male and female—were usually consumed with boredom. There was a very short list of acceptable occupations of one's time, and those things often grew wearisome—especially after years of having little else to do. Therefore, positive social interaction was a great treat to such people. Given that Oliver and Viola were both very outgoing in nature and also very generous in sharing all they'd been blessed with, having people over to visit was a genuine pleasure for them. However, they had no interest in entertaining people who were snooty or gossipy. Although it had never actually been articulated, Amala knew that her parents carefully gauged people's attitudes toward Amala being accepted as their daughter; it was like some kind of social barometer that determined whether or not people were ever invited more than once.

Amala's insides were swarming with butterflies when their visitors arrived. Initially she felt a little worried about being able to maintain her and Henry's secret around other people; she wasn't certain she could keep herself from staring at Henry or from allowing her feelings to show. But she felt a deep relief just to see him enter the drawing room with Chit at his side. His greetings to everyone were comfortable and amiable, and within minutes he was chatting and laughing with the others, appearing completely relaxed. Occasionally he tossed a glance in her direction that was too discreet to alert anyone to his having a particular interest in her, but it was just enough to remind Amala that this man loved her. And she loved him. The more she observed him in such a setting, the more enamored with him she became.

Amala noticed how thoroughly her parents were enjoying themselves, and even Kat seemed comfortable and not so bored and eager to leave as she had been the last time both men had visited. Even their talk of India—which generally made Kat either bored or uncomfortable—didn't seem to be bothering her. As the afternoon progressed, with seemingly endless things to talk about, Amala noticed that Henry seemed happy. In fact, there was a light in his eyes she'd not seen since she'd met him that night at the ball. Except that now it was brighter. She wondered if she was the reason for it. Was it possible that she could be responsible for making a man like Henry Beckenridge so happy? If so, could she make him happy enough to compensate for all the difficulties she would bring into his life? It was certainly a question worth pondering.

The two men *did* stay until after supper, and the day was delightful—except that not once could Amala find a reasonable excuse to have even a moment alone with Henry. After he'd left with Chit, she sat with her family while they revisited the highlights of the day, and they discussed the fine qualities of these men. Amala noticed they were being careful to respect her wish that they not speculate over the possibility of any gentleman being a good match for her. But they *did* speculate about one of these men being a good match for Kat. Hearing Kat analyze what she found favorable in both men, Amala felt decidedly uncomfortable. She'd not anticipated that keeping her secret would subject her to the possibility of Kat taking an interest in Henry. And her parents were very supportive of the idea of her doing so. Thankfully, at this point, Kat didn't exhibit any more interest in Henry than in Chit; she considered them both equally good men and potentially good husbands. But what if her feelings changed? What if she became drawn to Henry? Amala wasn't worried about how Henry would handle Kat's attention should it come to that. If she didn't know him to be a man of integrity, she would not have agreed to this absurd arrangement. But she was finding it much more difficult than she'd expected to keep herself from just telling her family that Henry was secretly courting her—as much as it was possible to do so and keep the matter a secret.

Two days later, Kat received a different gentleman caller, and she was clearly very fond of him as well. Amala realized that Kat really had no idea what real love felt like, and while she was conscious of seeking out the right characteristics in a man that would make him a good husband, she was seeing the men who came within her circle much the way she would consider choosing the right gown for an upcoming ball. Amala felt certain she had nothing to worry about in regard to Kat.

The day after that, Henry came to visit without Chit, and her parents were overtly thrilled to see him. But Henry was no less thrilled. Amala thought of what he'd told her about his own parents and the home he'd grown up in—and lived in now—and she found the interaction between him and her parents rather touching. Oliver and Viola had so much love to give, and they gave it so effortlessly. And Henry was sorely in need of the elements of home and family that he'd never received in his life—at least not since his father's death. She noted how comfortable and relaxed he had become and how eagerly her parents invited him to make himself at home in every way. Her father even went so far as to say, "If you feel like taking a nap or something, find a spare couch and do so. If you're hungry, just follow your nose to the kitchen."

Henry chuckled and thanked Oliver for his kind hospitality, but she could see that the invitation was meaningful to him, and she wouldn't be surprised if eventually he did those very things.

That afternoon it began to rain, and Kat received an unexpected visitor, a female friend she'd been acquainted with for years who had been traveling by carriage through this part of the county and had impulsively stopped to see if Kat might be at home. The two women went off to a parlor to visit at about the same time that Viola declared she was feeling the need for a nap and went upstairs. Noting that her father looked a little sleepy himself, Amala graciously offered to show Henry the library.

"A lovely place to spend the afternoon when rain keeps us away from the gardens," Oliver declared before adding that he'd leave Amala to see that Henry had what he needed, and that he was going to follow his wife's example and indulge in a nap.

"Don't hold back on my account," Henry said. "There's no need for you to feel like you need to entertain me every minute I'm here."

"Oh, we're past that," Oliver said with a chuckle. "But you'll stay for supper?"

"I'd love to," Henry said. "Far better company here than at the pub; the cook at my house won't be expecting me."

"Wonderful!" Oliver said and went off to take his nap.

For a long moment Amala just stared at Henry and he stared back in a way they never would have dared while there were other people in the room. Realizing the doors were open and there was risk of being overheard, she quickly said, "I think you'll like the library. It's one of my favorite rooms in the house."

"I'm sure I will," he said and followed her out of the drawing room, down the stairs, through two long hallways, and into the room that Amala considered the greatest representation of wealth in this or any other home—simply because it was filled from floor to ceiling with books.

"Oh, it's remarkable!" Henry declared as he entered and she closed the door behind them. She watched him as he took in the massive shelves of books and the many long windows that emitted the overcast light of a rainy day over the furnishings that were fine but simple and designed for comfort in a room that was meant for long bouts of reading.

Amala was about to comment on what she particularly liked about the room when Henry turned to look at her, all pretense gone from his expression. In the time it took her to exhale, he closed the distance between them, pushed his arm around her waist and his other hand into her hair. He looked into her eyes for only a moment before he kissed her.

"Do you realize," he asked softly, "the number of hours I have been in the same room with you, wanting to do that?"

"Yes, I'm well aware," she replied and urged him to kiss her again.

Recognizing the need to behave rationally and keep their affection in check, Amala eased away from him and drew his attention to her reasons for loving the library—most specifically, all of the books.

"I loved to read even as a child in India," she said, running her fingers over the spines of a long row of novels. "After I came here, reading was something familiar and safe. Of course, Kat and I had our lessons with tutors, and our play time, and we usually got along fairly well. But I couldn't go a day without spending time with a good book. Reading is one of the few things that Kat and I firmly agree on. We would often lounge about here for hours, each taking one of the couches, throwing off our shoes, and just getting lost in another world."

"What a lovely image that brings to mind," Henry said, sitting on one of those couches while Amala continued to affectionately touch the books.

"Do you like to read, Henry?" she asked, still more focused on the books than on him.

"I love it," he said. "In fact, it's one of the things I do *not* have in common with Chit. He always wants to be up and doing something. He loves to learn new things, but he prefers to do so by meeting new people and being actively involved in whatever it is they do. I often chose relaxing with a good book over following him about on his adventures."

"But you *did* follow him to India."

"Yes, I certainly did. And I confess that nothing in a book could have ever described what I saw and experienced there. Still, I've learned from the experience that being a world traveler does not necessarily agree with me. I suppose I'll just have to learn about other places in the world by reading about them."

"That sounds perfectly reasonable to me," Amala said and smiled, loving the way he smiled back.

Chapter Five
THE DECISION

AMALA SAT DOWN A SAFE distance away from Henry—close enough to hold his hand, but far enough away to avoid the temptation of his kiss. Should anyone come into the library looking for them— or for any other reason—they both agreed it was wise to avoid spending excessive time in close physical proximity. She was so glad to finally be alone with him—as she sensed that he was—but all of the conversation she wanted to share had gone completely out of her head. Following a stretch of silence that began to feel awkward, Henry said, "May I ask you something . . . sensitive? You don't have to tell me if you don't want to, although I confess to wanting to know everything about you. Still, I know some things can be difficult to talk about."

"Ask me and I'll tell you whether or not I want to talk about it." Amala sensed what the question might be, but couldn't be sure until it was actually spoken.

"How did your mother and father die?"

Even though she'd suspected this was what he wanted to know, hearing the question aloud took her off guard more than she'd expected. The incident hadn't been discussed in her family for many years. She looked away, wanting a moment to gather her thoughts and compose her expression. He squeezed her hand more tightly, as if he sensed the difficulty of speaking about this.

"Do you want the simple answer or the story as I remember it?"

"You should know me well enough by now to know my response to that. I'm not a casual acquaintance, Amala; I'm the man who wants to marry you."

Amala took a deep breath. "While I can't begin to understand all of the implications, I believe from the way my parents—those I have now—spoke of the incident, that there was perhaps some . . . scandal or controversy. For that reason, I ask for your confidence. I don't believe any ramifications would come back to my family, but to be truthful, I'm not certain."

"Of course, you have my strictest confidence in anything you share with me."

Henry felt a little nervous as he watched Amala turn to smile at him briefly, expressing silent appreciation for his discretion. Then she looked straight ahead, giving him a view of her profile while she was clearly gathering her words *and* composing her emotions. He'd expected to hear that it had been an accident, or illness. Disease was prevalent in India; he knew that well enough. He had *not* expected the kind of preamble she had already given, nor the evidence that after all these years, speaking of their deaths was still so difficult. He'd lost his father at a young age, and the loss had torn him apart. But he could talk about it and not be so affected. He gave her hand another gentle squeeze of encouragement and patiently waited for her to speak.

"They were shot," she said, "by British soldiers."

Henry caught his breath but refrained from uttering the curse that came to his mind and nearly escaped his lips. He didn't want to prevent her from saying whatever she felt inclined to tell him.

"They had been accused of treason, although I've been reassured by Oliver and Viola that it wasn't true. But there was no trial, no opportunity given to prove their innocence. Soldiers came into our home and . . . shot them."

Amala drew in a quivering breath and said more matter-of-factly, "Mata and Pita both worked for the Hepworths, who were among the few Britishers who treated the Indian people with respect. Whenever Mata and Pita were at the Hepworth home, I was there with them."

Henry liked the way she referred to her blood parents by an Indian version of the words for mother and father, and how it distinguished them from the people she had come to call her parents. He also appreciated that he actually knew the words well from his own time spent among Indian people. He felt increasingly comfortable with her, and his compassion deepened in regard to what he was hearing. Already he could understand why she would hold so much fear over the issue of prejudice and social barriers.

"I was tutored along with Kat," Amala went on, "and we were together practically from infancy. Kat also spent time in my home; she liked it there. And there were times when social events were taking place at the Hepworth home, and it was better if the children were out of the house, so Kat would spend the night at *my* home, and we'd have great fun together."

As Henry sensed where this was leading, he put a hand over his mouth as an added measure to keep himself from uttering some inappropriate expletive. He tightened his hold once again on Amala's hand and waited for her to go on.

"Kat was there when it happened. When Mata and Pita realized soldiers were coming into the house, they told me and Kat to hide and remain very quiet. And so we did. We clung to each other while we heard the shouting: the soldiers were yelling accusations and threats; Pita was demanding justice, declaring their innocence; Mata was crying, begging for mercy. I had to put my hand over Kat's mouth when we heard the shots." She let out a weighted sigh. "The absence of Mata and Pita protesting made it clear what had happened. I could hear the soldiers rummaging around the house, searching for who knows what and talking among themselves as if executing Indian people was a normal part of their expected routine. After they finally left and the house became quiet, we still didn't come out of hiding; I think we were too afraid of what we would find, even though neither of us said a word—even to each other. It seemed hours before I knew Kat was asleep, and in spite of my horror—and my fear that the soldiers might come back—eventually I feel asleep as well. I woke up to the sound of Oliver calling our names, his voice frantic, terrified."

Amala stood up and went to the window, where she looked out with distant eyes. "I remember him holding both of us close and sobbing. I'd never heard him cry like that—not before or since." She sighed loudly. "Within a few days we were on our way to England, taking very little with us. The journey was long and . . . I think I were all dazed and shocked." Following a long moment of silence, she turned to look at Henry and concluded, "And here we are. I've now lived more than half of my lifetime in England. I could never bring myself to go back to India, even if I could think of a reason to consider doing so. I was too young to begin to understand the complicated politics going on with one country attempting to rule another, and that country being divided in and of itself. I still don't understand; I don't want to. I've chosen to focus my memories of India on its beauty and uniqueness in contrast to where I live now. There are things I choose to never think of. When such thoughts jump into my mind, I just force them away. Whatever sacrifices I might make to be an Indian woman living in England are nothing compared to what life might be like for me there. Even if I could live there with some sense of safety and security—which I could not, given that I have no relatives or connections—I would never want to be that close to the memories of what happened. I could never even pass a British soldier on the street without being reminded, and they were everywhere."

"And yet you live here among the British people."

"It's different," she insisted, but didn't expound.

"I don't even know what to say, Amala. I never would have guessed; never could have imagined."

"You don't have to say anything," she told him. "But I'm glad you know."

"How can you tell me that story without shedding a tear?"

"I've cried an ocean of tears over it, Henry. I believe I've healed inside as much as it's possible for a human being to do so. I accept what happened for what it is, and I try every day to be grateful for all that I've been blessed with."

"You are more brave and strong than I think you will ever be able to see for yourself."

She laughed softly. "I don't know about that. I'm just . . . trying to move beyond this horrible incident in my past. Every day I am one day further away."

"You said you accept what happened for what it is. May I ask exactly how you define *what it is?*"

She looked firmly at him, and he saw her eyes flare with a mixture of courage and indignation but a distinct lack of anger or hatred. She stated as if it were a memorized mantra, "The deaths of my mother and father were the result of human depravity and injustice. I choose to strive to make my life meaningful in the eyes of God in spite of it and not allow what happened to define my own character."

Henry was silenced by the summation. Was it any wonder he loved her so much? It was as if his spirit had sensed these very convictions in her the first time they'd met. He'd witnessed a great deal of the same human depravity and injustice she'd spoken of. It was the very reason he could never return to India. How could he feel pride in being British and be surrounded by the evidence of how British arrogance and wealth were impacting the Indian people? It had gone on for so long—and would likely continue to go on—that the possibility of correcting the problem was too complicated and overwhelming to believe that it was solvable at all. And so Henry had chosen to look away, return to his homeland, and be grateful for the good life he could come home to. But Amala was like a personification of his convictions that he could never even put into words. He loved her for far many more reasons than that. But he loved her more because she touched something in his soul that he couldn't define. India had changed him, made him who he was now. And it was the same for her.

Henry watched her looking out the window and struggled for minutes to think of something appropriate to say. He realized there were no words that could ever express his compassion, his sorrow, his empathy on her behalf. He finally concluded that there was only one thing he could say that mattered, and he said it with all of the conviction he felt. "I love you, Amala. I love you with every piece of my soul."

She turned slowly to look at him, and he was taken aback by her beauty showcased by the window at her back. It was like a painting he wished he could look at every day for the rest of his life, knowing that each time he did he would be moved. In that moment he didn't care what cruelty the world might throw at them for going against convention. He only wanted to build a protective cocoon around the love they shared and devote his life to keeping her safe and happy. He wanted to believe it was possible; he had to believe it could happen, that he could find a way to convince her. When she smiled at him, he was at least gratified to note that they were making progress in that direction.

Henry watched Amala walk back to the bookshelves and pull one out, then she crossed the room and handed it to him. "Eventually someone will come looking for us, and when they find us here we should perhaps at least give the illusion that we've been reading."

He looked down to see that he was holding a copy of *Sense and Sensibility*. He'd certainly heard of it but he had never read it, mostly because it was considered to appeal more to the feminine mind. But the pursuit of marriage was nothing if not two people striving to learn more about each other—and their gender—in order to better understand each other.

"Would you like me to read to you . . . or the other way around?"

"Both, perhaps," she said. "Mostly I just want to talk . . . and pretend to be reading."

"An excellent plan," he said and kept the book open on his lap while she sat down on the couch and he turned more toward her. Time passed quickly as they talked of many things that had nothing to do with India, or politics, or social injustice.

A maid found them there to announce that it was time for tea, and they went together back to the drawing room to find Amala's parents, and Kat and her friend, all seated for tea. Henry helped Amala with her chair, then sat across the table from her, next to Oliver.

Henry found Kat's friend mildly annoying, mostly because she didn't seem to find any interest in a topic of conversation that had any real depth. But he did appreciate how much Kat was enjoying her friend's company. The friend left after tea, and the rest of them lounged about the drawing room while the rain continued, and Henry felt completely at home. He wished that such scenes might have taken place in his own home, but they never had. He felt comfortable enough with these people to share his thoughts, and he was once again reassured that he would forever be welcome. Even in setting his feelings for Amala aside, their genuine acceptance and open invitation meant more than he could ever tell them.

Henry stayed until after supper and he returned two days later to spend as many hours as he could get away with. He visited a little with Everett upon his arrival and shared lunch with the family, after which he went riding with Oliver, since the weather had turned more favorable than it had been on his previous visit. After tea, he enjoyed a little time alone with Amala in the library, and he didn't leave until after supper. He returned home in time to check in on his mother before she settled down for the night. She didn't inquire over where he'd been or show any interest in what he might be doing with his time. She only grumbled about the servants, the food, the weather, and the gossip that had come to her ears about two members of the serving staff sharing a romantic tryst and perhaps wanting to marry. She treated the matter as if it were something criminal. Henry commented that any human being, no matter what their class or ethnic origin, had the natural right to fall in love and be with the person of their choosing. His mother looked at him with a harsh astonishment that made him feel like a naughty little boy who'd been caught at some kind of terrible mischief. He dropped the subject, wished her well, kissed her forehead, and hurried to his own room, where he felt like he needed a bath just to wash away the negativity his mother exuded, which seemed to cling to him.

Weeks eased into months while Henry never went more than a few days without spending a day with the Hepworth family. He *did* feel completely at home there and with every member of the family—most especially Amala. He loved every bit of time they might find alone together, but he also loved being with her when the family was there as well. They were indeed getting to know each other much better, and he hoped she was coming to believe—as he was—that they truly had the strength to be together and withstand the social and cultural challenges they would face.

Henry dearly loved Viola, who was loving and cheerful and had a broad perspective on many facets of life and the world, all of which she saw through the best possible lens. In a word, she was exactly the opposite of his own mother. He also grew fond of Kat, recognizing, as Amala had pointed out, that she was very different from her sister in many ways, but she was kind and lighthearted and completely without guile. Henry found it interesting that he had a sister who shared his blood but was a complete stranger to him, yet Amala and Kat had no blood connection but were completely integrated into each other's lives, the way that siblings should be.

Beyond his love for Amala, Henry was most drawn to Oliver—perhaps for the simple fact that he was the only man in the household. The two of them pored over Oliver's Indian mementos and artifacts and could talk endlessly about all the things they both loved and loathed about the country they'd temporarily attached themselves to. He heard the story of the death of Amala's parents from Oliver's perspective, and it was evident that the tragedy had affected them all very deeply. Technically these people had been servants in the Hepworth household, but given the nature of Oliver and Viola, they had also been good friends. Oliver felt certain that someone had specifically targeted Amala's father with the accusation of a crime in order to divert the guilt from the person actually responsible. It had been a conspiracy of the worst kind, reeking of horror and injustice. But the political climate of the country had made it impossible to even hope that any justice would ever be served, and Oliver felt good about his decision to have left India when he did, and he spoke of Amala with great pride, genuinely considering his opportunity to care for her as a privilege. He also expressed some concern for Kat over the fact that she had never once spoken of the incident, and he believed it was the reason she felt such discomfort regarding *any* conversation about India. In contrast, Oliver told Henry that Amala had talked freely of what had happened and how it had affected her, and he felt that she had appropriately healed from the death of her parents—as much as it was possible to do so.

During one conversation, Oliver brought up his concern about Amala's believing she could never marry or have children because of the social taint and strain it would bring into the lives of everyone involved. As comfortable as he'd come to feel with Oliver, it took great willpower for Henry to not share his views on the matter. He believed that Oliver would be pleased to know that Henry wanted to marry Amala, and if anyone could make her happy and help her deal with the repercussions, it was him. But Henry kept his promise to Amala and didn't say a word except, "I hope that perhaps one day she will find someone who will prove her wrong."

"I hope the same, dear boy," Oliver said and changed the subject.

Henry and Oliver often went out riding and they occasionally did a little hunting—although Henry preferred the riding more than the sport. Henry came to know most of the servants in the household by name, and he certainly did sneak into the kitchen sometimes to tease the cook and the maids and taste whatever they were making and offer his candid opinion. He also became comfortable enough to find a couch and take a nap, if he felt so inclined while the family went about their usual routine, seeming more and more to just take his presence there very matter-of-factly, with a complete absence of any formality.

Chit occasionally came with Henry—just as Henry still occasionally joined Chit for other social engagements or recreation. But over time, Chit joined him less and less; he'd become comfortable with other friends and in other households—and he also enjoyed just being at home, because his home and family were actually enjoyable.

Henry came to know Everett better by often stopping to chat with him as he was coming and going. He knew that Everett was very loyal to Amala and would always stand by her in whatever decision she made, but he also knew that Everett liked Henry very much and hoped Amala would choose marriage to him when all was said and done.

For all the reasons that Henry had found to feel comfortable and happy at Willenbrock House, Amala remained the bright star, shining above all else, giving him joy and hope continually. Their opportunities for conversation and spending time together had made them completely comfortable with each other, and the more they became acquainted, the more it seemed inevitable that marriage was the only course for them to take.

Henry thoroughly enjoyed stealing a kiss whenever the opportunity presented itself, and he had no doubt that Amala enjoyed the affection they shared every bit as much as he did. The only problem was that the more comfortable they became with each other, the more they both had to admit that it was becoming increasingly evident that their desires were wandering far beyond an occasional kiss. They talked about it in what he believed was a mature and appropriate matter; they both had strong feelings about reserving intimacy for marriage. The problem was that he felt more than ready to marry her, while she continued to want to give the matter some time. More than once they came close to arguing over the issue when it seemed evident to Henry that they still had the same problem they'd had from the start: he was willing to take on whatever challenges might come with their public union, and she preferred secrecy and clinging to the belief that it would likely never work out. When he realized she was likely just prolonging the inevitable and perhaps had no intention of marrying him at all, he felt a deep anger that he knew was only a reaction to the intense hurt and fear festering inside of him.

At the conclusion of yet another argument over the matter, they both agreed to just give their relationship more time. Henry wanted to believe that time would make a difference, but a part of him feared that Amala was so afraid of what making their relationship public would do to their lives, she might have preferred to forever remain in this clandestine arrangement in which they could share a portion of their lives and no one would ever know. But he knew it couldn't go on this way forever; in fact, he doubted he could bear for it to go on much longer. He believed that God had created men and women to feel these desires so that they *would* marry and have children. Keeping their relationship a secret while maintaining his desire to remain chaste was becoming more and more of a dilemma. Aside from his own personal, moral convictions, he knew he could never do anything that would make Amala feel disrespected or taken advantage of. The result was that he found himself *avoiding* any opportunity to spend time alone with her, when he knew it should have been the other way around.

On a particularly cold afternoon in late autumn, Henry couldn't refuse Amala's mention to her family that she hoped Henry would accompany her to the library and read to her.

"I do so love the way he reads," Amala added.

Oliver and Viola encouraged it, since they were about to set out to call on some neighbors who'd had a recent death in the family. And Kat wasn't feeling well and was going to lie down. Henry was glad to know they were in a house full of servants so that they could never be *completely* alone. He didn't trust himself in regard to the path he often found his thoughts taking in regard to Amala, and he often had to fight very hard to stop himself from nurturing such thoughts.

Once alone in the library with Amala, he wasn't surprised by the way she took his face into her hands and kissed him. He returned the kiss eagerly and drew her into his arms, wanting to hold her this way for the rest of his life. But temptations began filtering into his mind, tainting an experience that should have been nothing but pure and precious.

"Amala," he whispered and stepped back, "we must be careful. All of this secrecy is not good—now that we've come to know each other so well."

She turned her back to him, either to conceal her emotion or to let him know that she didn't want to talk about it. But he knew that they *needed* to talk about it and that the status of their relationship couldn't continue to be ignored.

"Amala," he pleaded, "I love you more every day. Just . . . let me speak with your father, and we'll get all of this out in the open so we can be properly chaperoned until we're married. We can be married soon, as soon as possible. I see no reason to wait. Please, Amala. Talk to me. Tell me you'll marry me. Have I not proven my love and devotion to you sufficiently?"

"I have no question about your love and devotion," she said, still keeping her back to him.

"Then tell me what to do. I cannot go on like this."

"There is nothing that you or anyone else can do to change the circumstances."

"So . . . it's true. Your views haven't changed. What has been the purpose, then, of all the time we've spent together these many months? Am I some kind of entertainment or distraction to you?"

"No, of course not!" she insisted, finally turning to look at him.

"Did you *ever* intend to sincerely consider marrying me? Or did you always believe in your heart that it would never happen? Was this just a prolonging of the inevitable for you?"

"You should know the answers to those questions," she countered.

"I *thought* I did," he said, hearing the sorrow in his own voice. "But we both know it can't go on like this. We always knew a day would come when we would have to make a decision—one way or another. I want to marry you, Amala. I don't ever want to let you go. But I'm not certain at all what *you* want. I know you love me, but perhaps your fear of how others will treat us is more powerful than your love. I honestly don't know." When she said nothing in response, he had to add, "It seems you don't know either."

"Maybe I don't," she admitted.

"And maybe you never will until we actually exhibit some courage and come out of hiding. Just . . . let me talk to your father, and—"

"No!" she insisted. "Not yet."

"Not yet? Or not ever?" he demanded. "I think you know as well as I do that your family would be nothing but pleased with our getting married, and they would be nothing but supportive. You don't want me to talk to them because they'd side with me, and you know they would."

"Their love for both of us blinds them to the reality of how it would really be; you have that in common with them."

"Oh, for the love of heaven, Amala, give us all some credit for being something less than inane fools. Do you not think your parents are well aware of the situation? Of the possible challenges? Do you not think that I've not considered the ramifications—over and over and over? Do you think I would still be here if I weren't willing to take that on?"

"You're letting your feelings blind you," she insisted, and he felt angry.

"So . . . you're saying *you* know more than I do, more than your parents know, about the kind of life we would live? We—who have all lived in India. We—who have all seen for ourselves how cruel society can be. We—who know the reality of what life can be like for half-caste children. It's as if you're standing there calling us all a bunch of ignorant fools while you believe you have all of the answers, and you're willing to be a martyr for this cause. What is it, really, Amala? Do you feel guilty because your parents died as a result of prejudice and injustice? Do you believe that laying any claim to happiness for yourself is . . . what? Dishonoring them, somehow? What is it? Help me understand. Talk to me. Tell me the truth. The whole truth. The real truth. Because I'm not playing games here. This started out as a rational option to be courting and still keep the social mongrels at bay. But it's grown beyond that. It *has* become a game, and I won't be a part of it. So marry me or don't. But if you don't, at least be humane enough to give me a *good* reason, a reason I can understand, so that I don't have to spend the rest of my life wondering why it all went wrong between us when I tried so hard to do everything right. I'm willing to give up anything and everything for you. I don't *care* what people say or do. Because there are only two things that really matter to me: my devotion to God and my love for you. And I already know in my heart that God sees us as equals, and I can live with that. But apparently you can't. So what's it going to be, Amala?"

"I'm not ready," she said with a surprising lack of anger, considering how upset he was.

"Will you *ever* be ready?" he asked, and she didn't answer. He took in a deep breath to try to calm himself. "I don't understand why we can't at least talk to your family. They would understand. They would help us to talk things through and—"

"No," she said but offered no explanation. It occurred to him that the things he'd just said to her were perhaps even more true than he'd feared, and she couldn't come up with any reasonable argument to everything he'd already laid out.

In spite of all that, Henry opted to share something more. "Your father has expressed to me his concern about your belief that you could never marry and find happiness." Amala looked astonished. "He doesn't agree with you, but he's trying to respect your wishes."

"You didn't tell him that . . ."

"That what? That I'm ready and willing to marry you? That I love you with all my heart and soul? No, I didn't tell him. It was tempting, but I would never break my word to you. And again I say you don't want your family to know because they would agree with me."

Amala said nothing. She turned away and walked to the window, where she stood and looked out, keeping her back to him. Henry could feel his heart sinking, and his stomach was tightening into knots. Was the inevitable finally coming to pass? Had he been a fool to even believe—in spite of her own declarations to the contrary—that changing her mind would even be possible?

Henry had one other idea that he'd been hesitant to bring up, but it was something he'd been considering for a long time. He considered it a possible last resort. "Then let's go and talk to the vicar; just you and me. He's obligated in his position to keep anything we tell him in confidence. Perhaps he can help advise us."

Amala turned to look at him without moving. Her eyes were wide with astonishment. "Do you believe that man speaks for God? Is that what you're saying?"

"Given his position, I believe he could perhaps offer some sound advice. It's up to us whether or not we heed his advice, but it might be a step in the right direction to solving this problem."

Amala looked out the window again. "You know—because we've talked about it—that I too believe God sees us as equals. I'm not worried about what God thinks, but I don't believe our local vicar will see the situation as God sees it. God did not *choose* him. *He* chose to become a vicar; it's his profession. He teaches a fair sermon and looks after his congregation in all the ways that most people believe he should. But he barely acknowledges *me*. I don't trust him, and I don't necessarily like him."

While Henry was trying to reason that out with his idea that speaking with the vicar might help, Amala turned and said with resolution, "Fine, we'll go talk to the vicar. I'll meet you there tomorrow afternoon at two. For obvious reasons, I believe it would be better if we arrive separately."

She hurried past him and out of the room, and a part of Henry knew it was over. Something inside of him instinctively believed that Amala's willingness to tell this man their secret was because she knew he would be opposed to the marriage and his attitude would help prove her point. He wished now that he'd never brought it up. But what else was he supposed to do?

Later that night while he wrestled with his thoughts in a sleepless bed, Henry wondered if—in spite of what he suspected would happen—going to see the vicar was still the right course of action. His months of *courting* Amala had convinced him that they were indeed meant to be together, that their love could withstand the persecution. But Amala was no more convinced now than she had been when they'd met. And if she was never going to change her mind, then he was just wasting his life away waiting for something to happen that never would. His heart felt so broken at the very idea that he could hardly breathe. But he didn't want to be alone. He wanted to marry a fine woman and have children and lead a normal life. And if Amala wasn't willing to share that life with him, he'd be a fool to keep hoping for what was hopeless.

Henry could never add up the hours he'd spent praying that he and Amala could be together, that her heart would be softened, that she would be willing to commit herself to him and know that he would do everything in his power to make up for the sacrifices she would be making. It occurred to him just before dawn that perhaps his idea to speak with the vicar had been an answer to his prayers. Perhaps God was guiding him to a path that would illustrate to him—without question—that it was time to move on. Now he could only pray that God would help heal his broken heart. He had a sick feeling that today would be the official ending of his relationship with Amala, and since no one had known he'd ever shared anything more than friendship with her, no one would be able to understand his grief. There would be no one to talk to about it, no one to confide in. Perhaps Everett, he thought. But how much time could he spend loitering around the carriage house pouring his heart out to a man who preferred to be alone?

Henry finally rose from a sleepless night feeling like a man going to the guillotine—except that he believed death might be preferable. Instead he had to go on living and do his best to find a life without Amala. At this moment, the very idea was impossible to comprehend.

* * * *

Amala informed her family at lunch that she wanted to have Everett drive her to the church. She felt the need for some solitude and prayer. She avoided their polite inquiries over what the problem might be and assured them she was fine and there was nothing anyone could do. She simply needed some time alone.

Amala spoke with Everett about the purpose of this little excursion, and she was glad to be able to do so openly. He expressed concern over her reasoning and didn't hesitate to say that he personally didn't believe this was a wise course of action, but, as always, he respected Amala's decision, and they were on their way in plenty of time to arrive at the church before two. Heavily overcast skies matched her mood perfectly.

During the drive, Amala had to use all her willpower to not start crying; if she started now she wouldn't be able to stop. She could cry later. Henry's declarations yesterday in the library had haunted her all through a restless night, and they were haunting her still. Looking back to the time she'd agreed to this arrangement with Henry, she honestly didn't know if she'd been hopeful that it might actually work out between them or if she'd simply wanted the time with him. Had she unwittingly used him in order to simply have the experience of romance in her life? If that were the case, she wondered if she could ever live with the guilt and regret threatening to smother her. She felt wicked and cruel and horrible. And in her heart she knew how the vicar was going to respond, and therefore she knew the outcome of this meeting—and her relationship with Henry. Her heart was breaking, crumbling into pieces. But a part of her felt like she deserved it, although Henry did *not* deserve to feel this way. But she knew that he did, and she knew that it was her fault. She couldn't imagine ever being able to look at herself in the mirror again without being overcome with shame and regret.

When she knew they were getting close to the church, a little voice in the back of her mind told her there was one way to remedy all of this. *Just marry him*, she thought, as if to try it out. They didn't need the approval of this particular vicar to choose marriage. They could elope. They could do it with or without the knowledge of her parents. Either way, she knew her family would support her in the decision. They loved Henry. They would help create a buffer around them through whatever consequences they might suffer. *Just marry him*, she thought again. But loud, booming voices of fear quickly drowned out the idea. The absurdity of an English gentleman marrying an Indian woman and expecting to live any kind of a normal life washed over her. The cruelty their children would inevitably endure put a final exclamation point to the sentence she was firmly passing upon herself. It was impossible!

At the church, Everett helped her step down from the carriage. He wished her well and she went inside with trepidation. Daylight illuminated the little chapel, but with the same cloudiness that was present outside. The vicar was seated on a pew near the front, reading from the Bible. Amala had never before come here alone seeking refuge *or* advice. But she assumed the vicar likely spent his free time here to make himself available for anyone who might seek him out. She was almost disappointed to see him. Perhaps if he'd been off visiting someone in need, this could have been prolonged. But she squared her shoulders and reminded herself that it was better to have it over with. Now that she'd become brutally aware of how unfairly she'd been treating Henry, she couldn't bear to have this charade go on any longer.

A quick glance let her know that Henry hadn't arrived yet, but, then, she was early. The vicar looked up when she entered, but he didn't stand.

"Hello, Miss Hepworth," he said. "What brings you here today?"

Rather than trying to explain that she needed to speak with him but couldn't do so until Henry arrived, she simply said, "I'll just sit and pray for now, if that's all right."

"Of course," he said and turned back to his reading.

Amala tried to pray while she gripped the wooden bench cruelly, trying to channel all of her turmoil and regret down to her fingers and into the wood that she clutched so hard her hands began to hurt. When minutes passed she began to wonder if Henry wouldn't come. Perhaps he knew the probable outcome of this meeting and had changed his mind about pursuing it. A minute later she heard the door open behind her, and the vicar immediately rose to his feet.

"Mr. Beckenridge," he said with overt respect and an obvious pleasure at seeing him here. Assessing the difference in his greeting to her left little doubt as to what his attitude would likely be over their seeking his advice and guidance.

"Mr. Guthrie," she heard Henry say. The sound of his voice quickened her heart; his words made her realize that she'd actually forgotten the vicar's name, even though she'd been present in this building to hear his Sunday sermons for many years.

"What may I do for you?" Mr. Guthrie asked with a slight bow and an expression of adoration, as if Henry might be royalty.

"I may need to speak with you," Henry said, and Amala considered the ambiguity of the word *may*. "But I'd like to just sit for a few minutes, if that's all right."

"Of course," Mr. Guthrie said. "I'll be right here if you need me."

"Thank you," Henry said.

The vicar sat back down, and Amala became keenly aware of the sound of Henry's footsteps coming closer before he sat beside her and reached for her hand, but she had trouble letting go of the bench in order to allow him to take it. He noticed and whispered, "I'm guessing you're rather upset and trying very hard not to show it. How typical of you." There was the tiniest hint of snideness in his voice; but she couldn't blame him. She knew it was only a symptom of the way she had treated him so cruelly.

Amala noticed a glance from Mr. Guthrie, which made his surprise evident that Henry Beckenridge was sitting close to her, speaking to her, when he'd likely assumed their both being here at the same time had surely been coincidence.

"I know," Henry added quietly, very close to her ear, "why you agreed to this without the kind of protest you are so famous for. You know he will be wholeheartedly against the possibility of our union, and you will feel utterly vindicated to prove that you were right all along."

"I only know for certain that he doesn't approve of me in any way. I would assume he'd be opposed to a fine gentleman such as yourself being associated with me at all."

"Then let's leave. We don't have to talk to him. It was a bad idea. Come away with me now."

"And what?" she asked, continuing to whisper. "You told me yesterday that it couldn't go on this way. If we're not going to marry, it has to end."

"Then marry me. We'll leave now and go to Scotland. Everett can take a message to your parents. Forget your fears, Amala. Trust me when I tell you that I love you enough to make up for all else."

Amala fought hard to swallow the hot, burning threat of tears in her throat. She closed her eyes and felt tears leak out, but it was only a tiny portion of the unshed ocean of tears threatening to overtake her. With all the courage and strength she could muster, she took a deep breath, drew back her shoulders, and said what she needed to say, keeping her voice too low for the vicar to hear her. "Forgive me, Henry. I now question my own foolishness in allowing this relationship to go forward at all. You were right; what you said yesterday was all true. I didn't do it intentionally; I would never hurt you intentionally. But I know that I've hurt you nevertheless. I think a part of me always knew it could never be, but I was blinded by my love for you, and I wanted time with you—any time at all. I take all of the blame for any pain this has brought into your life. I can only hope that one day you will find it in your heart to forgive me. But I would understand if you didn't."

Amala took another deep breath and forged ahead, fearing she'd never get another chance to say what needed to be said. "I don't want the change between us to affect your relationship with my family. I want you to continue to be comfortable in our home. My parents love you, and I know you love them. It would break their hearts if you stopped your visits. I beg you to not add to my guilt and regret by hurting them with your absence."

Following a stretch of silence that made it clear she had nothing more to say, Henry finally whispered, "So, that's it. All we've shared has come to nothing. All we feel for each other is irrelevant."

"Forgive me, Henry. It's the way it has to be. One day perhaps you'll understand that it's better this way. The pain we're feeling now would only be magnified in the future if we were to pursue marriage."

"That's what *you* believe," Henry said, the bite in his voice becoming more evident. "But I believe the love we share would more than compensate for the difficulties."

"Then it appears we have come to an impasse."

"It appears there always was an impasse," he whispered, sounding angry now.

Without warning, he took hold of her arm, forcing her to stand, and she had no choice but to walk with him toward the front of the chapel unless she wanted to create an unsavory scene in front of the vicar.

Mr. Guthrie stood as they approached. He took note of the way Henry was holding Amala's arm and was clearly trying to hide his astonishment. Amala felt certain that Henry was holding to one last hope that this man might understand and become their ally. She wished now that she had protested more boldly yesterday over this idea and that they'd never come here.

"Mr. Guthrie," Henry said with no hint of the hurt and anger Amala knew he was feeling, "we have somewhat of a predicament, and I'm hoping you can help us." Mr. Guthrie nodded and Henry went on. "You see, I very much wish to marry Miss Hepworth and . . ."

The vicar's eyes widened with either astonishment or horror—or perhaps one attempting to disguise the other.

"And . . ." Henry continued, "in spite of knowing there could be obvious challenges, I would like to believe that someone like yourself, who represents God to the people of our community, could recognize that surely God sees all of His children as equals, and that you might offer your blessing and support to us in this endeavor and perhaps help the people of this community be more understanding."

Amala felt a little dizzy and took hold of Henry's arm with her free hand in order to remain upright as the vicar immediately broke into a tirade of the abomination of even considering such a marriage. He boldly declared his belief that people of color were cursed by God and their seed should not be mingled with that of the pure, white English. Amala wondered how she was even managing to stand there while this man said everything to her face that she felt certain the people of this community were frequently saying behind her back. And yet it was far worse than even she had imagined.

In spite of barely maintaining her composure, Amala couldn't help but be aware of Henry's shock. It was as if he'd been struck by a hot gust of wind that had hit him with such force it was threatening to knock him off his feet. When Mr. Guthrie finally paused to take a breath, Henry declared with heated indignation, "And you have the nerve to call yourself a man of God. I should very much like to be present when you meet our Maker, and see the look on your face when He asks you to explain your hatred and bigotry."

Henry turned to leave, keeping hold of Amala's arm as they walked—both trembling—toward the doors at the back of the building. A thousand thoughts raced through Amala's mind in a matter of seconds, but they brought her to one firm and solid conclusion. It was over. She could never be with Henry. She wasn't even certain she could look him in the face. The moment they came through the doors and into the open air, she broke free from him and ran as fast as she could manage on her quivering legs. She prayed he wouldn't try to follow her, not wanting a scene in the churchyard, where people might be passing by and notice. Everett saw her coming and opened the carriage door for her. She didn't even allow herself to glance back over her shoulder before she stepped into the carriage and collapsed onto the seat, heaving with sobs before the carriage was even in motion.

Chapter Six
RUNNING AWAY

BACK AT THE CARRIAGE HOUSE, Amala was glad that Everett left her alone to do her crying privately and that he didn't even ask what had happened. She knew they would talk about it, and he likely knew that too. But at another time, when she wasn't so upset. After Amala's tears had finally settled into a numb kind of shock, she composed herself enough to go into the house, asking one of the maids to inform her parents that she was home, she was not feeling well, and she would not be joining them for tea. She hurried up to her room, kicked off her shoes, and crawled into her bed, not caring how it would wrinkle her dress. Her head hurt from all of her crying, and her heart felt so broken that it seemed to physically ache in the center of her chest. She couldn't even think about Henry, what he might be doing, how he might be feeling. She couldn't think about what the vicar had said or everything that had led up to such a horrible exchange. She couldn't think of what a fool she'd been to even allow herself to get caught up in her feelings for Henry and ignore the inevitable repercussions. There was nothing at all she could think of that didn't amplify the pain in both her heart and her head, so she just tried to force all thoughts out of her head and found herself simply staring at the wall, seeing nothing, feeling nothing, caring about nothing.

When her mother peeked in to check on her, she pretended to be asleep, and she wished long afterward that she *could* sleep. At least then she would be oblivious to this all-consuming, numbing, inconsolable pain.

* * * *

For three days Amala clung to her bed, claiming to not feel well, barely eating any of the food brought to her, and reassuring her family members that it was nothing serious when they came to check on her. She wasn't lying about not feeling well, even though she led others to believe it was a physical malady. The doctor was called again in spite of her protests. He checked her over and declared it was nothing serious and that it would pass with some good rest. After he'd left, Amala decided she was glad for his visit; his declaration on her behalf gave her more validity for just remaining in bed and doing nothing. Nothing was all she could manage beyond minimal personal hygiene and barely eating enough to keep hunger pangs from making her nauseated. While her heart was manifesting just how broken it had become, and her mind rumbled with regret over how her behavior had affected Henry, she felt physically drained of all strength, and the knots in her stomach often had a nauseating effect. Sometimes she believed her heart was experiencing literal pain, and her head often hurt—either from trying *not* to cry, or from crying inconsolably when no one was around.

Amala was told two days after she'd run away from Henry at the church that he had come to call and had spent most of the day—as he often did. Viola tried very hard to talk Amala into rallying herself to at least come and have tea with the family while he was there, saying with enthusiasm, "He does so enjoy your company." But of course Amala had to decline, emphasizing that she just didn't feel well enough to make herself presentable. Knowing he was in the house made her cry while she was alone; she missed him and wanted to spend time with him, but that would only drag out the painful inevitability more than it already had been. She was glad at least that he was here and spending time with the family. She didn't want that to stop, even though she wasn't certain how she could ever be in the same room with him and not be upset. She wondered how he was doing and knew that it couldn't be good. But perhaps he was a better actor than she was; or perhaps he was just stronger in holding himself together. After his visit, Kat reported that he seemed a little down but otherwise he was the same old Henry. But then, Kat was not necessarily known for her powers of perception.

On the fourth day following the nightmarish episode with the vicar, Amala opened her eyes after a somewhat restful night, completely surprised by who was sitting casually in a chair near her bed, relaxed and reading and looking beautiful in the glow of morning light.

"Auntie Paulina," Amala declared with delight, barely awake.

"Hello, my dearest," Paulina said with the remarkable smile she was known for. She immediately set her book aside and moved to the edge of the bed and hugged Amala tightly.

"What are you doing here?" Amala asked; the timing felt like a miracle, especially considering how rarely Paulina actually set foot in England.

"Just visiting between my travels," she said as she always did.

Paulina was a younger sister to Oliver Hepworth and his only sibling. They were close in the respect that they shared a loving, comfortable relationship. But Paulina's continual desire to travel had forced their relationship to mostly consist of letters that were usually very slow to arrive due to the faraway places from which they came. The Hepworth family wealth had been inherited by Oliver and Paulina in great abundance, and Oliver did not hold to the convention that he had more right to it simply because he was male. He'd made it clear that the house was huge enough for Paulina to live there should she choose, and she always felt completely at home there when she came. But with her own portion of her inheritance, she had chosen to travel and take in many diverse experiences. And Amala knew that her travels were not purely for recreation; she also involved herself with actively assisting those who were less fortunate, and she was involved in projects of many kinds in faraway places that made positive contributions toward easing the suffering of those in need. It was one of many things that Amala admired about her aunt.

Paulina was a beautiful woman whose age had only enhanced her dignity and grace—something that could not be said of many women in their fifties. Her hair had prematurely gone completely white, but to Amala it gave her the look of an angel. She dressed with a style and flair that was neither ostentatious nor gaudy. She was confident without being arrogant and kind without ever allowing herself to be treated badly in return. The fact that she had never married and yet had lived a full and exciting life had always hovered in the back of Amala's mind as an example of the kind of life she might possibly emulate.

"Oh, I'm so happy to see you!" Amala said, clinging to her more tightly than usual.

Paulina didn't question the intensity of their embrace; she just returned it as if she sensed that Amala needed to be held. That very feeling spurred tears from Amala that she could find no power to hold back. Paulina didn't question her need to cry either; she just continued to hold her and let her spill her sorrow until Amala calmed down.

"Now, then," Paulina said, easing back from their embrace to take Amala's shoulders. "I'm told you're not feeling at all well, that you've not been out of this room for days. I'm also told that the doctor can find nothing obviously wrong with you. Perhaps my visit has some serendipity in it, hmm? You know how I have an extra sense about these things."

Amala knew all about Paulina's *extra sense.* Oliver had often mentioned how his sister had always just been able to perceive more deeply than most people. Whether she simply had a strong sense of instinct or discernment or it was actually a spiritual gift depended on the opinion of whoever might be discussing Paulina's sometimes uncanny abilities. In Paulina's opinion it was a little of both. Whatever it was, Amala was glad for it now. It had been a few years since she'd even seen Paulina, and she'd hardly thought of her for weeks, but if she'd ever needed her unofficial aunt, it was now. She didn't want to talk about what had happened, but Paulina's extra sense often made it easier to talk about sensitive matters when Paulina was so good at filling in the blanks. And since she didn't know Henry, she wouldn't be biased toward him the way her other family members were. She didn't want any of them to have their own relationships with him tainted by what had happened. But Paulina would be able to see the matter objectively and offer sound advice. She'd always been that way. The timing of her visit couldn't possibly be a coincidence; she could call it serendipity if she liked. Amala considered it a miracle.

Hoping to divert the topic of the source of her ailment just a little longer, Amala asked Paulina, "When did you get here? Where have you been? Will you stay long?" Amala hoped that she would, certain that Paulina's presence would help her get through this transition with more strength and dignity.

Paulina laughed softly. "One question at a time, my little chocolate sweet." From the day her brother had officially taken Amala into his family, Paulina had always called her and Kat her chocolate and vanilla sweets. It was her way of distinguishing their differences and uniqueness in a completely respectful and loving manner. Paulina had never made Amala feel unloved or less valuable in any regard; in fact, she had taken Amala in with perfect acceptance, and in some ways they were closer than Paulina and Kat. Perhaps Paulina's life— which had never quite fit into the conventions of society—helped her relate more to Amala. Perhaps she had sensed that Amala needed an ally in the world. Whatever the reason, Paulina had always been one of Amala's favorite people, and her visits were far too rare and brief.

"As you should know from my letters," Paulina said, "I've been to India, but I spent some time in the islands before returning. I've felt drawn back home for reasons I couldn't explain, and I confess I've missed *you* most of all." She winked and lowered her voice to a whisper even though they were alone. "But don't tell anyone." She laughed softly and went on. "But truthfully I don't know how long I'll stay; funny how I already feel restless and I only arrived very late last night. I've considered a few different possibilities of where I might go next."

Amala sighed, determined to make the most of every minute her aunt chose to remain here and to not to let her departure be as upsetting as it had been for her at times in the past.

"Enough about me for now, my precious girl. You must tell me what ails you. And I'll not settle for the barely truthful explanations you've been giving everyone else. I'm your auntie, and you know I'll keep your secrets. You *do* have secrets, don't you?" It was not a question, which reminded Amala how unnerving Kat's extra sense could be at times. "The others might not see it, but I knew as soon as my brother told me your 'symptoms.' This is not something physical that ails you, even if it makes you ache and consumes you with exhaustion. This is a broken heart if I've ever seen one. And yet I'm told there have been no gentlemen suitors. So a secret it must be. What *have* you been up to, and why has it come to such a dreadful outcome that would put someone so strong and willful into this devastating state?"

Amala's tears came again, if only to hear the truth of her situation voiced so accurately. To not feel alone, to feel heard and understood—even without having said a word—warmed her so deeply that she could only cry once again in her auntie's arms. But Paulina seemed to have expected such a response, and she was well prepared with a handkerchief tucked into each of her sleeves. Her feminine embrace felt safe and secure. The shoulder Amala cried on felt strong and able to share any burden, and her tender words of comfort and reassurance filled Amala with strength.

A knock at the door startled Amala, but Paulina came to her feet and said, "It's all right. Just hide yourself in the bed for a moment. I asked that breakfast be brought here for the both of us and told the family I'd be spending the morning seeing to my niece and her 'illness.'"

Amala did as she'd been told and quickly lay back down with her back to the door, pulling the sheet up to cover most of her face in order to hide any evidence of all the sobbing she'd been doing. She heard Paulina conversing kindly with Pearl, who brought in a tray and set it on the table near the window. Paulina assured Pearl that she would take care of Amala for the morning, and Pearl said she would be available if they needed anything at all. Amala knew Pearl had been concerned, and she'd been nearby to help with little things when Amala needed them. Perhaps Pearl too sensed that Amala's ailment was more emotional than physical, but they weren't close enough to discuss such things. Which made Amala all the more grateful for Paulina's timely visit and her insight in making it possible for them to spend this time together.

"Come and eat, precious," Paulina insisted after Pearl had left and closed the door. "You must keep up your strength, and you can tell me all about what ails you. There will be no secrets between *us*."

"Does that mean you'll tell me all about the *real* adventures of your life?" Amala asked as she stood up and put on the robe Amala handed her.

"One of these days," Paulina said with a wink.

They sat down across from each other at the little table, where Paulina spoke a brief prayer over their meal before she began loading Amala's plate with scones and sausages and fresh fruit from the serving dishes.

"Put lots of marmalade on those scones," Paulina ordered. "You need some sweetening up; and those sausages will put some substance into you." She also put a boiled egg still in its shell in front of Amala and poured her a cup of tea, putting exactly the right amount of cream and sugar in it, as if she'd served Amala tea according to her personal preference just yesterday.

"Now, talk to me while you eat," Paulina insisted, loading up her own plate. "Talk with your mouth full; I don't care. It's just the two of us here; no need to be ladylike or eat like birds."

Amala suddenly felt hungrier than she had in days; perhaps the fact that she'd barely been eating had finally registered, and her body had given her the message that it would no longer tolerate being starved. Perhaps Paulina's presence—and her assertiveness—had given her the nudge she needed to get some sustenance into her. With the distraction of eating and the comfort and trust she shared with Paulina, it was easy to start telling her aunt the story of how Henry Beckenridge had shown up in her life and turned it upside down. She told Paulina everything, even her own doubts and fears about how poorly she'd handled the situation and how much she might have hurt Henry. She wasn't worried about Paulina trying to talk her into changing her mind; she simply emphasized the same thing she always had, reassuring Amala that it was following her own heart that mattered and emphasizing if she couldn't put her whole heart into committing to a life with Henry, then it was best for everyone if she didn't. "You must do what *you* feel is best," Paulina said, and it was far from the first time Amala had heard her say it, but never had it meant more. For the first time since she'd left Henry alone at the church and run away from him, she actually felt some real confidence in believing she'd done the right thing.

The two women talked long after they'd eaten every morsel of food that had been on the tray, although Paulina mostly listened and offered comfort and encouragement. It was nearly lunchtime and

Amala was actually beginning to feel hungry again when Paulina rang for Pearl and asked for lunch to be brought up and a hot bath prepared for Amala. Pearl seemed eager to do anything she could to help. The bath was prepared while Paulina and Amala ate lunch, then Amala was soon soaking in steaming water, clouded with the aromatic jasmine bath salts that Paulina had brought with her from her travels.

"After your bath," Paulina instructed while she fluffed Amala's pillows nearby and straightened the bed (she'd never been one to wait around for a maid to do what she could do herself), "get yourself into a clean nightie and back into bed. I advise *more* rest, for your heart and your mind to catch up to all that's happened. I need to spend some time with the rest of the family this afternoon, but I'll have tea sent up for you, and I'll come check on you after I've had tea with my vanilla sweetie and my dear brother and sister. I can't leave them wanting for my delightful company too terribly much." She laughed softly in a way that exuded her confidence in knowing that her family *did* enjoy her company, but also exhibiting a gracious humility that was so naturally a part of her character.

"Thank you," Amala said, "for everything. I'm so glad you came. I feel better already; truly I do. With you here, I think I can get through this."

Paulina kissed the top of Amala's head. "I love you, my chocolate sweetie."

"I love you too, Auntie," Amala said.

Paulina left the room and Amala closed her eyes, breathing in the jasmine steam of her bath and mentally reviewing the simple but wise advice and reassurance her aunt had given her. Perhaps there was light on the other side of this darkness, after all.

* * * *

Amala took Paulina's advice and went back to bed after her bath, but unlike most of the time she'd spent there the last few days, she actually slept. She woke up just a little before Pearl brought a tray of tea and biscuits for her. She enjoyed them very much and went back to bed, uttering a silent prayer for Henry that he would be comforted and strengthened—and that she would be as well.

Paulina came back as promised, and they talked mostly of her travels, which helped Amala feel distracted from her own problems. She suspected that Paulina knew Amala needed a distraction now that she'd been able to share her burdens and not feel alone in them.

The following morning, Paulina was there again to share breakfast with Amala, but as they were finishing up she declared, "Apparently the famous Mr. Beckenridge is coming to spend the day."

"I'm glad," Amala said. "I would not want what happened between us to deter the way he's become close to the rest of the family."

"I agree," Paulina said. "From the way they all talk about him, it's evident they've grown to care for him very much. It would be a shame for them to lose that. And luckily for me, I get to spend the day making myself acquainted with the young man. Don't you worry. You know your old auntie won't let on at all that she knows a thing. I will gracefully plead your case once again to the family that you need rest and assure them that you're doing a little better and you'll be right as rain very soon. I'll come back this evening and give you a report— maybe sooner if things get boring."

Amala felt restless throughout the day. She'd grown tired of clinging to her bed, and now that she'd resumed her eating habits and had gotten some good rest, she felt a desire to return to the habits of her normal life— except that her normal life included Henry coming and going from her home. She couldn't avoid him forever, but she wanted to. She felt ashamed of how she'd led him on—however unintentionally—and she wasn't sure she could even look him in the eye. She didn't want her family to sense any negative tension between them, although they'd never seemed to sense anything *at all* between them for many months. Still, Amala didn't feel ready to face Henry yet, and she felt impatient over the fact that he was apparently settled in here for the day.

After supper when Paulina had still not yet returned, Amala got herself dressed in a simple dark-blue dress that was easy to get in and out of. She brushed through her hair, grabbed a cloak, and went quietly down the back stairs, hoping to get out of the house without being seen.

Instinctively she went to the carriage house, seeking the habitual refuge she'd always found there. She went inside and quickly determined that Everett was not there; but a couple of lanterns were still burning—so he hadn't closed the place up for the night. Just coming into the carriage house seemed to help her breathe a little more deeply. It was habitually a place of comfort and the best place she could be while wanting privacy but needing to get out of her own rooms. Amala just stood there for a few minutes, soaking in a vast array of memories, some of them warming her, others causing torment. She heard the door and turned, expecting to see Everett. She lost her breath when she saw that it was Henry. He was so obviously surprised to see her there that it was evident he'd come expecting to talk to Everett and had no idea she'd be there. She wondered then just how much Henry and Everett might have been talking, but that was fine. She was glad to know Henry had someone he could confide in who was wise and kind.

"You're feeling better, I see," he said at last.

"Slowly," she admitted.

"Dare I guess that your malady is entirely my fault?"

"More accurately my own fault," Amala said, looking down.

Following an awkward pause that made it evident Henry might not entirely agree but didn't know how to comment on that, he said, "Paulina is delightful."

"She is," Amala said eagerly, appreciating the change of subject. Although she herself jumped right back into it when she confessed, "My aunt has a way of helping me put things in perspective; she's helping me pull myself back together."

"That's good, then," Henry said. And another lengthy pause stretched out before he added, "I must apologize, Amala, for any grief I've caused you. It was never my intent."

Amala fought back tears. "It is *I* who must apologize, Henry," she said, managing to look at him. "It was never my intention to lead you on with false hope. I just . . . got carried away with my feelings, but . . . I was so unfair to you. I pray that one day you can forgive me."

"There's nothing to forgive, Amala," he said with such sincerity that she *couldn't* hold back her tears. "I too got carried away with my feelings. A part of me will always wish that everything we shared could have gone on forever, but I do respect your position. I just . . . want you to know . . . need you to know . . . that a part of me will always love you."

"You mustn't think that way, Henry," she said, looking away again. "You must . . . let go and find someone who can share a real and complete life with you. You deserve every possible happiness."

"I appreciate the sentiment, Amala; I do. But right now I can't even comprehend that being possible. I just need you to know that I'm not harboring any ill feelings toward you over any of this. I want there to be peace between us, and I don't want you to feel as if you have to hide when I spend time with your family. I miss you. Surely at the very least we can be friends."

"I'd like to think so," she said. "I just . . . might need a little more time."

"I understand," he said, and there was another taut silence.

"Amala," he finally went on, "I have one favor to ask of you."

Her curiosity urged her to look at him, then she wished she hadn't when the love and adoration in his eyes was so evident. But perhaps part of making peace with all of this was facing both his feelings and hers and accepting what had to be in spite of them.

"What is it?" she asked, not willing to make any promises until she knew what he might ask of her.

She heard him take a deep breath and sensed him gathering courage. "The last time I kissed you, Amala, I didn't know it would be the last. If I'd known—if *we'd* known—surely it would have been different. Let me kiss you good-bye, Amala. One last time."

Amala didn't know if she could bear it, while at the same time she desperately wanted the very experience he'd just described: one last kiss, knowing it would be the last, with an opportunity to savor the experience and the sweet, albeit poignant, memories it might offer her in the future.

"Promise me it will be the last and not the beginning of more turmoil for both of us."

"I promise," he said and stepped tentatively toward her, almost as if he were approaching a wild animal, afraid it would bolt. Considering all the times she had run away from him—both literally and figuratively—she couldn't blame him.

"Amala," he whispered and took hold of her upper arms in a way that was so familiar, and she did the same to him, loving the strength she could feel in his arms. "I will always treasure," he said close to her

ear, "everything we shared. I refuse to regret a moment of it. Every
kiss, every embrace, every conversation—they have all been rich and
precious to me. And I will forever treasure each memory."

Amala closed her eyes and felt tears slide down her cheeks the
same moment his lips came to her forehead and lingered there.
"Please find a way to be happy, Amala. I can't be happy without
believing that you are too. I know it's complicated for you in ways I
can't begin to understand. But please . . . find a way to be happy."

"I will," she promised, grateful in that moment for Paulina's
example of living a fulfilled and happy life without marriage and
children. Otherwise, she wasn't certain she could make such a
promise. "And you," she said. "Promise me you'll move on, that you'll
open yourself to love. You shouldn't be alone in this world, Henry.
Promise me you'll do your best, even if it's difficult."

He hesitated but said, "I promise . . . if that's what you want."

"It's what I know is right; I can't be happy if I know you're alone."

He drew back slightly, and she opened her eyes to see him gazing
at her. "I love you; I'll always love you."

"I love you too, Henry," she said, and he kissed her with a kiss
that seemed to encompass everything they'd shared, all they'd hoped
for, and even the heartbreak of letting go of those hopes. His kiss was
lengthy but still far too brief. He looked at her with silent yearning
in his eyes, and a glisten of tears, then he turned and walked away,
leaving in haste as if he had to before he changed his mind and
backed down on his word.

Amala stood where she was, trying to hold on to the moment,
until her legs felt tired and she crawled into the nearest carriage,
curling up on the seat to try to fully accept that the remarkable and
wondrous romantic journey she'd shared with Henry was over. And
logic told her that it would be the one and only romantic experience
of her life. She needed to keep her promise to him; she needed to
find a way to be happy. But it would take time. For now, she simply
needed to grieve over all she had lost. Still, she couldn't deny that the
ache in her heart seemed strangely worth it. She wouldn't trade away
all she'd shared with Henry in order to be free of it. All the extremes
of joy and heartache made her feel more alive, wiser, more a part of
the human race. He had taught her the meaning of love, and he'd

given her the knowledge that one had to truly know love in order to know true loss. She felt as if she better understood the impact of her parents' deaths for that very reason. It would take time—and plenty of it—to fully come to understand all she'd gained from these experiences, but she would forever be grateful for all that Henry had taught her about life and love, about devotion and loss. Oh, how she loved him!

Amala heard Everett come into the carriage house, and she wondered if she should make herself known; perhaps it would be good for them to talk. But she decided to remain hidden and just be alone with her lingering memories of the farewell she'd shared with Henry. Everett extinguished the lamps, leaving the carriage house dark, before she heard him go. The darkness was not unfamiliar. She'd many times come out here in the middle of the night, and she knew her way around well enough. She just wanted to stay here and be alone a little longer.

When Amala finally returned to her room, she wasn't completely surprised to find Paulina waiting there. "I'm glad to see you're up and about. Your parents were concerned, but I assured them you likely just went for a walk and said I would wait up and make certain you were well. They're not accustomed to keeping the late hours that I do. Are you all right, my dear?"

"Better, I think," Amala said and kicked off her shoes before she curled up in the middle of her bed. Paulina kicked off her own shoes and sat beside her, leaning back against pillows propped up by the headboard, urging Amala's head into her lap.

"Talk to your old auntie," Paulina said, and Amala told her about her encounter with Henry in the carriage house.

"Serendipity," Paulina declared, and Amala couldn't deny that the timing had been remarkable, especially since their formal good-bye seemed to be an important step for both of them. When she expressed the thought to Paulina, her aunt agreed completely. They talked through the situation as it stood, and Paulina helped Amala to get her bearings and to decide on some simple steps for moving forward. Amala committed to spending some time with her family tomorrow, finally feeling ready to be around others without the fear of bursting into uncontrollable tears that she could never explain.

Paulina asked if Amala felt up to being present when Henry should decide to call again and spend time in her home. She believed that she could do it now that she'd faced him and shared a proper conclusion to their romantic relationship.

"If it becomes too much," Paulina said, "you only have to excuse yourself and make a graceful exit. I'll help make an excuse for you."

"Thank you," Amala said. "For everything. I'm so grateful you're here. I just don't want you to leave. I feel lost here, Paulina. I've always felt completely comfortable and safe in my home and with my family, but with Henry coming and going, it's changed. I'm glad my family doesn't know anything of what's happened, but it's still difficult to not be able to talk about or behave the same way that I feel."

"I can well imagine," Paulina said with compassion.

"Nothing is the same."

"And it likely never will be," Paulina murmured gently. "Time will help heal the wounds, but you are forever changed. And this is an experience that you must mostly keep in your heart. But you know you can always show your whole heart to me, my chocolate sweetie."

"I know," Amala said. "That's why I don't want you to go."

"I'm not going anywhere yet," Paulina said. "By the time I decide where I'm going next, I'm certain you'll be much stronger."

Amala could only hope so, and she determined to enjoy Paulina's company and support while it lasted.

* * * *

Throughout the next week or so, Amala spent more time with her family, but she still chose to spend more time alone than usual in her rooms, acknowledging with Paulina's support and insight that she was grieving the loss of her relationship with Henry and that it was a sorrow that her family could not understand because they were unaware of it.

On Sunday she declared she was feeling too unwell to attend church and stayed home; Paulina stayed with her. Amala didn't know how she could ever face the vicar again, and she told Paulina so. But she couldn't keep telling her family that she felt ill every Sunday.

Henry came to visit, and Amala managed his presence better than she'd anticipated, although she definitely felt herself reach a point where she could no longer maintain her acting abilities and she feigned a headache, escaping to her room. While she sat alone and cried, longing to be alone with Henry so much that it hurt, she couldn't deny her gratitude that her foibles had not interfered with the relationships he shared with her family members. It truly would have broken their hearts if he'd stopped coming to visit, and they never would have understood why.

The following day at lunch, Paulina announced that she was making plans to travel across the channel to the continent and spend a significant amount of time in three different locations where she had previously put down some roots and had friends and connections, people she'd not seen for a long time and wanted to spend time with. Amala's heart felt immediately heavy, and she found it difficult to keep eating when her appetite lessened suddenly. She listened while Paulina talked of her plans to go to Spain, Italy, and France, and of the friends she had in all of these places, since she'd actually lived in each place at one time and in fact owned living quarters that would be there for her whenever she chose to return. She intended to send off letters that very day to those who could make preparations for her arrival at her first intended destination in France. She would, of course, be taking with her the two servants who traveled with her all the time.

Ivy had been a personal maid to Paulina since her youth, and Miles had been a manservant to her since she first started traveling in her twenty-seventh year. Miles provided male protection, as well as his masculine strength to any task that required a man. Both Ivy and Miles were loyal and devoted to Paulina because they had earned her complete trust, and she treated them more like friends than servants—as someone like Paulina would. Amala knew that Ivy and Miles had been here at the house along with Paulina, and she had crossed paths with them a few times. She hated to think of *them* leaving as well. It all felt horrible, and she wanted to yell at Paulina for having this ridiculous wanderlust that was luring her away from home right when Amala needed her most.

Amala's thoughts stumbled to a halt when she heard Paulina declare to her parents, "I've been giving it a great deal of thought, and I'm hoping you will allow me the privilege of taking Amala with me."

Everyone stopped eating, but no one said a word. Amala barely managed to keep from choking.

Paulina spoke directly to Kat first. "I don't want you to think I'm showing Amala any favoritism, my dear vanilla sweetie. But we are family and I know we can all speak openly and honestly. You have many advantages, my dear, that are not available to our dear Amala. I'm well aware of the challenges Amala faces socially, and I think it might be wise for her to have the chance to spend some time away during this season of *your* life while you are needing to explore the possibility of seeking appropriate suitors. Perhaps you hesitate doing so because you don't want to hurt Amala or make her feel left out, and perhaps Amala struggles as well." Paulina took a bite of her food and added gracefully while she chewed in a very ladylike manner, "I have an extra sense about these things. You must trust me. Although, if anyone has any argument, you'll have to speak up."

No one spoke, and Paulina turned her attention to Oliver and Viola. "You have been the best parents to Amala that she could ever hope or ask for; I know because I've seen it, and she's told me many times." This made Viola dab at her eyes with her napkin. "But I think you're being entirely selfish to think you can keep her all to yourselves. I'm her auntie, and I desperately want her company for a season. If she grows weary of our adventures and wishes to return home, it can be arranged. The continent is not so very far away. But I think it would do her good to get away from this stuffy community with all of its bigotry and ridiculous social snobbery. She simply needs to see a bit of the world beyond this place, I think; but someplace that doesn't resemble her homeland, with its challenging memories."

Paulina took another bite of her breakfast and said nothing more, as if to let the idea settle in. No one else ate, or spoke, or even moved. Amala's heart was pounding, and she felt quivery all over. The very idea appealed to her so deeply that she wanted to jump out of her chair and start packing her things immediately. But she wondered what Kat and her parents were thinking.

Amala saw Paulina give each one of them a long, severe gaze, as if to silently challenge them to speak their opinions on the matter. She had certainly set a marvelous example for speaking up and telling the truth about the situation as it really was without skirting around the sensitive matters.

Kat surprised Amala by speaking first. "I would miss Amala more than I can say," she said, reaching across the table to put a hand over Amala's, "but I understand." Her chin quivered and she bit her lip, but her voice still cracked when she spoke, looking directly at Amala. "I know how difficult some things are for you; I try to understand, but I'm not very good at it. Sometimes I just don't know what to say. I would miss you, but . . . I think Paulina is right. Some time away might be very good for you. If you want to go . . . I think you should. We will need to write letters every day, though, and . . ." She pressed her napkin over her mouth as she became too emotional to speak, and Amala squeezed her sister's hand.

Paulina turned to look at her brother in a way that seemed to threaten that if he didn't speak up she might lean over the table and give him a hearty slap on the face.

Oliver took the cue and looked directly at Amala. "What do you want to do, my dear girl? Paulina's offer is very kind and generous, and I can't dispute her wisdom and insight. But what matters most to me is what *you* want to do. I know there are difficulties here that we can't change or fix. And you know that running away from them will not change them. But sometimes distance can give a person perspective. You are at a time in your life when you need to learn who you really are inside and what you want to do with what you've been given, and . . . I suppose to be able to accept the limitations that are outside of our control." He paused and sighed. "What is it that you want, Amala darling?"

Amala looked at her father a long moment and then at her mother, who nodded as if to echo her husband's question and to express her agreement with all he'd said. Amala realized then that they'd all been concerned about her far more than they'd let on. And it seemed that Paulina's directness was something they could all benefit from exemplifying.

"I want to go with her," Amala said, trying not to betray just how enthusiastic she felt over the idea. She didn't want them to think she wouldn't miss them. She discreetly reached for Paulina's hand beneath the table and squeezed it, expressing paragraphs' worth of gratitude for her insight and the opportunity she'd put before Amala. She felt an enormous burden lifted to think that Paulina wasn't abandoning her; these travel plans had likely been motivated by Paulina's insight in being able to see that some time away might be the best remedy for Amala, to give her a chance to heal, away from Henry and away from Kat's desire to pursue marriage.

"Then you should go," Oliver said.

"Yes," Viola added, again dabbing at her eyes, "you should go. I don't know what we'll do without you, but it's only temporary. And I agree that it would be good for you."

"Then it's settled," Paulina declared with a little laugh. "We'll be leaving before dawn tomorrow, so we've got a busy day ahead."

Again Amala was bathed with relief. Now that the opportunity was before her, she couldn't get out of here fast enough. Perhaps running away from problems would not solve them, but in this case, she believed it would. She exchanged a smile with Paulina and thanked God for bringing this wonderful woman back to her right when she'd needed her most. She *did* have an extra sense. And it had guided her to be the means of making a miracle happen for Amala. She left the bulk of her breakfast uneaten and hurried up to her room to get on her knees and thank God for providing such a miracle; then she rang for Pearl and began packing her things, pausing through the day only long enough to eat and to write Henry an appropriate note of explanation, which she sealed and put into her Everett's hands for safe delivery. By evening she was mostly ready to go, counting the hours until she could remove herself from this place with all of its bigotry and piousness and social snobbery. And especially until she could get very, very far away from Henry. She believed it was the only way they could both truly heal and be able to find happiness in this life without each other.

Chapter Seven
DISTANT HEARTS

HENRY AVOIDED GOING TO WILLENBROCK House for a few days, uncharacteristically overcome with the motivation to do many things that he'd been procrastinating. He took care of some estate business that needed his attention, met with the doctor in regard to his mother's health issues, and made a formal visit to Chit's home, since he'd been avoiding their dinner invitations—because he'd preferred being at Willenbrock House prior to the demise of his relationship with Amala, and since then he'd preferred being completely antisocial. Focusing entirely on business and practical matters helped him keep his mind off of his broken heart, except at night when he was completely alone, and then he felt as if he'd lost her to death—except perhaps this was worse. She was alive and well, and so was he—physically at least. But their separation had become a chasm that was apparently impossible to bridge.

Following a fine dinner with Chit and his family, the two friends went to a parlor in the house that had been a favorite of theirs ever since childhood.

"Now that we're alone," Chit said while he poured a small amount of brandy into two snifters, "I'm hoping you'll tell me what's *really* going on with you. Your ability to behave as if everything is normal is impressive; I'll give you that, old boy. But I know you better than that, and I can see through it." He handed Henry a snifter and sat down across from him, staring him down while he took a long sip of his drink. "Out with it, man."

Henry sighed. He didn't want to talk about it, but if something like this had been going on in Chit's life, Henry would have felt insulted to not have his closest friend share. Now that the relationship had ended, his promise of secrecy to Amala no longer applied, and he didn't have to wonder if he could trust Chit to never repeat anything confidential. Knowing that Chit preferred just getting to the point, Henry simply said, "I asked Amala to marry me."

"You're joking, surely!" Chit said with an astonishment that made Henry angry—or at the very least defensive. "I know you have a great fondness for the girl, but you can't honestly believe that such a marriage would ever bring anything but grief."

Henry heard the agitation in his own voice as he countered, "I believed that the depth with which I love her would compensate for the obvious challenges. I realize I'm the sentimental one here, but I'm still not a fool. Don't think I didn't consider the implications very carefully. I love her."

"I see," Chit said in a way that indicated he was listening, even if he didn't necessarily agree. "From that look on your face, I'm assuming she doesn't share your affection."

"Oh, she does," Henry said and took too big of a swallow of brandy, which made him cough. "She also agrees completely with *you*. She's committed herself to a life without marriage or children, believing that it's simply not possible for a woman like her to have those things living in this society."

"She's probably right."

"You say that as if it's nothing at all. I don't believe that *anyone* should spend their life alone . . . without love in it."

"And yet . . . many people do," Chit said, his voice now expressing more compassion. "Unfortunately, being married and having love in your life are not necessarily synonymous in this world. But you are obviously not currently in a place where hearing such things is going to make you feel any better."

"Right now I don't think anything can make me feel better," Henry admitted.

"So she's refused you, I take it? Not because she doesn't share your affection but because of the obvious challenges of such a relationship?"

"That basically sums it up," Henry said and swallowed more of his drink.

"Well," Chit said as he stretched out his legs and eased lower into his chair, "everyone certainly has a right to grieve over such a disappointment."

Henry looked at his friend and resisted the urge to shout at him, knowing that it was his own grieving that made him feel so angry. *Disappointment?* He wanted to yell. *Disappointment?* His heart had been shattered into millions of irreparable pieces; he felt as if he could barely force himself to function. There was nothing in this experience that could be described as disappointment. But he reminded himself that Chit had always been practical and somewhat lacking in sentimentality. For all the closeness they'd shared and the great adventures they'd been on together, Henry had recognized years ago that there was little point in trying to converse with his friend about emotional insights or his observations of beauty or suffering. Chit might listen politely, but he didn't really understand Henry's need to analyze his perceptions of life and the world around them in ways that Chit had admitted mostly seemed silly to him. They'd joked about it lightheartedly; there was no judgment or ill feelings between them. They'd simply accepted that they saw the world through very different eyes. And the present heartache weighing on Henry was something that Chit could simply never understand. He'd never been in love, and Henry suspected that if Chit ever did marry and settle down, it would more likely be due to finding a comfortable and practical relationship with a woman than it would be due to the kind of love that Henry felt for Amala.

Now that Henry had informed Chit of the reasons for his recent moods and behavior, he had no desire to speak of it any further. He changed the subject, and one topic of conversation led to another until Chit informed Henry of the plans he was making to travel back to India. They'd both known before they'd even returned to England that Chit would likely go back, and Henry had no intention of ever doing so. But discussing the reality of it coming to pass only disheartened Henry even more. He couldn't rely on Chit for deep, analytical conversation, but their friendship was deeply precious to Henry and they'd been integrated into each other's lives since boyhood. Considering the grueling months of travel it took just to get to India, they both had to accept the possibility that they might never see each other again. The way Chit spoke of his plans made it sound as if he knew he would settle there permanently, with no intention of ever returning to England.

Henry went to bed that night feeling doubly depressed. He'd lost Amala, and now he was losing Chit. He reminded himself that it would be months before Chit actually left—but he still had to get used to the idea. He also reminded himself that Amala and her family were still there at Willenbrock House and he could go and visit anytime. He needed to adjust to letting go of his romantic inclinations and hopes in regard to Amala, but he found hope in thinking that she could always be his friend. In light of his feelings, it seemed like a sore compensation, but it was better than no compensation at all.

Deciding he'd stayed away from the family that felt like his own long enough, he made up his mind that he would go there tomorrow and spend the day. He thought of how glad Oliver and Viola always were to see him and how loved and accepted they made him feel. And Kat too would always kiss his cheek and smile at him, expressing how genuinely pleased she was to see him. Amala would kiss his cheek and smile as well, and they would both have to pretend that nothing more had ever existed between them. But at least he would be in the same room with her, with all of them. He felt at home there among them, and that's where he needed to be. In spite of not being able to speak openly with Amala's family about his grief, he knew that being among them would afford him the best source of healing he could ever find in the present state of his life.

* * * *

By the time Henry had ridden the distance between his home and Amala's, he felt surprisingly prepared to be able to handle the situation and just enjoy the day as much as possible. Upon arriving, he went into the carriage house to say hello to Everett, as he often did, but Henry couldn't find him. So he went to the house as usual, where a maid showed him to a familiar drawing room. He knew that he could relax and make himself at home here; he could even go to the library on his own if he got bored. Given his established habit of calling without any prior message or announcement, he knew there were occasions when it took time for any—or all—of the family to be ready to receive guests. And he was used to making himself comfortable.

Henry felt nervous about seeing Amala, but he felt prepared, and he hoped that his visits would not be too difficult for her. She had insisted that he continue to visit; he was more grateful for that than he could comprehend. In many ways Oliver had become a friend with the characteristics he'd never found in Chit. This wonderful man was *very* sentimental and analytical—at least he could be at certain times when they got into deep conversation. And the women were all delightful and kind. He looked out the drawing room window of what he'd come to consider his second home and silently thanked God for such a blessing in his life. He was determined to focus on what he *did* have and not preoccupy himself with what he wanted but *couldn't* have.

Henry turned from the window when Oliver entered the room and greeted him with a handshake and then a quick, familiar embrace.

"Good to see you, my boy," Oliver said. "It's been nearly a week, hasn't it? But you did send a message that you had some business to attend to."

"Yes," Henry said, and the men both sat down in their usual comfortable chairs across from each other. "But I do believe the estate is running a little more smoothly now, thanks to good overseers."

"And how is your mother?"

"The same," Henry reported. "Very cranky," he added, managing a chuckle. "But I spoke with her doctor; he tells me that, truthfully, he can't believe she's remained alive this long, given the many complications of her health. It's his belief that she's too stubborn to die."

"And maybe she is," Oliver said, and they talked a few minutes—not for the first time—about the complicated emotional impact of the situation between Henry and his mother. Henry felt comforted to hear this good man validate his feelings on the matter. He loved his mother, but he knew it was more a dutiful kind of love, as opposed to feeling any strong affection toward her; she was simply difficult to love, and Oliver understood. He had encouraged Henry to keep doing what he was doing—to visit his mother every day and do his best to see that she was cared for in the best possible way so that he would have no regrets when she *did* finally pass away.

When that topic ran its course, Oliver glanced at the clock and said, "Viola and Kat are certainly taking their time with all that feminine primping today." He chuckled. It was a common source of humor for him to tease the women about all the fussing it took for them to even leave their rooms.

"And Amala?" Henry asked, his heart quickening to say her name while at the same time something tightened inside of him at Oliver's obvious omission of her name.

"Oh, my goodness!" Oliver said and slapped his knee. "It seems I lost track of how long it's been since you were here last. Now that it's become old news here, I'd forgotten you didn't know."

"Know what?" Henry asked, proud of himself for sounding only politely interested—as opposed to how he really felt: utterly terrified of what her absence could mean.

"Well, Paulina—you met my sister, Paulina."

"Yes," Henry said, trying not to sound impatient.

"Paulina got it into her head that she was off to the continent; she does that. Just suddenly decides it's time to move on and she's gone before you can say boo. And she invited Amala to go with her; thought it would do her good to get away."

Henry found it difficult to breathe and even more difficult to not allow Oliver to see how the news was affecting him. He was glad that Oliver kept rambling without paying too much attention to Henry.

"I dare say Paulina was probably right; she does have that extra sense, you know." He chuckled. "I don't understand it, but she certainly does have a way of knowing things. Anyway, it seems she had a sense about it being difficult for Amala and Kat to be at this season of their lives and be in such dramatically different situations. At least that's what Paulina told me when we spoke privately about it before they left. She put it a little more delicately when she spoke of it in front of the girls. But I suppose a father misses the clues about such things, and perhaps their mother is just too close to them every day.

And Paulina swoops in and tells me it's obvious that Kat is hesitant to attend social events and seek out potential marriage suitors because she doesn't want to hurt Amala, who is determined that she will never be able to marry—and unfortunately none of us can argue with the challenges in that regard. So, Paulina thought it would be good for Amala to do some extensive traveling while Kat focuses on her social life. I guess that about sums it up. Paulina announced her plans one day and they were off before dawn the next morning. I'm sorry you didn't get a chance to tell her good-bye."

"I'm sorry for that too," Henry said, his voice surprisingly steady. Practically speaking, he could see perfect wisdom in Paulina's insight. And given what the rest of them didn't know about the nature and current status of his relationship with Amala, he couldn't deny that getting her away was probably best in many respects. But, oh, how he was going to miss her! He was grateful for the numbness that dulled his emotions and willed it to remain in place for as long as he was in the company of others. He couldn't believe it! She'd been gone for days and he hadn't even known. He wondered how it might have been if he *had* been given a chance to tell her good-bye, and he immediately knew it was far better that he'd not known. He likely would have caused a scene and only made things more difficult for both of them. It was surely better this way. But, oh, how he missed her!

Olivia and Kat arrived in their usual feminine flurry, creating a distraction from Henry's dismal thoughts, but also making Amala's absence all the more keenly felt. Henry managed to maintain an unaffected facade through lunch and into the afternoon, although he was asked more than once if he was all right.

"You just seem somewhat . . . distracted," Kat commented.

"I'm fine," he insisted, offering her a convincing smile. "I've just been very busy, that's all. I confess I've been keeping late hours and likely need to catch up on my sleep." The statement was certainly true, and Henry was glad when they seemed to accept it as sufficient explanation.

"It surely doesn't seem right without Amala here," Oliver commented, and Henry felt as if Oliver had read his mind.

"No, it certainly doesn't," Viola said.

"I miss her terribly," Kat added. "I don't remember what it's like to not have her nearby almost constantly."

The ensuing silence implied that Henry should also comment, so he simply said, "It's just not the same without her."

"Of course, we're repeating the same sentiments several times a day," Viola said. "I assume that with time we'll become more accustomed to her absence. I only wish I had any idea how many months Paulina intended to keep her away from us."

"Or years," Kat said with chagrin, and Henry's stomach tightened.

"We'll all feel better when a letter arrives," Oliver said in a tone that seemed meant to assuage the concerns of the women. "She promised to write often; I'm certain she'll have something posted at the first possible opportunity."

"I'm certain you're right, my dear," Viola said to her husband, and thankfully the subject of the conversation changed to Oliver's concern over a health dilemma with one of his best horses. Henry only listened enough to not be rude. He couldn't believe Amala was gone, but then he wondered how awkward it might be if she were here. Given the choice, he'd take the awkwardness over her absence.

Henry stayed for tea, then made a graceful departure, pleading the need to have an early supper at home so he could catch up on his sleep. Once out of the house, he went again to the carriage house, grateful when he entered to see Everett there, who turned toward Henry, his eyes immediately betraying that he'd been expecting—and perhaps dreading—this moment.

With no greeting whatsoever, Henry said, "Please tell me she left me some kind of—"

"I'll get it," Everett said and went into a room where he kept his tools. He returned a moment later and held out a sealed envelope toward Henry.

"Thank you," Henry said, taking it from him with equal portions of relief and trepidation. At least she had been considerate enough to leave him with some kind of formal good-bye, but he suspected the letter would hold words of finality that would truly put all they had shared to an end. Logically, he should have already accepted that it was officially over and there was no hope, but with her letter in his hand, he realized he'd still been holding on to some tiny grain of belief that a miracle might happen, that she might have a change of heart. Now, the last sparks of hope sizzled cold inside of him, as if they'd been doused with water.

"Did she . . . say anything . . . to you . . . about her reasons for going?" Henry asked.

"Just said she felt Paulina's idea was an answer to her prayers . . . that she needed to get away; that it would be easier for everyone."

"I see," Henry said and tried not to think only of himself. "You must miss her terribly."

"I do, indeed," Everett said. "As I'm certain you do." He nodded and walked away, saying over his shoulder, "I'll give you a few minutes."

It took Henry several seconds to realize what Everett meant. He walked with leaded feet to the carriage that was Amala's favorite, the old one that was never used anymore, and stepped inside, thinking of all the times they'd sat here together, talking, laughing, crying—kissing. He forced his mind away from that and moved into the light shining through the carriage window before he broke the seal, unfolded the page, and read.

My Dearest Henry,

By now you will know that I'm gone, and I pray that you can forgive me for not being able to tell you face-to-face of our plans. Everything happened so quickly, there simply wasn't time. I need you to know that in spite of the pain we are both experiencing, I know in my heart that this is for the best. I truly believe it will be easier on both of us if I am away, even if it feels more difficult initially. Surely our wounds will heal with time, and we will both find fulfillment and happiness in our lives.

I feel I must make it clear, Henry, that I want you to go forward without me. Please do not let this keep you from finding love. I'm certain there is the right woman for you, one who can offer her whole heart and bring much good into your life. I plead with you, and I pray to God that you will make every effort to marry in spite of any hurt I may have caused for you. Knowing you will do this gives me peace and the hope that I can one day forgive myself for creating such turmoil for you. Find love, and be happy. Do it for me if not for yourself, I implore you.

When I return I hope to find you visiting my parents frequently enough that we will be able to share the friendship that I treasure and miss. I wish all the best in every aspect of your life.

With my fondest regards, Amala

Post Script: I believe it would be prudent for you to destroy this letter once you have read it.

Henry found it difficult to read the letter with the way his eyes kept misting over, especially since the light was far from optimal for reading. He finally managed to read it through twice, unable to even imagine doing what she was so adamantly requesting of him. He had no heart to offer *any* woman except Amala. Right now he could only resign himself to go on living from day to day, putting one foot in front of the other, and doing his best to pretend that somehow everything would be all right, and maybe—just maybe—with time these wounds would heal enough to consider accepting a life without the woman he loved.

* * * *

Amala was overcome with a deep relief to leave England. The sadness she carried within herself couldn't be left behind, but she wouldn't have to contend daily with the fear of whether or not Henry would show up at her home and wondering if she had the strength to resist her temptations to let her heart rule her head. Even with her belief that her willpower was strong enough to allow her to keep her wits about her while knowing Henry would remain involved with her family, she wondered if her acting skills would hold up to the test of continuing to pretend she didn't feel agitated and ill at ease in his presence. Carrying on their clandestine relationship had been a different matter entirely. There had been joy and delight in the secrecy. But to try to hide her broken heart, knowing all the while that he was trying to hide his, seemed more than she could bear. She knew that going away would be much easier for her, and given some time to adjust, she believed Henry would come to accept that it was easier for him too.

It didn't take as long as Amala had expected to reach the channel, and she wondered if she had related traveling of any kind to her memories of the journey from India to England that had taken months and had been mostly miserable. They crossed the channel on a beautiful sailing vessel, and although it was daylight, she could see very little due to the fog. But they were assured the captain was well accustomed to dealing with such challenges and they would arrive safely.

The captain was proven right when they docked safely in Calais and Miles hurried off to make arrangements for a carriage to take them to Paris, although they only traveled for a few hours before getting rooms at an inn for the night. Paulina declared they were traveling for pleasure and there was no rush. There were sights she wanted to see along the way, although for Amala, knowing their destination was the very south of France, the overall journey still felt somewhat daunting.

But Paulina kept her promise of making frequent stops, where they stayed in lovely inns and ate fine meals at places where she'd obviously been before and knew all of the best menu items to choose from. She spoke French fluently, which helped Amala with her minimal knowledge of the language. Amala noticed that some people were put off a little by Paulina introducing her niece, who was obviously not related by blood in any way, but Amala was used to that. She was surprised, however, to realize that some people were only curious and asked courteous questions, delightfully inquisitive over Paulina having such a beautiful, exotic relative. Paulina had told her early in their journey that in many cases the people of Europe were more open-minded than the British, and while Amala could see that was not *always* the case, she met more people who were kind to her than she ever had since she'd left India.

Paris was a great wonder to Amala, and Paulina made a fine guide since she knew the city well. Miles and Ivy generally accompanied them on their outings, and even though they were there as paid servants, Paulina always treated them with a kindness and respect that reminded Amala of Oliver and Viola. Miles and Ivy had obviously been to all of these places before in their many prior travels with Paulina, but they took in the sights with some of the same wonder that Amala felt. And it was always nice—if not wise—to have a man in their company who was strong and capable enough to see that the women were all kept safe.

They toured museums and attended operas and ballets and went shopping for frivolous things. At first Amala insisted she didn't need pretty, new clothes or anything else, but Paulina's delight in the simple act of shopping and in providing such niceties for Amala gradually won Amala over and she began to understand why Paulina so thoroughly enjoyed the vast variety of shops in Paris.

They also experienced the pastries and confectionaries of Paris with equal delight. Amala had never eaten such wonders, and every time she tasted something new and declared her pleasure, Paulina behaved as if she'd never been happier, like a child who had just received exactly what she wanted for Christmas. A great unexpected treat in Paris came when Paulina took Amala to dine at an Indian restaurant, which was run and owned by a family who had traveled from India many years ago. The patriarch of this family and his wife personally greeted Paulina as if they were old friends, and they were thrilled to meet Amala and wanted to introduce her to their every child and grandchild, a family so large Amala couldn't keep track. But they were all working together to cook the food, serve the customers, and keep the establishment in pristine cleanliness and order. Amala loved eating the food of her country and she indulged in the good memories that were brought to mind by her aroused taste buds. The spices and sauces were so unique compared to anything she'd eaten in England, where the food was rather bland.

While Amala had her eyes closed, slowly savoring the food in her mouth and inhaling the fragrances in the air, she heard Paulina say, "Did your parents never take you to an Indian restaurant in London?"

"They never took me to London," Amala said, and Paulina gasped. "But before you get upset with them"—Amala opened her eyes—"you need to know that they offered. I believe I was afraid of such a large city. Memories of the crowded cities in India had become frightening to me after what had happened. I told them they were welcome to go to London and I would be well cared for by the staff, but they refused to go without me." Amala took another bite of her food, chewed, and swallowed. "That is one of many reasons I think my being away will be beneficial to Kat. She deserves a season in London; I believe I restrained her social life in many ways, even though I never tried to."

Paulina shook her head but said nothing, as if no polite words could be found to declare her opinion of such a ridiculous situation. She then distracted Amala with a discussion of the food they were enjoying, and Amala was glad to know that the influence of India had found its way to England and Europe.

Late that evening, back at their hotel suite, Paulina came into Amala's room to say good night. It was a typical way for their day to end. They were both in their nightgowns and often sat on the bed like a couple of little girls—much as Amala had done with Kat—to recount the day's events and talk about anything that might come to mind. Tonight Paulina began the conversation by saying, "I have a thought I want to share, and since it will be many months yet before we return to England, you have a great deal of time to think about it, but I believe it's worth considering."

"I'm listening," Amala said, feeling a measure of excitement. Paulina's insight most often led to very good ideas.

"You've always been made to feel completely accepted and loved in your home, and I highly respect my brother and his wife for all they've done for you. You're a precious girl and we all love you dearly. However, it occurs to me—and perhaps all of my time spent in India contributes to this way of thinking—that everything in your home is still so *English*. You have become so English."

"What do you mean?" Amala asked, wondering now if she felt intrigued or unsettled by whatever Paulina might be thinking.

"I understand that when going out into society, certain measures must be taken to not ruffle feathers—at least not too much—although I believe a little feather-ruffling offers some balance in all the stuff and nonsense of people's ideas. But at home, my dear, should you not be allowed to live in an environment that offers you a life that is more of a balance between your two worlds? Have you ever worn Indian clothing since you came to England? Eaten Indian food?"

"No, I have not," Amala said.

"And there is my point. You are an Indian woman, and your life is completely *English*. Within the confines of your own home, you should be able to experience more of your heritage—beyond the presence of your father's precious mementos. I'm only thinking that it might help you feel more at peace with yourself, perhaps happier."

Amala thought about it a long moment. "I confess I'm . . . fascinated by the idea. You may well be right."

"And of course we have time to think about it."

"But . . . how would we acquire such things? How would we make adjustments to the menu when the kitchen staff is all English? It seems a huge undertaking in some ways."

"Not so overwhelming if gone about the right way," Paulina said. "We have time to work on that as well. Why don't we get some sleep and let the idea settle in." She kissed Amala's forehead. "I love you, my chocolate sweetie."

"I love you too, Auntie," Amala replied and hugged Paulina tightly. "You are very good to me."

"Ah," Paulina said as if it were nothing, "that's easy. You bring me much joy. If you're having a good time, just know I'm having a much better time." She winked and left Amala alone for the night, contemplating how it might be to make India more a part of her life, even though she'd chosen to always make England her home.

* * * *

Amala loved the distractions of her days with Paulina; it was only at night when she was completely alone that she had trouble not thinking of Henry. She couldn't go to sleep without some measure of tears overcoming her, but Paulina had kept her so busy that she was usually too exhausted to cry for long. It occurred to her more than once that perhaps that was part of Paulina's motive in keeping Amala involved in one activity after another. Whatever her reasoning, Amala felt grateful, and she often told Paulina so. Every day Paulina would ask Amala how she was doing in regard to Henry, and Amala would generally give her simple answers to indicate that she was adjusting and she felt confident that with time she would heal and find peace. But they didn't talk about him any more than a few minutes a day, as if they were on a quest to allow Amala to put some distance—both in miles and time—from the source of her broken heart.

Amala wrote home every few days, and Miles gladly posted the letters for her. Since they were traveling, she asked that the family not attempt to write back yet, but as soon as they were settled in Paulina's home in the south of France, she would let them know and she would look forward to hearing from them.

While in Paris they went back to the Indian restaurant a few more times, and one night they stayed very late, until after all of the other customers had left, and they had a wonderful visit with the owners. Amala loved their story of how they had sacrificed a great deal to leave India behind and come here to bring their love of their own food to Europe. She asked questions about the spices they used, loving the sound of the words they spoke that mingled with childhood memories.

Amala and her aunt revisited many of their favorite spots while in the city, and Amala loved writing the details of each day in her journal. She also loved how every minute that she was distracted by everything going on around her kept her from thinking of Henry. She was already starting to feel a glimmer of hope in having the heaviness in her heart lightened, and she hoped and prayed it was the same for him. She was surprised to also find another weight lightening. Until she'd actually had the opportunity to have some distance from her family, she hadn't realized how much she'd been carrying a burden of guilt and regret in believing that she was holding Kat back in her own social life. She felt more and more certain that Kat had restrained herself to some degree in seeking out suitors and attending social events because she'd not wanted to hurt Amala's feelings. Amala felt some joy on Kat's behalf to think of her sister now enjoying a full social life without any such strain in the family to hold her back.

Leaving Paris behind was difficult in some ways, but a part of Amala had grown weary with the bustle of the city. She loved the river and the bridges and a certain beauty that was unique to the city, but she was more accustomed to country living and looked forward to getting settled at Paulina's home.

The distance from Paris to the southernmost part of the country felt daunting to Amala, but again Paulina insisted on never being in a carriage for too many hours a day before they would stop in some city or village where she always knew the best places to stay and to eat. Amala absorbed every piece of the experience into her memory, and at Paulina's suggestion she had begun a journal of her travels soon after they had left England so that she could always remember this season of her life in detail and recall it fondly. Amala enjoyed writing in the journal; she filled up one book, and Paulina bought her another. And tucked between the pages were tickets and brochures and other little mementos of their adventure.

When they finally arrived at Paulina's French house, Amala was pleased to discover that it was only a few minutes' walk to the beach, but the little cottage was surrounded by enough land that it didn't feel as if the neighbors were too close. And yet they could walk a few minutes in the opposite direction from the sea and be in the center of a delightful village that had everything available they might need.

The cottage was functional and cozy, with bedrooms upstairs for Amala and Pauline, as well as a spacious bathing room. On the ground floor were rooms for Miles and Ivy, a kitchen, dining room, and parlor. But the rooms were not necessarily large, and Amala liked the dramatically different atmosphere after having lived years in a place like Willenbrock House.

Since word had been sent of their arrival, a couple of local women who had worked for Paulina in the past had aired out the house and cleaned it up, putting everything in order for their arrival. The kitchen had been stocked with bread, cheese, fruits and vegetables, and some wine. However, Paulina told Amala they would eat simple meals at home for breakfast and occasionally for lunch, but very little cooking would actually take place in the kitchen, since she preferred to take advantage of the colorful cafés in the village, and there were also many friends there who always insisted on inviting her and whomever she might be traveling with over for dinner whenever she stayed there.

Amala settled quickly and comfortably into the pace and rhythm of life at Paulina's seaside cottage. She loved the little house, the sea, the village, and the people. Some were snobbish toward her for being different, but many were only curious or fascinated by her origins, and some didn't even seem to notice.

Amala also loved the food and the relaxed atmosphere of the social life—something she'd never experienced in England. She and Paulina talked a great deal about the contrasts and how remaining in one place for the whole of one's life could restrict one's way of thinking. Amala only knew India and England. But her memories of India were dominated by the horror of her parents' deaths, which had accentuated her memories of all of the negative and frightening things about her home country. She *did* remember its beauties as well, but she couldn't think about them without thinking of the ugliness. Amala's experience of England—as she realized now—had been very limited. Her parents had clearly been trying to protect her, but the result had been that she'd only been exposed to a certain level of society in one part of the country. Paulina told her stories of wonderful people she knew in quaint English villages that were not terribly unlike where they were staying now. And she talked of treasured areas of London where diversity was not so looked down upon and where there were kind, selfless people who ran quaint shops and bakeries and eating establishments. It seemed these were the kinds of people Paulina sought out wherever she went; she was interested in the common people, and while she was a little too flamboyant to ever blend into *any* crowd, she had learned to make friends among them because she respected and admired all people, no matter their class or profession—or the color of their skin.

Amala began exchanging regular letters with her family now that she was settled in one place for a long while; how long, she didn't know yet. And she didn't care. She was glad for every piece of mail that came from home, and all the lovely details of life that each of her parents and Kat shared in their letters. She missed them, but her relief in being away from the complications there overpowered any longing she might feel. In turn, Amala wrote back lengthy letters about her adventures and all she was learning and experiencing. The exchange of missives back and forth became a highlight for Amala, allowing her to feel that she was remaining close to her family while still maintaining a comfortable distance and continuing to enjoy all the things she loved about this place that had quickly come to feel like home.

Amala loved to read her letters aloud to Paulina, as much as Paulina loved to hear them, and they would talk about her family and their personalities and strengths and weaknesses in a way that Amala believed was aiding her education in understanding the behavior of people in a broader and deeper perspective. From a distance she could see more clearly both the strengths and weaknesses of those she loved. It all combined to make her love them more, but it also helped her learn to love herself as well, given that she could see her *own* strengths and weaknesses. Paulina truly had an extra sense about people and life, and Amala thanked God every day for putting this remarkable woman there for her at this time. While Kat was coming out socially and entertaining many different men with the hope of finding a suitable husband, Amala realized she was having her own version of *coming out*. She was becoming more comfortable with her acceptance that marriage was not a viable option for her, because she was learning that she could have a fulfilling life and be completely happy with or without a husband and children—all depending on how she chose to view herself and the life she lived. The lessons Paulina taught were invaluable.

Amala was surprised to receive a letter from Henry. Since Paulina knew every tiny detail of Amala's relationship with Henry and her complicated feelings for him, Amala read that letter to Paulina as well. It was written in a polite and gentlemanly manner—as she would have expected—but he didn't write as if he were pretending that no relationship had ever existed between them. He wrote to tell her that it had been a struggle to try to move beyond what they had shared, but he was doing a little better and he hoped that she was too. He wrote of his commitment to trying to do as she had asked of him and seek out the possibility of opening his heart to another woman, although he admitted it wasn't easy. He expressed his hope that she was finding peace for herself and that her life would be good in every respect.

Amala was glad to hear that he was regularly spending time with her family—even though she already knew that from their letters. But it was nice to hear funny and tender moments about her family from Henry's perspective. He mentioned that he had accompanied Kat to a couple of social events, given that they were good friends and comfortable with each other and that it was a way for them to get out and be sociable and not feel too alone or conspicuous.

"Good heavens," Amala said to Paulina after she'd read aloud that part of the letter, "you don't think that . . . he and Kat could ever . . ." She couldn't put it into words.

"I don't know," Paulina said. "What do *you* think?"

Amala put a hand over her heart, feeling pain there as the idea settled in. "I want them both to marry and be happy; I want them to not be alone. But it never crossed my mind that . . ."

"That they might find those things with each other?" Paulina asked, and Amala turned to stare at her.

"But it crossed *your* mind?"

"It did," Paulina admitted. "I don't know if they would ever find a spark of love between them, or if it's even a remote possibility. Maybe they could never feel that way about each other. But we would be naive to think it's not possible, my dear." Paulina took Amala's hand. "I can't imagine how difficult that might be for you, but I do think it's something we should perhaps talk about—in case their friendship evolves. He's so very comfortable with your family. What *if* he grows to love Kat enough to make her his wife?"

Amala gasped for breath and dropped the letter as she stood abruptly and went to the window, holding to the sill to help her remain upright.

"Obviously the idea upsets you," Paulina said.

"How could it not? I'm trying very hard to make peace with accepting that Henry will never be a part of my life, but how can I live with knowing that he might share with my sister . . . everything that I can never have?"

"That's a very good question, my dear," Paulina said with compassion, "and a very difficult one. Perhaps it will never happen, and I don't think you should get yourself all worked up over something that *hasn't* happened. But I do believe—all things considered—you should prepare yourself for the possibility."

"Of course," Amala said and was aware of Paulina leaving the room. Because of her extra sense, she seemed to know when Amala needed time alone. She was able to cry some tears that needed to be shed, but she believed that no amount of time alone or otherwise could ever make her comfortable with the possibility of Henry courting—or marrying—her sister.

Contemplating the matter during quiet moments throughout the course of many days, Amala felt no closer to believing she could cope with such a thing. She was grateful to be able to talk openly about her feelings with Paulina, who eventually offered the suggestion, "If you can't live with it, you don't have to."

"What do you mean?"

"There's no reason why you *have* to return to England and live out your life in your parents' home, observing the man you love living a happily married life with your sister. You always have the option of remaining with me, wherever I go, my dear. We can make brief visits home, but you don't have to stay there and endure such a thing. Or you can create your own life, following my example but making it the way *you* want it to be. You have been blessed with financial resources that make many options available to you. Your parents will support you in your choices, even if they might prefer to have you there. Again, I don't think we should be jumping to conclusions based on so little information. The possibility of a union between Henry and Kat may not have even crossed either of their minds, and maybe it never will. So let's give the matter some time and not fret too much."

Amala liked hearing there were possibilities open to her that would not doom her to being too directly involved with her sister's life if such a thing were to happen. Still, the possibility felt heartbreaking. In her mind she'd believed that when this season of healing was complete, she would return home and be forever close to her sister and parents. But if Henry ever officially became a part of the family, she doubted she could ever do that. She prayed that such a thing would never happen; it felt like too much to bear. But who was she to dictate the course of other people's lives—or their hearts?

Amala tried very hard to follow Paulina's advice to give the matter time and not fret. She forced the possibility to the back of her mind and immersed herself in the experiences around her while months slipped by and a part of her never wanted to leave this peaceful haven. But a day came when Paulina declared she was feeling restless and they would be going to her home in Italy to stay for some months— until Paulina became restless again, presumably. Amala only wished that her heart could let go and move on in the same way Paulina could move her life so easily from one place to the next.

Chapter Eight
LETTING GO

AMALA HAD DIFFICULTY PARTING WITH all the things she'd come to love about this home away from home in the south of France. But she focused on what adventures might lie ahead. And she was not disappointed.

Paulina's Italian home was similar to her French one only in its size and the number of rooms. Rather than being separate from any other dwellings, this was a home built tightly between similar homes on a curving, narrow street where there was a continual bustle of people. But Amala quickly became accustomed to the sounds from the street, realizing it was conversation and laughter among neighbors who gathered to visit, sometimes sitting together to share wine and bread, or occasionally a meal. On sunny days, the children played in the street, and their laughter floated through the open windows.

Just as in France, Paulina was fluent enough with the language to be able to interpret for Amala, who knew much less Italian than she did French. But with time she learned enough to exchange minimal conversation with the local people. She enjoyed walking into the center of the village to shop and explore. She enjoyed the food and the quaint cafes and restaurants where they often dined. And she especially enjoyed the people. She quickly realized that in Italy most of the people had darker skin and hair, which made her blend in more easily. Anyone looking closely at her or hearing her accent would know immediately that she wasn't Italian, but she still didn't stand out nearly as much as Paulina with her pale skin.

"Perhaps you will find a handsome Italian husband, hmm?" Paulina teased more than once.

Amala humored her with the teasing, but she sincerely felt no appeal in permanently settling here. It certainly was a lovely place to enjoy an extended stay, but she was finding herself longing for England and for home.

Just as she had done in France—and at home—Amala filled her spare time with reading novels or other books from which she learned about places and people and other things that fascinated her. Paulina introduced her to new books and new authors, and she discovered new adventures and experiences through the written word. The books she loved best were stories that somehow touched on her own sorrows and joys; even if her life had nothing in common with any particular plot that she read, being able to relate to the dilemma and poignancy of a character's experiences moved her deeply.

Letters continued to go back and forth between Amala and her family. Kat spoke of a few different gentlemen suitors who had been giving her a great deal of attention, and she wrote detailed descriptions of the many social functions she had attended. Henry's name came up, but not in any way that implied even a hint of what Amala feared most. She prayed it would remain that way.

Once in a while a letter came from Henry, but not often. He told her that he was stepping more outside of his tendency to be reclusive and attending some social events, although he declared that he rarely enjoyed them. In one letter he wrote of how Chit had returned to India, taking his personal servants with him. He missed Chit, and it was difficult to think that he would likely never see him again, but he admitted that their personalities had grown more different as they'd matured and he didn't miss him as much as he might have in previous years. The next letter that came from Henry informed Amala that his mother had passed away. He confessed that while it caused him some sorrow simply because she was his mother and almost his only remaining blood relative, he couldn't feel guilty for admitting that he'd shared no loving relationship with her and that her loss mostly meant the relief of not feeling he had to please her. He explained that he felt some peace in knowing that she was surely in a better place, where perhaps whatever had made her so cantankerous in this life might be resolved and she could be happier. He liked imagining her that way.

Amala wrote back to offer her condolences and her understanding of his complex emotions. She also expressed an understanding of his mixed feelings about Chit's departure. She expressed a hope that he could find the right woman and start a new family so that he wouldn't be alone. While a part of her sincerely desired it, wanting him to be happy, she knew that when it happened she would likely have to face an entirely new assault of grief in having to let him go. And all the while she kept a prayer in her heart that when he *did* marry, it would be to anyone but Kat.

Not many weeks later, Amala received word from her father that Everett, her beloved friend who had always worked in the carriage house, had died suddenly from what was likely a heart attack. Amala grieved for the loss of her friend, and she wrote a letter to her family in which she expressed how dear Everett had been to her. Since Everett had had no family, there was no one else for Amala to connect with over his death. For her, it was one more piece of evidence that life was fragile and that even the things that felt secure and stable could be gone in an instant. But just as she'd learned with the deaths of her parents, there was nothing to do but go on living.

After months in Italy, Paulina took Amala to her home in Spain, which was also located in a quaint village where people knew her and she knew how to enjoy the good and simple pleasures of life. Of Paulina's three homes Amala had lived in, she decided she liked the one in France the best, although she certainly couldn't deny the beauty and opportunities for enlightenment in each country, and she could understand why Paulina was drawn to such diversity in her life. She was like a grand and beautiful butterfly, flitting from country to country, spreading joy wherever she went and loving all people with the goodness of her giving heart. In fact, Amala came to see firsthand the way Paulina very carefully and privately managed to help those in need wherever she went. Amala now believed that part of her motive in spending time among the common people was to learn who was struggling and why, and she managed—with the help of Ivy and Miles—to find ways to anonymously assist them with food or money or medical care, whatever might be needed. Amala came to believe that this was the truest source of Paulina's fulfillment and happiness. While she was seen by others as being a world traveler who was addicted to appreciating the good things of life, she was secretly spreading joy and relief to others, which in turn created a joy within herself that nothing else could.

Amala loved and respected Paulina more and more, and she enjoyed their time together. She had learned much about life and the world in the seventeen months since they had left England. And she had learned much about herself. She had felt healing in her heart and felt better prepared to face the rest of her life with courage, dignity, and a stronger sense of honoring herself. But she had also learned that she differed greatly from Paulina in the way she was coming to miss her home in England; she was a person who needed a home, *one* home. The traveling was nice, and she believed she would like to have times in her life when she would leave home for a time in order to experience new things and gain perspective. But she would always need a home to go back to, a home where she could stay rooted. And the more time that was passing, the more Amala was feeling the need to reconnect herself with the place that had become her home.

Just as she did with everything, Amala shared her every thought and feeling with Paulina, who was not at all offended or upset to hear that Amala would like to work toward returning home as opposed to continuing to travel with her aunt. "I will miss your company greatly," Paulina said, "but we have created some wonderful memories together, and we will always be close in our hearts. And perhaps we will have more escapades in the future." Paulina squeezed Amala's hand. "In truth, I'm proud of you for finding what your own heart wants and having the courage to declare it. You will be happier for it."

"Yes," Amala said, "I believe I will."

* * * *

Amala had been away from home for nearly two years when she felt the urge to reread all the journals she had written during the course of this season of her life. She began at the point where she had first started recording her feelings, with Paulina's encouragement, and she filled her spare time with reading her own story as opposed to what she might normally read—a novel or a book about science, or theology, or faraway lands, or great people. She had always craved learning and enjoyed the way books offered that in so many forms. But now she was learning something about herself.

After reading all she'd written up to the present, Amala wrote about how she'd been reading the journals, and she summarized what she'd come to learn about herself as she had evolved through these experiences. Paulina had taught her so very much, both through her example and her sound wisdom and insight. And she had offered Amala opportunities of diversity and perspective that Amala never could have imagined possible. But it was the change inside of Amala as a result of all these things that mattered most to her. She had discussed these feelings and observations a little here and there with Paulina through the course of her reading, but now that she'd finished the project, they sat together on an upstairs balcony watching the Spanish sun setting in the distance while the now-familiar sounds of a nearby outdoor café emitted a pleasant background of people talking and laughing and dishes clanking as an indication of these people enjoying good food. There was also—as always—the pleasant sound of music gracefully intermixed into all the other noises; the café employed a well-skilled violinist who always worked during the evenings, and other than his short breaks, the sound of his music was nearly constant.

"I've come to see," Amala said, "that I've had a great deal more fear inside of me than I'd ever realized in regard to my parents' deaths—and the way it happened. I closed myself off from the world—and perhaps from love—because of that fear. I could never see the connection until I began to see the pattern of it written in my own words. I can see now that whatever I choose to do with my life, I need to go forward with confidence and hope and faith, and not make decisions based on fear."

"That's a very impressive evaluation of yourself, my dear," Paulina said. "Most people leave this world without ever understanding themselves so well." She paused as if to give Amala time to be prepared for a difficult question; Amala had come to recognize the meaning in Paulina's long pauses. But this time, the question was more difficult than Amala had expected. "If you could go back two years, knowing what you know now, would you have chosen differently? Would you have married Henry?"

"It's too late to wonder about such things," Amala said quickly, hoping to divert attention away from how the question bristled her.

"Is it? Do you think if you went back now you would find circumstances changed too much to reconsider?"

"I think it's more likely than not," Amala declared. "I've been pleading with Henry to move on and to find someone; it would be ridiculous of me to believe that such a thing has not taken place—at least to some degree. And to be completely truthful, I'm still not certain if I would have decided any differently. I loved him dearly—I love him still and doubt that I will ever stop. But that's just it—I love him enough to recognize that I *would* have brought hardship into his life. Perhaps to some my decision might appear to be overly self-sacrificing, perhaps even some form of martyrdom; that was never my intention. The truth is that I never felt at peace with balancing out the good that could come of a marriage between us with all the difficulties we might face—and particularly our children. Time and distance have not changed that, which makes me believe all the more that it was the right decision. I wish him every happiness, and I feel better prepared to find happiness and fulfillment in my own life—whatever form that might take."

"You have come a long way," Paulina said. "There's a serenity about you that was very much absent when I whisked you away from England."

Amala took her aunt's hand. "You deserve much of the credit for that, Auntie."

"Oh, no," Paulina chuckled humbly. "I have offered you opportunities; what you have chosen to do with them has been entirely up to you."

A thoughtful silence fell between them until Amala declared with all sincerity, "I feel ready to let him go, to completely let him go. I cannot deny my feelings, and, as I said, I believe a part of me will always love him. But I've felt the nature of my love shift inside of me. I truly want him to be happy, and the idea of him marrying someone else is not nearly so painful as it once was. It's as if . . . the attraction I felt and the romantic notions we shared, have settled into a more solid and mature kind of love. I sincerely feel I can wish him all the best and mean it."

"And again I say that you have come far," Paulina declared.

As a perfect conclusion to their conversation, sounds of celebration floated up from the café. A large group was obviously making a toast to honor someone, followed by the sound of clinking glasses and cheering. The two women stood and went to the balcony to look down. The celebration centered around an elderly couple who had obviously been together many years; this was likely a wedding anniversary, and they were surrounded by a large group of family and friends. The violinist began a lively tune, and members of the anniversary party took advantage of the music to start dancing in the street, making Amala smile. To observe such beauty and joy in the good things of life lifted her spirits and added to the serenity of which Paulina had spoken.

It was not many days later that Amala's declarations of being ready to let go of Henry were put to the test. She received a letter from Kat in which she joyfully shared with Amala the news that she was engaged to be married. Amala could feel nothing but joy for her sister, except for the sentence in the letter she had to keep reading over and over to try to convince herself that the words really said what they did.

I hope it will not come as too big a surprise to you, and that you'll be happy for me, when I tell you that it is Henry who has won my heart, and I've grown to love him so dearly that I can't imagine how I ever existed with the absence of such feelings.

Amala stared at the letter and reread it several times, overcome with such an onslaught of mixed feelings that she could hardly discern them. Shock overrode all else initially while she tried to accept that her worst fear had come to pass. She couldn't deny some jealousy and knew she'd be a fool to try to pretend it didn't exist inside of her. How could she stand back and see her beloved sister have everything that Amala had wanted but couldn't have? Henry would now officially become a part of the family; he would always be there, involved and in the middle of everything. Amala had hoped that when he found a wife and settled down, he would settle into his home and she would rarely encounter him. But how would she ever be able to manage this? Perhaps she was not nearly as over him as she'd believed. Or, as Paulina suggested, perhaps his marrying Kat—as opposed to some nameless, faceless woman—put the matter far too close to Amala's heart.

Paulina was compassionate to Amala's shock and encouraged her to talk through the complexity of her feelings, and Amala found the need to grieve all over again for the love she and Henry had shared that was clearly now in the distant past—at least it was for him.

The following day a letter from Henry arrived, and Amala insisted that Paulina sit with her while she read it. Her hands trembled, and her eyes misted over before she could even break the seal. She was grateful more than ever for the ally she'd found in Paulina, who already knew every detail of the situation and knew Amala's heart inside out. It was only natural, then, to read the letter aloud and therefore not feel alone in hearing whatever Henry might have to say.

My dearest Amala,

I'm not certain if Kat's letter will have reached you already or if mine will be the bearer of news that is difficult to share. You, more than anyone, have encouraged me to find love and to settle down. Your concern on my behalf has always been admirable and even touching, but I wonder how you will feel to learn that I have finally found the right woman to marry, and that woman is Kat.

Amala took a deep breath and tried to steady her voice, wondering how she would have felt if Henry's letter had arrived first. She was glad it hadn't.

I hope and pray that you have come to terms with the past enough that you can be sincerely happy for us, and I especially hope this will not create any awkwardness or difficulty between us in the future as I become more fully a part of your family. I want you to know that time has healed the wounds in my heart, and while I will always hold a place in my heart especially for you, I must now put all that you and I shared behind me completely and commit my future to your sister.

Again, Amala had to pause, this time to wipe her hands over her cheeks to be rid of the tears that had fallen there. She went on to read details of how it had been his time with her family that had more and more become his strength and his comfort. As Oliver and Viola and Kat—and even the servants of the household—had become more and more a comfortable part of his life and their home had come to be increasingly more home to him than his own had ever been, he had naturally been drawn to Kat's company, and over time their feelings for each other had evolved. He reassured Amala that he'd carefully examined his motives for marrying Kat, not wanting to be unfair to her, to himself, or to anyone else. He declared that even though Kat was very different from Amala in so many ways, he had sincerely grown to love her and he was fully committed to devoting his life to her and to making her happy. His feelings for Amala had taken their proper place in his past, and he was ready to move forward with Kat in every respect. He declared how happy he felt at the prospect of marriage to her, and his hope that Amala would be happy for them and that with time all would be well for all of them together as a family.

"I don't know if that's possible," Amala said to Paulina, temporarily turning the letter upside down on her lap. "How can I face having him share his life with Kat? How can I make peace with that?"

"These are not the words of the young woman who told me just a few days ago of how far she'd come," Paulina said. "You *will* make peace with it, even if it's not easy. You love them both; you want them to be happy. It will be all right."

"I'm glad you think so," Amala said, wishing it hadn't sounded so snide. She then picked the letter back up and continued to read, only to discover that Henry had made the decision to sell his own estate and accept the eager invitation of her parents to live with Kat under their roof. A buyer for the estate had come forward with a generous offer near the time of Henry and Kat's engagement, and to him it had felt like the hand of Providence. He'd never liked the home he'd grown up in and was glad to be free of the burden. The sale would give him even more financial resources that would more than last him a lifetime and give him plenty to pass on to his posterity, and, of course, he would contribute to the living expenses of the home he would now share with his wife's family. It was all very practical and made perfect sense, but Amala felt consumed by a level of confusion and heartache she didn't know how to face. She bolted out of her chair and tossed the letter at Paulina before she began pacing and wringing her hands.

"I can't . . . take all of this in," she said. "I can't . . . go back there and stand at my sister's side for the wedding. I . . . I can't . . . live under the same roof with them like this. It's as if . . . my home is not my home anymore. How can I go back there?"

"You don't have to go back," Paulina said, "at least not until you're ready. You can choose whatever life suits you. With time you'll be able to be happy for them. But . . . we don't have to go back yet, Amala. We don't."

Amala stopped pacing and looked at her aunt. "If we'd decided to leave here and do more traveling a few days ago, I wouldn't have received the letters. They would not have found us for who knows how long."

"That's true," Paulina said with a slight smile, as if she liked where Amala's thinking was headed.

"What happens to your mail when you move on?"

"Friends or those who watch over my houses receive it. Ivy keeps everyone informed through letters of where I am traveling, and where to send the mail. She can take care of having it all sent to the house in France, for instance. I know you'd like to go back there, but we could do some sightseeing here in Spain and take our time getting there. It could take weeks—maybe months—for the mail to catch up with us at my French home. They would be married by then; it would be unfortunate that you were unable to attend the wedding, but they would all get over their disappointment. We can return to England for a visit when you're ready, and we don't have to stay long if you prefer not to."

Paulina stood and took both of Amala's hands into hers. "I will support you in whatever you need, my dear, so that you can get through these challenges in your life with as little heartache as possible. Tell me what you want to do."

"I want to leave here tomorrow, and I will pray that God forgives me for pretending that I didn't yet receive these letters. I need time to come to terms with this, and I believe God will understand."

"Yes, I believe He will," Paulina said and kissed Amala's forehead. "I'll tell Miles and Ivy that I have a hankering to get out of this routine and go see some sights, and we'll all start packing today. Arrangements can be made for us to leave before dawn."

Amala breathed a sigh of relief. "Thank you," she said, far more relieved than she could fathom that she could gracefully avoid the wedding and allow herself some time to be ready to face the man she loved and her sister as husband and wife. Right now it was simply too much to bear.

* * * *

Amala lost track of the weeks and months that she traveled with Paulina, keeping her focus on the fascinating and unique experiences they shared. During her time alone—which was minimal—she read books or wrote in her journal, doing everything she could to avoid thinking about Henry and Kat, knowing they were married by now, and that all written communication her family may have sent to her was likely waiting at the house in France, which she didn't feel ready to face. But Paulina was only too happy to indulge Amala's desire to put off returning there, which would mean facing up to the full extent of how she felt about all of this.

Amala knew that eventually she would need to return to England, at least for a significant visit. And she would. But not yet; not until she was ready. She grew increasingly grateful for the comfortable companionship she shared with Paulina, who often declared that she didn't know how she would ever get along without Amala should she ever decide to take a different course in life beyond traipsing around the world according to Paulina's whims. For now, Paulina's wanderlust suited Amala just fine, even if a part of her knew she was hiding and running away. She preferred to think of it more as simply giving herself time to adjust; perhaps it was some of both.

Paulina occasionally mentioned a desire to travel to America, just for the adventure of it, and said that perhaps they could do that after they'd worked up the courage for a brief visit in England. Amala liked the idea of having a plan that included extensive travel and a great many miles between herself and the happiness being shared by two of the people she loved most. It was Paulina's view that some years had now passed since the end of that dreadful civil war in America, and as long as they restricted their travels to certain parts of the country, the dust had surely settled by now and they would not be affected by it. They had conversations about how much of the basis of the war had been rooted in the slavery of black-skinned people and how President Lincoln—prior to his tragic death—had written a proclamation to declare them now free. But Paulina and Amala both agreed that being declared free and actually being treated fairly by those with white skin were two vastly different things, and it would likely take a long, long time for such people of color to truly feel equal to their fellow human beings—if such a thing were ever even possible.

A day came when Amala realized she'd grown weary of traveling, and she asked Paulina if they could return to the house in France, of which Amala had grown so fond. Even though she knew there would likely be many letters waiting for her from home—which would surely be difficult to read—she believed the safe atmosphere of Paulina's French home, combined with the time that had passed, would make it possible for her to do so and come to terms with them. She couldn't find words to explain a restlessness she felt in needing to finally face all of this and reconnect with her family, but Paulina with her extra sense completely respected such feelings, and they were quickly on their way to France, arriving there more quickly than Amala had expected. Since a message had been sent ahead, the house had been aired out and freed from dust and was all ready for them to settle in. And two stacks of letters had been left on the table in the parlor. There were a few letters for Paulina, that were set apart from the large quantity of those addressed to Amala.

Amala unpacked, freshened up, and got a little something to eat from the variety of fruit and bread and cheese that had been left for them. She then found she couldn't put it off any longer. Paulina suggested that Amala have some time alone and said they could talk later.

Amala sat down on one of the pretty little couches in the parlor and looked at the ominous pile of mail in front of her. A glance through the stack made it evident that the woman Paulina hired to take care of things in her absence had carefully stacked the letters according to the order in which they'd been received, indicated by the postmark on the envelopes. Since the most recent letter was on top, Amala turned the stack upside down and opened the first letter, which was from her mother.

Amala remained in the parlor for hours, reading her letters and rereading some of them, and weeping a great deal. She read of her family's great disappointment in not being able to reach her, since Paulina had written to tell the family they were traveling not long after letters had been sent to tell her of Kat's engagement. Her family assumed that those letters had crossed in the mail, and Amala was fine with allowing her family to believe that. In spite of everyone's disappointment at her not being present for the wedding and all of its delightful preparations, she received reports from both of her parents and from Kat about how lovely it had all been. Henry wrote only a couple of brief notes in a very brotherly tone, politely expressing his well wishes on her behalf and reporting that he was doing well.

Occasionally she got up to go walk outside for a few minutes or to go upstairs to freshen up. Paulina checked on her now and then, and Ivy brought tea and something for Amala to eat. She picked at the food but felt little appetite as she read of how Henry and Kat had been away for some weeks on their honeymoon and upon returning, Henry had quickly settled in as a permanent resident at Willenbrock House; none of them were surprised with how easy the transition was for all of them, given how much time he'd been spending there for years.

After Amala had read everything she possibly could in order to feel caught up with life back at Willenbrock House, she was relieved to discover that she didn't feel as downhearted as she might have expected.

While she and Paulina shared a light supper, Amala told her aunt that she believed the months she'd spent working toward this day had truly been healing; she'd been able to adjust to the idea, and she felt more at peace and more able to feel confidence in having truly let go of Henry. She could sincerely say that she felt pleased for Henry and Kat and the happiness they'd found together. Of course, she expected that some difficult feelings might arise now and then in the future, and she believed her first visit home might entail some initial awkwardness, but where she'd once wondered how she could ever go home at all, she now felt much closer to being ready to do so, and as long as Paulina went with her, she believed everything would be fine and that after initial greetings were exchanged, she would surely be very happy to see all of them again. In spite of her gratitude for this necessary time away from home, she couldn't deny that she missed her family—including Henry. She was coming to think of him as her brother and becoming comfortable with the idea.

Amala concluded her report to Paulina with the news that had come in the most recent letter. "Kat is pregnant; the baby is due to arrive in the autumn."

"That's lovely news," Paulina said cautiously. "*Is* it lovely news?"

"It is, of course," Amala said with sincerity. "I'm very happy for them, truly."

"And now you will be an aunt. Being an aunt has brought me a great deal of joy; perhaps it will be the same for you."

"I like the thought of that," Amala said and felt surprisingly serene and at peace. "Kat and Mother both want very badly for me to be there when the baby comes," she added. "I confess that I miss them; I believe that I should think about returning home, perhaps before the end of the summer."

"If that's what you want, it can certainly be arranged," Paulina said. "I confess that I wouldn't mind being around when the baby comes, myself. Such moments in life are rare and precious, and I'd like to be involved. I don't think anyone would mind my being there if I don't make a nuisance of myself."

"You never make a nuisance of yourself," Amala insisted, "and I'm sure they'd be delighted. I was hoping you'd feel that way, because I think I will manage the adjustment much better if you are there. After the baby comes and things have settled, we will decide what to do."

"Perhaps you will feel comfortable enough that you'll want to remain at home," Paulina said. "And though I don't know what I'll do without you, I would certainly understand."

"And perhaps I will go to America with you."

"We'll see," Paulina said with a smile and a wink. And Amala's mind wandered to the fact that she was going to be an aunt to Henry Beckenridge's child. When she'd first become smitten with him, she never could have imagined such a turn of events. But she was glad to note that she felt nothing but happiness for both Henry and Kat. And her parents' excitement about becoming grandparents couldn't help but make her smile. Perhaps this baby would be the means of healing any residue of difficult feelings that might remain. Amala considered the possibility a pleasant thought and clung to it, wondering what it would be like to have a baby become a part of the family.

The following day Amala and Paulina went to church—as they'd done nearly every Sunday throughout their travels. Together they had attended many different churches of different denominations and many different atmospheres. They'd worshiped with tiny congregations in little village chapels, and large congregations in enormous cathedrals. Amala definitely felt closer to God in some settings than others, but recalling her horrible encounter with the vicar back home, she especially enjoyed being able to attend church without having *him* look down from the pulpit at her with his judgmental eyes.

Wherever Amala and her aunt might be on any given Sunday, they found a place to express their mutual devotion to God and to seek for something inspirational or uplifting in the sermons they heard and the hymns they sang—as much as it was possible for Amala to understand these things in Italian and Spanish, which had been more difficult for her than French. After church, Amala typically enjoyed discussing that day's particular experience with Paulina, and often they would read together out of the Bible and discuss their favorite passages. Amala often felt grateful—and she shared her feelings with Paulina—that she had been taught the Christian religion from her childhood, and it was something that she had come to embrace eagerly of her own free will, not simply because it was the way her family or community worshiped. She held a deep respect for the religious beliefs of the people of India, but she could honestly say in her heart that she was more suited to the teachings of the Bible. Perhaps that was one of the biggest reasons she knew she could never return to India and feel comfortable there.

On that first Sunday back in France, Amala sat in the little village chapel she had grown to love during her previous visit to this place. Looking back over the diverse Sabbath experiences scattered throughout her journey of healing, she knew that God's hand had played a very large role in that healing. Without Him she surely never would have found the peace she was feeling now. Deep within herself she carried a strong sense that God loved her every bit as much as He loved any fair-skinned person, that He had compassion for the struggles of her life, and that His peace was there to strengthen her. It was this very peace that gave her the hope of being able to return home and know that everything would be all right, and she was glad to now have a plan of when they would return. She could begin preparing herself for the reunion with her family, holding to the expectation that more healing would take place once they were all reunited—even if no one but Henry had any understanding of Amala's true reasons for leaving and being away all this time.

That evening Amala wrote a long letter addressed to the entire family, telling them that she and Paulina had just returned from a long excursion through parts of Spain and Italy and that they were now back at the house in France, where all of the letters had been waiting. She expressed her sincere joy about Henry and Kat's marriage and the forthcoming arrival of the baby, and she told them that she and Paulina were planning to return home before the end of the summer.

Amala walked into the village the following day to post the letter, soaking in the details of this place she'd grown to love but longing for her home in the English countryside more than she had since she'd run away from there. She'd actually lost track of how long she'd been gone. She felt no need to count the months and years; she simply felt it was the amount of time they had all needed. She wondered if Henry and Kat would have been able to discover their love for each other if she had been there; and she wondered if she would have wavered and struggled and caused more grief for Henry. And she absolutely knew she would have not been able to heal and make peace with herself had she not been given the distance from home in order to do so.

Feeling a light and peace inside of her that she'd not felt in a long time—or perhaps ever—Amala took her time wandering through the village and buying some odds and ends. When she came across some baby apparel, she found delight in picking out a beautiful crocheted gown with a matching bonnet. With the delicate purchase wrapped and put into a box to keep it safe from damage, Amala returned to the cottage to share with Paulina her thoughts and feelings of gratitude and peace and her anticipation of becoming an aunt.

* * * *

With summer coming on fully, Amala settled into what she knew would be her final stretch of time in Paulina's idyllic French world. They had a set a tentative date for their return to England, with the intention of spreading the journey out so that traveling across the entire country of France would not be too cumbersome. Amala was truly beginning to feel confident that she would be emotionally prepared when the time came, only to have a letter arrive from her mother with a sincere request for her to return as soon as possible. The letter didn't come right out and say that something was wrong, but Amala knew her loved ones well, and through the exchange of seemingly countless letters, she had developed a sense of what might not actually be written in ink.

Amala showed the letter to Paulina and asked for her opinion without saying anything at all to influence her. The moment she'd finished reading the brief missive, Paulina declared, "Something's not right. It's my guess that she doesn't want to alarm you, but there's a reason she believes you should be at home."

"What should we do?" Amala asked, hoping Paulina would agree with her own feelings. It was rare when they weren't in tune with each other.

"I think we should prepare to leave as soon as we can manage," Paulina said. "What do *you* think?"

"I agree," Amala said, both relieved and concerned—not only about what might be wrong, but about whether or not she was ready to face all that had changed at home.

"And I think we should make our journey with some haste," Paulina added. "It won't be enjoyable or relaxing, but . . . I do feel there is a need for us to get there as quickly as we can."

Amala only nodded, feeling a sudden urge to cry. She'd come to trust Paulina's extra sense, and Paulina's response to the letter was even more concerned and determined than Amala had expected. She wondered what might be going on at home. Was someone ill? Or had someone been injured? Or was it something she couldn't even imagine? Writing to inquire wouldn't do any good. They would be back in England before a reply could ever be received.

Amala had difficulty saying good-bye to the cottage and the village and the sea where she had come to feel so at home and where so much healing had taken place for her. But her mind was preoccupied with her true home and her loved ones there. She wondered if she would ever return to this place with Paulina; logic told her it was highly likely, given the status of her life. But a subtle, chilling sensation coming from deep within herself led her to wonder if she ever would.

Chapter Nine
MUCH CHANGED

Setting out to cross the channel, Amala was exhausted and aching from the long carriage rides with little rest between stops. They had made fairly good time, but her body certainly felt the effects of their hasty journey. The fatigue and sore muscles seemed a tangible manifestation of the concern and worry consuming her mind. Paulina had cautioned her more than once not to leap to assumptions that would only cause her grief when she had no idea what might actually be taking place at home. But Paulina couldn't deny that she too felt something was not as it should be.

Crossing the channel felt soothing to Amala, even though she felt somewhat impatient with how long it took. Still, being able to walk about the ship was far better than being confined to a carriage rumbling over bumpy roads. As soon as they arrived in England, they were quickly whisked into yet another carriage with more miles of hasty travel, being jostled about on seats that were not terribly comfortable under the best of circumstances.

When the hired carriage finally drove onto her family's land, Amala could hardly breathe for all of the relief she felt at having the journey behind them, the concern she had for whatever might be wrong, and the fear of her initial reunion with Henry and Kat.

"We should arrive in plenty of time to have tea with the family," Paulina announced. Amala just stared out the window, taking in scenery that hadn't changed even a tiny bit through all the time she'd been away. As the house came into view, her joy at returning home soothed her concerns, and she could only think how glad she would be to see everyone, and to sleep in her own bed, and to spend her days in this place that was her truest home.

Only a minute after the carriage halted in front of the house, servants whom Amala knew well came out the door to investigate their unexpected arrival. They were pleased to see Amala and Paulina, and she was certainly pleased to see them.

While the luggage was being unloaded, Viola rushed out the door, exclaiming with a combined burst of laughter and tears, "Is it true? Is it really true?"

Amala didn't have time to answer before her mother embraced her tightly, not letting go, vacillating between her ongoing tears and expressions of joy. Amala held to her mother fiercely, knowing now that she'd not fully acknowledged how very much she'd missed her family. She was glad she'd come home earlier than planned and wished that she hadn't waited so long.

Oliver came out the door with a similar reaction to that of Viola, stealing Amala away from her mother's embrace only to hold her even more tightly. "Oh, my precious girl!" he said close to her ear. "We have all missed you so very much!"

"And I you," she said, looking up at him. "It's good to be home."

"I am very glad of it," Oliver said and smiled. "You have grown even more beautiful, if that's possible."

"Indeed, she has," Viola said with her arm still around Paulina following the embrace they'd shared. Oliver laughed when he saw his sister and hugged her tightly as well.

They all went into the house while Viola was telling Amala and Paulina that they should go to their rooms and freshen up. She said they would all gather for tea in a couple of hours and be able to catch up on all the news. Amala hoped some of that news wouldn't be whatever awful thing might be going on—the nature of which she couldn't possibly imagine. Her parents appeared to be in excellent health as always. That was a good sign.

Amala was nearly to the stairs when she heard Kat call her name and turned to see her coming from a side hallway. She looked very much the same except for the obvious evidence that she was pregnant. Her belly wasn't terribly big, since she had months yet to go, but there was no hiding the fact. Amala was taken aback for only a quick second by the thought that this was Henry's baby; then she focused on her sweet reunion with her sister.

"Oh, Amala," Kat said softly, her voice quivering as they walked toward each other, coming together with an embrace that felt as if they were twins who had been joined in the womb and their being reunited now took them back somehow to that crucial and essential bond. They touched each other's faces and wiped each other's tears while Amala considered the evidence that Kat seemed well and strong, which alleviated one more source of Amala's concern.

With their parents and Paulina looking on, Kat and Amala talked for a few minutes, throwing questions at each other and trying to answer them in a way that made their conversation a jumble that just ended in laughter and a declaration that they had a great deal they needed to talk about and plenty of time to do it.

Amala was relieved at the evidence that everything seemed fine with her sister and her parents, and her concerns shifted as she asked, "Where is Henry? Is he—"

"Oh, he's just outside the west parlor, near the garden," Kat reported. "He likes to read there in the afternoon sun. You must go and say hello to him."

Amala quickly debated whether to do so now or wait until she'd had a chance to freshen up. She decided she didn't want to dread it any longer and said, "I think I'll hurry and just let him know we're here." Keenly aware of the dramatic change of circumstances and wanting to maintain perfect propriety, she took hold of Kat's hand. "You'll come with me?"

"Oh, you don't need me," Kat said with a little laugh. "I confess that I was on my way to get a little something to eat; I'm feeling a bit nauseated."

Amala scanned the other faces of her family members, wondering how to ask if someone would come with her, but Oliver declared with a grin, "Just go and surprise him and we'll see you at tea."

Paulina offered a nod of encouragement, as if she believed this would be better; and Paulina was the only one who knew everything about her history with Henry. Amala wasn't certain she agreed, but she didn't want to behave awkwardly and draw any undue attention to her angst.

"Very well," Amala said. "I'll see you all in a while, then."

Amala walked slowly toward the west parlor, where she knew that doors opened onto a large patio that bordered the garden. She had often enjoyed the afternoon sun there herself. She entered the open door into the room, her footsteps completely silent on the carpet. She stopped when Henry came into view, lounging comfortably in one of the chairs that always remained on the patio during the summer months. Just the mere sight of him caused Amala to catch her breath. He looked different, but that was easily credited to the neatly trimmed beard on his face and the fact that she'd never seen him dressed that way before. She was glad to have a minute to take it all in while he was unaware of her presence. She found it funny that she could clearly recall how much she'd loved him and how difficult it had been to adjust to dissecting herself from his life and then to accept his marriage to her sister. But she could honestly say that her feelings were even more controlled and proper than she'd believed possible. Now that she was here, she knew that everything would be all right and, perhaps more importantly, that everything was as it should be—for all of them.

Amala finally stepped through the open doorway onto the patio, saying quietly, "Hello, Henry."

"Amala!" he said with a gasp of surprise as he stood and turned and dropped his book all in a matter of seconds.

"Forgive me for startling you," she said as their eyes met and memories flooded over her. He said nothing, and she could imagine him contending with the same memories. For a moment she feared he might revert to the kind of interaction they'd once shared when they were alone together, which would have been completely inappropriate for a married man. But it only took a second for her to realize that his countenance and demeanor expressed nothing but friendship and the love of a brother—just as it should. There was not even the tiniest hint of the attraction he'd once exhibited so readily. He'd changed, and Amala was glad to realize that she felt nothing of the awkwardness she had feared might be present between them.

"Amala," he said again with a breathy laugh and hugged her tightly but briefly, the way he had done many times during his visits to her home when they had been around other people and they had wanted their relationship to appear as it had now become, like a brother and sister, like the dearest of friends. "You're really here," he added, stepping back to fully take her in with his eyes.

"I really am," she said and took him in as well. "What is this?" she asked, momentarily touching the cream-colored linen fabric of his sleeve. He was wearing clothing she had commonly seen worn by men in India, which was a linen shirt that hung loosely down to his hips over the top of loose-fitting trousers of the same fabric. He wore sandals on his feet. "I never saw you dress like this."

"You never came to *my* home. I've dressed like this while at home for over a decade, Amala. It's not as practical here in England during the colder months, but during the summer I find it quite accommodating."

"Well, it suits you," she said and smiled.

"We weren't expecting you for at least a couple of months yet," he said and motioned her toward a chair. "Why the surprise?"

Amala didn't want to explain their reasons for hurrying home, nor did she want to sit and visit with him right now. "We just decided it was time to come home," she explained. "I need to freshen up before tea. I just . . . wanted to say hello and . . . let you know we're here."

"It's so good to see you, Amala. I'm very glad you came back early, and I know that Kat will be all the better with your company."

The way he said it prompted Amala to ask without thinking about whether or not she should, "Is something wrong?"

Amala's heart quickened when she realized she had expected him to assure her that everything was fine, but she immediately saw something very contrary to that in his eyes. She found no comfort when he said gravely, "That is a conversation you need to have with Kat."

Amala heard herself gasp as the implication of his words settled in. "Henry, you're scaring me."

He looked down abruptly, as if he had no reassurance to offer her on that count either.

"Henry?" she pleaded, glad to feel as comfortable in his presence as she once had.

"Please," he said, "just . . . talk to Kat." He reluctantly lifted his eyes to meet hers, and Amala gasped again to see clearly in his expression that he was not only upset about whatever she needed to talk to Kat about, but that he was also terrified.

Amala didn't bother saying another word before she rushed into the house and up the stairs, going to her rooms for only a few minutes, barely long enough to ensure that she could be comfortable, before she went to Kat's room and knocked at the door, wondering if she still used the same room now that her husband had moved into the house with her.

"Come in," she heard Kat call softly, and Amala opened the door to see Kat resting on the bed. "Oh, I was hoping it would be you!" Kat grinned and held out a hand toward Amala, who hurried to sit on the edge of the bed and take Kat's hand.

"Are you unwell?" Amala asked, recalling now her mention of feeling nauseous.

Kat laughed softly. "I have all the normal symptoms of pregnancy," she said and went on to share details of the nausea, which was improving but had been dreadful the first couple of months. She talked of needing to always keep food in her stomach and said she never went to bed without making certain there was something within reach on the bedside table that she could eat the moment she woke up. She talked of her excessive fatigue and of how she couldn't get through the day without a nap and was going to bed much earlier than usual. Kat told Amala she'd had some occasional light-headedness as well, but she assured Amala that the doctor had told her all of these things were a completely normal part of pregnancy. But Amala wondered what Kat *wasn't* telling her. Whatever it was, she needed to know. She had to understand what she'd seen in Henry's countenance that made her feel cold from the inside out just recalling it.

"Kat," Amala said carefully, "is something else wrong? Is there something you aren't telling me?"

"Why would you ask me that?" Kat asked with a hint of defensiveness, and Amala knew she was trying to keep something from her.

While Amala was trying to come up with a reasonable way to explain all of the different hints she'd accumulated that let her know there was a problem, the door opened and Henry came in. He didn't look surprised to see Amala there, but he did say, "Forgive me if I'm intruding. I'll leave the two of you alone to talk if you prefer."

"We're just chatting," Kat said, reaching her free hand toward him.

Amala mentally adjusted to the dramatic changes that had taken place as she observed the way Henry kissed Kat on the forehead before he took her hand and sat on the opposite side of the bed from Amala.

Amala took full advantage of having Henry there as her ally. She knew he wanted her to get answers from Kat, but she'd also just realized that Kat was not eager to be forthcoming. With Henry in the room, perhaps she could get the information she needed.

"Kat was just telling me about all the undesirable symptoms of pregnancy," Amala said. "It sounds rather challenging."

"But well worth it," Kat said, smiling at Henry.

"Although I get the feeling there is something else going on," Amala said, keeping her gaze keenly on her sister. "Something she doesn't want to tell me."

"And again I ask," Kat said to Amala, "why you would ask me that? Why would you think that?"

"I'm your sister," Amala said. "There are a number of reasons I just feel that something isn't right, Paulina's extra sense being one of them."

"Is that why you came home early? Paulina's extra sense?" Kat sounded mildly angry, which Amala saw as another sign that she was attempting to hide something.

"Mother wrote and asked if we might come home earlier than planned. She said nothing about a problem, but her request did make me wonder if something was wrong. Paulina sensed that there was. So here we are. In spite of my absence, I *am* a part of this family, and I know when something isn't right. And I know you better than anyone. I know you're married now, but I'm your sister, and we have been together practically our entire lives. So talk to me."

Kat looked toward the wall in a way that clearly indicated she didn't want to look at—or talk to—either one of them. In a slightly huffy voice she said, "I just don't want anyone making a fuss. I'm certain it's nothing to worry about."

Amala was startled not only by how quickly Henry retorted but by his mildly angry tone of voice. "I don't know if this is some kind of misguided bravery or if you're just not facing up to the truth. We've talked about this, Kat. Whether or not you truly believe it's nothing to worry about, the rest of us are worried. Amala is your sister. She deserves to know the facts, and then she can decide whether or not *she* should be worried. Your pretending that everything is fine and normal will not make it so."

Amala saw Kat squeeze her eyes closed as if to block out what Henry had just said. Amala exchanged a glance with Henry and saw something in his expression that she knew all too well. She felt a little nauseous herself as she reexamined the expression in his eyes when he turned to look at his wife. And sure enough, it was true. Henry's heart was breaking. But there was more anger than sorrow in his voice when he said to Kat, "If you won't tell her, I will." Amala could easily sense that his anger was an attempt to cover his sorrow, but she knew him well enough to see the truth.

Kat sighed and opened her eyes, but she didn't look at either of them as she said, "I've had a little bump for a long time, and it's gotten a bit bigger."

"A *little* bump?" Henry countered. "A *bit* bigger? Show it to her." Kat obviously didn't want to, and he added, "Your parents have seen it. She's your sister," he reminded her again. "Show it to her. She has a right to know."

With an exasperated sigh, Kat rolled more onto her back, pulling up her dress with one hand while she pushed down the drawstring waist of her petticoat and drawers with the other to expose her belly. Amala was distracted for only a moment by the thought of Kat doing so in Henry's presence. The evidence of their marital status was quickly sinking in, but Amala was more concerned by this *bump* she was about to see. She didn't know what she'd been expecting, but she sucked in a sharp breath and very nearly let out an expletive that she knew no lady would ever utter. Low on the side of Kat's pregnant belly, just above her hipbone, was a protrusion about the size of an orange but distorted in shape.

"What *is* it?" Amala demanded.

"It's just . . . a bump," Kat insisted. "I've had it for years. And it didn't hurt at all until it started . . . getting bigger."

Amala sensed Henry's frustration rising, and something close to panic began to erupt inside of her. She waited to let him handle this, mostly because she didn't know what to say. She wondered for a moment if he might express his anger toward Kat, and she felt momentarily caught between them. She could understand Henry's anger over Kat's apparent flippancy about something that was obviously serious, but she would never want her sister's husband to be unkind to his wife. She reminded herself that—in spite of how long she'd been away—she should have known Henry better than to believe him capable of such a thing. She'd certainly seen him frustrated, and even angry, but she couldn't fathom him being unkind.

Henry proved her right when he let out a long sigh and spoke to Kat gently. "Forgive my frustration, my darling; I'm just worried. We all are. And Amala needs to know what's going on. Whatever *you* might believe, we know what the doctor has said, and we can't pretend that the situation is otherwise."

"I know this is difficult for you," Kat said to Henry, "but nothing is more important right now than this baby, and that's what I choose to think about." She glanced at Amala and added, "You can tell her what she needs to know. I don't want to hear it again."

The implications of all Amala had heard—and seen—pressed the panic in her closer to the surface. Fearing that *she* might say something that sounded unkind, she hurried out of the room but didn't get very far, since her legs had become shaky and she felt a little dizzy. She took hold of a balcony railing with both hands and tried to catch her breath while questions and assumptions whirled in her mind. She could hear herself breathing hard and fast and tried to focus on drawing each breath slowly in and then out in order to calm down—which was the reason she didn't hear Henry approaching until he was standing next to her, putting his hands on the railing in the same manner, as if he too needed something to hold on to.

A minute or more passed and he said nothing, which made Amala wonder if he was searching for the right words or waiting for her to ask. When the silence began to feel torturous, she finally found the will to speak her most urgent thought. "So . . . my mother asked me to come home early because . . . that thing . . . whatever it is . . . will eventually . . . kill her?"

"The doctor didn't ever say that exactly," Henry said.

"What exactly *did* the doctor say?" Amala countered. "You said I needed to know."

Henry sighed loudly. "The growth—which is what Dr. Cowell calls it—was there when we got married. It was significantly smaller. Kat told me it had been there for a couple of years and it didn't hurt and was nothing to worry about. More than once I encouraged her to have a doctor at least look at it, but she insisted that it was surely nothing. When I noticed that it was getting bigger, I insisted she see a doctor. We argued about it numerous times." He chuckled humorlessly. "Your sister is a stubborn woman, Amala."

"And you're wise enough to have known that when you married her."

"Yes, of course. It's actually one of the things I love about her. But I never believed her stubbornness could be an issue regarding something like this. I finally had her convinced to see a doctor when she started getting pregnancy symptoms. And with a doctor coming to attend to her pregnancy, it was easy to seek out his opinion. He was immediately concerned, and he did a procedure to remove a small sample of whatever is inside of the growth."

"That sounds dreadful!" Amala said, certain it must have been painful for Kat.

"It wasn't as bad as we'd expected it to be; it was over very quickly." Henry turned and leaned back against the railing, folding his arms over his chest. "He had the sample tested in a laboratory and told us it was undoubtedly a cancerous growth. In essence, he explained that these things can behave very differently from patient to patient, depending on where the growths show up; it's very unpredictable, except for one thing."

"And what's that?"

"If it cannot be removed and it gets out of control, it will eventually lead to death—most often a difficult and painful death."

"So, he *did* say it would kill her?"

"Not in those exact words, but the implications were clear. With the size of the growth and the fact that it is now causing Kat pain, he believes it's far too late to attempt removing it, which would only be a difficult operation with a painful recovery, and he's certain they could never remove enough of it to keep it from growing. From the descriptions of Kat's pain, he believes it's . . ."

"What?" Amala insisted when his pause lasted far too long; then she realized he was struggling to maintain his composure. She wanted to put her arms around him and hold him so they could cry together. And even though she absolutely knew there was no motive in her desire except for their common love of Kat, she also knew it would never be appropriate—especially given the history they shared. Instead she gently touched his arm.

Henry cleared his throat loudly and kept his face turned away. "As I understand it, the pain is an indication that the cancer is . . . destroying bone and muscle."

"Oh, good heavens!" Amala said and again took hold of the railing tightly.

Following another lengthy silence, Henry cleared his throat again and said, "I sent for a doctor from London who specializes in cancer. I had no reason to believe our local doctor wasn't right; he's bright and competent. But he actually encouraged me to seek out another opinion, feeling perhaps there were things a specialist might know that he didn't. This doctor concurred in every respect."

Amala again became aware of her breathing. Her sister was dying. She heard—as if from a distance—Henry telling her they had no idea how long it would be or how much she might suffer. Henry had obviously become well-educated on the disease with the way he repeated facts and statistics from his long conversations with the doctors with whom he'd consulted. Sometimes there were miracles and people held on for years. But he also said that sometimes— when a person was in a great deal of pain—the miracle could be not holding on at all. Kat had a strong will to live; he spoke of her courage and dignity over the matter with the exception of rare moments when she had broken down over the fact that this had happened to her.

"She feels cheated," Henry said. "We dreamed of having many children and growing old together." He coughed in a way that indicated once again his struggle for composure. "I feel cheated too."

"And the baby?" Amala asked and wiped a hand over her face as tears fell there.

"There's no way of knowing. So far everything seems fine. Kat can feel it moving inside of her. But Dr. Cowell said the growth could be at least as big inside as what we can see. I think the question is which will grow faster. If the baby can reach full term without the cancer invading the womb, then it should be fine. Of course, Kat's priority is the baby. She doesn't want to take anything for the pain, fearing it might harm the baby. She considers her life worthwhile if she can bring this child safely into the world."

"But whether or not she can, she will still die," Amala said and sniffled.

"Eventually."

"I can't believe it," Amala muttered.

"I've known for months and I *still* can't believe it."

"One of you should have written to tell me . . . sooner than this." Amala heard a tinge of anger in her own voice as she realized the opportunity to spend time with her sister was being measured in increments that were far too small.

"It's not the kind of thing any of us wanted to tell you in a letter, but let's just say that we all hoped with your mother's request for you to come—and our faith in Paulina's sense about such things—that you *would* come home. And you have." He finally turned to look at her and added with solemnity, "You are such a strength to Kat; she loves you and admires you so very much. Your presence with her will help to keep her spirits up, and that will help all of us. You're a strength to all of us, Amala—more than you will ever know. Even from a distance you have buoyed up your parents and your sister. I've seen how they light up when they talk about you and how your letters became the highlight of their lives. You need to know how your strength and courage are needed here, but at the same time you need to know that you don't have to be strong all the time. This is at least as difficult for you as it is for anyone else, and it's all right to admit that."

"You sound as if you know me so well," she said in a tone that was a sore attempt to lighten the mood.

"Don't I?"

"As I know you," she said.

"Yes, you do."

Amala sighed and asked a question she'd always worried about— ever since she'd received word that Henry and Kat were getting married. "Does she know . . . about us?"

"I never told her," he said. "It's in the past, and I believe you and I are both strong enough—and wise enough—to leave it there. But

I never wanted Kat to have to wonder if I still carried those kind of feelings for you."

Amala didn't even have to ask if he did; she only had to look into his eyes to see that his love and devotion were centered wholly on Kat—as they should be. She was grateful, however, that they were comfortable enough with each other as friends to be able to talk as they were now.

"I agree," Amala said. "It's better that she doesn't know."

"Paulina knows?" Henry asked, and she wondered how long he'd wanted to ask her *that* question.

"Yes, she knows everything, but she would never break my confidence."

"I'm not worried about that," Henry said. "And just so you know . . . because I think it has to be said . . . I do sincerely believe now that this is how things were meant to turn out. This is what's best—for everyone."

"I agree with that as well," Amala said, but she couldn't put a voice to her next thought. He'd already admitted to feeling cheated out of the life he'd hoped to live with Kat. But it was evident he was still grateful for whatever amount of life he would have with her.

Suddenly overcome with far too much to think about and a storm of unvented tears, Amala hurried to say, "Thank you for telling me what I needed to know, Henry. I need some time alone. Please . . . let me know if there's anything I can do to help Kat."

"I will," he said, and she walked briskly to her room, where she curled up on the bed and cried until her mother found her there and they cried together.

* * * *

Amala and her mother both managed to control their emotions enough to go down to tea. But the family gathering didn't feel at all like old times. Paulina was there but Kat was not, since she was still resting. Oliver and Viola had given Paulina the horrible news while Amala and Henry had been talking; therefore, they were all able to talk about their feelings—something they likely couldn't have done if Kat had been in the room. In fact, Viola came right out and said that

Kat had asked that the subject not be brought up in her presence. She wanted to enjoy life while it lasted, and they all felt it was important to respect her wishes. So they would all do their grieving when Kat wasn't around—and when she was, they would all pretend that nothing was wrong. It seemed like a horrible way for a family to live, Amala thought, but she couldn't deny the wisdom in it. She'd just never believed that something like this could happen in *her* family, to *her* sister. And she also found it difficult to believe that Henry was here, in the very middle of the drama. When she'd been stewing about how it might be to adjust to living under the same roof with Henry, this was certainly not what she'd imagined.

Amala was understandably surprised when the woman who entered the drawing room to serve tea was Indian. And not only Indian, but dressed in traditional Indian clothing rather than the English clothing worn by the other servants in the household.

"Hello," Amala said to her, which she hoped would ease any awkwardness over the fact that she knew she was staring at this woman. It was rare for Amala to come face-to-face with someone who shared her Indian blood, but to see this woman in her own home felt delightfully exciting.

The woman, who was somewhere between her own age and that of her mother, had lovely features and glossy black hair that she wore in a long braid that was hanging over the front of one shoulder. She paused after setting down the tray she'd been carrying and looked at Amala, smiling in response to the greeting she'd received.

"Memsahib," the woman said, and Amala felt a thrill just to be addressed with that word. She knew it was a simple, respectful greeting offered to a woman, but the last time she'd heard the word had been in India, when she'd been nine years old. "Your family has spoken of you with great admiration." She spoke with an accent far thicker than Amala's. "It is a genuine pleasure to meet you at last."

"It is a great pleasure to meet you," Amala said and glanced at her parents, then Henry, then again at this lovely woman. "I assume my family will tell me what great miracle has transpired to bring you to my home."

The woman smiled shyly, but she didn't seem uncomfortable having conversation in the drawing room with the people she worked for. But, then, Amala would never expect her parents or Henry to make their employees feel anything less than comfortable.

"This is Lekha," Oliver said with great pride. "She is as kind as she is competent and helpful. It's been a joy to have her here. Lekha, it's high time you finally meet our Amala."

"Memsahib," Lekha said again, nodding slightly.

"I think Lekha should tell you herself how she came to be here," Oliver added. "Why don't you sit down with us for a few minutes and briefly tell Amala your story; I'm certain the two of you will be getting better acquainted over time."

"Thank you, sahib," Lekha said to Oliver, offering perfect respect toward him, using the male version of the word she'd used to address Amala. Lekha was clearly appreciative of being asked to join the family for a few minutes and didn't seem at all timid or embarrassed about doing so, but she still offered perfect respect for her employers. Amala already liked her, even though they'd barely met.

Lekha sat down and pressed her dark hands over the sari she wore, smoothing out the wrinkles on her lap. She looked directly at Amala as if she were equally happy to see another dark-faced woman. "In India I worked for Mr. Henry's friend, Mr. Chit." Amala tossed a quick smile toward Henry; she could see where this was likely heading, but she enjoyed the fact that in India Henry and his friend had chosen to be called such by their household servants. Lekha went on. "Mr. Henry had asked that when Mr. Chit returned to India, he might ask if any of us would like to come to England, where we could live and work for him. I was very grateful for the offer, since I have no family there, nor does my husband—who also worked for Mr. Chit—and we have often dreamed of coming to England. I am happy to say that I like it here very much. Mr. Henry and your family have been very kind to me."

"I'm very glad to hear it," Amala said. "I do hope that you will indulge me whenever possible and we might talk of our homeland."

"I would like that very much," Lekha said. "Thank you, memsahib."

"It's lovely to hear such a word spoken here," Amala said. "But you may call me Amala; there's no need for such formality."

"Miss Amala, then," Lekha said, rising gracefully to her feet. She turned toward Viola, "Will there be anything else for now?"

"No, thank you, Lekha."

Lekha nodded and left the room with the grace and beauty of a rare butterfly. For a long moment, Amala looked toward the door through which she'd exited, pondering how inexplicably soothed she felt by Lekha's presence in the house. She turned to look at Henry, since the silence implied that everyone was waiting for her reaction. He looked positively pleased with himself, and she couldn't help but smile.

"Aren't you clever," she said.

"It was never part of my plan to end up living in *this* home and bringing some of my servants with me," Henry said. "But when it worked out that way, I can't say it didn't occur to me that it might be good for you to have people from India around you. . . whenever you finally chose to come home."

"I'm ashamed I didn't think of it before," Oliver said. "Henry's right; you should have people around you who might help you not feel so out of place—at least at home."

"People?" Amala asked. "Lekha did say she's married. Her husband is here, I assume."

"Yes, and one other man," Henry explained. "Ravi is Lekha's husband, and a fine man. And Ravi's father, Manik, is also with us. He actually assists in the kitchen since he originally worked as a cook in India and he has a distinct talent with culinary arts. You will soon discover that our menu has more variety now."

"Yes, and it's delightful," Viola said. "I must echo my dear Oliver and say that I'm ashamed I didn't think of such a thing myself a very long time ago. It's Henry's theory that while he prefers to live in England, there is much about India that he grew to love, and having elements of that world integrated into this one offers the best of both worlds."

Oliver added, "When Henry and Kat were married, and he made the decision to sell his estate, most of the staff remained with the home, but he insisted these three must come with him because they were not only his personal responsibility but they helped enrich his life and he believed they could do the same for us. He was certainly right."

"Your parents have been more than gracious," Henry said, "not only in allowing me to make my home here but to humor me in making these changes to the household."

"It's been nothing but a blessing!" Viola insisted. "We've loved every minute you've spent in our home right from the start. And far better for you to be here than for us to rarely see our dear Kat."

"It's worked out marvelously," Oliver declared, but his words were followed by a silence that became taut, as everyone was obviously thinking of the same thing but no one wanted to say it and break the lightness of the mood. Everything had worked out marvelously except for the fact that Kat was dying.

Amala was relieved when Paulina said with her typical enthusiasm, "Well, I think it's absolutely marvelous!" She said to her brother in a teasing tone, "Shame on you for not bringing more of India here with you when you came back in the first place! It seems Henry is a good influence on you."

"He is indeed." Oliver chuckled.

Viola said with enthusiasm, "Henry also asked Chit to send many things from India. We have many new and wonderful spices in the kitchen, some beautiful decor about the house here and there, and we all have clothing from India should we choose to wear it."

"I made it clear that I was not trying to impose my own preferences on anyone," Henry said. "I was simply offering it as an option. As I told you, I find certain Indian dress much more comfortable, especially during the warmer months. And forgive my boldness, but—"

"Nothing to forgive," Oliver interjected. "We like your boldness." He chuckled. "As if you would hold back on our account."

Henry and her parents *all* chuckled, and Amala assumed it had become somewhat of a joke among them.

Henry continued. "Well . . . I honestly don't know how you ladies can survive in all those corsets and petticoats—especially when the weather is warm. As a gentleman I often feel strangled by the need for a waistcoat *and* a coat; not to mention needing to wear a tie in public, as well. I figure that at home we should all wear what is most comfortable."

"I confess I've taken to it now and then," Viola admitted. "There are some days when wearing a sari just suits my mood better, and it is certainly very comfortable."

"I have conformed on occasion as well," Oliver said as if it were a grave confession, but it was followed with a little burst of laughter.

"Kat prefers her traditional English wardrobe," Viola said, "but, then . . . with the exception of Amala, she never did favor anything Indian. I suppose that's because her memories of India are not good."

"Each of us has the right to our own opinions," Henry said. "And Kat has been very gracious about allowing me to make such changes in the household in spite of her aversion to some of them."

Amala pondered the depth in what had just been said about Kat's aversion to all things Indian—except for Amala. It was a strange kind of sisterhood they shared, given their unique history.

"I mentioned to Henry awhile back," Oliver said, "that when you came back, my dear Amala, you might enjoy wearing more traditional Indian clothing that could be more to your liking."

"I think I *would* enjoy that," Amala said. It had certainly crossed her mind many times, but she'd never felt it would be appropriate to ask for such a favor.

"I confess I had Chit send some clothing specifically with you in mind," Henry said. More lightly, he added, "And I'm certain Kat would be more than happy for you to take what I got for her off of her hands."

"I hope there's enough for me to try it out," Paulina said.

"Of course." Henry smiled at her. "That would be delightful."

"Indeed it would," Amala said, exchanging a warm glance with her aunt and best friend.

While they drank their tea and passed around the little cakes and biscuits Lekha had brought to the drawing room, the conversation remained more focused on lighter things—which meant steering it away from talk about Kat's health. Amala and Paulina were encouraged to describe their travels, and Amala enjoyed the memories. She was also glad to hear that Paulina intended to stay at least until after the baby was born, declaring she didn't want to miss such an event. Amala suspected that Paulina would likely stay and offer her gracious support to the family through whatever challenges they would face in regard to Kat's illness. At least Amala hoped that was the case. She couldn't imagine how she would ever get through this at all, but having Paulina around would inevitably make it easier. She was simply that kind of person.

That evening Kat came down to supper, apparently feeling fine and behaving very much like herself. Amala was relieved to note that it didn't take much effort to settle into old habits of how it had been to be together as family prior to her leaving with Paulina, which made it fairly easy to pretend that everything was all right. In truth, Amala was glad to know they could share time together and talk and laugh with the prospect of creating good memories that would help carry them all through when Kat was no longer with them.

After supper Henry and Kat went for a walk in the garden, and Amala didn't allow herself to even think about how it had been when she'd gone for long walks in the garden with this man she had once loved. She still loved him, but it had genuinely settled into a familial kind of love, and she felt no jealousy or regret—only sorrow to think of how brief Henry and Kat's life together would be and to know how difficult all of this surely had to be for both of them.

With Henry and Kat gone, Amala was able to sit with Paulina and her parents and express her own shock and horror that hadn't yet begun to settle in. She needed to talk about her feelings, and she was grateful for the support and compassion—and perfect empathy—of these people who loved her and cared for her more than anyone else.

Soon after Amala had gone to her room for the night, she answered a knock at her door to see Lekha standing there with beautiful, brightly colored fabrics draped over her arms. "Mr. Henry asked that I bring these to you. He hopes you will enjoy them."

"Thank you," Amala said and motioned Lekha into the room.

They chatted comfortably while Lekha showed Amala the saris in a variety of colors, as well as choli tops and many different choices of a skirt which Lekha referred to as a pavada, and also many scarves— all of which were used together in certain ways to create ensembles. Lekha proved her insight when she said, "Because you have lived in England since your childhood and have only worn English clothes, I am happy to help show you how to wear them."

"I would be very grateful for that," Amala said.

After Lekha had shown the clothing pieces to Amala, she carefully draped them over the backs of the chairs in the room, promising she would put them away properly in the morning. From the way she spoke, it became evident that Lekha would be available to Amala as her personal maid, and Lekha seemed pleased with the change of duties now that Amala had returned, as if she preferred caring for a lady's clothing and personal needs more than serving tea. Pearl, who had once assisted both Amala and Kat, had become busier, focusing all of her attention and energy on Kat, whose needs were more complicated and likely would become more so. For that and many other reasons, Amala was glad to have Lekha as a new part of her life.

Once she was alone, Amala pressed her hands over the fine fabrics, allowing memories of India to filter into her through her fingers. She then succumbed to exhaustion and went to bed.

Amala hardly slept at all that night while she tried to accept Kat's diagnosis as a reality rather than a horrible nightmare. She also had to recount how dramatically things had changed since she'd left here. This was still her home, and in some ways she felt even more at home here with the touches of India Henry had brought with him; yet her home and her life were considerably changed, and it would take time to acclimate herself to those changes.

Chapter Ten
SISTERS

AMALA FINALLY FELL ASLEEP AT dawn and didn't awake until nearly noon, which meant she'd missed breakfast and would likely miss lunch if she didn't hurry and get dressed. She felt sure that Paulina or her mother would have peeked in on her and found her sleeping and left her undisturbed; they both had enough insight to realize she probably hadn't slept well.

Impulsively, Amala decided to wear some of her new Indian clothing, and she was grateful when Lekha came to her room to offer assistance, as if she'd been sitting in the next room waiting for evidence that Amala was awake. When Amala came right out and asked, Lekha admitted she had been reading in a comfortable chair in the sitting room adjacent to Amala's bedroom.

Lekha helped Amala with the new clothing, explaining how to drape the pieces of fabric appropriately in order to be sufficiently covered but also to wear them according to tradition. Amala loved the feel of the fabric, and she loved even more the way she felt about herself when she looked in the mirror and observed the transformation.

"Oh, you look so very lovely, memsahib," Lekha observed with enthusiasm.

"It feels very good," Amala admitted. "And again . . . you don't need to call me that."

"You said it was a lovely word to hear spoken; therefore, I will speak it at least some of the time."

"Fair enough," Amala said.

While Lekha helped Amala with her hair—insisting that she do so because it was something she enjoyed doing very much—Amala asked the woman questions about herself. Lekha loved reading very much, and the fact that she'd been given permission to read anything from the library in the house felt like a miracle to her. She also loved England and expressed great humility and gratitude for being given the opportunity to now live in this new country. In that way, Amala understood her completely. They both loved their homeland and could appreciate its beauty, but they had also both observed its many challenges and were glad to live a more peaceful life than any they would have been able to live in India, given their lack of family or money prior to being taken in by such a generous English family. Amala was glad that Lekha had been able to come here with her husband and father-in-law, which meant she had family of her own who shared her racial genetics. In that respect, Amala couldn't deny some degree of envy. It seemed Lekha had gotten the best of both worlds. Amala would have gladly taken on the work required of Lekha in order to have a fuller life. But that choice was not open to Amala, and she needed to remind herself that she had already come to terms with that.

Amala felt as if she could have talked with Lekha all day, but it was time for lunch, and she hurried off with the promise that they would continue their conversation later. In the dining room, Amala found her parents and Paulina were already seated but had not yet begun to eat. Henry was eating lunch upstairs with Kat, and Amala wondered if the fact that Kat remained in her room so much of the time was due to her pregnancy or the cancer-related pain Henry had told her about.

Paulina and Amala's parents were very complimentary about Amala's apparel, and she couldn't deny how comfortable it was in contrast to *all those corsets and petticoats*, as Henry had put it.

After lunch, Amala went straight to Kat's room. Now that she'd had some time to get used to what was happening, she felt a strong need to just be with her sister, even though it meant avoiding any talk of cancer. They had always been close, had always spent a great deal of time together. And now Amala had been gone a very long time and Kat was married. But their sisterhood had not changed, and Amala wanted Kat to know that. She also wanted to spend as much time with her sister as she possibly could without intruding upon

Kat's time with her husband. She knew that Henry was with Kat now, but she at least wanted to check in on her sister and find out when it might be a good time for them to catch up.

At the top of the stairs, Amala turned a corner and nearly bumped into Henry, who was coming from the other direction. Before either of them could even exchange a hello, she saw his eyes widen as he took in the way she was dressed, and he said, "You look . . ."

"What?" she pressed when he didn't finish.

"So . . . comfortable; at home. I was searching for the right words."

"I like it," Amala admitted, pressing her hands down the soft, blue silk she was wearing. "I want to thank you . . . for being so thoughtful. It means more than I can say."

"I think I understand," he said.

"Yes, I think you do."

"And you're welcome."

"I . . . was just going to check in on Kat," Amala said. "Is she resting? Should I wait to—"

"She's more comfortable lying down, but she's often restless. I'm certain she would enjoy your company."

"We have a great deal of catching up to do," Amala said.

"I'm certain you do." Henry smiled, and it was easy to pretend there was nothing wrong. "And since I have promised to help your father with some estate business, I will leave the two of you to gossip and giggle to your hearts' content."

Amala laughed softly at his words, mostly because she couldn't deny it was true. She suddenly felt the deprivation of being away from her sister for so long; she was surely in need of a great deal of sisterly gossip and giggling, and she had to assume Kat was as well.

Before they parted ways, Amala hurried to say something she'd wanted to say to him long before she came home, but there had been so much drama taking place. "I was so sorry to hear about Everett."

Henry looked down and heaved a deep sigh. "Yes, it was difficult. He was a very good friend to me."

"And to me," Amala said and allowed their shared memories of his part in their relationship to speak for itself.

"I still find myself wishing I could go out there and talk to him," Henry added.

"Yes, I've been feeling that way myself since I got home," Amala said.

Henry told her a little about the funeral service her father had arranged. They talked for another minute or two before Amala hurried on to Kat's room while Henry went down the stairs. She found Kat propped up with pillows, reading a book, but her face brightened to see Amala enter the room. She raved about how beautiful Amala looked in her new clothes and went on to declare that she personally didn't feel suited to the Indian clothing, but she loved seeing Amala dressed that way.

Amala sat in the middle of the bed in a way that had always been common for her and Kat, but she loved the comfort of the clothes she was wearing, recalling how her most relaxed conversations with Kat had usually occurred when they'd both been wearing their nightgowns. Kat was still wearing what she had slept in, but Amala was glad to not be wearing a corset and petticoats.

Their visit stretched all the way to teatime while Kat asked all kinds of questions about Amala's travels, and she also shared details she'd not written in letters about how she'd grown to love Henry and about their courting and getting married. Amala initially felt a little disconcerted to think of the relationship she'd once shared with Henry, but she'd come to terms with all of that and it only took a minute or two to feel completely comfortable with hearing all about the love that Kat and Henry had come to share. Amala was not at all surprised to hear Kat describe what a kind and loving man he was and how her observance of many other men in her social circles had quickly drawn her to the conclusion that she would never find a better man than Henry Beckenridge. She had been thrilled with Henry's idea to sell his home and combine his resources with those of her own family, and Amala loved hearing of how her parents had burst into joyful tears when Henry had presented the idea to them. In spite of their pleasure over Henry and Kat getting married, they had both been dreading the thought of Kat living elsewhere; even with regular visits back and forth, it just wouldn't have been the same.

Pearl brought tea to Kat's room for the two of them, along with a message from their mother for them to visit as long as Kat felt up to it. The entire family knew that the sisters would have much to talk about. Amala loved every minute with Kat as the strength of their bond was rekindled. She knew these years apart had been absolutely necessary—in ways Kat didn't know about—but Amala was glad to have now come home and to renew her sisterhood with Kat. And for now she chose not to think about how what they were sharing would be temporary. Later, when she was alone, she could cry if she felt the need. While she was with Kat, she was completely all right with following Kat's example of enjoying the present and making the most of the time they had together.

* * * *

Suppertime was drawing near when Henry went to the room he shared with Kat to see if she felt up to going to the dining room or if she preferred to have a tray brought up. Some days were more difficult than others, and he never knew exactly what to expect. However, he suspected that the bad days would become more frequent until she would never be able to leave her bed at all. But he couldn't think about that. He just had to keep moving forward, day by day, and not think about the past or the future. He could only think of the present and try to do as Kat had pleaded with him to do: make the most of what they had.

Henry knocked lightly, not certain if Amala might still be here with Kat and not wanting to intrude on their sister time. When he heard no reply he opened the door carefully and peered into the room to see that both women were asleep. They were facing each other as if they'd drifted off in the middle of relaxed conversation. Beyond that, the only thing they had in common was their bare feet. There was no similarity in their appearance or coloring, nor in the way they were dressed. Kat had changed from her nightgown into a red dress since he'd last been in the room; Amala must have helped her. He carefully closed the door and leaned against it, just taking in the sight as if it were a painting that he never wanted to forget. *Sisters*, he would have called it. And the stark contrasts in the two women made the bonds they shared all the more beautiful.

Henry didn't want to disturb them, but he knew that if he didn't remind them that supper would soon be served, someone else would do so. He sat carefully on the edge of the bed next to Kat and pressed a kiss to her face while at the same time letting his fingers comb through her golden curls. She turned to look at him and smiled, so he kissed her lips.

"Sorry to wake you," he said, "but it's nearly suppertime. Do you feel up to coming downstairs?"

He saw her shift slightly, which he'd come to recognize as an indication of her pain. He was pleased when she smiled again and said, "I would love to come downstairs. Is Amala . . ."

She paused when he pointed to the other side of the bed, and Kat turned her head to see Amala sleeping.

"Oh, my," Kat said. "The poor dear must be exhausted."

"It was a long journey to get home," he said, and didn't add that he suspected she likely hadn't slept well last night, given the news she'd received. "I'll let you wake her," Henry whispered. "I don't want to embarrass her. Would you like me to wait for you in the hall or—"

"We'll see you in the dining room," she said and kissed him again. "Let them know we're coming."

"Don't be long," he whispered close to her ear. "I've not seen nearly enough of your beautiful face today."

Kat laughed softly, and Henry slipped quietly out of the room. He wondered for a moment—as he often did—what it would be like when she was no longer here. But a moment was all he allowed himself before he forced his mind to the present and went down the stairs.

* * * *

The weeks of summer slipped by while Henry often felt as if he were an observer of his own life, looking at it somehow from the outside in. Everyone in the household was pleased—although no one more than himself—when Kat's pain seemed to have reached a plateau. She was troubled by it more some days than others, but it wasn't worsening, and she was actually getting around quite well and living a fairly normal life. Seeing Kat like this made it easier for everyone else in the family to follow her example of pretending that nothing was wrong, even though Henry couldn't forget for more than a few minutes that all of this was temporary, and he knew the other members of the family felt the same. They talked about it amongst themselves here and there when Kat wasn't present. Being united in their love and support of Kat, they had all agreed that they should express their feelings and concerns to each other when they felt the need, rather than holding them inside. And so the days became a balancing act between living life in the present—with Kat at the center—and making the most of it, pretending it could go on this way forever, while at the same time contending with feelings too frightening and horrible to comprehend. Having others who shared those feelings proved more invaluable every day, but it sometimes felt like a game of cat and mouse to make certain Kat never caught any of them expressing their grief or talking about her illness and their feelings about it.

Henry made a point of spending time alone with Kat every day. They would lounge in the library or sometimes just in their rooms, and occasionally they would walk in the gardens or even go on a picnic when the weather was fair. He knew it was important for himself—and for her—that they spend this time together. He didn't want to have any regrets in regard to his marriage in spite of—or perhaps especially because of—its brevity. And he could easily see that Kat was happier and more at ease when she was given regular doses of evidence of his love for her. The theory certainly went both ways; he felt as if he were starving for every morsel of her love and her life, and he could feel the sand running through the hourglass of her time in this world. He wanted to hold that sand securely in his hands and not let it fall, but every day he felt it slipping between his fingers while he could do nothing to stop it.

While Henry believed that his personal time with Kat was absolutely essential, he also felt it was equally important for her to spend time with her family. Her parents, her sister, and even her aunt, were all struggling with their own grief over the prospect of losing

Kat, and they all wanted to share in the present with her as much as possible. It would be ridiculous for Henry to think he could give Kat everything she needed. Every member of her family loved her and contributed greatly to her happiness. And he felt happier when he observed her father teasing her, her mother fussing tenderly over her, her aunt regaling her with tales of her adventures around the world, and he was especially pleased when Amala strengthened her with the bond of sisterhood they shared. He was quite in awe—though he figured he shouldn't have been surprised—by how integrated Kat and Amala were in their relationship and how Kat thrived on her time with Amala. Even while he gave them their deserved privacy, he often couldn't keep himself from checking on them or hovering nearby. He never eavesdropped, but he regularly overheard them caught up in girlish laughter, or sometimes he heard them crying together. He hoped that meant Amala might be helping Kat come to terms with her impending prognosis, but he didn't ask either of them about their conversations. He just gratefully put his wife into the care of her sister for a few hours every day, and he dreaded the time when they would have nothing to do but talk about all the things that had been said and done when Kat had been alive and with them.

Very few visitors came to the house. Dr. Cowell came once or twice a week, and his bedside manner was as welcome as his medical expertise. He always made Kat laugh and helped put the matters of her health into perspective. From all the evidence he could gather, the cancer growth wasn't changing much, and the baby was growing at a normal rate and everything appeared to be progressing well in regard to the pregnancy. Everyone agreed that prayers were being answered, since they all had the sincere hope that the baby would be born normal and healthy in spite of the cancer. Henry had difficulty even comprehending there would be a baby. He could admit that he found it challenging to place too much hope in that eventuality when he was so focused on wishing that Kat would somehow escape the evil menace of cancer and have a miraculous recovery. He knew that Kat's greatest hope was to give this child life before she lost her own, but Henry couldn't tell her that the idea of having a child without her around to share in that child's life just didn't hold any appeal for him at this point. He could only pray that if it turned out that way, his feelings would change and he would be given the strength to get through it. For now he simply appreciated the doctor's regular visits and how he had a way of lifting Kat's spirits.

Besides Dr. Cowell, there were only a few local people who came by to visit occasionally. These were the friends of Oliver and Viola who had no problem with the fact that they had an Indian daughter and that their household now included Indian servants. These people also appreciated the Indian cuisine that was sometimes served when they might stay for a meal. As friends of Kat's parents, they had been made aware of the cancer, but that meant they were also sworn to the household pact of not discussing it in front of Kat. Henry liked these people well enough, but he most often left the older generation to visit with them, and he was most comfortable when there was no company in the house.

In fact, it was becoming more and more evident that choosing to remain mostly isolated from the world was a character trait he shared with the family he had married into. Paulina was the exception in the way she seemed to need regular social interaction outside of the family, and she sometimes went into the village just to be among people, eat at one of the pubs, or do a little shopping. She usually took Miles or Ivy—or both—with her, and they often came back with little gifts for Kat, Amala, and Viola. And sometimes for the servants. Henry's admiration and respect for Paulina grew the more he got to know her, and he could understand why Amala had grown so close to her. She was wise and kind and confident in her own place in the world as an unmarried woman who chose to live a full and happy life, seeing only the good and handling difficulties with courage and dignity. She had much in common with Amala, and he could see that her influence on Amala had been nothing but good. And Paulina's presence in the home through this time of crisis proved to be a blessing in numerous ways. Kat always loved her time with her aunt, and Paulina had a unique knack for making Kat feel pampered and cared for.

The family all attended church together on Sundays; Kat was able to attend about half the time, although Henry knew she would gradually become less able to go out. Henry had no illusions over the kind of man the vicar really was; he'd seen for himself the evidence of this man's prejudiced and judgmental attitudes, which made his sermons on the teachings of Jesus feel nothing but hypocritical to Henry. But he couldn't refuse to attend church without appearing offensive to Kat and her parents, and he couldn't very well explain the reasons for his intense dislike for the man. So he learned to allow his mind to go elsewhere during the sermons, trying in a way to come up with his own version of how Jesus Himself might have taught— and shown by example—the principles of love and kindness to *all* people. And he secretly felt rather proud of himself to think how scandalized the vicar would be if he came to their home and saw how much the servants—both English and Indian alike—were all treated more like friends and companions. The man would be appalled! He would also be horrified with the way members of the household often wore Indian clothing while at home. The thought made Henry smile. He knew it was perhaps prideful for him to believe that Jesus would likely be offended with this man for preaching sermons that contradicted his own behavior toward his fellow men. But Henry believed it anyway.

His belief was strengthened by the fact that the entire community was aware that Kat had cancer and it was serious, but not once had the vicar or his wife come to call on the family to inquire about the situation and to see what they—or their congregation—might do to offer support. Henry knew they were blessed as a household to have everything they needed and more. But he believed in prayer, and he would have liked to think that a clergyman could offer support and compassion and urge his congregation to pray for someone in such a situation. Henry believed that if it was a person's time to go, expecting a miracle to change that would be foolish. It was more accurate that he believed prayers and faith could strengthen and sustain the people facing severe challenges. He would have liked to think of people praying for them, but as it was, he knew there were only a very few outside of the household who were, and they were the loyal friends of his new family. Still, he felt enormously blessed to be part of such a family, and he devoted a great deal of mental energy each day to counting his blessings.

As Kat's pregnancy progressed, Henry found himself more able to think of what it might be like to have a child. The baby was moving a great deal; he'd even felt the evidence himself and marveled at the miracle. With the cancerous growth not appearing to be getting any larger, and Kat's belly growing *much* larger, the baby took over his thinking and helped him be less preoccupied with the cancer. The family all took on much the same attitude, and many of the servants became caught up in the excitement of the pending arrival.

A room across the hall was cleared out, and the walls received a fresh coat of paint in a pale yellow color that offered the effect of sunlight, even on cloudy days. The room was then gradually filled with all the furnishings needed to care for a baby, and after that, little clothes and diapers and blankets began accumulating. Paulina never came back from one of her shopping excursions without bringing one more thing for the baby. All of it made the idea of a baby more real, and Kat loved to sit in the nursery in the comfortable rocking chair there and just talk about the baby. Henry knew that Kat often had Amala or her mother take out all of the little pieces of clothing so they could look at them and speculate over the joy the baby would bring to their home, and together they'd refold everything and put it back. Henry found the ritual endearing, and he could only hope and pray that the cancer had not caused problems they couldn't see or imagine, and that this baby would be born whole and strong—and that Kat would be strong enough to deliver the baby safely and not be set back by the ordeal too greatly. His fears regarding childbirth would have been inevitable even without this dreadful cancer issue intermixed with it. As it was, he felt engaged in a nearly constant battle within himself to counteract his fears by counting his blessings and focusing on the good of the present, and hoping and praying the future would offer him something worth living for.

* * * *

As the expected arrival of the baby drew ever closer, Henry became keenly aware of the shift in Kat's habits. She stopped leaving her rooms at all and rarely got out of bed for more than a few minutes at a time. Dr. Cowell had explained to Henry that most women found the final stage of pregnancy to be difficult and uncomfortable. As the baby growing inside of a woman became large enough to consume every tiny bit of space, women naturally experienced much discomfort, and often pain, and in that regard Kat's symptoms were normal. But the doctor suspected that the cancer growing in Kat likely contributed to her pain. Even though the cancer hadn't been visibly growing for a few months, there was no way of knowing what it might be doing out of view inside of Kat's body, and there was evidence that Kat experienced pain from it, even if she did well at trying to conceal it.

With the approaching birth of the baby, Henry couldn't help but grow more and more anxious over the matter. Dr. Cowell's kindness and candor in their private conversations meant a great deal to him. He would far rather feel educated and informed about Kat's condition than be kept in the dark and taken off guard. There was so much the doctor did *not* know, but he talked to Henry about things he'd personally witnessed in regard to cancer, and he also talked to him in detail about what childbirth typically entailed and how it might—or might not—be different for Kat. There was no way of knowing until it actually happened, and then the doctor admitted he would do everything in his power to help her safely through with as little pain as possible. He told Henry about some relatively new methods of helping a patient be safely unconscious during painful procedures, or if used more sparingly, it could at least help a patient remain more relaxed and less conscious of the pain. He explained that while a woman needed to be conscious enough to assist in pushing a baby out, he felt confident he could monitor her closely through the ordeal, and he promised Henry she would not suffer any more than absolutely necessary in order to bring the baby into the world. And they could only pray that the baby would be born without any ill effects from the cancer.

Henry always shared with the family a general summary of the doctor's regular reports, and he also shared them with Kat, even though she preferred not to talk about it. In this one way, Henry ignored her edict, believing she needed to understand what was happening to her own body. "We don't have to talk about it and analyze our feelings over it if you don't want to," he'd told her more than once, "but that doesn't mean you shouldn't be informed about what's going on and why. If your highest priority is giving birth to a healthy baby, then you need to know what the doctor is doing to help make that possible."

She didn't protest his reasoning, but she still had very little to say. Henry knew her well enough to know that she was likely terrified of what childbirth would be like—as any woman would be. But she had the extra complication of not knowing how this painful cancerous growth might affect the process, the level of pain, and the outcome. He did his best to reassure her that many people were praying for her, and they had to believe that everything would be all right. Every time Henry tried to offer such reassurances, he felt somewhat hypocritical. If Kat was able to safely deliver this child without too much trauma, they would all consider that a triumph. But then what? Everyone knew that cancer would take her life; they just didn't know how long before that happened or how much she might suffer before God took her home. Henry sometimes wondered whether that was gradually becoming his own version of believing that everything would be all right; when this was over and Kat was no longer suffering, would everything be all right? For her, perhaps. For him, facing that day only felt like the beginning of a long and dreary existence of attempting to make it through this life without her. But he couldn't think about that now. He had to focus on being there for his wife, and he offered frequent and fervent prayers that all would go well with the birth of this child. If something was wrong with this baby, or it didn't survive, it would surely break all of their hearts—most especially Kat's. He far preferred to imagine Kat leaving this world with the satisfaction of having left a part of herself behind. And Henry wanted that too. If he couldn't have Kat, then he at least hoped God would be merciful enough to leave him a child that would be living, breathing proof of the love they'd shared and the fact that Kat had lived a meaningful and valuable life—however brief it might have been. And even though the priority of passing down titles and wealth was of little importance to Oliver and Viola, they had both admitted that with Kat being their only child by birth, the idea of their bloodline ending with her was disheartening, to say the least. For that and many other reasons, they were all praying the baby would arrive safe and strong.

Kat's labor began on a rainy, autumn afternoon. The doctor was summoned, and the maids saw to every preparation according to previous instructions. Then all they could do was wait. For the first few hours, Kat's pains were not terribly severe, and she had time between each one to relax and take deep breaths according to the doctor's instructions. Henry sat next to her and held her hand, trying to remain positive, talking about how wonderful it would be to have a baby in their lives and teasing her about ridiculous names they might give the child, which would always make her smile. Amala and Viola were also nearby, offering support but allowing Henry his moments of privacy with his wife. But as Kat's pains became more intense and closer together, Henry was sent away—as he'd been forewarned would happen—to wait downstairs with Oliver and Paulina. While a part of him longed to remain with Kat, he couldn't deny his relief in not having to be in the room and witness her suffering, wondering if something awful might happen and she might not even come through alive. He was well aware that even women without cancer sometimes didn't survive childbirth, and the very idea made him ill. He had accepted it was a possibility that he'd shared his final communication with Kat in this world, but he didn't think he could bear to be present and witness whatever might be happening.

They chose to wait in the library, since it had larger, more comfortable couches and it was closer to the stairs that went up to the room where Kat was undergoing an ordeal that Henry couldn't even imagine. A light supper was brought to the library for them, but Henry couldn't eat in spite of all of Paulina's encouragement. Her presence kept his mood more light and positive than he felt sure it would have been without her, and he was grateful for that. Oliver was mostly somber and quiet. Henry knew all of this was very difficult for both him and Viola, even though they'd both been incredibly brave and stout over the whole thing. They likely shared a great deal of grief together privately, and they'd admitted that their dreams of becoming grandparents had never included the complications of Kat's condition, and the knowledge that their daughter was dying. Henry had never imagined becoming a father to be complicated by such drama. But he had no regrets. He'd married Kat for all the right reasons and had given her his whole heart in every way he knew how. She was kind and remarkable, and he wouldn't trade away anything of what they'd shared, in spite of the extreme challenges. The fact that marrying her had made him a part of the most wonderful family he'd ever known was an added bonus that he considered nothing less than a miracle. He was grateful beyond his ability to express to know that even when Kat finally left them, he would always be a part of the family and that their love and acceptance of him was no less than his was of them. They would be able to help each other through this, whatever happened, even if none of them could comprehend at this point how getting through such a loss might even be possible.

The evening turned to night, with a maid occasionally coming through the open doorway to offer a brief update, which mostly consisted of telling them that according to the doctor, labor was progressing normally and Kat was doing all right. Oliver and Paulina eventually stretched out on two of the couches with blankets and pillows that a maid had brought to the room earlier. But Henry couldn't relax. Sometimes he could sit for a while, but he never could have slept. More often he was prone to pacing and wringing his hands, wondering if he would ever see his precious Kat alive again, wondering if their child would survive this ordeal and be born without any kind of deformity. Each time his mind wandered into fear, he fought to battle that fear with prayer, trying sincerely to trust that God knew the plan for Kat's life—and his own—as well as that of this child. Without that belief he felt certain he would surely lose his mind. Overcome with exhaustion but too distressed to get any rest, he mostly sat with his head in his hands, trying very hard to remain positive and believe that his time with Kat was not yet over and that all would be well with the baby.

Not long after the clock in the library had chimed four, Henry heard footsteps enter the library and shot his head up to see Amala instead of a maid.

"What?" he demanded, bolting to his feet.

He didn't say it loudly, but Paulina and Oliver both sat up, which meant they'd either been awake or only dozing lightly.

Henry saw tears in Amala's eyes and undeniable strain in her expression, but he couldn't tell if it was joy and relief in her countenance or if she had something unthinkable and grievous to report. He held his breath, grateful she didn't hesitate another moment before declaring, "Kat is fine; the baby is fine."

Henry fell back into the chair, made dizzy by the assault of relief. He silently thanked God while Oliver and Paulina laughed and embraced each other tightly. Henry looked up again at Amala when she added, "It *was* very difficult for her." Oliver and Paulina both paused in their joy to listen. "But Dr. Cowell was wonderful, and it's his hope that this will not set her back too terribly much." Amala nodded at Henry. "You can go up now." She turned to the others. "And you can see Kat and the baby in an hour or so, the doctor said. If you want to rest some more, I'll come and get you."

Henry hurried out of the room, barely muttering a thank-you to Amala over his shoulder before he fled down the hall and up the stairs, pausing a long moment outside the bedroom door to catch his breath and steady his composure. It was over, and Kat was still alive. For now, nothing else mattered.

Henry entered the room timidly, where Doctor Cowell greeted him with a smile, declaring in a soft voice, "Your wife is a brave, strong woman, Henry. She did remarkably well; childbirth is never easy, but you should be very proud of her." His smile broadened as he added, "You have a son, and as far as I can see, he's perfect."

Henry only nodded in response, since he could feel his composure dissipating. The doctor motioned him toward the bed, and Henry crept tentatively closer. Kat was propped against pillows, looking so pale and still that for a moment he felt some strange presage to how it might be when she died. Her lips were the same unnatural whitish hue as her face. And even though she was apparently relaxed, the strain she'd endured was readily evident. She opened her eyes as he sat on the edge of the bed and took her hand, relieved at the evidence that she was very much alive.

"My darling," he murmured and kissed her brow. "It's over."

She smiled as if she'd never been happier and slowly turned her head, drawing Henry's attention to the infant at her side, wrapped tightly in a little blanket. "He's so beautiful, Henry," Kat said, her voice weak and raspy. "He's so perfect. And he looks like you. I can see it already."

Henry could see no sign of life from the baby until an impossibly tiny hand reached up out of the blanket as if to stretch, and at the same time he heard a silly grunting sound that increased his curiosity.

He couldn't remember the last time he'd been exposed to an infant of any size, but he'd never seen a newborn, and he had no idea what to expect. He'd been so focused on Kat getting through this alive that he'd not allowed himself to ponder what this moment might be like.

"Pick him up, Henry," Kat said. "He won't break. Meet your son."

Henry leaned over to get a better look at the baby and gasped at his tiny, red face—amazingly adorable even for being wrinkled and puffy. He couldn't see anything of himself in the face, but he felt the immediate connection of fatherhood surge through him as he carefully lifted the infant into his hands, marveling at how tiny he looked and how little he weighed. He considered a ten-pound sack of flour and knew his son was definitely smaller than that. He chuckled and adjusted the baby into the crook of one arm, cradling it against his chest while he used his other hand to touch the baby's face and wispy blond hair, and those amazingly tiny hands.

"Ten perfect fingers and toes," Kat said. "I already counted them."

"He *is* perfect," Henry said, looking at Kat. "I never imagined such a miracle."

Henry saw a deep solemnity in her eyes and knew they were thinking the same thing. For all her positive attitude and his cautious skepticism, neither of them had known if this day would come, if she would be able to safely deliver a baby under the circumstances. But it had happened, and it *was* a miracle. No words were needed for both of them to acknowledge that fact, but Kat smiled and said lightly, "O ye of little faith."

Henry smiled in return, saying simply, "Point taken." He couldn't deny that Kat's faith was an inspiration to him, and her determination to give this child life—no matter what cancer might be doing to her body—made him agree completely with the doctor: his wife was a brave, strong woman.

Henry sat next to Kat on the bed and leaned against the pillows at her side so he could continue to hold the baby and they could admire him together. They had rarely discussed possible names for the baby, but now that he had arrived—a new living and breathing human being—they agreed it didn't seem right for him not to have a name. It was Kat's strong opinion that he should be named after his father, who had been given *his* father's name.

"It's a fine name," Kat said. "Henry George Beckenridge . . . and he shall be the third."

"It's a big name for such a tiny baby," Henry said.

"You do realize you were a baby when *you* received the name," Kat said with a little laugh. He could tell she was completely worn out and sleepy, but she was determined to get acquainted with her son before she rested.

"I *do* realize that," Henry admitted with a chuckle. "But how do we distinguish him from me? My father went by George, so it was easy, but this little man doesn't look like a George to me."

"I should like to call him Harry, a respectable form of the name Henry. And I think it suits him well."

"I think I agree with you," Henry said, attempting to comprehend the entire spectrum of how his life had just been altered permanently. He was a father, and this child would be taking his name and changing the lives of everyone who would have the privilege of knowing him. He refused to think of Kat leaving him to raise this child alone; such thoughts could wait for another day. Little Harry was surrounded by family who loved him already, and Henry would make certain he had a good life and that he wanted for nothing—most especially love.

"Harry it is," Kat declared and let out one of her girlish giggles that he found so endearing. "I can't believe how darling he is."

"With such a beautiful mother," Henry said and kissed the top of Kat's head, "how could he be otherwise?"

"But he looks like you."

"If you say so," Henry said and chuckled as Harry grunted and stretched his arms again, his little face contorting in a way that was adorably comical. Henry absorbed the moment into his spirit, taking the entire experience deep into himself, wanting to hold on to this memory forever. In that moment, life had never been more perfect. He only wished it could last.

Chapter Eleven
KATARINA'S WISH

WITHIN A DAY IT BECAME evident how popular Harry would become in the household. His grandparents were beside themselves with joy, as was Paulina. The absence of children in her own life seemed to be soothed by her admission that she'd never felt such joy over being a part of this child's life right from the beginning. It seemed likely that Harry might be the one to help soothe her wanderlust, and she was likely to spend a great deal more time at home in the future. The maids who had personal contact with Kat and the baby fussed over little Harry as if he were a prince, but it was Amala who took to him in a way that seemed to prove even further that she was a sister to Kat in any and every possible way. Everyone wanted to hold the baby, and he was rarely not in the arms of one family member or another, but it was Amala who instinctively seemed to know exactly what the baby needed. No one would ever have guessed at her lack of experience in caring for a baby. While Kat struggled with the pain and exhaustion of her recovery, Amala oversaw the care of both her sister and the baby with great finesse. The nanny they had carefully hired a couple of weeks earlier was on hand with solid knowledge and experience in caring for infants, but it was Amala who loved Kat and had a keen sense of her sister's needs, and that sense had apparently flowed over into an uncanny awareness of the baby's needs. Henry never felt unwelcome or pushed aside from being with Kat and Harry as much as time and practicality permitted, but he quickly came to depend on Amala to see that his wife and son were well cared for. They had servants aplenty at their disposal, but it was Amala who knew exactly what to ask for and when. And his gratitude for her place in their lives grew greater each day.

* * * *

The passing of weeks made it evident that Kat was not bouncing back from childbirth the way most women did. She remained pale and weak and barely able to get out of bed with assistance for a few minutes here and there. She insisted she was not in much pain, but Henry suspected she'd become accustomed to a certain degree of pain; either that or she was lying in an attempt to be brave. Dr. Cowell told Henry it was probably a little of both. While the cancerous growth had not visibly changed much in months, the doctor suspected more and more from her symptoms that it was likely spreading inside of her body where they couldn't see it. They had been blessed to not have it adversely affect her pregnancy, and they were all keenly aware of the miracle of Harry's existence. But bearing a child had taken its toll on Kat, and it seemed that in her weakened state the cancer was quickly taking over.

The family all tried to continue on as they had before—not talking about the cancer in front of Kat unless she chose to bring it up, which happened rarely. But they were all concerned, and the inevitable seemed to be creeping ever closer and increasingly beyond their control. It came up in conversation often when Kat was not present, but more and more there was nothing to say that hadn't been said many times already. Kat was dying and they all knew it. None of them wanted her to suffer, but neither did they want to lose her. It seemed that both were inevitable.

The great light in the midst of this unspeakable heartache was little Harry. With the perfect innocence of his new life, he radiated a glow of hope and happiness that helped them all keep perspective. He also kept them all gratefully distracted from Kat's worsening health. If Kat was awake, the baby was with her, and while she slept each member of the family took turns holding him, often joking that he rarely if ever was not in someone's arms, and he would become so accustomed to sleeping while being held that getting him to sleep in his own bed eventually might prove impossible. But nobody cared. Holding Harry, whether awake or asleep, was a soothing balm for all of them.

A wet nurse had to be hired to feed Harry when it quickly became evident Kat wouldn't be able to do so. But she was a kind, sensitive woman who fit nicely into the household, as did the nanny, who was always on hand to help but never intrusive on the family's desire to care for the baby as much as possible and to give Kat every opportunity to spend time with her son.

As the weather became colder, Henry reverted somewhat reluctantly to his English style of clothing. He couldn't dispute that the fabrics and layers of a waistcoat—and a jacket or coat when going out—as well as the typical boots he wore, were more practical for English winters. Even in the house, every room had a slight chill unless fires were kept blazing in every fireplace, and remaining in close proximity to them was preferable. Still, he preferred the change in season in England, which was more dramatic than that of India. The summer heat of India had meant always feeling sweaty, and even the cooler season there had never been dramatically different. Here in England there was a vast difference between summer and winter, and Henry liked it. He especially liked autumn and spring, when the transitions between seasons were taking place. The changes suited him, keeping a variety in his life that spoke to his spirit.

Henry noticed that Amala too reverted to her English clothing as the weather got colder, although it was impossible not to notice that she was forgoing any corsets or enormous petticoats beneath her dresses, and he liked the way she was choosing to remain more comfortable, which seemed to correlate with how she'd become more serene and at peace with simply being who she was, apparently not caring nearly as much as she once had that she was so different in appearance from the rest of her family.

The Indian servants in the household had trouble adjusting to the cold, even though it was now their second winter in England. But apparently they'd figured out—with the help of English servants in the household with whom they'd become friends—how to wear a layer of warm underclothing beneath the traditional Indian fare, which helped them remain comfortable. Henry noticed that Amala sometimes did the same. In fact, he never knew which style of clothing she would appear in each morning, which seemed to represent her love of both sides of her heritage and her desire to express herself accordingly.

The winter cold encouraged even more solitude and isolation, but since Henry loved his new home and the people with whom he shared it, he didn't mind. He went riding occasionally, or walking in the garden, in order to get some fresh air. And he was grateful for the wealth he'd been blessed with that made it possible for servants to regularly take a wagon into town to acquire needed supplies. He became more and more comfortable with this lifestyle that combined his love for both of the countries that had so greatly influenced his life. And since no one came to visit who didn't respect and appreciate the unique atmosphere of their home and their blended family, the entire situation settled in quite nicely.

If not for Kat's deteriorating health and the ever-present cloud of inevitability of her life drawing to a close, Henry would consider life as close to perfect as a man's life could be. Every day he thanked God for all he and his family had been blessed with, and he begged God to be merciful with Kat and all of those who loved her and were grieving over the prospect of her loss and the daily evidence that it was drawing closer. Henry came more and more to appreciate and respect the principle of accepting God's will and trusting that He and only He knew what was best. Henry wouldn't want the responsibility of determining when it was the right time for Kat to go. He had moments when he saw evidence of her increasing pain, and he wanted to see it end, if only so that he could know she was no longer suffering in any way. There were other moments when she was doing better and he couldn't imagine life without her and he desperately wanted her to never leave him. So he did his best to put the matter in God's hands and prepare himself to accept the end when it came and to gracefully endure the dreadful anticipation, day by day.

The family had developed a comfortable routine with Kat, where they each had their time with her every day, sharing in her company and helping her with whatever she needed. Servants were on hand for certain things, but the family was committed to taking on the greatest responsibility of caring for Kat and for little Harry. The baby was rarely not in Kat's room, so that she could enjoy him whenever she felt up to it. But for those who spent time with Kat every day, her deterioration was becoming more and more evident. Dr. Cowell came two or three times a week, monitoring her closely and teaching the family about the body's natural process of death and how to appropriately give Kat the medication available to help ease her pain as much as possible. There were times when Kat didn't want the medicine; she wanted to be awake and able to talk to her loved ones and enjoy her baby—who would always make her light up in spite of her persistent pain. But she always reached a limit when she would ask for the medicine, knowing it would make her sleepy and ease her suffering.

As winter settled in fully, with bitter cold winds and occasional snow, Kat was sleeping with the aid of the medicine far more than she was awake. Spending time with Kat had now become more an exercise of simply being in the room and watching her sleep. Still, Henry found some peace in that. Just observing the evidence of her breathing soothed him. And strangely enough, the evidence of her increasing thinness and pallor helped him feel a little more prepared each day to be able to let her go. He pondered how it might be to lose a spouse very quickly to an illness or accident that offered little or no warning. In such a case, the grief would surely be overwhelming and consuming, and that kind of adjustment seemed impossible in his mind. But to lose a spouse—or any loved one—slowly to disease in this way was an entirely different experience. He had grieved deeply at his first awareness of the disease, then later as he'd struggled to accept that it would take her life. He had been warned by the doctor—who had become as much a trusted friend in this journey as he was a wise medical advisor—that the actual shock of death could likely send loved ones into a new level of grief, but it generally tended to be briefer and easier to overcome for people who had been coming to terms with their grief for many weeks or months prior to the death.

Henry prayed more than he ever had in his life, and as a result he felt closer to God than ever before. In his darkest moments he could always eventually find a glimmer of light in an inexplicable warmth that soothed him from the inside out. He knew in his heart that this was God's plan for Kat and that her spirit would live on in a better place. He found a peace with this knowledge that made it possible to believe he could let her go and find happiness again being a father to their child and a part of her family as a brother, a son, and a nephew. Still, he had many moments when his grief felt raw and unbearable.

He couldn't fathom his life without Kat in it and didn't know how he could even function without her there at the center of everything— even if that meant his simply being at her side while she remained mostly oblivious in medicated slumber. As long as she kept breathing, as long as he could put his fingers to her throat and feel her pulse, he felt connected to her, and his love for her filled him. The very idea of her breath and heartbeat leaving her body, of having her turn cold and being put into the grave, sometimes made him feel physically ill.

Henry continued to vacillate between peace and acceptance and a horrifying grief too intense to manage. He simply needed to believe that with time the peace would become stronger than his grief and he would be able to move forward. He often shared his feelings with the family and found they were each having similar feelings in regard to their own relationships with Kat. Henry knew that marriage constituted a relationship that was not comparable to any other, but that didn't diminish his respect for the fact that her parents and sister—and even her aunt, who had not physically been present much of the time—all had their own unique and powerful bond with Kat, and this was difficult for all of them in different ways. The commonality they all shared was their love for Kat and their grief over losing her. But it was a commonality that strengthened their family bonds, and he was grateful beyond words to have been given the privilege to be part of this family and to not be facing this dreadful thing alone. More than once he'd tried to imagine how it might have been if his own mother was still alive and he'd taken his bride to live in the home of his upbringing. The thought made him shudder. There wouldn't have been even a degree of the love and support and comfort he'd found here at Willenbrock House.

On an especially cold afternoon, the wind wreaked havoc outside with flurries of snow that were not coming down in quantity but were made vicious by the wind's influence. Henry chose wisely to stay in and spent the morning with Kat, even though there was very little evidence that she was still alive. In fact, he had noticed the last few days that Viola and Oliver would come to briefly check on Kat for a few minutes; they'd hold her hand and kiss her cheek, but they never stayed long. He knew it was difficult for them to sit with her when she rarely showed any sign of life and when she did it was generally tainted by evidence of pain. Paulina's visits to Kat were even more rare, but for all her devotion to Kat, she had never shared the ongoing closeness with her that the other family members did. Therefore, it was Henry and Amala who each spent significant time with Kat each day, and there were some maids especially devoted to Kat and Amala who would take shifts at other times to be certain Kat was never left alone and to notify him or Amala if anything changed.

Henry held his son and talked to him and played with him until Harry became cranky due to hunger and needing his morning nap. The nanny took him, and Henry knew that the baby would be kept in the nursery for the remainder of the day; unless Kat specifically asked to see him, Harry was mostly kept away since Kat had requested it when she'd felt her own symptoms worsening.

Henry sat in an increasingly familiar location on a chair he often moved close to Kat's bedside so that he could just sit and hold her hand. Sometimes he kissed it or held it against his face; sometimes he talked quietly to her, not certain if his words would reach past her sleep and into her mind, but he felt certain it was therapeutic for him. He verbally shared memories of how they had first become friends and how their feelings had grown and changed into something that had taken him completely by surprise. He told her how her love had healed many wounds inside of himself and had helped him come to terms with things he'd not even shared with her.

A maid brought lunch to Kat's room for him, and he thanked her before he sat at the little table by the window to eat. He'd been eating lunch in this room for weeks now, alone with Kat while she slept; and he tried not to think about how she had come to a point where her very minimal appetite had diminished down to eating nothing at all. He knew death couldn't be far away due to the simple fact that a body needed nutrition to survive and she was getting none. She rarely even took a drink of water and insisted that the smallest amount of broth or diluted wine made her nauseated.

After Henry had finished his lunch, he sat again beside Kat, holding her hand but remaining silent now while his thoughts sifted through memories and fears. He wasn't surprised when Amala came to the room, since she always did after lunch, which was her usual time with her sister. He generally left her alone, but he felt hesitant to leave—or perhaps simply incapable of finding the strength to stand up and walk out of the room.

"May I have just a few more minutes before I go?" he asked quietly.

"Of course," Amala said. "Do you prefer to be alone or—"

"No," he said. "Please stay. She's hardly stirred all morning. I think it's getting close."

"I've had the same thought," Amala said, sitting exactly opposite Henry on a chair that had been placed on the other side of the bed. She took Kat's other hand. "I feel so many thoughts and emotions bubbling up inside of me, but there is nothing to say that we haven't all said so many times before."

"Yes," Henry said. "I know exactly what you mean."

They sat together in silence while the clock in the room audibly ticked off seconds that stretched into many minutes, until Amala asked, "Are you going to be all right, Henry?" He looked up at her, feeling confused, or perhaps the full meaning of the question was too much to take in. "If the question is too personal or you don't want to talk about it, I understand. But I still have to ask."

Henry thought about the question for another minute or more. "Do I have a choice? I have to be all right. The only other choice is . . . what . . . to spend my life in misery . . . become a drunk or a burden to my family?"

"That would never happen; it's not in you to become that kind of person."

"I appreciate your faith in me, but I'm not sure I share your confidence. However, thanks to the blessing of marrying Kat, I have a wonderful family. And I have a son who needs me. I have plenty to live for and many reasons to strive to be the kind of man Kat would want me to be. Therefore, I *must* be all right."

"And I believe you will be, but that doesn't mean it will be easy."

Henry looked at Kat's face. "No, it won't be easy." He sighed with all the breath that was in him. "Although I'm well aware that it's not necessarily more difficult for me than it is for you or your parents. Perhaps Paulina will not be as personally affected, but it's still very difficult for her."

"I know we all share a different kind of bond with Kat," Amala said, "but the relationship between a husband and wife is surely something that makes this more difficult to bear."

"Maybe," was all Henry could say. Who was he to judge the level of difficulty from one person's grief to another? Perhaps he was closer to Kat in many ways, but he'd not known her nearly as long as Amala. And her parents were just that—her parents. Now that he was a father himself, he couldn't even imagine how this must be for them.

Kat began to stir, and both Henry and Amala leaned closer to her, eager for any interaction they might have during these increasingly rare moments when she was awake. He was glad that Amala understood his desire to stay, and he expressed to her that she should also be there. In spite of their previous schedules of each spending time alone with Kat, her condition had changed dramatically, and it would be absurd to think that Kat might conveniently be conscious at times that might adhere to their schedule.

"Hello, my darling," Henry said, using his free hand to brush her hair off her forehead so he could kiss her there. "How are you feeling?"

"Water," she said, barely audible.

Henry carefully lifted her head and put a glass of water to her lips, helping her take a few slow sips while Amala held a clean handkerchief against Kat's chin to absorb the water that didn't make it past Kat's parched lips. Henry set the glass back on the bedside table and asked, "Is that enough for now?"

"Yes," Kat said a little more clearly with her mouth moistened. "Thank you."

Henry gently guided her head back to the pillow, and Amala asked, "Is there anything we can get for you?"

"No, I'm fine," Kat said. "Thank you."

"Are you in much pain?" Henry asked.

"Not much," Kat said. "I want to stay awake . . . for now. I'll let you know if . . . I need more . . ." She didn't finish; they all knew what she meant. "I'm so glad you're both here. You're never here . . . at the same time. I've been . . . praying . . . to talk to you . . . together . . . and you're both here."

Henry exchanged a glance with Amala that let him know she was as ignorant as he over what Kat might want to talk to them about.

"We're listening, darling," Amala said. "Just don't wear yourself out."

Kat kept her eyes closed, either too weak or still affected by the medicine that made her so sleepy. In a voice that carried an almost dreamy quality, she said, "I know it won't be long now. A part of me doesn't want to go . . . I would never choose to leave any of you . . . I hope you know that."

"Of course, darling," Amala said at the same time Henry said, "We would never doubt it."

"But my being here has come to a point where I am only keeping the rest of you from living as you should. Having my family hover in this room simply because I'm here is ridiculous." She coughed a little and asked for more water, and they repeated the procedure of moistening her mouth and throat enough for her to keep talking. Henry was amazed at how lucid she was; she'd already said more consecutive words than she had in several days. Another glance at Amala let him know she had noticed the same.

With Kat's head again relaxed against the pillow and her eyes closed, she went on. "I'm not worried about any of you being able to move on and be happy; I know that all of you are strong, and you all have each other. I worry least of all about Harry. He is so loved and will live a good life. I feel so much peace to see how happy and healthy he is."

She paused for so long that Henry wondered if she'd drifted back to sleep. He said quietly, "He is a great joy to all of us, and he will always be living proof of your life and your love, my darling."

He felt Kat squeeze his hand in response; then she spoke again. "There is only one thing that worries me, one thing that I need to know is taken care of before I can go." She turned her head on the pillow slightly and opened her eyes, looking directly at Henry. "There's one thing I need you to do for me, my dearest. You must promise me that you will, or I cannot leave you peacefully."

It was easy for Henry to say, "Anything, my darling Kat. You've given me such a good life and made me so very happy. I would do anything you ask of me."

"Promise me," she said.

"I promise," he stated with conviction.

Kat smiled weakly and turned her head with some difficulty to look at Amala. "I must ask the same of you, my dear sister. I cannot leave this world knowing that something very important is undone . . . unfinished; something is not right, Amala; something is not as it should be. You're my sister, my best friend, my confidant for my whole life. You must promise me . . . that you will grant me one final wish."

"I promise, dear sister," Amala said. "I promise. Anything."

Kat sighed with such obvious relief that Henry almost feared it might be her last breath, that she might leave without either him or Amala knowing what they had promised to do. He couldn't begin to imagine what it might be, but he'd meant it when he'd told her he would do anything she asked of him. Kat settled her head back so that she was looking at the ceiling but she could glance back and forth between Amala and Henry. With her eyes now open, she seemed intent on watching them both while she concluded whatever she intended to say. But rather than speaking, she used what very little strength she had to move both Henry's and Amala's hands together over the top of her belly. When she urged their hands into each other's and let go, Henry heard Amala gasp at the same time that he felt his chest go tight with a sudden inability to breath. What was she trying to say?

Henry exchanged a confused and astonished glance with Amala; then they both looked at Kat, and he still couldn't draw breath. He felt Amala attempt to pull her hand away at the same moment he was tempted to do the same, not liking the implication at all given the entire spectrum of the situation. But again Kat exerted energy from some unseen source and pressed her hands over theirs, forcing them to maintain their grasp.

"The two of you must be together," she said, glancing back and forth between them to assess their reactions. "You must be Harry's parents. You must allow yourselves to make each other happy."

Henry finally began to breathe, but it came in sharp bursts that he knew both women could hear, and he could see Amala's shoulders rising and falling to indicate a similar reaction. If either of them had any doubt over the full depth of Kat's request, it was clinched when she added, "No one could be a better mother to Harry than you, my sweet Amala. He needs you, and you need to give Harry siblings that he can grow up with, a beautiful family he can be a part of. He mustn't be alone, just as neither of you should be alone."

A sound erupted from Amala's throat that was a combination of pain and protest. She pulled her hand away from Henry's abruptly, and Kat didn't have the strength to stop her. But Kat looked at her sister with an intensity that had always been rare in Kat. She'd always been lighthearted and able to see the world through an innocent kind of wonder that could sometimes come across as naive. But there was nothing innocent or naive about the way she said to her sister, "You promised me. It's my dying wish, Amala. And you promised me."

"You cannot ask such a thing of me," Amala said, quietly but with anger, and in a way that seemed to imply she'd forgotten Henry was in the room. "How *can* you ask such a thing of me? You're asking me to marry your husband after you are dead?"

"Yes," Kat said, leaving no room for doubt. Henry leaned back in his chair, again finding it difficult to breathe. The irony and poignancy of all of this was impossible to take in.

"Well, you can't do that!" Amala said, sounding even more angry. "This is not India, where marriages are arranged."

Again Kat's strength came through in a way that Henry could hardly believe was possible, given the state she'd been in for days. "Do you think I would ask something of either of you that I believed would make you unhappy? It is quite the opposite, dear sister. If it's my dying wish for the two of you to be together; then anyone else who chooses to be critical of the marriage or look down upon you will be defying *me*. And don't think for a moment that I'm foolish enough to not know that it's right and it's what both of you would want." Henry felt startled by that last sentence, but before he could comment, she added, "When that grief you both feel over losing me settles, you will need each other, and this is what you will want. I'm giving my blessing to that end."

"What are you saying?" Henry demanded, and she turned to look at him. "You know this is what we both *want*? Since the moment I first realized I was falling in love with you, I have never thought of, or felt attracted to, *any* woman but you. Never!"

Kat coughed again, and the drama of the conversation was paused to help her sip more water before she settled back onto the pillow to continue.

"I know that, my darling," she said, taking hold of Henry's hand again. "I have never questioned your love and devotion to me. This is not an accusation. I know beyond any doubt that you have been faithful to me in every way—in your mind and in your heart. I've never questioned it. But . . . before you fell in love with me . . . before Amala left . . ."

Again Henry found it difficult to breathe, and a quick glance let him know Amala was suffering from the same ailment. "What are you saying?" he asked his wife, looking firmly into her eyes.

Henry was naturally surprised by the way Kat laughed softly and again closed her eyes, perhaps because she was weak and tired, or perhaps because it was easier to say what she wanted to say without looking at him. Maybe both. "I know the two of you believed you were being very clever, sneaking off together to be alone, thinking that the rest of us wouldn't give it a second thought. But I knew. We all knew. How could we not with the way the two of you would steal glances at each other every chance you got, thinking we were oblivious?"

With Kat's eyes closed, Henry looked at Amala a little more boldly, validated by the shock and dilemma in her expression that mirrored his own reaction. He felt foolish for having believed he'd been able to conceal what had once been such powerful feelings for Amala. He felt guilty for having kept it a secret from Kat all this time when she'd always known. And he felt utterly terrified to consider facing up to everything that had happened in order to even consider keeping the promise he'd just unwittingly made to his dying wife.

Henry was glad when Amala spoke, and he felt complete empathy for the reasons her voice was trembling. "Are you telling me," she asked Kat, "that you knew all along? That Mother and Father knew?"

Kat opened her eyes and looked at her sister. "Of course we knew, dearest. It's one of the reasons we were all so upset over your declaration that you would never marry. When things seemed to be going well for you and Henry—in spite of the secrecy—we all hoped you would change your mind. We wanted to tell you we would support you in your decision, and we would have eventually when we felt the time was right, but Father felt we should give you time to come to terms with it, and then . . . you just . . . left. And we could all tell that Henry was heartbroken." Kat turned to look at him. "You did well at keeping it concealed," she said, "but I could still see it in your eyes. We all could. And we were all so grateful that you continued to be a part of our family."

Again Kat closed her eyes, but not before she made certain she had a firm hold on each of their hands at her sides. Her voice sounded weaker now that she'd said her piece, which was apparently moving toward a conclusion. "Amala," she said, "I want you to know that I didn't try to fall in love with Henry." Tears leaked from the corners of her closed eyelids. "In fact, I tried very hard not to. I cried more than I want to admit over the matter. I talked with Mother and Father a great deal about my feelings. In the end they told me you had made your decision quite clear and I needed to follow my heart. They also told me they knew Henry was a man of deep integrity and that he would not love me falsely or betray your love in any way."

Kat opened her eyes again but not as widely. She looked at Amala with great effort. "I need you to know that a day did not pass when I didn't feel that you had sacrificed your own happiness for mine, the same way you had protected me when your parents were killed, and the way you've protected me all of my life since. But I believe now that this is how it was always meant to be." She squeezed Amala's hand, and Henry noticed that both women were crying, with their gaze locked firmly. "Now it is your turn to be fully happy, my dearest sister."

"I *am* happy," Amala insisted. "It is only losing you that breaks my heart. I have made peace with all of that."

"I know," Kat said. "But you must trust me when I tell you there is a kind of happiness that you've never known, and that is my last wish for you." She turned her head slowly and with effort to look at Henry, and he could tell she was becoming more lost in her pain and her burst of strength was now depleted. "Love her, Henry, the way you have loved me. Let her be a mother to our son, as she should be. You mustn't be alone, my darling. You're far too sensitive and tender a man to be left alone for so much of your life. I must know you have someone, and no one but Amala could ever understand the beautiful mixture of life and culture that makes you who you are."

Henry couldn't speak. He too was now crying. And what could he say? He still hadn't recovered from the shock of everything she'd just told them. Kat sighed deeply, and peace washed over her countenance as she settled her head back into the center of the pillow and closed her eyes. "Now you both know how I feel, and I will come back to haunt you if you disappoint me." The hint of a smile touched her weak lips. The smile faded, and she said in a voice that was severe in spite of becoming raspy, "Mother and Father already know my wish; they are completely in agreement that it's the right thing. And on the chance that I was never able to tell you how I feel, it's all in writing . . . a part of my will."

"What?" Henry blurted before he could think that it might be better to remain silent. He felt suddenly more angry than sad, even though he knew that expressing anger to Kat at such a time would be completely inappropriate and something he would regret. Still, he had to say, "You left us to each other in your will?"

Kat was unaffected by his appalling question. With perfect calm she said, "Something like that. Could you get my medicine? The pain . . ." That seemed to be the last word she could muster the strength to say, but she grimaced, and he knew she was hurting a great deal more than she'd been letting on. Her determination to say what she felt the need to say had given her an illogical measure of strength, but it was all used up now. She'd stated her edict, and she would now go back into her oblivion, leaving him and Amala to deal with the repercussions.

With Amala's help, Henry gave Kat the usual spoonful of foul-tasting liquid that eased her pain and helped her sleep. Another drink of water followed before he carefully guided her head back to the pillow, where she became so still so suddenly that she already looked dead. If not for the sound of her shallow breathing, he might think that her declarations had come with her dying breath. But even if she still held on for days, he had a feeling she'd spoken the last of anything significant she might say. She'd obviously had serious conversations about her final wishes with her parents. She looked serene and at peace. Henry was glad for that; he only wished that he could feel anything close to the same.

Since it was typically Amala's time to sit with Kat, he pressed a kiss to Kat's forehead and hurried from the room without uttering a single word to Amala. He could feel the anger inside of him growing, even though he knew it was only masking a barrage of other emotions that he didn't know how to face or deal with. He only knew that he had to be alone until he could find a way to gain some control over what Kat had just thrown in his face—on her deathbed, no less. He rushed down the back stairs, wanting to avoid running into anyone in the family, and hurried out to the carriage house, ignoring the bitter cold and the fact that he'd not even bothered to grab a coat. He was grateful to find no one there, which wasn't unusual since Everett had died. The stable hands who had taken over his tasks never put the time or care into their work that Everett had.

Henry climbed into a carriage that was never used, the same one he'd once sat in with Amala many times while they'd talked and speculated over a future together. The irony didn't fully sink in until he was seated. After she'd first left, he'd come here to feel close to her, and then it had just become a habit when he'd wanted to be alone. He'd rarely come here since he'd married Kat and had become completely comfortable in his new home, and with his wife. Now, memories of being here with Amala wreaked torment and confusion, given the shock that Kat had just dealt him. He didn't know what to do or how to feel. He could only bury his head in his hands and cry. And once he got started, all of the tears he'd been trying to keep in check while he'd watched his precious Kat wasting away now rushed into the open like a tidal wave that threatened to obliterate everything in its path.

* * * *

Amala was so stunned and overcome with a torrent of roiling emotion that she could hardly breathe, let alone move, after Henry had left the room. When she knew for certain that Kat was deep in medicated slumber, she allowed herself to let out a gasp of harsh breath that carried a sob into the open on its wake. Another came, and then another, until she dropped to her knees beside Kat's bed, keeping her sister's hand tightly in hers while she pressed her face into the bedding and cried the way she'd wanted to for weeks now. She'd been unable to fully feel the grief surrounding her over Kat's impending death, but now everything had become so much more complicated and difficult in ways that Kat could never understand. Or could she? Kat had admitted to being able to see right through Amala's attempt to hide her feelings for Henry. What else had Kat observed? She projected herself as always seeing the best in people and situations, to the point of what had appeared to be a degree of naiveté. She had always insisted on not wanting to talk about things that were sad or difficult, and that had been interpreted as perhaps being somewhat unobservant or superficial. But it was evident that even though Amala likely knew Kat better than anyone, she'd underestimated her—and even misread her. And now Kat was dying. Now there was no opportunity for long conversations where they could sort out and analyze all of this.

Amala felt mortified to realize that Kat and her parents had known of her feelings for Henry all along. Had they purposely encouraged the two of them to go for walks in the garden, or to spend uninterrupted hours in the library or the carriage house, or to go riding? Probably! Had they truly been hoping that she and Henry would have married? Had they not shared her concerns about the difficulties it would cause? Those inevitable difficulties had not changed with the passing of time or the change of circumstances. She had worked very hard to come to terms with her feelings for Henry. And now . . . *now* . . . Kat had peeled away all masks and veils and pretending. It was too much! It was just too much!

Amala's sobbing finally subsided into a numb kind of shock, as if Kat had already died. She lay down on the bed near her sister, as she often did, and wished that she could sleep, wanting the same oblivion Kat was presently experiencing. But her thoughts raced in circles and her heart frequently quickened its pace, making it difficult to breathe deeply.

When tea was brought to the room for her, Amala thanked the maid and picked at the offering a little, mostly just wanting it to appear that she had eaten something and enjoyed her tea. She found herself staring into a nearly empty cup of cold tea, wondering how to cope with losing her sister, wondering how to face her parents with her newfound knowledge that they'd been aware all along of feelings she'd tried so hard to pretend didn't exist. And how would she ever come to terms with the promise she'd given her sister, even if she hadn't known what she'd been promising at the time? She knew that Kat had planned the conversation carefully; she'd purposely led them into making the promise before telling them what it was, likely knowing that neither of them would have ever dreamed she would ask such a thing and that they would be willing to do anything to appease her on her deathbed.

Amala wondered where Henry was and what he was doing. If this was difficult for her, she couldn't imagine how he must be feeling. She didn't question to any degree that he had appropriately let go of his romantic feelings for her before he'd married Kat. She had felt the conviction of that in his letters, and she had certainly seen it in his eyes since she'd come home. He loved Kat as a husband should love his wife. Amala was a sister to him now, a friend. After all they had gone through to come to this point, how could they ever go back? What had once felt so wonderful and perfect now felt entirely wrong.

Amala heard the door opening behind her and straightened her back. A maid would have knocked lightly before entering. She steeled herself to face her mother or father, wondering what she should say, or if she should say anything yet before talking to Henry about how they should handle this. She hoped it might be Paulina, who was her closest confidante. She sincerely hadn't expected it to be Henry until she heard him say, "I was hoping you'd still be here."

Amala's heart began to pound at the sudden realization that she now felt completely awkward and uncomfortable about even being in the same room with him. She heard the door close and set down her teacup but remained as she was. He walked slowly past her and stood at the window, his back to her. Silence echoed around them, making the awkwardness more evident. Amala turned to look at Kat, seeking evidence that she was still breathing while she slept deeply. The subtle rise and fall of the sheet covering her chest assured Amala that she'd not left them yet.

Amala wondered if she was supposed to speak, but minutes of thinking brought no words to mind that she dared utter. Henry finally said, "I don't know what I'm supposed to do with this, Amala. I don't know how I'm supposed to feel."

"I don't think how you're *supposed* to feel is the issue, Henry. It's how you really feel that matters."

"I don't know that, either."

"Nor do I," Amala admitted, "other than feeling like a fool for believing that no one would have figured it out."

"Yes, there is that," Henry said sourly.

Amala tried to think sensibly and put some sound reason into the situation. "As I see it, Kat is nearing the end, and that's what we need to focus on now. We can discuss the other when all of this is . . . behind us."

"That sounds very practical," Henry said in a slightly acrid tone that reminded her of the times when she'd been trying to convince him they should not court publicly, let alone be married. "You've always been very good at being practical . . . sensible." It almost sounded like an insult.

"I don't know how else to be . . . especially now. Losing Kat this way is likely one of the most awful things that will ever happen to any of us. If I allow myself to think too much about the rest right now . . . I will completely fall apart. And I can't. I need to be strong. My parents need to be strong. And so do you."

She heard him sigh loudly. "Yes, I probably do." He sighed again. "But I do believe your parents have to know . . . that Kat told us . . . what she wishes. If she's already told them, they'll be wondering if it's up to them to tell us . . . that they knew . . . that they know . . . that we know."

"At any other time the way you said that might have been funny."

"Maybe," he said and moved toward the door without having even looked at her. "I'll see you at supper; I think we just need to tell them."

Amala couldn't bear the thought of him leaving the room without her knowing just a little bit more about his frame of mind. She heard the door open and hurried to ask, "Do you intend to keep your promise to Kat?"

"How in heaven and earth do you expect me to answer that question now?" he retorted, clearly angry in spite of keeping his voice hushed. "Do *you*?"

"Forgive me for asking," Amala said. "It's as I already told you . . . not the time to be concerned over how to handle the situation."

Amala heard the door close and felt certain he would have slammed it if not for Kat sleeping in the room, although Amala suspected Kat would sleep through anything with the amount of medicine she'd been given. Amala turned again to look at her sister and felt a distinct desire to trade places with her. It was far from the first time she'd thought it. Kat had a husband and a son, and she didn't have the challenge of being a dark-skinned woman in a society of light-skinned people. For Amala to leave this world, having lived a good life and experienced so much, would not have been nearly so tragic. And now with Kat's edict hanging over her—and Henry—she wanted all the more to be the sister with cancer, the one who could gracefully leave this world and leave all of her problems behind.

Chapter Twelve
WITHOUT COLOR

WITH ALL HER SOUL, AMALA dreaded going down to supper. But she knew it had to be faced; they just had to get all of the secrets out in the open and stop pretending about everything. Still, the very idea felt terrifying, and she knew that if she felt terrified, Henry surely did too.

Lekha came to sit with Kat, and Amala updated her regarding when Kat had last taken her medicine. Lekha reported that she'd just come from the nursery and that Viola and Paulina had been spending time with Harry there, and he was doing fine. Amala was glad to hear that Harry was being held and cared for more by family than by servants, although she found it ironic that while she and Henry seemed to instinctively feel the need to be with Kat as her time drew closer, the others had a difficult time being with Kat at all. But they were apparently comforted by spending time with Harry. She knew that every person grieved in their own way, and she was glad for the perfect joy and innocence that Harry had brought into their home. She was also glad that Kat was never lucid long enough to really know who was with her and for how long.

Amala thanked Lekha and went to her own room to freshen up before going downstairs. She also took the time to kneel by her bed and pray, asking for strength in all they had to face and for her family members to be strengthened also. She prayed that Kat's passing would be painless for Kat and bearable for the rest of them. And she asked that this strange dilemma that had been stirred up by Kat's final wish would be sorted out according to God's will and that they would all be strengthened in dealing with that, as well.

Drawing courage, Amala went with trepidation down to the dining room, where she found everyone else already seated. As usual, her father sat at the head of the table, with her mother next to him across one corner and Paulina sitting opposite her mother. Henry sat—due to her father's request—at the opposite end of the table from her father, as the *other* man of the house. Kat's chair across the corner at his side had been empty for many weeks now, and Amala always sat across from that chair, each time mourning the fact that her sister was not there facing her, talking and laughing and adding a lightness to everything they might discuss. Kat's absence felt more stark than usual as Amala seated herself and apologized for being late.

The family engaged in minimal conversation during the first half of dinner; then Henry set his napkin next to his plate and took hold of the table with both hands, and Amala could feel it coming. He glanced at her as if to warn her; then he looked directly at her father and said, "There's something I need to say." He cleared his throat and took a deep breath. "Kat had a fairly lucid conversation with me and Amala today. I fear it could well be her last, not only because of the evidence of her growing weakness and pain, but because of what she said. I suspect she now feels that she can go in peace." He took another deep breath, and Amala sensed the expectation of her parents and her aunt. "I'm well aware that Paulina knows the truth about the situation between me and Amala prior to her leaving. But neither Amala nor I knew that the two of you"—he glanced at both Viola and Oliver but kept his gaze mostly fixed on Oliver—"knew all along what we had believed we'd been able to keep secret."

"Oh, my," Paulina said quietly and also set her napkin down. In fact, no one was eating anything at all.

Henry forged ahead, and Amala was grateful at least that he'd taken the lead and was handling this. "She also told us her final wish but made us promise to do as she wished before she told us what it was. And she told us that you were both well aware of her desires and that it's in her will."

"That's right," Oliver said, taking his wife's hand across the table. "And how do you feel about that?"

"How do I *feel?*" Henry countered, clearly angry but not speaking disrespectfully. "My wife is dying. I can't even begin to process any other circumstance beyond that. There are, however, a couple of things I want made clear, so there is no room for any misconceptions about all of this."

"Say whatever you need to say," Oliver said with a compassion in his tone that indicated he had no difficulty understanding why Henry would be so upset.

"First of all, I need you to know—all of you—that I let go of my feelings for Amala long before I married Kat. I was never divided in my love for her or my—"

"You *don't* have to tell us that, son," Oliver said, and Viola nodded in agreement with her husband. "We know you. Enough said."

Henry took a deep breath and glanced again at Amala as if to give her a silent warning before he said, "Forgive me, Amala, but I have to be completely honest with your family. Obviously there are no more secrets, and no more pretending that what happened in the past didn't happen." He turned again to look at her parents. "I feel like an absolute fool for believing you wouldn't have noticed. In no way do I wish to blame Amala or be cruel to her, but I want you to know that keeping my feelings for her a secret was her idea, not mine. I wanted to speak with you almost as soon as I met Amala. I wanted to court her, to marry her. She insisted that no one know. I still don't fully understand her reasons, but I cared for her enough to respect them. I just wanted you to know that." He pushed back his chair and rose from the table. "That's all I have to say, and I really don't have much of an appetite. I'm going to sit with my wife. If you have any other questions, I'm certain my dear sister can answer them."

Amala couldn't help but hear that tiniest bit of snideness in the words *dear sister*, as if he wished to emphasize the current state of their relationship. But she knew him well enough to know that he was far angrier than he was allowing himself to show.

Henry turned to walk away and was almost to the door before Oliver stood and said, "Henry."

"Yes," he said, and Amala glanced over her shoulder to see him face his father-in-law.

"There's something that *I* need to say, and I know I speak for your mother because we have discussed it many times." Amala hoped that Henry noticed the reminder of how Oliver and Viola considered themselves *his* parents, too. "You have been such a great blessing in our lives, son. We have never questioned your integrity nor your wholehearted commitment to our dear Katarina. As much as we love her and can't even fathom what's happening, we can't imagine how difficult it must be for you. If I were to lose my Viola, I . . ." He paused and struggled for composure. "We just want you to know that your becoming aware that we knew about you and Amala changes nothing. We love you, son; we respect you, and we're grateful to have you here with us. Whatever your future decisions might be, this will always be your home. We couldn't bear to lose you, too."

Amala glanced at Henry again to see him lift his chin, and there was a slight softening in his eyes and in his voice. "I couldn't bear to lose you either." He straightened his shoulders and added, "I believe you should send for the doctor. And perhaps when you're done here, you should each have some time with her. I could be wrong, but I don't think it will be long now."

Amala turned to look at her father, who nodded stoutly while his chin quivered and he bit his lip. Viola bowed her head and put her napkin over her mouth as if to keep from crying out. Henry left the room. Oliver sat back down. Viola wept quietly. Amala stared at the food on her plate that she'd barely touched and had no desire to eat. After long moments of silence, Paulina said quietly, "Forgive me if this is not the right time or if it's none of my business to say so, but apparently Kat's final wish has caused a great upset. Amala has shared a great deal with me, but—"

"She wants Henry and me to get married," Amala said, wanting her to know and unable any longer to bear the tension in the air. Paulina gasped before Amala continued. "Until today neither Henry nor I even suspected that any of you knew about me and Henry—except for what I had told Paulina. I believe Henry is quite upset—understandably so—to consider what Kat might have been thinking about the entire situation all this time and the fact that he never told her. She was completely kind and understanding—as one would expect—but the implications are . . . complicated and confusing at best."

"Yes, they certainly are," Paulina said with the perfect compassion she was known for—and one of the reasons Amala loved her so dearly.

Amala rose from the table as well, unable to sit there with a meal she had no intention of finishing while the tension in the room felt unbearable. They all knew the truth; there were no more secrets. But Amala had trouble reckoning with her reasons for keeping it all a secret to begin with. At the time it had all made sense to her; now she wasn't so sure she'd done the right thing. And yet, if she'd made a different choice, Kat and Henry would not have come together, and precious little Harry would not even exist. How could she feel regret when considering such things? And yet she did. She felt certain that Henry's anger was mostly *her* fault, but she didn't know how to rectify it when Kat's death was at the door.

"I need some time alone," she declared. "I'm certain we'll have plenty of time to talk about this ludicrous situation far more than any of us probably want to." Hearing her own tone of voice, she knew that Henry wasn't the only one who was angry.

* * * *

Henry had to stop twice on his way to the room he shared with Kat just to catch his breath and calm himself. He was glad to have said what he did; he couldn't live even a day under the same roof with Oliver and Viola and not have the issue out in the open, knowing what he knew now. He was afraid he might have hurt Amala, but he still didn't regret what he'd said. He'd only stated what was true, and he knew she had enough character and insight to understand, and when they were not so overwhelmed with the present drama, he knew she would forgive him. Right now he was glad to simply have that dreaded conversation out of the way, and he could only focus on one thing. Kat was dying, and he needed her to know how very much he loved her.

When he entered the room, Lekha was sitting beside Kat on the bed, holding her hand.

"I am glad to see you, Mr. Henry," she said. "I was about to call for someone to come and get you. I believe she's coming around and will soon need more medicine, but it is best if you or her sister take care of that. And I know you want to talk to her when she's awake."

"Yes, Lekha, thank you," Henry said, grateful for her kindness and insight, as well as her ability to follow his instructions carefully. She also had an endearing quality of always repeating the obvious so that he would know she *had* followed his instructions.

Lekha moved away so that Henry could take her place, sitting on the edge of the bed, taking hold of Kat's hand.

"I will be in the sitting room should you need me," Lekha said.

"Thank you," Henry replied, looking only at Kat's face. "Have someone bring the doctor directly here when he arrives."

"Yes, Mr. Henry," she said and gracefully exited the room.

Kat groaned softly and shifted in a way that indicated to Henry that she was experiencing pain. As always with these increasingly rare moments of lucidity, he didn't want her to suffer, but he felt desperate to share any conversation that might be possible. She appeared even more weak and sallow than she had earlier in the day. His confidence in his own theory that the end was drawing near increased. She'd made declarations to him and Amala that she'd felt the need to make; she now had no other purpose in living, especially when she knew that dying would release her from the awful pain she'd been enduring for so long.

"I'm here, my darling," Henry said, leaning close to her face.

Kat's eyes barely flickered open for a few seconds. "Henry," she said with a raspy voice, but her love for him was evident even as she simply spoke his name.

"Do you want your medicine, my dear?" he asked. "I know you're in pain."

"Not yet," she said. "Just . . . give me a few minutes . . . with you."

He nodded and asked, "Water?"

"Just . . . a little."

Henry carefully lifted her head and helped her drink, and he knew its purpose was more to moisten her mouth and throat than to give her body any fluid. The doctor had told Henry that Kat's body had stopped feeling the need to take in any sustenance or liquids because it was slowly letting go. Henry found some comfort in learning that the lack of sustenance in her body seemed to actually reduce the pain. Oh, how he didn't want her to suffer!

After helping make Kat comfortable again on the pillow beneath her head, Henry instinctively went to his knees beside the bed, where he could hold her hand and lean his face more comfortably toward hers. There was something he needed to say, and he knew his time was brief. Before he could form the words, she murmured in little more than a whisper, "Forgive me . . . if what I said earlier . . . upset you. I knew that it likely would, but . . . it had to be said."

"I understand," he said, even though he was, in truth, still only *trying* to understand. More accurately, he could understand why Kat needed to let them know that she was aware of the situation of his past relationship with Amala; her edict for them to marry was not something he felt pleased about. But she was dying, and he wasn't going to argue with her. Whether or not he made the decision to honor her wishes was something he couldn't even think about right now.

"I need you to know, Kat," he said gently, "that once I committed my life to you, I never harbored feelings for Amala. Never! I need you to know that."

"I *do* know it," she muttered. "It's one of many reasons . . . I love you . . . so much." She took a long moment to try to catch her breath, as if the effort to say that much had taken all her strength.

"I will always love you, Kat; always. It breaks my heart to lose you this way." He couldn't hold back tears, but if a man couldn't cry when his wife was dying, when could he cry? It wasn't as if he'd ever been opposed to crying when he needed to, anyway.

"I know it, Henry," she whispered, her strength waning, "I do. But you mustn't pine for me. It's my time; I know it is. I . . . feel peace . . . over leaving. You must find . . . the same peace. God will comfort your heart . . . if you let Him. Promise me . . . that you will let God . . . into you heart. Be sad for a time if you must, but . . . don't be angry. Promise me."

Henry marveled at the profound depth of insight he was hearing and inwardly chided himself for the times he'd believed Kat wasn't necessarily a deep thinker. She understood life and the world around her far more than he'd given her credit.

"I promise," he said, knowing it wouldn't be easy, but still a far easier promise to keep than that which she'd tricked him into making earlier. He couldn't think about that.

"And Henry," she said, at the same time grimacing, while her difficulty in breathing became more evident, "you mustn't think that . . . you have to wait . . . to move on." While he wondered if she meant what he thought she meant, she forced her eyes open more fully and gave him a penetrating gaze he would surely never forget. "Move on . . . with your life, Henry. Don't . . . worry about . . . what anyone else thinks. Just . . . listen to your heart . . . trust it . . . follow it." Her eyes closed as if they'd reached their limit. "Don't think . . . that you need to . . . honor my memory . . . by waiting."

Kat sighed and offered a weak squeeze to Henry's hand, as if to conclude the last of what she wanted him to know. Her eyes flickered open for only a long moment more as she added, "I love you, Henry. You've been . . . so good to me; . . . made me . . . so happy. Remember . . . only that."

"I love you too, my darling," he said and kissed her brow, her closed eyelids, and her cheek, even while he noted the evidence that she was no longer able to suppress evidence of how much she was hurting.

"Medicine," she muttered in a voice he could barely hear. He helped her take it and swallow enough water to get it down, then waited for it to take effect, telling her twice more that he loved her while she slowly drifted into oblivion, and he wondered if she would ever regain consciousness. He was glad for what they'd been able to say to each other but heartbroken and shocked to even consider that this could really be the end. When he knew she was sleeping deeply, he climbed carefully onto the bed beside her, pressed his face into her hair where it was splayed over the pillow, and cried like a lost and frightened child.

Oliver and Viola found him there when they came to check on Kat, and Henry was glad at least that these good people loved him enough that he didn't feel the need for embarrassment at being caught in such an emotional state. They each kissed his head and whispered words of comfort to him as if he were a child—*their* child—and he wished he could remember his own mother ever having done the same. Oliver sat in a chair on one side of the bed, keeping a hand on Henry's shoulder as if to just silently let him know he was there. Viola sat on the other side of the bed, crying silent tears and touching her daughter's face and hair while she slept.

A while later the doctor arrived and they all moved away so that he could examine Kat. He listened to her heart, checked the pulse in her wrists and ankles, opened her eyelids briefly, then put a hand on her forehead that was more a gesture of concern than any part of the medical evaluation. He then turned to face the husband and parents of his patient and said with compassion, "I would be surprised if she makes it through the night." Viola cried out before putting her hand over her mouth to suppress the sound. Oliver teetered slightly until Henry put an arm around his father-in-law's shoulders to help steady him. "I would recommend," Dr. Cowell went on, "saying your good-byes. Even if she is not conscious, I strongly believe it's important for loved ones to speak what they feel they need to say. And in my own personal opinion, I think it's highly likely that in some spiritual way she will hear you."

The doctor sighed and added, "I'm going to stay until it's over, as we have discussed previously. I'm familiar enough with your home that I think I can find what I need. I know you already have maids taking shifts with her at night; it would be good if at least one of them is on hand. But this is a sacred time for you as a family, and I will stay close but keep my distance so that you can share this time together. If you have questions, I'll most often just be in the next room."

"Thank you," Henry managed to say, since Viola and Oliver were both weeping. The doctor went into the sitting room next to the bedroom, where he had previously spent considerable time while he'd assisted them all through this long and arduous journey toward death.

Throughout the following hours, Henry hardly left Kat's side, taking only brief breaks now and then, mostly for the purpose of allowing another member of the family to have a few minutes alone with Kat. Paulina came and talked quietly to Kat's unconscious, barely living form, and Henry took the opportunity to splash cold water on his face and to drink the cup of coffee a maid had brought into the room a few minutes earlier.

Paulina said her good-byes and left weeping, and Henry knew she wouldn't be back until it was over. He'd been aware of Amala hovering nearby, sometimes sitting, sometimes pacing the room, but they said nothing to each other; in fact, she said nothing at all.

Oliver and Viola spent a significant amount of time at Kat's side, making it clear that Henry was welcome to stay nearby, and he was grateful to not feel that he needed to leave. They each spoke to her of the joy she'd brought into their lives, sharing memories aloud and expressing their hope of being together again one day in heavenly realms. Henry found himself wondering if he truly believed that life after this world was real. He'd always passively believed it, but in that hour of the darkest part of the night, knowing that his wife's life was being measured most likely in the minutes remaining before daylight, he asked himself if he *really* believed that Kat's spirit would live on and that one day this family would be complete again in another time and place. He was surprised by a quickening of his heartbeat and a warm tingling in his eyes that manifested itself in tears that held no trace of sorrow. He felt only peace, and he had to concede that he not only believed it, but something divinely unexplainable had just witnessed the truth of it to him. He thanked God for such a profound personal witness that would surely aid him in making peace with Kat's death, as she had implored him to do.

When it became increasingly evident that Kat was not likely to regain consciousness, Oliver and Viola both expressed tearful farewells and left the room together, leaning on each other for support as they slowly walked away. Henry believed it was better that way. He personally felt a desire to be with his wife until the very end, but they'd been warned by the doctor that it was impossible to know what to expect. Sometimes patients slipped quietly away, but it was common for some to struggle toward consciousness as the body attempted to take its final breaths. Henry preferred to think of Kat's parents remembering her in this peaceful state.

Now that only Henry and Amala were in the room, Henry said to her, "You need to spend some time with your sister. I'll give you some privacy."

"I . . . don't want to intrude," Amala said, wringing her hands while her chin quivered.

"Your relationship with her is no less important than mine, Amala. I'll be back shortly, but you're welcome to stay as long as you want."

"Thank you," Amala said and briefly met his eyes with a silent echo of her gratitude. Had she believed he wouldn't want her here with all that had happened earlier?

For the sake of clarification, he put a hand on her shoulder and said with firm sincerity, "Right now . . . sharing these final moments with Kat is all that matters. We both love her, and we both need to be here. It's all right."

Amala nodded, and he could tell she was trying very hard not to burst into tears. "I'll give you some time alone with her," he added, which would give her the opportunity to let those tears come forth in privacy, if that was what she needed.

Henry checked on the doctor in the sitting room and offered him a fresh cup of coffee. Dr. Cowell thanked him and continued reading from a book he'd brought with him, and Henry wondered how many hours of this man's life he might have spent waiting for people to die. He thought of this man using his expertise to bring Harry into the world, and considered the irony. Death was as much a part of life as birth, and both required a great deal of waiting. And Dr. Cowell did it with such kindness and finesse. Henry felt a renewed gratitude to have the services of such a skilled and compassionate man at their disposal.

The two men exchanged a few words; then Henry hovered near the open doorway between the bedroom and the sitting room, aware that Amala was lying on the bed next to Kat and talking quietly to her. He couldn't hear what she was saying, but neither could he keep himself from observing them together in the dim glow of the lamps on the bedside tables. For all of the heartache and poignancy of such a scene, he couldn't help seeing the beauty in it. Their deep and profound closeness in life was now culminating in their sharing the experience of death. He thought for a moment of how they'd been together when Amala's parents had been killed, and found the present experience all the more poignant.

When Amala became quiet, as if she'd said all she needed to say, but remained on the bed beside her sister, Henry moved tentatively into the room, asking quietly, "Is it all right if I intrude now?"

"Of course," Amala said. "Is it all right if I stay?"

"Of course," he insisted, hoping his firm tone would let her know that he would never want to deprive her of her right to be with her sister to her last breath if that was what she wanted.

Henry sat for a long while in the chair next to the bed, holding Kat's hand, keenly aware of every tiny bit of evidence that she was still alive. He wondered how long this waiting might go on. He felt tired but not sleepy; still, he feared he might fall asleep and miss that moment of transition. He wanted to be with her when she left, even if she had no awareness of his presence. He focused on her face, still so beautiful in spite of the way it had become painfully thin and gaunt. Given how much time he'd spent watching her sleep like this for weeks now, he couldn't help noticing that a change had taken place in her countenance. He pondered it for several minutes before he said to Amala, "She looks different. She looks more . . . at peace."

"I noticed the same," Amala said. "She's ready to go." The statement came with tears, which provoked the same from Henry, and he wiped them off his face with a quick brush of his free hand. "If only I felt ready to *let* her go," Amala said.

"Yes, I know what you mean. She's barely been aware of life for so long, I thought I'd be more prepared. But the finality of it all still feels . . . unbearable."

"Exactly," Amala said, reminding Henry of how well they had always understood each other, how much they thought and felt the same. Their eyes met briefly as if to exchange the silent declaration that they were of one mind; then they both turned their full attention to Kat.

More than an hour passed in complete silence except for the doctor coming in every fifteen or twenty minutes to check Kat's pulse, each time telling them it was slowing down and the end was getting closer.

Henry began to feel more tired and more afraid he would drift off to sleep in the chair and Kat would slip away without him knowing. He finally followed Amala's example and lay down on the bed next to Kat where he could relax more but also be more aware of any slight change in her condition. He put a hand over Kat's belly where he could feel her breathing—however slight and shallow—moving through her. He whispered in Kat's ear that he loved her, and he was aware of Amala crying quietly where she lay on the other side of Kat, her head resting on her sister's shoulder.

As Henry focused keenly on Kat's breathing, he felt calm and at peace and less afraid than he'd thought he would be when the end came. He was able to relax and close his eyes but still remain alert and completely aware of his wife. When he heard the sound of Kat's breathing change, sounding noisier and perhaps strained, he lifted up on one elbow to look at her. She didn't look different, but something was happening. The doctor appeared at his side, declaring that this was exactly what he'd expected; it was completely normal. He called it the *death rattle* and said it wouldn't be long now.

Henry and Amala both remained at Kat's sides, neither of them speaking but both acutely aware of Kat's every breath. Time passed while nothing changed, and then Kat seemed to stop breathing, and the sound of the death rattle stopped completely. Henry held his breath, wondering if she could be gone as simply as that, and then she drew another noisy breath. For interminable minutes it went on like that, with her breathing becoming noisier, with the time between each breath growing longer. He knew the doctor was hovering in the room now but keeping a polite distance, as if he held a deep respect for the ritual of death.

Henry was leaning his elbow on the bed, his head in his hand, just watching Kat's face, when her eyes came open, making him gasp after so many long hours of no indication of life at all except for her faint pulse and strained breathing. Amala lifted herself up at the sound of Henry gasping. Kat turned her head slightly toward Henry, and he hoped for some final words between them, but her eyes became focused more past him, so much so that he turned his head to see who might be standing behind him, but there was no one there. She blinked and muttered in a voice that was barely audible, "The light . . . the light . . . hurts my eyes."

Henry exchanged a brief, astonished glance with Amala before they both watched Kat shift her eyes and turn her head ever so slightly, as if she could see movement that they could not see. A faint smile touched her lips, enhancing the peacefulness of her countenance. "Mata," she whispered, and Amala gasped. "Pita," Kat said, and Amala gasped again.

Henry knew Kat had just uttered the Indian words for mother and father that Amala had used in reference to her blood parents. Could it be possible that she was seeing them? Looking at her face and the fixed intensity of her eyes, he found it impossible to believe any other explanation. Kat's eyes closed as if a deep sleep had overcome her instantly. She drew a long, rattling breath. There was silence for several seconds, and she drew another. And then she became silent and still as death settled over her with absolute finality.

For more than a minute, Henry felt stunned, frozen, in shock over the loss as much as the evidence of the miracle he'd just witnessed. He was aware of Amala sobbing, her face buried in the pillow at Kat's side. When he finally felt jolted to the present reality, Henry sat up and did what he'd been wanting to do for months, but Kat had been in too much pain for him to hardly touch her. She was now free of that pain, and he lifted her frail, lifeless body onto his lap and into his arms, holding her like a child while he wept into her hair, desperately wanting these final moments of closeness before she began to turn cold. Amala held Kat's hand that had fallen limply to the bed at her side and wept just as intensely. The doctor discreetly left the room. There was no need for him to tell them it was over.

* * * *

Once Kat's body had been taken way, and after Henry had spent some time with his son, he slept until it was dark again, then he ate just enough to sustain him and slept through the remainder of the night. He felt certain that his deep exhaustion was not just from being up all through the night of Kat's death, but from all the weeks and months leading up to it when his sleep had been sporadic and he'd been in continuous emotional turmoil.

When Henry finally came around enough to feel like he could function, he got himself cleaned up and had some time to spend with Harry in the nursery before he went down to breakfast. The rest of the family were there, all looking as grim and solemn as he felt, but he was glad to not be alone in his grief and the adjustment of truly knowing Kat was gone and of not being continually aware of wanting to spend time with her. He learned through brief conversation that the others had also slept a great deal the previous day, but Oliver had taken the initiative to put funeral plans into action. Since the plans had already been discussed weeks earlier—mostly initiated by Kat—they had already been in agreement about how everything should be handled, and Henry was glad to not have to face dealing with what Oliver had already done.

Henry noticed that Amala appeared more grave and quiet than the others. He completely understood how she felt, and he was grateful that they'd been able to share Kat's death in such a peaceful and intimate way. But now that Kat was gone, the echoes of what she'd made them promise were becoming more prominent in his mind, making him not want to exchange any conversation with Amala at all. He knew that was ridiculous and told himself that she was still his sister and his friend, and to avoid her due to the awkwardness of the situation would only make it all the more awkward. Neither of them was anywhere near ready to discuss the implications of or their feelings on the matter. He simply forced himself to focus on the present and try not to think at all of Kat's final wish.

The days leading up to the funeral were heavy with dark clouds and occasional drizzling, making the world outside seem completely without color. Henry most often found himself staring out one window or another, thinking of how the weather perfectly mirrored how he felt. In fact, he believed that if the sun were shining he might resent it for contradicting him. He too felt without color, often needing to cry just enough to release the overwhelming grief consuming him, just as the sky seemed unable to stop emitting regular bursts of rain, rarely stopping for more than a few minutes here and there.

Henry spent a great deal of time with his son, deeply grateful that Harry was unaware of the grief and drama taking place around him, but saddened to think that he would not even remember his mother. Nevertheless, Henry would always tell him about her and would never allow her place in their family to be forgotten.

Now that Kat was gone and the family no longer had the need to spend time at her bedside, Harry became the center of attention even more than he always had been, and every member of the family became drawn to him. He was a literal part of Kat that lived on, and to Henry he was living proof of the love that he and Kat had shared. This precious child was a soothing balm to everyone who loved and missed Kat. Even while grief hung heavy in the air, Harry could make them all laugh with his funny expressions and comical noises. He had come to be able to focus more on what he could see, and he'd often smile or make sweet googling sounds when he was spoken to. The family could be entertained and distracted every moment that Harry wasn't sleeping or eating simply by passing him around and savoring the joy he offered so freely without even trying. Henry marveled at this great gift that Kat had left behind, and he knew the others felt the same way. And he felt pleased with the way that Kat's parents expressed their gratitude to have Henry living in their home, knowing that Harry would be raised there under the same roof and they would always have the privilege of being a part of his life. Nothing could make Henry happier in regard to his son; he knew he couldn't raise him alone, and this arrangement of sharing a home had never felt more right than it did now. Perhaps without Harry he might have felt out of place here now that Kat was gone, but, if anything, he felt all the more as if he belonged with these people. Given how he'd never felt completely at home in the house where he'd been raised, he considered that to be a miracle.

Henry dreaded the funeral, and he hated every minute of it. The only thing he found redeeming in the experience was the beauty of the flowers surrounding Kat's casket during the service, and even more beautiful were the three women—Viola, Amala, and Paulina—all dressed exquisitely in black. He didn't know why he felt so fascinated by the way they looked dressed that way, all hovering together, their faces heavy with grief, but he found it difficult not to watch them, especially when doing so kept him distracted from listening to the vicar—a man he loathed—saying words about his wife's life and death that felt hollow and meaningless. Henry knew for himself the real truth of those things; he didn't need this self-righteous hypocrite pretending to actually care about what was taking place.

As the casket was carried from the church to the adjoining cemetery that would be Kat's final resting place, the sky was heavier and darker than it had been since her death. Before the final portion of the service was completed, umbrellas were erected all around the grave to ward off the sudden downpour that didn't show any hint of letting up for a good, long time. Henry just stood with his hat in his hands, letting the cold winter rain fall over him, disguising his tears and empathizing with his aching spirit. Feeling the rain cease, he glanced up to see Oliver standing at his side, sharing the shelter of his umbrella as he said quietly, "You'll become ill if you're not careful."

Henry wanted to say he didn't care, but he knew that would sound immature and irresponsible. He had a son who needed him, and he didn't need to add to the family's burden by needing to be cared for himself.

Oliver had to practically force Henry away from the grave after everyone else was gone. Once they were in the carriage, Henry couldn't keep himself from saying, "I'm glad that's over. If I had to listen to that hypocritical imbecile say one more word, I think I would have given him a bloody nose, and that wouldn't have been very appropriate for my wife's funeral."

He was surprised when Amala added vehemently, "I was seriously considering that I should hit him myself. Given that he already believes my very existence to be an abomination, it shouldn't have been nearly as shocking to him for *me* to do such a thing."

"What on earth do you mean?" Oliver demanded, and Henry realized from a quick glance at everyone's expressions that Paulina knew exactly what they were talking about, but Kat's parents did not. He had to remind himself that they didn't know the *whole* story, and even though he didn't really want to explain right now, he was the one who'd brought it up.

Henry turned more toward Oliver, who was sitting beside him, rather than looking at the three women who were sitting on the opposite seat of the carriage. He cleared his throat and tried to think of the simplest way to answer the question, well aware that Amala was highly uncomfortable with the topic, but given what she had just said about the vicar, he figured that some part of her would likely prefer to have this out in the open along with everything else.

Henry just stated the facts as simply as he could. "When Amala and I were considering marriage, we went to speak with the vicar. I sincerely believed that he might be able to offer us some sound advice that would come from a Christian way of thinking. I mistakenly believed that a man who declares himself to be representing God would acknowledge that all human beings are equal in God's eyes. To this day I cannot think of the things he said without cringing and feeling angry—especially on Amala's behalf."

"He said that she was an *abomination*?" Oliver said as if *he* might ask the carriage driver to go back so that *he* could give the vicar a bloody nose.

"Actually," Henry said, recalling the encounter all too well, "I believe he said that to even consider such a marriage was an abomination. And he held nothing back in his heated declaration that he believed people of color were cursed by God and their seed should not be mingled with that of the pure, white English." He heard Oliver and Viola both gasp in horrified shock while he looked directly at Amala, wondering if he should have kept his mouth shut when he saw her head bowed and tears running down her face. But he believed her parents needed to know, that it would help them understand what had happened and why honoring Kat's wish could likely be ludicrous considering how deeply he'd been convinced that Amala had been right from the start: their marrying and having children would be difficult in too many ways to count.

To finalize his point—and give Amala an opportunity to speak if she felt the need—Henry said, "Am I remembering the event correctly, Amala? Feel free to correct me."

Amala sniffled and briefly pressed her handkerchief beneath her nose. "That's how I remember it. Such words are hard to forget. In fact, that's all I hear in my mind every time I have to sit through one of his sermons."

"As do I," Henry added with a long pause between each word to emphasize how deeply true the same was for him and how much he hated it.

"I'm stunned," Oliver declared.

"I never would have believed," Viola added.

"I think it's disgusting," Paulina said. "I've attended many congregations of many different faiths throughout my travels, but I've never encountered such bold hypocrisy. I wonder how he can even call himself a Christian when he stands up there every Sunday and preaches the words of Christ and then contradicts himself in the way he lives his life and supposedly serves his congregation. As I've heard, he caters very much to those who have the most money and influence. But did he once come to visit Kat through the course of her illness? Forgive me if it sounds disrespectful; perhaps it's even blasphemous for me to assume the attitude of God, but I do not believe for one moment that Jesus would at all approve of such supposed representation of His teachings."

"If such feelings are blasphemous," Oliver exclaimed, "then I think we are blasphemers all."

"Amen," Amala muttered quietly and looked out the window.

Chapter Thirteen
MAKING PEACE

THE DAYS FOLLOWING THE FUNERAL continued to be dark and rainy, and the adjustment to living without Kat proved to be difficult. Henry knew that Amala was struggling at least as much as he was, but his ability to be a friend to her had become tangled up in the things Kat had said to them and the awareness that everyone else knew the whole truth.

It felt strange to Henry—as he knew it did to everyone in the household—that their schedules had changed so dramatically, or rather that they spent their days trying to get back the normalcy they had once had. Life had come to revolve around Kat, and the entire family hadn't been together for a meal or tea in months. Now they were sharing *every* meal *and* afternoon tea, but the normalcy had yet to return. With rare exception, they were all unusually quiet. At times it felt right and necessary to talk about Kat and about how they missed her, and to share their thoughts about believing she was in a better place. They all enjoyed talking about Harry and every adorable thing he was doing, as he seemed to change every day. But often there was nothing but thoughtful silence, as if no one had anything to say that wouldn't initiate some kind of pain or awkwardness. If someone brought up any speculations about the future or moving forward from Kat's death, it always led to implications—unspoken or otherwise—about whether or not Henry and Amala would heed Kat's final wish and work toward marriage. Neither of them was ready to even think about that yet, let alone discuss it over the dinner table. Henry couldn't even imagine opening his heart again to *any* woman, and in the rare moment when he could consider that one day he might be ready to move beyond the love he'd shared with Kat, his mind would always immediately go to the fact that Amala had broken his heart. And as much as she loved her sister, he wasn't sure that Kat's desire would be enough for Amala to overcome her initial belief that their getting married was a bad idea. He simply wasn't willing to even consider the idea only to live through *that* drama all over again. For now, all he could do was live one day at a time, keep putting one foot in front of the other, and try to acclimate himself to living without his wife, grateful at least to be a part of her family. In spite of the awkwardness hovering over the situation between him and Amala, he still felt that he belonged and he was loved and accepted, and that alone was dearly precious to him and not something he took for granted.

When Saturday evening came, Henry was surprised to hear Oliver announce near the end of supper, "You are all welcome to do as you please, but I won't be attending church services tomorrow. I've not missed a Sunday during the whole of my life unless I was too ill to attend, but I'll not be attending any further as long as that man is leading the service. I cannot tolerate such hypocrisy, especially knowing how much his attitudes have hurt you, my dear." He nodded toward Amala, who looked astonished. "Therefore, I will remain at home, where we have copies of hymnals and the Bible, and I'm certain I can express my devotion to God without the distraction of wanting to stand up and expose this supposed clergyman for the charlatan that he is."

"I fear that if you did so," Amala spoke up, making Henry realize how very little she had spoken at all since Kat's death, "most of the congregation would agree with *him*."

"All the more reason to remain at home and worship God in the privacy of my own home," Oliver declared. "I will honor the Sabbath as I always have, but I will not be attending church services. You are each welcome to do as you wish."

No one made any further comment, and the topic of conversation was changed, but the following morning at the time they would usually be getting into the carriage to go to church, the entire family showed up in the drawing room dressed in their finest as if they *were* going to church, which seemed appropriate for a gathering—even such a small one—meant to express their devotion to God. They sat down together, and Oliver—being the head of the household—led the family in singing hymns, praying together, and reading passages from the Bible, which they discussed in depth. When their little family service was over, Henry felt better emotionally and spiritually than he'd felt following *any* Sunday meeting since the vicar had treated him and Amala so cruelly.

Later that day, after spending a couple of hours in the nursery with Harry, Henry went to his room and found the door slightly ajar, when he knew he had left it closed. He thought as he did every time he came to this room that he hated the memories of sharing it with Kat—and of her dying here—and that he should approach Oliver about moving to a room in a different wing. But he'd put off the conversation, given the fragile emotions they were all experiencing. As he quietly pushed the door open now, he knew it was time to start sleeping elsewhere. This had been Kat's room long before he'd married her, and apparently it needed to remain Kat's room. Amala was curled up in the center of the bed in the very spot where Kat had died, crying so hard that she had no awareness of his entering the room.

For a long moment Henry just stood there, debating whether to slip quietly back out undetected or to make himself known. He hated the chasm that had grown between them since their comfortable friendship had become lost in Kat's attempt to become a matchmaker. He knew that no one would understand his grief more than Amala—and perhaps the other way around. And yet they could hardly talk to each other. Suddenly deciding he wanted to put an end to such discomfort between them—or at least try—he left the door open for the sake of propriety, picked up a chair, and moved it to the side of the bed, where he'd spent endless hours sitting at Kat's side during her illness. As he put the chair down and sat on it, Amala was startled and sat up abruptly.

"What are you doing here?" she demanded.

"This is my room," he reminded her, and she looked immediately embarrassed, putting a hand over her eyes, which didn't stop the flow of tears running down her face.

"Oh, I wasn't thinking," she murmured, scooting to the other side of the bed. "I'm so sorry. I just . . . I just . . ." She put her feet on the floor, but before she could stand, he noticed how she dropped her head to her knees, as if she felt dizzy from sitting up so quickly while in such a state.

"It's all right," he said. "I understand why you would want to come here. I'm going to move to another room tomorrow anyway. The memories are difficult for me here. This should remain Kat's room—at least for the time being. Perhaps one day we'll decide we no longer need a shrine to her memory, but right now . . . it seems to still hold her spirit somehow."

Amala raised her head slowly, but with her back turned to him, he couldn't see her face. He'd longed to talk to her about their shared grief, and at least she was listening—so far. Therefore, he kept talking.

"Sometimes I like to think of her spirit being here with me—with us—and I want to be closer to that feeling. And sometimes the very idea just makes me miss her more. I'm so glad she's no longer suffering, but I think I spend way too much time feeling sorry for myself for being left behind. It's not that I want to die; I have so much that's good in my life, so much worth living for—not the least of which is my son. It's just that . . . Kat's gone, and I'm here, and it feels all wrong."

Henry allowed enough silence to give Amala the opportunity to speak if she wanted to. He could hear her sniffling and saw the way she was wiping at her face with a handkerchief. She finally said, "Yes, it *does* feel all wrong. I . . ."

She hesitated far too long, and he urged, "Please talk to me, Amala. For all that's happened, you're the best friend I've ever had, and I'm going through the most difficult thing that's ever happened to me. I know you're struggling with it too. We both love her; we always will. Please talk to me. Tell me how you feel. Help *me* feel better by letting me know that I'm not alone in this. Your parents are wonderful, but . . . it's different. Please talk to me."

Amala lowered her head, and Henry heard evidence that she was fighting back the urge to start sobbing again. With her back still turned to him, he could see her shoulders heaving with unvented grief. He wanted to sit next to her, to wrap her in his arms and let her cry on his shoulder. But he thought it was more prudent to remain seated where he was and adhere to conversation. For all that he wanted to bridge the gaps between them, he didn't want to do or say anything to imply—even in the smallest way—that he could even consider honoring Kat's deathbed request.

Henry wondered what else he might say to offer some comfort or to encourage her to talk about her grief, which might help ease it. When he came up with nothing, he was relieved to hear her finally find her voice again. "I . . . keep wishing it would have . . . been me."

Henry was so shocked that it took him a long moment to even be able to utter, "What? What do you mean?"

"She . . . had a husband and a child who need her. She . . . was always . . . so very much without guile. She didn't have to live with . . . the color of her skin being a source of controversy and scandal and grief. She could have lived a long and happy life without any of those things ever mattering to her or anyone else." Amala let out a little sob that sounded more like a loud hiccup. "Why couldn't it have been me, Henry? It should have been me!"

Henry lost all concern over propriety or implications in their relationship as he shot out of his chair and walked around the bed, going to his knees in front of her. He took hold of her shoulders and looked into her moist, swollen eyes. "Now you listen to me. Life and death are not some kind of random lottery, Amala. And it's certainly not about what's easy or convenient in regard to whatever it is we are meant to be learning or accomplishing through this mortal journey. It's no accident that you survived when your parents were killed, and it's no accident that you came here to live. You are a remarkable woman with so much to offer this world and the people who love you! Do you hear me? If we believe in a higher power and a bigger plan—and we do—then we must trust that God is in charge, and He knows what He's doing. We must trust Him! I miss her, Amala, as we all do. It feels impossible and often too horrifying to grasp. But I have to believe it will get easier. Still, even in my most difficult moments of grief, I know it was her time to go. Her death was not a random accident, any more than your being alive and here is. I *know* it was her time to go! Do you hear me?"

Henry saw her looking into his eyes, probing deeply for evidence that he truly meant what he was saying. He knew well enough that she could see right through him; he could never get away with lying to her. So he just gazed right back at her, giving her all the time she needed to accept the truth of what he'd just said, to know that he meant it. The very idea that she had been believing she should have died in Kat's place made him feel ill. Did she truly see her own life as having so little value? For all of her outward confidence and determination to make the very best of her circumstances and live a fulfilling life, did she somehow believe what society may have conditioned her to believe, that she was somehow inferior? That she had less right to live than an English woman with fair skin? While he allowed her to search for the sincerity in *his* eyes, he saw the truth in hers. She *did* believe it. Somewhere in the deepest, most private places of Amala's heart, she believed she was inferior, less than equal to even the members of her own family, who had done nothing but give her love and acceptance in every way.

Henry's thoughts wandered boldly into territory that broke his own rules on the present situation. He couldn't help it. He had to ask himself: Was *that* why she'd so adamantly refused to marry him? For all the logic and practicality of her reasoning over the difficulties it would have brought into their lives—and into the lives of their potential children—was the true heart of the problem her own perception of herself? For as long as he'd known her—and loved her— and for as well as they had grown to understand each other, Henry saw for the first time what life might really look like through the eyes of a young Indian woman, orphaned and transplanted to a place where she could never blend in and never be treated as an equal by the whole of the society in which she lived. His heart cracked in a way that made him momentarily forget about his own grief, and he felt tears slide down his face before he even felt their presence in his eyes.

Amala looked surprised by his tears, and he saw a glimmer in her countenance that allowed him to believe she had heard what he'd told her and it had left some impact that might help her come—in time—to know for herself that her thinking about dying in Kat's place had been completely distorted. But he saw something else in her eyes that made his heart pound and his mouth go dry before he even recognized what it was. She was trying to hide it; but he knew her too well to not see the truth. And it scared him. It scared him so badly that he let go of her shoulders and stood so quickly that he almost fell over. He caught himself with a couple of steps backward, moving away from her as if that might put distance between himself and the thoughts that had just rushed into his mind.

Not wanting to create a new discomfort between them when they'd just begun talking again, he cleared his throat and fought to pretend that everything was the same as it had been a few minutes ago. Needing to leave the room but wanting to do so gracefully, he said in a gentle voice, "You spend as much time here as you need to; I'll be sleeping elsewhere from now on. And if you need to talk, you know where I live." He finished on a light tone that he hoped would ease any tension she might have sensed in him. Fearing she would see through him, he hurried from the room and started to run as soon as he knew Amala could no longer hear his footsteps. He ran down the back stairs and out of the house, as if he could run away from what he was feeling, from what he now knew Amala was feeling.

After more than an hour of pacing inside the carriage house, Henry had neatly placed *all* of his difficult emotions behind a wall of anger. A rational part of his mind knew that doing so wasn't healthy and that it wasn't going to aid his sorrow over Kat's death or his uncertainty over the future, but he sincerely felt so overwhelmed with the drama going on in his life that he couldn't find any other way to cope at the moment. Anger he could handle. The rest was just too much for any man to take in when it had not yet been a week since his wife had been put into a grave.

* * * *

Amala was glad when Henry took up residence in a different wing of the house and Kat's room was left very much as Amala had remembered it before she'd gone away with Paulina. Since Henry wanted his own room to be next to the nursery where his son slept— wanting to help care for him as much as he was able—the move created quite an ordeal because the nanny and the wet nurse both needed rooms near the nursery for obvious reasons. But once they were all settled in their new quarters, Amala found a safe respite in going to Kat's room, where she could be alone with her memories and her grief.

A month after Kat's death, Amala felt mostly lost within herself and wondered if she would ever recover. Her family began to express concern for her, which she always managed to brush off. Viola had defended her more than once, declaring to the others that every person needed to grieve in his or her own way, and there was no set time for how long it took to come to terms with such a loss. Amala agreed and she appreciated her mother's declaration, but secretly Amala wondered if there was something wrong with her. The rest of the family showed signs of grieving, and conversations about Kat were always a mixture of fond reminiscing and sorrow. But they all seemed to be doing much better than she was—at least as far as she could see.

Amala and Henry had never shared a private conversation since the day he'd found her crying in Kat's room. In fact, they hadn't so much as exchanged a glance in spite of all the meals where they'd sat at the same table, all the time spent with the family—whether visiting or participating in their private Sunday service—and all the times they had both ended up in the nursery together to play with Harry. Recalling his declaration that they should talk more and help each other through this—since she was his best friend—his behavior seemed especially contradictory. They exchanged necessary, appropriate words as if they'd never been friends at all; as if they weren't as good as brother and sister, the way they'd become prior to Kat's death. She assumed he was managing all right in regard to his own grief, although her father mentioned once that he was concerned about Henry for reasons he didn't expound upon. He'd taken to leaving on a horse nearly every day—sometimes after breakfast, and sometimes after lunch—and being gone for a couple of hours, with the only explanation being that the fresh air and speed of riding helped clear his head. But he'd become very quiet. Amala wondered if he was grieving privately, much as she was. But she longed to talk to him, to share their thoughts and feelings, and she couldn't help being confused over the fact that the last time they'd spoken privately, he had admitted the same to her. And then he'd left her alone and had not said a personal word to her since.

Amala had to assume his behavior toward her was directly related to Kat's desire for them to marry. But Amala had no idea how to feel about all of that, and she certainly didn't know what to do. She had definitely convinced herself a long time ago that marrying him was not a good idea, and she'd apparently done a good job of convincing him. She'd broken his heart, and he had put all of that behind him. She had no reason to believe that Kat's request would prompt such a man to change his beliefs on any matter. And she certainly didn't want him feeling obligated to marry her simply because her sister had asked him to. She also had to consider that even *if* he decided he was all right with the possibility, she wasn't certain that her original concerns weren't just as valid now as they'd ever been.

When Kat had been gone more than two months and signs of spring were beginning to show, Amala still didn't feel anything but sorrow and confusion. Paulina and her parents had often urged her to talk to them, but she had resisted, insisting there was nothing to talk about. But on a rainy afternoon, Paulina found Amala alone in Kat's room, staring out the window. Her aunt sat down nearby and said, "I'm not leaving this room until we get to the bottom of whatever is troubling you."

"My sister died," Amala said. "Beyond that, what could—"

"Don't give me the same old speech. I know your sister died. I also know how strong and wise you are. But the strong, sensible woman I came to know before Kat's death is nowhere to be found, and I know you well enough to know that it's not only losing Kat that's weighing on you."

"I have no idea what you're talking about," Amala insisted.

"All right, fine," Paulina said. "I'm going to tell you what *I* think, and you can tell me if I'm wrong. But you need to speak from the heart, not from this defensive, troubled place where you've been hiding. Is that fair?"

Amala thought about it for a long moment, knowing she completely trusted Paulina—and her judgment and wisdom. "Yes," Amala said, already feeling a little sheepish to realize she *had* been hiding in a defensive and troubled place.

"Well, then," Paulina said, "it's my belief that you're not only grieving for your sister's death, you're finally truly grieving for having given up Henry years ago. The possibility hanging over you of perhaps resuming that relationship is too terrifying for you to even think about, let alone talk about, even though you know that talking through such feelings is the only way that you can really come to terms with them. And on top of that, a part of you is angry."

Amala felt the truth of Paulina's words permeating through her, making her tremble from the inside out. But she turned in astonishment toward her aunt at that last word. "Angry?" she echoed in that defensive voice Paulina had predicted.

"Yes, my dear, angry. I've experienced a great deal of life and have cared for a great many people. I have seen people grieve, and never once have I observed grief that didn't come with some degree of anger. It's natural to feel angry over losing someone you love. But who can you be angry with? God, perhaps? And yet I know you believe it was Kat's time to go, and you have a strong faith in God. So, I suspect you're angry with Kat."

"Why would I be angry with Kat?" Amala retorted, sounding even more defensive.

"Because she left. A part of you knows she didn't choose to go, but she still left, and however irrational it might sound, you're angry with her for leaving. But even more importantly, my dear girl, you are angry with her for the predicament she has put you in. You thought you had it all worked out, that you had come to terms with it. And you did. If Kat had lived, everything would have moved forward smoothly according to the peace you'd made over the situation and the possibilities of what you could do with your life. And then Kat had to go and die. And not only did she die, she looked into your eyes and made you promise to marry Henry. And you are *so* angry with her for doing that to you. But you, who are always so self-composed and dignified; you, who always tries to do the right thing and be appropriate, have no way to express that kind of anger. It's trapped inside of you and it's slowly killing you, my dear, as surely as cancer killed your sister. Until you can see and accept how angry you are, you will never be able to make sense of any of this."

Amala moved unsteadily toward a chair and sat down as that inner trembling reached her extremities and she found herself shaking violently. The truth of Paulina's words assaulted her with the force of a strong wind, the kind that could uproot trees and overturn all that might lie in its path.

"And what about Henry?" she muttered in a quivering voice.

"What *about* Henry?" Paulina countered, but Amala couldn't find words to clarify her question. Seeming to sense this, Paulina said, "I have no idea where his head is in regard to you, other than his obvious avoidance of the matter entirely. Whatever the future might bring for the two of you is something you'll both have to discuss when the time is right. But I can assure you, my dear, he is every bit as angry as you are. It's my belief that neither of you can make peace with Kat's death until you both recognize how utterly furious you are with her."

Amala put a hand over her mouth as the shock wave of truth rushed out of her with a painful sob, followed by another, and another. Paulina scooted her chair closer to Amala and put her arms around her, encouraging her to just let it all out and cry as hard and as long as she needed to.

* * * *

Henry sat down to share tea with Oliver and Viola, wondering where Amala and Paulina might be. Since he'd brought Harry with him, they were all distracted by the baby's antics while he grabbed at things he shouldn't have, then promptly pushed a biscuit into his mouth when it was placed into his chubby little hand. When Harry became quietly distracted by his biscuit, Henry asked, "Where are the others?"

He saw Oliver and Viola exchange a concerned glance before Oliver said, "Lekha went in search of Amala, since she'd not seen her for hours. She found her in Kat's room, and Paulina is with her. She told us that Amala is very upset, and Paulina asked Lekha to let us know that they wouldn't be joining us for tea."

Viola dabbed at her eyes with her handkerchief. "I just hope Paulina might be able to help her get to the heart of whatever is holding her back."

"I hope so too." Oliver took his wife's hand. "They are very close; I've been hoping Paulina could help her."

"Perhaps Paulina's extra sense will help her know what to do," Viola added, then took a deep breath to compose herself and focus on pouring out the tea.

Henry didn't comment, but he felt a tangible ache in the center of his chest over their concern for Amala. He shared their concern completely, but he could hardly help her when he could barely get through any given day without being continually tempted to break something or fly into a rage. Harry had a soothing effect on him and helped keep his self-discipline in check. The tears he shed while alone at night and during his long, brisk rides every day were likely helping to keep him sane. But he knew he couldn't go on like this forever. He just didn't know what to do about it.

Amala and Paulina didn't show up for supper either, and Lekha reported that they were still in Kat's room, that Amala was still upset, and she'd had a tray of food sent up for both of them.

That night, Henry couldn't sleep; it was a common problem, but definitely made worse by his concern for Amala. A part of him wanted to seek her out and be there for her, but a larger, more dominant part of him was terrified of doing so. All he could do for now in order to remain in control of his senses was pray for her and hope that whatever drama had been taking place with her and Paulina had offered her some cathartic benefits.

The next morning both Amala and Paulina were at breakfast, but Amala looked strained and exhausted in addition to her typical solemnity. Henry wanted to ask her how she was doing, but the possibilities of how she might answer kept him from speaking.

A few days later, Henry found himself having tea alone with Paulina, since Amala had apparently been holed up in the library with her parents for quite some time and they didn't wish to be disturbed. Henry wished he could eavesdrop at the library door, and he certainly felt no appetite for the tea and biscuits on the tray Lekha had brought into the drawing room. Feeling awkward with the silence between him and Paulina, he nearly got up to leave, but something inside his mind, something that almost felt as if it had come suddenly from a force outside himself, told him this was a golden opportunity and that Paulina might just have the answer to his prayers if he simply exerted the courage to ask.

Henry thought about that for a couple of minutes, considering what he'd been praying for. Peace. Clarity. Hope. Could Paulina really have such answers? He liked her and respected her, and she *did* have an extra sense about some things; he'd seen evidence of it for himself. But he felt barely alive and spent every day wondering how to move forward. He felt skeptical that she would know how to fix such deep and overwhelming grief, but he figured it couldn't hurt to ask, and knowing her as well as he did, it didn't take as much courage as he might have believed.

"So, Auntie," he said, as he'd come to call her sometimes, usually in a light tone that was partly teasing. But there was nothing light about the way he said, "I've heard rumors that you spent some time with Amala, and I assume you had some sound advice for her."

"I shared some observations with her," Paulina said. "I suppose advice came along with that."

"And what advice would you offer me? Given your observations, I'm certain you have an opinion."

"Oh, I do," Paulina said with such confidence that Henry felt more than mildly uneasy, and the need for courage became more apparent.

"And what might that be?" he asked.

"I never give advice where it's not wanted," Paulina declared. "Amala and I are close enough that I know when she's ready to hear something, even if she doesn't want to hear it. I don't share that kind of relationship with you, in spite of how much I've grown to care for you."

"I'm asking," Henry said.

"All right, then," Paulina said, looking at him almost fiercely. "I'll tell you what I told Amala because I believe you're both suffering from the same problem when it comes right down to it."

"And what's that?" Henry asked, his heart now pounding as the need for courage became even *more* apparent.

"I told her she would never make peace with Kat's death until she came to terms with the reasons why she's so angry with Kat for putting her in this predicament."

Henry felt as if he might turn to warm butter and slide off the chair onto the floor in a puddle. She had hit a hammer precisely upon the nail of what ailed him, so much so that he wanted to scream or cry or break something. No wonder Amala had been debilitated with tears for hours after Paulina had shared her observations.

When Paulina said nothing more, Henry asked in a barely steady voice, "And what do you suggest I do to remedy such a thing?"

"You're an intelligent man, Henry, and surprisingly sensitive and caring for a man. Find a way to get through the anger. You can't go around it or bury it; you have to just go through it, look at it, and get it over with. Then decide what you want your life to be like and make it happen. Make your decisions based on what *you* want, not what your dead wife wanted for you. Even if it's the same thing, it has to come from your heart, not because you were tricked into making a promise with implications that dear, sweet Kat could have never understood." Paulina stood up. "There, that's what I think . . . for whatever it's worth."

She walked out of the room, and Henry blessed her keen sensitivity; it was as if she knew that he needed to be alone but he didn't have the strength to get up and leave or to even speak. When he finally *could* get up and walk, he hurried to his room as quickly as he could get there, pausing only long enough to tell one of the servants to let the family know he wasn't feeling well and that he was going to bed and would not be joining them for supper. Once alone with the doors locked, the grief and anger he'd barely been keeping at bay rushed at him like growling beasts, threatening to destroy him. He wondered if this was the reason Amala had not been able to come out of Kat's room for so many hours. At the moment, all he could do was pray that he might know how to do as Paulina had suggested, to go *through* the anger and the pain, as opposed to trying to go around it or bury it. He had a feeling it was going to be a long night; he could only hope that with the light of dawn he might feel even just a little bit closer to the hope and peace he'd been praying for.

* * * *

Amala was both grateful and somewhat overcome by the lengthy and tearful conversation she'd had with her parents. She had so much to think about and a long way to go in finding the peace and resolution she was seeking, but she felt as if she were at least moving forward as opposed to being stuck in the dark and helpless place where she'd been for many weeks.

She couldn't help but be concerned when a servant informed the family at supper that Henry was ill and wouldn't be joining them. When Paulina mentioned that he'd asked for her advice at tea and a brief conversation had followed, Amala felt certain that Henry was suffering from the same ailment that had kept her confined to her room not so many days ago.

"Perhaps it's contagious," Amala said in a tone of mild sarcasm, knowing the others would understand exactly what she meant. Of course, she'd hardly exchanged a word with Henry for weeks. But perhaps their ailment had been contracted years ago when they'd first dared admit to their love for each other.

When Henry remained confined to his room all the next day, allowing only Ravi access to see to his minimal needs, Amala and her parents grew increasingly concerned, but Paulina felt certain he just needed time alone and he would come around. She suggested that if it went on too long, they would know when to intervene, and then Oliver would be sent to speak with him—man to man.

The following morning Henry came to breakfast as usual, declaring that he felt better. Amala recognized the strain in his countenance from having seen the same on her own face when she looked in the mirror, but she also saw a subtle clarity in his eyes that she'd not seen there for a long time, and she wondered if the others knew him well enough to see it.

A few more days passed in much the same way as the last several weeks—with her and Henry both pretending there wasn't some enormous, invisible cloud hanging over them that would never go away until they talked about it. But neither of them brought it up. Amala prayed very hard to know what to do, what to say, how to say it, and when. She wondered if her prayers were being heard until a thought occurred to her that seemed to hold an answer, or perhaps the beginning of an answer. She recalled very clearly how it had been *she* who had once insisted they keep their relationship a secret, and it was she who had demanded that he not try to court her officially, and it was she who had insisted they could never be married. She had discussed these very things with her parents recently, wanting to understand what had happened and why, in ways she'd perhaps been unwilling to look at when it had occurred. But she'd not considered until now the real possibilities of how the impact on Henry of her refusing him then might be the very reason he was so unwilling to even talk to her about it now. Perhaps it needed to be up to her to open the conversation, even if she didn't want to. She doubted that Henry was consciously thinking that it needed to be up to her, but perhaps something within him had good cause to not want to bring it up. Given her growing awareness of how her choices had affected everyone in the family—most especially Henry—she couldn't blame him.

Amala went to the nursery for a while after breakfast as she often did, not surprised to find Henry on the floor, playing with his son. The nanny was in the next room with the door open, on hand in case she was needed.

"Good morning," Amala said, and Henry returned the greeting. She sat in the rocking chair, as she usually did. Everything appeared to be normal, but inside she was trembling, struggling to gather enough courage to open up a real—and likely difficult—conversation with Henry as soon as the opportunity presented itself.

They both played with the baby and said very little to each other until Harry began to fuss, which they knew was the signal that he was hungry and ready for his morning nap. Harry was turned over to the wet nurse, and Amala put a hand on Henry's arm to stop him before he could leave the room. He looked at her hand, then her face, and she distinctly saw her own fear reflected in his eyes. He surely knew every bit as much as she did that they needed to talk, and he was likely dreading it too. Amala felt tempted to dismiss it for now, to wait, to simply say something kind and let him go. But she reminded herself that this was only going to get worse until it was addressed, and it likely wouldn't be nearly as difficult as they were both imagining.

"I need to talk to you," she implored quietly, even though no one else was in the room and they wouldn't be overheard. "Is now a good time, or—"

"Now is fine," he said, but he didn't sound happy about it.

Amala nodded and led the way through a series of halls to the sitting room just off of Kat's bedroom. She'd considered the best place for them to have this conversation. If they went to the library or one of the parlors, they were more likely to be interrupted. This room felt neutral, and yet it had a nearness to Kat that seemed appropriate.

Amala sat down on one of the small sofas, and Henry sat down across from her, crossing his ankle over his knee and staring at her as if he dared her to say something that could ease his own heartache. She prayed that might be possible. Knowing she needed to focus this conversation on *her* feelings, as opposed to expecting him to open up about his, she took a deep breath and began.

"I'm not going to state all of the things that are already clearly obvious, but—"

"Such as?" he interrupted.

"You *want* me to state what is obvious?" she asked.

"Maybe what's obvious to me isn't obvious to you—or the other way around. What makes you think my struggles and my grief are the same as yours?"

Amala drew in another long breath with more difficulty. "Very well. What I believe to be obvious is that . . . you and I are both struggling to make peace with Kat's death and at the same time come to terms with her final wish and how it has brought up some dramatic complications for both of us. Our experiences and our feelings may vary, of course. But I believe that is the basis of the problem."

"All right," he said. "I agree with that. I just want to be clear that we're talking about the same thing."

Amala felt an inkling of relief. At least the conversation had been opened and they were in agreement about *something*. She forged ahead.

"I know the situation is complicated at best, and I don't think either one of us has the strength or the desire to analyze and debate everything that's happened and what we should do about it. But we have to at least start to talk about it. For now, I mostly need to admit to you . . . aloud . . . as difficult as it is to say . . . that I've been so *angry* with Kat." Tears came with her confession, but she'd expected it, and he'd seen her cry nearly as much as her parents had—and they'd known her all of her life. "I've struggled to be able to admit to it . . . and could hardly believe it was true when Paulina first suggested that it was at the heart of the problem. How could I be angry with Kat? She never would have intentionally hurt anyone—

especially those she loved most. But once I admitted to myself that I was angry, I began wishing that she might somehow be haunting me, that her spirit might be close enough to hear me say all the hateful, awful things I was thinking. Whether or not she heard me, I don't know. But I said it all anyway. I told her that I loved her, and I understood, and I could forgive her. And I also told her that what she'd done to us was cruel and selfish."

Amala heard her own tone of voice reflecting the anger she'd been feeling and she saw Henry squeeze his eyes shut. Could he not bear to hear what she was saying? Or was she expressing his own difficult feelings? She wanted to ask but needed to finish what she'd begun.

"I told her it was all fine and well to leave this world without any secrets, but to expect that her husband and her sister might just be able to somehow magically leap past all that had happened—and all we had struggled to come to terms with—in order to honor some whimsical idea she had of a happily ever after coming out of all this . . ." She paused to breathe. "Well, I told her it was unconscionable, and it wasn't fair, and she had no idea what she'd left us to deal with. While she's in some peaceful, heavenly realm, we're here in this wretched world trying to make sense of things that don't make sense and solve problems we're not capable of solving."

Henry kept his eyes closed and hung his head. Amala could only keep talking, although she managed to sound a little calmer now that she'd gotten past the worst of it.

"I ranted like that for a very long time, and then I cried so hard that every muscle in my body was in knots. When I finally calmed down, I somehow knew that Kat understood, and that she could forgive me for being so angry, and that I could forgive her for making this so difficult. But acknowledging my anger is obviously just a step in resolving all of this. Another step is that I need to tell *you* how angry I've been—even if I didn't realize it for a long time. And you need to know that I'm not angry with you; not even a little."

He lifted his head then and looked at her. "You're not angry with me for marrying your sister after I'd declared my undying love for you?"

His brutal honesty took her off guard, but she knew it needed to be said. And what had she expected when she'd opened this conversation?

Attempting to be equally honest, she said, "I was hurt initially. A part of me hoped to never see you again because I believed that would be easier for both of us. It took time to accept that you would always be a part of my family. But I *did* accept it, Henry. I made peace with it, and I was happy for both of you. I never felt angry."

"At least not that you were willing to acknowledge," he said, again taking her off guard. "Well, you know what?" He leaned his forearms on his thighs and glared at her. "As long as we're admitting to our anger, I was *so* angry with *you*! I understood your concerns, and the vicar certainly made it clear that your concerns were not unfounded. But I wondered what I had ever done to make you have so little faith in me as to believe that we couldn't have made it work, that *we* were not worth it. I was *furious* with you! And before we could even attempt to let the matter settle, you left. And then I was *really* furious. But I was determined to get over it and to do it right—even though I had to keep it completely to myself in order to honor *your* desire for secrecy. Without your family I would have crumbled. And Kat was so kind to me, and so genuine. How could I not fall in love with her? And now? Now I look back and realize that she *knew* I had loved you first, that my heart had been broken. And it all feels . . . tainted somehow. So, if you want to talk about being angry, Amala, I'll tell you about being angry. After I fought like a soldier in a losing battle to put myself back together after honoring the wishes of one of the Hepworth sisters, I find myself thrown right back out there, being forced to figure out how I'm supposed to honor the wishes of the *other* Hepworth sister. And I wonder sometimes how my greatest blessings in life can also be my worst curse. I have hated you, and I have hated her! And yet I love you both so much that I can barely breathe if I even try to think about the fact that I have lost her and I can't have you. And yes, that makes me angry!"

Amala was trembling too much to speak beyond a whispered squeak as she muttered, "I'm so sorry, Henry."

He stood abruptly and walked around the sofa where he'd been sitting to stand at the window, where he pushed his hands into the pockets of his breeches and leaned his shoulder against the window frame.

"You have every right to be angry with me," she managed to add in spite of the way she was trembling. "If you—"

"I don't believe *anyone* has the *right* to be angry. Perhaps my anger is understandable, but it's not a right; it's my responsibility to figure it out and make peace with it."

"Easier said than done."

"Yes, well," he said, sounding mildly cynical, "most things in life are." He sighed loudly. "I'm not nearly as angry as I used to be, Amala. I too had come to terms with our not ending up together . . . until Kat said what she did. And after she died, I think it just all came rushing back and it was too much. I think I'm more afraid than angry; it's just easier to be angry than it is to think about the things I'm afraid of."

An idea occurred to Amala, and she spoke it before she had time to consider it too deeply. "Are you afraid of thinking about them, or of admitting them to me?"

He turned his head abruptly to the side as if the question had jolted him, and she had a perfect view of his profile against the light coming through the window. She knew she'd hit on something sensitive, but he turned to look outside again without commenting.

Amala reminded herself that there was something else she needed to say and that her goal in speaking with him had not been to try to resolve things that would need a great deal of time and consideration. She just had to clarify where she stood and hopefully bridge the gap between them, even a little.

Setting aside her own reaction to his description of how much she'd hurt him, she hurried to get this over with. "There's something else I need to say, but it's difficult. I realize, however, that the trust between us is fragile, and trust cannot be rebuilt without some risk. I know I'm the one responsible for everything falling apart between us, and I know I didn't handle it well; therefore, I feel it's my responsibility to clarify something."

She paused to fill her lungs with air and consider her words. "I'm listening," he said, his back still turned toward her, and she continued.

"I'm afraid too, Henry. I'm afraid to admit this aloud because I've barely been able to admit it to myself. And I want you to know—without any doubt—that I never would have even allowed myself to think about it if Kat had lived. But now that we're here . . . like this . . . I need to tell you that . . . I'm not certain I did the right thing." She paused, waiting for a reaction, but he didn't move or make a sound. "I know my concerns were real, and valid, and they still are. But perhaps I was too . . . naive . . . or too ruled by fear . . . to make the right decision for the right reason."

Henry turned slowly to look at her, his brow furrowed, his eyes delving into her as if he might be able to find her motive for saying such a thing. The evidence of his ongoing struggle with anger sharpened the edge in his voice. "Don't you *dare* give me hope, Amala, if you will only end up breaking my heart again."

Amala was proud of herself for countering firmly, "And don't presume that my admission to having made a mistake means that I have any idea how all of this will turn out. Still"—she took in a deep breath and looked away, unable to bear his gaze another second—"it's a place to start, I suppose." She then repeated her hope that he would take it as a challenge. "Trust cannot be rebuilt without some risk."

He said nothing, and she stood, knowing she couldn't bear any more of this right now and he'd likely reached his limits as well. She had enough sense to know when a conversation was already far too overloaded, and this one certainly was.

"Thank you for listening, Henry, and for your candor. I would very much like to get past this awkward silence between us." She met his eyes firmly as she concluded, "I miss you."

Still he said nothing, and she left the room, again overcome with that trembling inside. She hurried to her own room, where she locked the doors and went to her knees beside the bed, praying that she'd done the right thing, said the right words, to help move them both forward on this impossible path.

Chapter Fourteen
FILLED WITH COLOR

HENRY WATCHED AMALA LEAVE THE room before he moved back to the sofa, suddenly weak. He pressed his head into his hands and groaned. He sat there for more than an hour, considering everything Amala had said—and his own words to her, some of them having come out far more brutally than he'd intended.

A maid found him there to remind him that lunch was being served, and he asked her to tell the others to eat without him; he'd get something from the kitchen when he got hungry. After another hour or more had passed, Henry realized he was tired. He was physically tired from all the months since Kat's death—and the many months before that—when he'd never gotten a good night's sleep. And he was worn out from the emotional whirlwind that had taken over his mind and his heart, wreaking havoc with both. He was especially tired of holding it all inside—except for the times when he had told Kat exactly what he thought about her dying and leaving him in this situation. He'd not felt ready to admit to Amala that he too had been talking to Kat's ghost, except that he'd been more prone to shouting at his dead wife, which was the main reason he took lengthy rides on many days, so that he could get far enough away from the house to not be overheard. But Kat had not been talking back to him, which he supposed meant he was still clinging to his sanity. However, the one-sided conversations were getting old, and he felt certain that if he didn't start talking to someone mortal, he would lose his sanity.

Once he'd made up his mind, Henry couldn't find Oliver quickly enough. He loved and trusted this man who had become a father to him, and he was relieved to find him alone in the library.

"Hello, my boy," Oliver said as Henry closed the door. He took off his glasses and added, "I do hope you've come to talk to me because I've been wishing that you would."

"Why?" Henry asked, sitting down across from him. "Because you think I need to talk? Or because *you* need to talk?"

"Both," Oliver said. "We both lost her, Henry. And women see things differently than we do in so many ways, bless them. But you have other things on your mind as well, I think."

Henry nodded and considered where to begin. He said the first thing that came to his mind. "I feel like a fool, Oliver, to realize that you knew Amala and I were romantically involved, which makes me feel like a bigger fool to consider what you and Viola must have thought when I then became romantically involved with Kat. And it feels like it's all exploded in my face, and I wonder why you haven't sat me down and given me a proper scolding. I wonder if you think that I deserve to be in this predicament. And maybe I do."

Oliver was silently thoughtful as he set the book and his glasses aside. "Henry," he said, "do you think that *I* am a fool?"

"No, never."

"Then why do you think I would allow *any* man to pursue one of my daughters if I believed that his intentions were not entirely pure? Do you think I would not have intervened if I'd believed there was any lack of integrity at the root of your affections?" Henry hung his head and tried to take that in while Oliver continued. "Viola and I knew from the day we met you that you were a man in need of a family, and we loved the way you fit so nicely into ours, and we would have been glad to have it be that way forever whether you had married one of our daughters or not. And we knew that you knew that, which means we both knew your feelings for them were not misguided or selfish. If I thought you'd done something wrong, son, I wouldn't be afraid to tell you. Truthfully, you are one of the finest men I've ever known and I consider it a privilege to call you my son."

"You really mean that?" Henry said, looking at him again, wanting to be certain.

"I really do. So, enough of this feeling like a fool. It's in the past. You kept it from us because Amala asked you to. We understand that."

"I'm not certain *I* understand it," Henry muttered. "I think I'm still trying to figure it out."

"I'm sure none of us ever could have predicted or imagined such a complicated and grievous course of events occurring in our family."

"No," Henry said, "we certainly couldn't have."

"But we know what the situation is, and Kat's been gone at least long enough for us to begin to think clearly again. I hope that's why you're finally here; I've been waiting, you know."

"Have you?"

"I have. Every night Viola climbs into bed and asks me if you came to talk to me yet."

Henry sighed. "And so the two of you can still see right through me."

"Let's just say we consider it somewhat of a parental duty to pay close attention to our children and their moods and behaviors. And not one of you could ever be pushed into something before you felt ready. But you're here now, so why don't you just ask me what you came to ask me. And, no, I have no idea what you came to ask me, but I know when I see the need to ask a question; it must be a big one from that look in your eyes. So get to it, son."

Henry sighed and crossed his arms over his chest. "If I *had* come to you back then . . . asking for your permission to court Amala . . . what would you have told me?"

"Funny," Oliver said with an expression that contradicted the word, "Amala asked me that exact question only a few days ago."

"Did she?" Henry asked. "And what did you tell her?"

"I would have joyfully given my blessing," Oliver said with conviction, "and then Viola and I would have sat down with the two of you and discussed the potential challenges of such a marriage in this time and place. We would have encouraged both of you to marry for love and to also be sensible enough to understand that such a marriage would inevitably be difficult, and that those difficulties would—without a doubt—be passed along to your children. So, to answer what I think might be another question spinning around in your head . . . you were right about believing that with a love that's strong and steady, two people can face and overcome anything. But Amala was right too; it would have been incredibly difficult. It *will* be difficult . . . if you decide to take Kat's advice."

"Advice?" Henry echoed with some chagrin. "She made us promise her . . . before we knew what we were promising. It was almost the last lucid conversation we had."

"I know that, Henry; we all do. But we also know that you and Amala are wise enough to know that she would never want either of you to make such an enormous decision just because it's what *she* wanted. If she'd been capable of talking for more than a few minutes at a time, I believe she would have clarified that. Either way, no one wants you to marry Amala just because Kat asked you to. Marriage for the sake of duty or obligation is a heavy burden and it would be far too much to bear along with the other inevitable challenges—should you ever decide to pursue that course."

Henry wished now that he'd come to talk to Oliver weeks ago. His common sense was validating, and his understanding was a comfort. But there was one more thing he *had* to ask, and he prayed he wouldn't regret it. "If I do decide to purse that course . . . if I came to you now and asked for your blessing . . . hypothetically speaking . . . what would you tell me? How do you feel about the situation, Oliver? How does Viola feel? I know you can speak for her because I know the two of you have no secrets from each other."

Oliver smiled slightly and leaned forward. "Henry, my boy, nothing in the world could make us happier. With the time that's passed since you first fell in love with Amala and all that's happened, we know we don't have to tell either of you how difficult such a marriage might be. But the two of you would never be in it alone; we're a family. And the entire household is practically like family. To my knowledge, every person who lives and works here loves and admires both of you. With so much love and support, surely there is nothing the two of you couldn't face and overcome. In a word, Henry, you have my blessing."

Tears stung Henry's eyes, and he drew in a quivering breath before he asked in a voice that was slightly shaky, "Is it too soon to be considering such things? I don't care what other people think; but I care what *you* think—and your good wife. Kat's not been gone so very long. Should I even be thinking that—"

"That what? That you should move on and find happiness? Kat wouldn't have wanted you to wait; I believe she as much as told you so."

Henry looked down, unable to hold back his tears now as he recalled well his final conversation with Kat. "You know, I'd actually forgotten. She *did* tell me not to wait. How did you know?"

"Because she told me that she was going to tell you," Oliver said, getting a little choked up himself as the memories of Kat's death hovered around them.

Henry sighed and pushed his fingers through his hair, feeling both overwhelmed and relieved. "But . . . what if Amala refuses me again? I don't know if I could bear it."

"Do you think she will?"

"I don't know."

"How could you when the two of you have hardly said a word to each other for so long?"

"We talked this morning," Henry was glad to say. He likely wouldn't be here talking to Oliver now if Amala hadn't forced him to start talking.

"I'm glad to hear it," Oliver said. "And?"

"And what?"

"Do you think she would refuse you again . . . after all that's happened?"

"I don't know. I honestly don't know. But I can't say if that's my own fear talking."

"Perhaps she's afraid you'll never ask, while you don't ask because you're afraid of her response. Sounds fairly ridiculous to me."

"When you put it that way," Henry said, "it does sound ridiculous."

"But don't take that to mean that I don't understand how difficult all of this has been for both of you. Don't be so hard on yourself, Henry. But for heaven's sake open your eyes and realize that the two of you have both been given a rare and wonderful gift, and to pass it up *would* make you a fool."

"What's that?" Henry asked.

Oliver whispered with a smile, as if it were a magical secret, "A second chance, my boy. You've been given a second chance." In a more normal voice, he said, "None of us would have wished for Kat to leave us the way she did, but I believe that God doesn't take things away from us without offering some kind of blessing to compensate.

We just have to pay attention and do our part. When God took our dear friends from us so tragically in India, He gave us their daughter to care for as our own. And now—as I see it—God is offering you and Amala a second chance, and I don't believe there is another man in all the world—of any color—who could make her as happy as you could."

"You really mean that," Henry said again, more than a little stunned.

"I think we've established that I don't say what I don't mean." Oliver smiled. "Now, why are you still sitting here? Go find Amala and tell her how you feel, or I swear to you I will force the two of you to talk over the supper table." He winked. "Are you willing to take that risk?" He picked up his glasses with an indication that he intended to return to his reading. At the mention of the word risk, Henry recalled Amala's words clearly: *Trust cannot be rebuilt without some risk.*

Henry stood but paused to reach out a hand toward Oliver, who looked at it before they shared a firm handshake. "Thank you," Henry said, "for everything . . . Father."

"Thank *you*, son," Oliver said with sincerity, and Henry hurried from the room, wondering how long it might take him to find Amala when he had no idea where to begin looking.

* * * *

Amala was startled to hear the door to the sitting room close, and she looked up to see Henry staring at her in a way that had once been common, except there was nothing familiar in the meaning of his gaze—the problem was that she had no idea what that meaning might be, and she'd once been able to read him so easily. When he hadn't come to lunch, she had felt concerned and eventually she had returned to where they'd been talking earlier with the hope that he'd still be here. She found it ironic that he'd now come looking for her. But she felt skeptical—perhaps even afraid—of what his reasons might be, and she couldn't keep from staring at him, feeling as if something had changed since they'd talked earlier.

"What's wrong?" he asked. "You look as if you're afraid of me. Have I changed so much that I would frighten you?"

Amala turned back to the view out the window. "You don't frighten me." She didn't add that her feelings *did* frighten her; perhaps they always had. Perhaps that was the heart of the problem. "But we are certainly not the same people we used to be."

"No, we certainly are not," he said, stepping slowly toward her. "But I have to believe that somehow . . . somewhere . . . deep inside both of us . . . what we once felt for each other is still there."

She looked up to see him standing directly at her side. The quickening of her heart seemed to verify what he was saying. "So, now that we've finally started to talk again . . . I have a question for you, Amala."

He hesitated, and she realized he seemed to be waiting for her permission to ask his question, which made her suspect it was perhaps something monumental. "I'm listening," she said and heard him take in a deep breath and let it out slowly before he went on.

"Do you think we *really* lost all of that love we both felt so intensely for each other? Or did we just put it away because it seemed the only option at the time? Because it was the right thing to do and we're both people who try very hard to do the right thing?"

Amala could hear her pulse beating in her ears as his implication began to settle in. This was not what she'd expected. But it was what she'd hoped for, although she'd believed it would take much more time and many more conversations before they would be able to talk about such things.

He took another step toward her, and she tried not to be affected by his nearness as he continued, his voice softening. "Do you think it's possible that a spark still exists somewhere deep inside each of us and it merely needs to be reignited? Or would getting married now simply be some kind of strange duty in honoring Kat's wishes?"

Amala couldn't bear to look at him. The fluttering in her stomach, the pounding of her heart, the dizziness in her head all seemed to verify that what he'd said was true. But she felt terrified to admit it. What if *she* had held on to that spark and simply stuffed it deep down inside, but he had not? What if Kat had eradicated any and all of the love he'd once felt for her? She couldn't bear to think of feeling this way without having her feelings reciprocated.

Fighting for practicality, Amala took a deep breath and said, "That was a great many questions, Henry. And none of them are easily answered. You can't expect me to—"

"You don't have to say a word," he murmured, taking hold of her chin with his fingers and turning to face her directly. "The answer to my every question is in your eyes." He leaned a little closer, and she added difficulty breathing to her list of symptoms. "Now that Kat is gone and our secret is out, you have no need to hide and pretend any longer."

Amala closed her eyes, unable to look at him. She was unprepared for the way tears leaked out from beneath her closed eyelids, surely giving her away.

"I saw it in your eyes the day I found you crying on Kat's bed, and it frightened me. I wasn't ready to talk about it. I wasn't ready to feel that way about you again. And I need you to know that I meant it when I said that not once while I was courting Kat and married to her did I allow myself to think of you in a way that I knew was not proper, but that doesn't mean I didn't think of you. I wondered every day if you were all right . . . if you were happy."

"I *have* been happy," she declared, still not opening her eyes, still unable to control the flow of tears running down her cheeks. "With the exception of losing Kat, I have been very blessed, and I have felt a great deal of peace. God has been kind to me."

"I could say exactly the same for myself," he said in little more than a whisper. "Perhaps what we both needed to say to each other earlier has allowed us to realize how far we've come in making peace with all of this."

"Perhaps," Amala said, still not looking at him.

"And perhaps it's time for both of us to accept that she really is gone, and she's not coming back, and maybe she was right about us. Maybe she knew that she needed to make us promise, or we would have both been too proud to ever come to it on our own."

"Perhaps," Amala said again, certain he was right.

His voice softened further. "What I need to know is . . . can you love me again, Amala?"

She opened her eyes at last, finding his face even closer than she'd realized. And she could feel nothing but relief to see stark evidence of the once-familiar love he felt for her glowing in his countenance. It was just as he'd said about her: he didn't need to say anything; the answer to her every question was in his eyes. She felt deeply compelled to admit to the truth, however vulnerable it might make her feel. "I never stopped loving you, Henry; I only learned how to put my love into its proper place. I will love you forever; I only pray that Kat can forgive me."

"Then may she forgive us both," he said as if to echo that his feelings were the same. "Although," he smiled only slightly, "I do believe she made it clear that she already had."

In spite of how close his face was to hers and the way he kept hold of her chin, Amala was still surprised when he kissed her, and even more surprised with how warm and familiar it felt after so many years. It only took a moment for that spark he'd described to come to life inside of her, and she took hold of his arms to save herself from the dizzying effect of the experience. Their kiss was long and slow, and it ended with a sense of reluctance to stop but a great hope of life beginning anew.

Henry looked into her eyes, his nose nearly close enough to touch hers. "Marry me, Amala. Let's make Kat's wish come true—and more importantly, let's make our own wishes come true. It doesn't matter what anyone else thinks or how the world views us or our children. I hope I've proven that our worlds can be integrated. We can teach our children to be strong; we can *make* them strong with the love we give them. Please, Amala," he implored with his eyes repeating an echo of his words, "please don't tell me no this time. Give me the hope of being able to enjoy a good and happy life in spite of losing Kat. No one is better for me than you are; no one will ever be more right for me than you. Please tell me you'll marry me."

Amala exchanged a long gaze with him that allowed her to fully absorb what he was asking her and what it meant—both in regard to the past *and* the future. There were aspects of this situation that still frightened her and left her concerned, but she had certainly learned that though there were certain things in life that could not be changed or controlled, the rest had to be up to her. Kat was gone; Henry loved her and she loved him. She didn't *want* to live her life alone. In spite of the fine example that Paulina had offered of how that was possible, Amala didn't share her aunt's wanderlust, and she truly longed for the companionship of a husband and the opportunity to be a mother. And Henry had proven over time how much he understood her plight and how his own love and personal regard for her homeland and her heritage made him the best possible match for her.

In the naiveté of youth, Amala had believed that every person likely wanted to believe that finding love was the answer to every problem in life, that true love could conquer all. Amala had grown past such childish notions at an age much younger than the average woman. The color of her skin and hair had quickly made her realize she could never expect the same out of life as the women around her. And yet she had observed that even in marriages in which race and skin color were not an issue, love in and of itself was never enough. Romantic love faded, attraction was likely relative, and it took a true and abiding presence of trust, respect, and commitment to make a marriage successful and to face the challenges of life. And Amala knew now what she hadn't known when Henry had first asked her to marry him; she knew that together they shared those things. Their love for each other was strong and true, but they also had the ability to communicate and be united firmly against the hardships of the world. She had carefully examined these things in her heart in the months since Kat had died and had likely been doing so at some unconscious level in her mind long before that. She knew that marrying Henry was absolutely the best thing she could do with her life and that with him at her side, she could live the best possible life available to her, given the facets of it that could never be changed. And maybe—just maybe—the two of them together *could* make a difference—even a small one in helping the world be just a little more accepting of a mixed family.

As a final point in the analysis that passed through Amala's brain in a matter of seconds—but perhaps one of the most important points— she knew they both shared the same firm belief in God, and they shared a mutual trust in Him to assist them throughout their lives. She recalled briefly a conversation she'd once had with Paulina about this very thing. It was her belief that if two people shared religious views and existed on a similar spiritual plane, then everything else was easier.

If Amala had held to the religious affiliation of her childhood, she and Henry might not have ever been able to make a marriage work. But Amala had quickly taken to the Christian beliefs of her new family, and her beliefs had brought abundant peace and understanding into her life. In that moment she felt certain that God approved of this marriage and that He would surely be with them.

"Your silence is making me nervous," Henry admitted, alerting Amala to the long moments that had passed while she had reassured herself that the answer she wanted to give him—and the one he was hoping to hear—was indeed the right answer for both of them.

Amala impulsively lifted her lips to his again, finding gratitude in simply being able to kiss him without guilt or secrecy or fear over the implications of wanting to share her life with him. She smiled at him and pressed a hand to his face. "Yes, Henry," she said, looking even more deeply into his eyes so he would have no doubt that she meant it. "I will marry you." She felt more than heard his breath escape him in a sharp burst. "I want nothing more than to share every part of my life with you. I believe we can take very good care of each other and of little Harry. Nothing could make me happier."

A laugh combined with a gentle sob erupted out of him and he pulled her completely into his arms. "Oh, Amala," he murmured. "I can't believe it." He looked at her but kept a tight hold on her, as if he feared letting go. "How can everything have changed so wonderfully in the course of a day?"

"I suppose we just needed to actually talk to each other. If we'd shared how we were really feeling, perhaps we could have solved this sooner."

"And perhaps this is the right time. Perhaps sooner would have been too soon." His expression sobered. "Do you think it *is* too soon? I don't care what people think, Amala; you know that. I intend to elope with a woman from India; what people think is more than completely irrelevant. But I want to do right by Kat . . . and your parents. Is it too soon?"

"I've asked myself that," she admitted. "And I think Kat would have been all right with you and I getting married the day after the funeral, and truthfully, I don't think my parents would have objected. I believe they understand a great deal more than we think they do."

"I'm sure you're right," he said and kissed her again. She felt a passion in his kiss she'd never experienced before, and she felt him withdraw with self-restraint, which made her love and respect him all the more.

"Did you say we're going to elope?" she asked while he pressed his lips to her brow.

"We obviously can't get married here," he said, and she knew it was true.

"I don't want to wait any longer," she confessed, holding tightly to his upper arms, wanting only to be in such close proximity to him night and day, never wanting to be alone again.

"Nor do I," he admitted, and she sighed with deep relief. "Let's leave for Scotland tonight."

In spite of her plea—and how she felt—she was still surprised. "Tonight?" she asked, looking up at him, but she couldn't help laughing as she said it.

"Give me one good reason why we should wait another day. If we take hired coaches and travel directly there, we'll have plenty of time to adjust to the idea."

"Oh, I don't think I need much adjustment," she said and laughed again, feeling nothing but pure joy.

* * * *

At the supper table, Amala made no effort to hide the fact that she was in good spirits—and perhaps feeling better about herself and her life than she ever had. The dramatic change in Henry's mood was also readily evident, and Paulina and her parents were quick to ask what had changed.

Henry looked at Oliver and said, "I'm assuming from our conversation earlier that if I ask for your blessing in making Amala my wife, you would give it."

Amala heard Paulina gasp and saw her mother put a hand over her mouth as if to suppress a great cry of happiness that was apparent in the sparkling of her eyes.

Oliver grinned and asked, *"Are* you asking, son?"

"I am," Henry said. Looking directly at Amala, he added, "I hope you know that I would devote my life to making her happy and keeping her safe with the belief that we can share a good life in spite of obvious challenges."

"I believe we all know that, Henry," Oliver said and came to his feet, extending his hand. Henry rose as well and firmly shook the proffered hand. "You have my blessing, son . . . with all my heart. And I think I speak for my wife and sister when I say that we are all very happy you've come to this decision."

"Amen," Paulina said at the same time Viola whimpered joyfully, "Oh yes!"

The men were seated, and Henry exchanged a warm smile with Amala over the table. She saw a sparkle of anticipation and perfect happiness in his eyes that made her heart beat a little faster and her stomach quiver. It had been a long time coming, and neither of them could have ever anticipated the journey their lives would take since the evening they'd met and shared a waltz and a garden stroll. But Amala had never felt happier and she knew with all her soul that this was the right course for both of them.

During the remainder of the meal, they discussed plans for the marriage, and Amala was glad that her parents agreed with Henry's reasoning in their need to just leave that night and elope. Oliver declared they'd waited long enough, and now that they knew being married was right—and they lived under the same roof—it was better for them to be married. He also declared that with the local vicar's attitude, which was shared by many residents of the community, their getting married quietly and out of the country was by far the best solution, given the extenuating circumstances. The plan was for Henry and Amala to travel to Scotland quickly, but then spend some time there for a honeymoon and travel home at a more leisurely pace, knowing that Harry was in good hands with so many people in the house who loved him and would work together to take care of him.

After supper, Amala went to her room with her mother and aunt accompanying her to help her pack. While both women took great delight in assisting the bride with her preparations as much as possible under such hurried circumstances, Amala couldn't help but feel her anticipation heighten. Amala was left alone when the others both declared they had something they needed to go and get, and she gathered what she considered to be the essentials onto her bed, wondering whether to try to get it all into an average-sized portmanteau she owned or if she should use a conservative-sized trunk. She knew from her vast experience of traveling with Paulina that a trunk was in some ways easier for the carriage drivers to handle—as long as it wasn't too heavy, which wasn't a problem. When her mother and Paulina returned together, she knew immediately that she would need a trunk.

"Oh, my!" Amala declared, seeing her mother carrying what she knew was the dress Viola had been married in.

"It's up to you if you want to wear it," Viola said. "Kat wanted a new gown that was her own, and I won't be offended if you decide you want the same. Even though you're choosing to get married this way—for obvious reasons—you should still have a proper wedding gown, so if you don't want to wear this, or it doesn't work for you, I want you to make certain Henry buys you a proper gown."

Amala nodded and said, "I would very much like to wear it—if it fits me."

Viola believed that Amala was near the same size she'd been when she'd married Oliver, and the dress had been carefully kept in Viola's wardrobe all these years and well preserved. Amala tried it on with great hope that it would work. The fit wasn't perfect, but close enough that no one would notice that it was slightly tight in a couple of places and a little loose in others. In truth, it was a magnificent wedding gown made from a variety of laces, with intricate beadwork sewn onto the bodice and sleeves in a floral pattern. All three women declared it to be perfect, and the gown was carefully wrapped in tissue paper and packed in a trunk, along with the rest of Amala's things. Some assistance from Lekha was very helpful, and the maid's excitement added to Amala's own thrill over what was taking place.

Amala had grown to care deeply for Lekha in the time since she'd returned from the continent. Pearl was also dear to her and still very much involved in their lives. But Amala shared a special bond with Lekha that had made it doubly comfortable to have her around. And now that Amala knew she would be marrying Henry and she had the hope of being a mother, she felt an added joy to know that Lekha was expecting a baby. Amala could never explain the peace it gave her to think that her children would grow up under the same roof as other children with Indian blood. But she felt certain that once she returned from her honeymoon, they would all have plenty of time to talk about what a blessing such things were for all of them.

Following many hugs and good wishes, Henry and Amala were finally off. The family driver would take them to a town that was a common crossroad for travelers—and far enough away from their own village to avoid having anyone local know what was taking place. From there, Henry and Amala would take hired coaches to Scotland.

Once alone in the carriage with Henry, Amala had believed they would have so much to say to each other. But he put his arm around her and she laid her head against his shoulder, feeling completely comfortable and at peace. He pressed a kiss into her hair and murmured gently, "I love you, Amala."

"Oh, I love you too, Henry," she replied. It seemed that nothing more needed to be said.

* * * *

Amala awoke in the quaint room of an inn somewhere in England. She didn't know where they were; she didn't care. Henry was sleeping beside her, and the angle of the early-morning sun filled the room with a light that seeped into her spirit like a tangible expression of the brightness she felt within. She looked around the room at the way the sunlight illuminated the beauty of every detail until her eyes came to rest on her husband and she could only stare at him in wonder. In the days since they'd been married, a realization had slowly settled into her. She had once naively believed that she could live without him and find a way to be happy. And although she still believed she would have found fulfillment and contentment with whatever life might have given her, she now knew she'd had absolutely no idea how thoroughly wrong she had been. But how could an innocent young woman possibly comprehend the absolute majesty and beauty of sharing every aspect of life with a truly good man? She knew now that it took common sense, and certainly enough humility to trust in God and listen for His guidance in order to come to such a place. She also knew that it took faith to be able to believe in something you could never know without experiencing it. And she knew that it took courage—the courage to follow your heart in spite of the odds being against you.

Amala watched Henry slowly come awake, and when he saw that she was watching him, he smiled, mirroring the same peace and contentment she felt, making the light in the room all the brighter.

"What are you thinking about so deeply?" he asked after he'd kissed her. He gently maneuvered his fingers through her tangled black hair and looked at her with eyes that needed no words to declare how beautiful she was to him.

"It's difficult to put into words," she admitted, "but I think . . . that it feels as if everything is more clear. It's as if . . . colors are more vivid . . . details are more beautiful."

"Everything?"

"Everything," she repeated. "My life, the world around me; everything I see, and taste, and experience is . . . more colorful, more exquisite."

Henry smiled again. "I think you just did a marvelous job of putting it into words. I've felt exactly the same way but never could have described it so perfectly."

Amala touched his face and kissed his lips, looking forward to every day of her life that they would spend together, a life that would surely be filled with vivid color and light.

* * * *

Nearly a year following their marriage, Amala had awakened with a strong desire to visit Kat's grave, and Henry had eagerly agreed to accompany her. It wasn't the first time they'd done so, but today was Kat's birthday, and Amala wanted to visit her sister's final resting place and leave flowers, especially on this day. She and Henry had talked a great deal about Kat, and time was making it easier to do so without having difficult emotions surface. Now that their lives had come to this place, they had more comfortably accepted their mutual love for Kat and her role in bringing them together.

While the carriage waited at the perimeter of the church cemetery and little Harry ran around between the gravestones nearby, Amala pressed her fingers over her sister's name where it was carved into the granite headstone. Henry did the same before he took hold of her hand and they stood there in silence together for a long moment until Harry wandered a little too far and Henry hurried to catch up with the toddler. Amala stood where she was, smiling as she observed from a distance the way Henry scooped their son into his arms and made growling noises that provoked giggling from the child. Henry laughed and shifted little Harry onto his shoulders, holding tightly to his little hands to keep him secure as he walked back toward Amala. She watched them while she once again touched her sister's name, trying to comprehend the happiness she felt. With a loving caress, she pressed her other hand over her rounded belly, anticipating the day when Harry would be getting a younger sibling.

Amala took a deep breath and realized that the vivid awareness of color and beauty in her life had not diminished since she'd married Henry; it had only become more and more defined. And she silently thanked God for blessing her life so richly. Challenges and concerns were by no means magically erased, but the love she shared with Henry, the support of her family and household, and the knowledge that God was in their lives had all combined to build her confidence in knowing they could face and conquer whatever might happen as a result of their unconventional marriage. Her love and admiration for her parents continued to grow as she observed how much selfless love and goodness they were capable of sharing. They expressed nothing but happiness over Amala and Henry being married and the prospect of more children joining their household. And they were still able to talk freely about their love for Kat and how they missed her. Paulina had still not had any urge to run off to visit faraway places and had in fact—through the help of an agent—sold her properties in Spain and Italy. The house in France was something she would hold on to indefinitely, and its value was proven when the entire family went there on holiday, and Henry and her parents had been able to experience why Paulina and Amala both loved the place so much. Nevertheless, they were all happy to return home and settle back into their comfortable routine.

As Henry approached, Amala heard a sound behind her and turned to see a man coming from the other direction. She'd never seen him before, but from the way he was dressed, she immediately recognized him to be a clergyman. She felt confused, knowing well enough who the local vicar was, but she also felt wary, given their past experience with the local clergy. As if Henry sensed and shared her concern, she found him standing strong at her side, and he moved Harry to one arm so that he could put his other arm around Amala as this man came closer, wearing a smile.

During the few seconds it took him to get close enough to speak to them, Amala wondered if going out into the public today had been a good idea. Initially, following their marriage, she had chosen to remain at home with the exception of occasionally going out riding with Henry or taking long walks. But the estate was so enormous that they'd never actually left the land they owned. She was blessed to live in an efficient household where everything she needed was brought into the home by other people, and she didn't have to face a critical public if she chose not to, and her family had made it clear that they supported her in that choice. However, Henry had repeatedly told her she shouldn't have to feel like she had to hide. He believed she was strong enough to face anyone with confidence in her own choices and not be intimidated. Gradually his belief in her had left her feeling challenged to go into public with him, just to see if she could do it.

A stroll through the village holding to her husband's arm had been their first outing. They had been met with many glares of disdain, which Henry had ignored, offering kind greetings in return. Amala had felt mildly upset even though she was not at all surprised. But the next time they went out, she was able to more easily ignore the way people looked at them, and with increased outings and a growing confidence in the reasons that she and Henry had made the choice to be together, she began to believe they truly were capable of teaching their children to confidently and appropriately deal with the challenges they might face by being half English and half Indian. Henry firmly believed that with time such marriages would become more common and more accepted. Amala wasn't certain they would live to see such changes, but she still wanted to believe it was possible.

And it was her father's opinion that perhaps his grandchildren could help facilitate even a little bit of that change. Amala wanted to believe that too.

Still, with all of Amala's growing confidence and her increasing ability to not care what people might think or how they might regard her, they had never ventured anywhere near the church—except for a rare visit to the adjoining cemetery, which until now had gone completely unnoticed. The family continued to have their Sabbath meetings at home, and worship was a high priority in their home. But in spite of all the progress she'd made, Amala felt entirely unprepared for whatever this encounter might entail, and she was grateful to have Henry at her side, knowing that he was not afraid to boldly declare exactly what he thought and that he would be efficient in whisking her away to the nearby carriage if the need arose.

"Good morning," the clergyman said, still smiling. His smile was a good sign, especially in light of Amala's memory of the terrible scowl on the vicar's face when he'd spoken to her so harshly.

"Good morning," Henry replied.

"It's a beautiful day to honor loved ones here," the man added, nodding toward the gravestone by which Henry and Amala were standing.

"It is indeed," Henry said, mildly cautious but kind.

"I should introduce myself," the man said, holding out his hand toward Henry in a genuinely friendly gesture. "I'm Mr. Reynolds, the new vicar here."

"New?" Henry echoed, and Amala wondered if he felt the same hope as she did.

"Yes, our previous vicar and his family were transferred to a new location, one that our superiors felt might be better suited to him."

Amala exchanged a brief glance with Henry, and she felt relatively certain that he too was wondering if the vicar's hypocrisy might have finally been noticed by his superiors. She felt certain that his disdain toward her was likely of no concern to them, since it was a generally accepted attitude that she was of an inferior race. But they had seen much evidence of their prior vicar exhibiting hypocritical and less-than-Christian attitudes about many things.

"I see," Henry said. "And how are you liking it here so far?"

"My wife and I like it very much," Mr. Reynolds said with enthusiasm. "Although," he chuckled, "I dare say some of the congregation will find that adjusting to . . . shall we say . . . my style . . . of the work I do . . . somewhat challenging."

Without allowing time for any questions regarding this comment, Mr. Reynolds looked at Amala, and his smile broadened, then he spoke to both of them in a way that Amala appreciated. Often when people spoke to them, they mostly disregarded Amala as if she were not present.

"I must be completely honest and admit that I know who you are." He tipped his head toward Kat's gravestone as if knowing the family connection had made their identity clear—but there was no other man in his congregation with an Indian wife, and he'd surely heard all about them. But exactly what he'd heard—and from whom—was impossible to know. "I've been wanting to come and visit your family and get to know you better, but I confess that we're trying to visit *every* family in order to become better acquainted, and we just haven't gotten very far yet."

He paused to catch his breath and smiled again, but Amala sensed he was gathering resolve for what he would say next. She prayed it wasn't something that would dash her hopes for a better relationship with *this* vicar as opposed to the trauma that had been caused for her and Henry by his predecessor.

"I'm not a man to beat around the bush," Mr. Reynolds said, "so I'm just going to come right out and say what I've wanted to say to the both of you ever since I was told about your situation." He looked more at Amala for a long moment. "My wife and I spent some time in India ourselves, and we grew to love the people there. I hope that counts for something, Mrs. Beckenridge."

Amala was taken off guard—first by his kindness, and secondly because no one had ever called her that except members of her family in a mostly teasing manner. She'd not been acknowledged publicly as Henry's wife by anyone at all in the community, and hearing it now left her slightly choked up. She nodded in response and continued to listen.

"I want to make it very clear that while I'm well aware of how unconventional your marriage is and that many people look down upon it here—as they surely would in India—I am a firm believer that God sees all of His children as equals; He is no respecter of persons, which I have always taken to mean that it is our devotion to Him that matters, and the way we treat others is a means of showing that devotion. It is my most fervent aspiration in my calling to spread the good news of the gospel of Christ by word and deed in the principle that He taught us to love one another—without exception. I hope you will not allow the opinions of my predecessor—or anyone else in this community—to taint your views on that principle."

Henry exchanged another glance with Amala, and this time she could see that he shared her amazement. He looked at Mr. Reynolds and said, "In spite of our lack of attendance at Sunday meetings, our family has diligently participated in a worship service in our home, and we certainly strive to live by this very principle."

"I'm so glad to hear it!" Mr. Reynolds said as if he'd just heard the best news of his life. "And if you choose to continue in that manner—given the situation and all that's happened—I would certainly understand. However, I am sincerely hoping you will agree to at least give me a chance and attend one of our Sunday meetings. I would very much like to help this congregation open their minds and take on a more accurate view of the teachings of our good Lord from the New Testament; some will never change their ideas, but I'm hoping some might come with humility and open hearts. And I would very much like your presence there to help people see the good that can come from living those teachings."

Feeling overwhelmed by such an idea, Amala was glad to hear Henry say, "Your offer is very kind, Mr. Reynolds, and I think I can speak for my wife when I say that it means a great deal to us." He glanced at her as if to ask her approval in speaking for her and she nodded. "I believe we would like some time to think about it and to discuss it with our family."

"Of course, of course," Mr. Reynolds said. "Perhaps later this week my good wife and I might come to your home and meet the rest of the family, and we can talk it through. You're always welcome— at any time—to ask me any question you might have about my beliefs and my feelings on any matter, and while I might fumble and stumble at times—as I'm prone to do . . ." he chuckled humbly, "I will always be completely honest with you."

"Thank you," Henry said.

"It's such a pleasure to meet the both of you," Mr. Reynolds said. "I should let you get on with your day . . . unless . . ."

"Unless?" Henry echoed when the vicar hesitated.

"I wonder if you might like to meet my wife now. It's not the conventional time for tea, but we can always put the kettle on. We have a couple of young children ourselves, so I can't guarantee the parlor will be tidy, but . . . my dear sweet wife is so kind to receive guests at a moment's notice. She's told me she would love to meet you." Again he looked more at Amala. "There are things about India she misses very much."

Henry looked at Amala, silently asking for her opinion, or perhaps he preferred that she simply make the decision. Amala felt completely comfortable saying, "I would love to meet your wife, Mr. Reynolds. We have no pressing matters this morning. If you're sure it's all right . . ."

"Couldn't be better!" Mr. Reynolds declared with a little laugh, again behaving as if their visit might be the best thing that had ever happened to him. But his diplomacy was completely natural and genuine.

Henry informed the carriage driver of their plans; then he took Amala's hand and followed the vicar the short distance to the cottage where he lived, which was not far from the church. Amala immediately loved the quaint coziness of the cottage, which reminded her a bit of Paulina's home in France—at least in its size and its warm mood. Even more, she immediately loved Mrs. Reynolds, who was so genuinely pleased to meet Amala and Henry that again Amala felt a little choked up.

They all sat down to share tea while Harry played with the Reynolds children, who were both a little older than Harry and did well at keeping him entertained and out of trouble. Mrs. Reynolds was full of kind and polite questions about their experiences in India and about how they'd come to be married. She declared that they were a beautiful couple, and noticing the obvious evidence that Amala was expecting, she predicted it would be a beautiful child and live a life of adventure and surely do great things in the world. Amala squeezed Henry's hand, feeling as if this woman had just soothed some of her fears away in regard to the future of their children. He squeezed back as if he understood.

Amala loved answering this woman's questions, and for the first time since Kat's death, she felt the possibility of actually having a friend in her life. Given that the Reynolds family had only recently moved here, this woman seemed in want of good company, and her love of India had already given them common ground. Her absolute lack of prejudice—much like her husband—made her easy to be with and easy to like. It was as if these people didn't even see the difference of color between Amala and Henry, and Amala felt as if the windows of heaven had opened. She knew in her heart that everything in their lives was just as it should be, and the journey ahead—whatever difficulties might arise—would be filled with joy and satisfaction.

As Henry and Amala walked back through the cemetery toward the carriage—pausing for another moment at Kat's grave—Amala was again overcome with the sensation that she could see the world around her with more clarity, with all its beauty enhanced and more vivid. She looked at Henry walking beside her, a sleeping Harry cradled in his strong arms, and she couldn't imagine anything more beautiful than the family they had become.

About the Author

Anita Stansfield has more than fifty published books and is the recipient of many awards, including two lifetime achievement awards. Her books go far beyond being enjoyable, memorable stories. Anita resonates particularly well with a broad range of devoted readers because of her sensitive and insightful examination of contemporary issues that are faced by many of those readers, even when her venue is a historical romance. Readers come away from her compelling stories equipped with new ideas about how to enrich their own lives, regardless of their circumstances.

Anita was born and raised in Provo, Utah. She is the mother of five and has a growing number of grandchildren. She also writes for the general trade market under the name Elizabeth D. Michaels.

For more information and a complete list of her publications, go to anitastansfield.blogspot.com or anitastansfield.com, where you can sign up to receive email updates. You can also follow her on Facebook and Twitter.